WHERE MAGIC
AND SCIENCE COLLIDE

JOSEPH J. SWOPE

Black Rose Writing | Texas

ISBN: 978-1-68433-531-2
PUBLISHED BY BLACK ROSE WRITING
www.blackrosewriting.com

Printed in the United States of America
Suggested Retail Price (SRP) $20.95

Where Magic and Science Collide is printed in Plantagenet Cherokee

*As a planet-friendly publisher, Black Rose Writing does its best to eliminate unnecessary waste to reduce paper usage and energy costs, while never compromising the reading experience. As a result, the final word count vs. page count may not meet common expectations.

Dedicated to my children, who are always my inspiration:
Chandra, Shane, Savanna, Marissa, Logan, Lucas and Emma

And to
Lynn Boyer Matz
She knows why

The World of Ambrasian

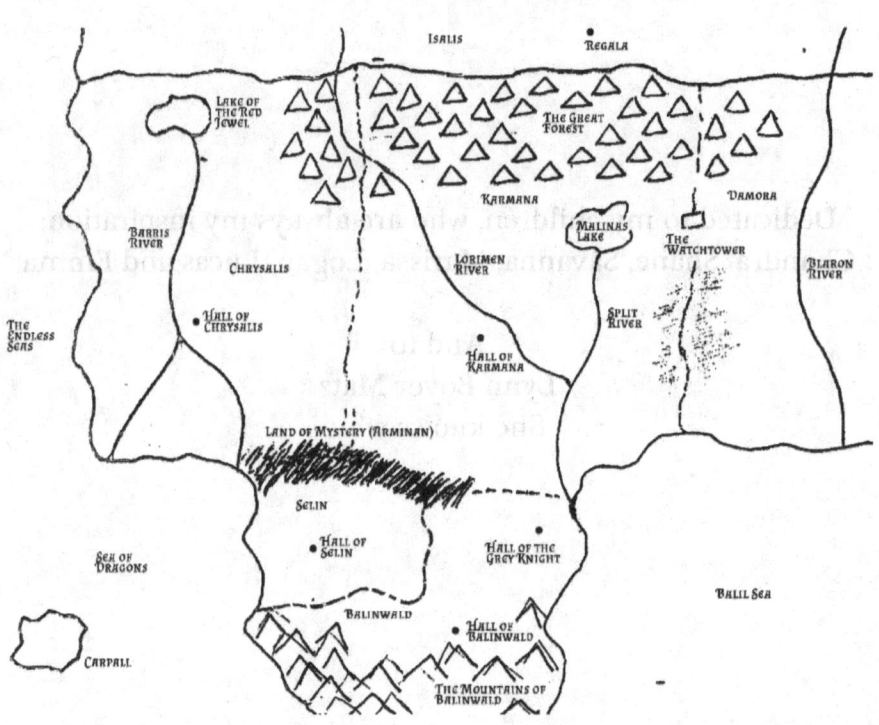

WHERE MAGIC
AND SCIENCE COLLIDE

CHAPTER 1
ANCIENT CORRUPTION
AMBRASIAN PRE-HISTORY

Far within the mountain range that defined the northern edge of Ambrasian and hidden in a workshop carved out of stone deep underground, Horan and his skilled craftsmen worked tirelessly to complete their all-important task. A cold wind howled outside.

"Taraz-El will arrive at dawn," Horan said. "There is unrest in the East."

Gareth looked up from his work, lines of concern creasing across his face streaked with age.

"I hear tales of strange creatures emerging from the forest," he said.

Horan grunted in disgust as the morbid possibilities passed through his brain.

"We can only imagine what abominations the Dranaki are capable of creating," he said.

"But surely our forces are strong enough to defeat such vermin," Gareth argued.

Horan changed tools as he shook his head in disgust.

"In a fair fight, surely," Horan answered. "But what chance do we have of a fair fight? Magic swirls unchecked, and one never knows how the whims of wizardry will turn on any given day. It can easily be corrupted this way or that by those who wish to do ill."

Horan gazed down at his work studying it carefully.

"That is why this Oracle is so important," he concluded. "We must finish our task, if not for us then for the future of Ambrasian."

With that, Horan had the craftsmen carefully lift their creation from the cauldron using an elaborate system of ropes and pulleys. The Oracle emerged from the mist that infused it with untold power and hovered in mid-air protected by a crystal case. The Oracle pulsated with hidden energy and glowed with an ethereal iridescence. Its beauty was unfathomable and wholly mysterious: a perfect diamond more than a thousand carats in size, with rubies, emeralds and *dalians*–a precious but mysterious stone brought to Ambrasian by the Wizards–somehow embedded within the diamond itself. Those most skilled with the elemental strength of the planet had locked special powers within the Oracle.

The Wizards had emerged from the Northern Mountains in the early days of Ambrasian and formed an alliance with the Cadaren, a people that had only begun to populate the landscape. The Cadaren were ambitious and resourceful, and the land and its people prospered to a far greater degree than before.

Yet just as in many cultures and worlds, on the fringes of success lie the seeds of jealousy and avarice. As the Cadaren population spread throughout Ambrasian, they encountered other species, some friendly and some more adversarial. Skirmishes broke out as various sides worked to exert their power and strengthen their claims. The Wizards had cast out the Dranaki, but in a young world where magic remained a natural and unharnessed force, the Dranaki retained powers beyond those of mere mortals. Those Dranaki who ventured too far into the east disappeared into the dense forests, only to re-emerge unrecognizable, full of hatred and malice. Wild tales suggested that an unknown force had somehow created some unnatural combination of Dranaki and beast, and the result was a race easily corrupted and stronger than any other species that walked the lands of early Ambrasian.

The Dranaki and their allies had begun to wreak havoc throughout Ambrasian. They had forced the free peoples of the land to form armies for the first time to defend their lands and their towns. Thus began the proverbial initial battle between good and evil on the world known as Ambrasian.

Even in battle, however, the Dranaki demonstrated their recklessness and disrespect of the balance of nature. Wizards and the Cadaren avoided using magic in battle, knowing that its surreptitious use could create unintended consequences, tearing apart even the very fabric of Ambrasian. The Dranaki, however, showed no such caution, and used magic and any other advantage they could muster without regard for repercussions. They slaughtered many innocent victims as these freed mystical forces collided with little consideration for life. The Wizards and the Cadaren eventually had to resort to using their own magic to neutralize that employed by the Dranaki.

To combat the threat to Ambrasian, the Wizards and the Cadaren, together with the Elvii–the mysterious peoples of the Great Forest in the West – began the project that would culminate in the Oracle's completion. The Oracle served as a beacon of strength and power, which captured the most vital energies of the land and sky and focused them on achieving the goals of only those with good intentions. The Oracle was intended to intensify the power of the just and neutralize magic intended for evil purposes. It was an incorruptible power in a corruptible world. Now, the Oracle was nearly finished and could be used to banish the invaders wreaking havoc in the East. Horan studied it in awe.

"At last," he said. "We can ensure our children and our children's children peace throughout the land. They will never had to endure the hardships we have seen."

At that moment, a disturbance outside the chamber startled Horan. Horan and his craftsmen rushed toward the entrance, only to find the guards in a fierce battle with a half-dozen attackers who had somehow found their way to this remote mountain retreat.

"Dranaki," Horan hissed. "They have spies everywhere."

The craftsmen armed themselves and sprinted toward the cave's entrance to support the guards. But in the chaos of the moment, neither Horan nor any of his companions noticed that one of their own had stayed behind. The few minutes it took to dispel the Dranaki warriors was all it took for Essira to alter the course of the future if ever so slightly.

Once the rest of his companions left the cave, Essira pulled a small flask from the folds of his robe and approached the Oracle still swimming in the magical mists. He pulled off the wooden cork from the flask. The liquid within the tube slowly turned to a gas, blending into the swirls that enveloped the Oracle. Essira threw the empty flask into the nearby fire, where it was quickly consumed by the flames.

"Incorruptible indeed," the Dranaki spy hissed. "Perhaps no good now, but the future is a long and unseen path. There will now be a chance to turn this weapon onto our oppressors after all."

The skirmish outside had become less fierce. The Dranaki force had been repelled. The last few soldiers had made one last mad rush, but the sheer number of their opponents overwhelmed them. Essira heard Horan and the others returning to the cave.

He pulled out a second flask, this one containing a bronze-tinted liquid. Quickly, he swallowed the entire contents, feeling the salinity of the liquid as it went down his throat. Essira again threw the flask into the fire.

By the time Horan and his companions returned to the inner chamber the cave, Essira was dead.

Chapter 2
A Breach of the Peace
Ambrasian Year 1384

The young farm family hid fearfully in their modest home, a wood and thatch structure perched in the soft hills of the countryside. While the two children burrowed into the corner and covered themselves with blankets, the mother and father barricaded the doors and windows as best they could. A fire blazed in the distance as the neighbor's farmhouse burned to the ground, and the band of five bandits rode their horses down the path toward their next target.

The farmer and his wife joined their children, the husband in front shielding his family from the coming attack. He held a four-pronged farm fork with a crudely carved wooden handle in his hands, a poor weapon against the sharpened blades of his foes but the only option readily available. He was a farmer, not a warrior.

"Whatever happens, I love all of you," the husband whispered. His wife grasped him in fear, unable to speak. "Never forget that."

A few minutes later, the roar of horses came to a halt in front of the house. Then, footsteps clapped hard across the ground, and a powerful knock shook the door.

"You know who I am and what I want," the first bandit roared. "We can do this the easy way or the hard. Your choice."

Harsh laughter echoed among the marauders.

"Go away," the husband croaked as bravely as he could. "We are poor farmers. There's nothing here you could possibly want."

The bandit roared again, more than a hint of impatience in his voice.

"I am Axela, and I decide what I want," he said angrily. "If nothing else, I saw your fair wife from the distance. Surely, she can provide us some amusement. And I'm sure your children can bring a fair price on the open market."

The husband stood defiantly trying to control his fury. He wanted to rush the door but knew it would be futile.

"Leave my family alone," he screamed. "You will not touch them."

"Or what?" Axela mocked. "You'll come out and single-handedly kill all of us with your farm tools? Or perhaps your oxen will fight at your side?"

The bandits tried to push the door open, but found it blocked.

"Idiot," Axela said once more. "Do you think you can keep us out of your shack with a few pieces of broken-down furniture? I will burn you out if I must."

Another member of the troupe came up to the house with a torch, its flames coming dangerously close to the thatched roof. The farmer knew the weather had been dry and the house would burn suddenly and violently should his adversaries set it afire. He realized his home would not stand long and he and his family would have to choose between surrender or a painful and gruesome death.

"What am I going to do?" he said quietly, desperately, looking about for some salvation.

"I'm going to count to three," Axela said. "After that, we'll turn you and your family to cinders. You still have a few animals here that will make our trip worthwhile."

The husband and his wife looked at each other in fear. She moved toward her husband and put her arms around him.

"One," came the voice from outside.

The couple held each other tightly.

"Two," the bandit said more threateningly.

"What should we do?" the wife asked her husband.

"They'll kill us no matter what," he replied.

"Thre . . . ," Axela stopped in mid-pronouncement as he heard a disturbance in the distance. Suddenly, two riders burst over the hill, their swords already drawn and ready for combat. With the sun behind the riders, the bandits were unable to identify the oncoming opponents, but they drew their swords in defense and quickly mounted their horses.

"This is our territory," Axela snapped. "Who dare challenge us here?"

Axela spurred their horses forward.

"More idiots," he said. "We have them outnumbered five to two."

Nevertheless, the two riders swept down on the five. With unexpected speed and fury, they pummeled the bandits, slicing open their bellies and hacking the arm from the one still holding the torch. The flames were doused as the rider fell from the horse.

Axela, the only one left of his once formidable gang, looked at his attackers.

"Who are you?" he asked.

"I am Roanan from the House of the Red Knight," the first rider said. "This is my cousin, Lasarion. You violate our land and our citizens. I order you to drop your sword and surrender."

Axela spit, intransigent to the last.

"Rich, spoiled, bratty princes," he mocked. "Acting like you are protecting your subjects for which you really don't give a rat's ass. I'll kill you both myself."

Axela pulled out a second sword, and holding a weapon in both hands, he charged toward Roanan and Lasarion. The brawny ruffian scowled in anger as he approached them.

The two knights glanced at each other for a moment, then turned toward their attacker, with Roanan riding to the left and Lasarion to the right. Lasarion blocked Axela's thrust, while Roanan easily avoided the bandit's wild swing on the other side and nearly severed Axela's neck with one blow. The body of the lifeless thief dropped limply from his horse.

The two knights surveyed the scene, ensuring all was safe. Then, they dismounted from their horses and approached the humble farmhouse. Roanan knocked on the door.

"Who is that?" came the frightened voice from within. "Please do not harm us."

"I am Roanan of the House of the Red Knight, son of King Broden," came the answer. "With me is my cousin, Lasarion, a fellow knight of the court of Chrysalis. You and your family are safe. You may open your door."

After a few moments, Roanan and Lasarion saw the young farmer peek out a small hole in the wall and verify what he had heard. Then he took a few more minutes to clear the barricaded door and welcome the knights inside.

"Prince Roanan, my name is Thelin, and this is my wife, Janellae," the farmer said, turning back to his spouse. "Welcome to our home and thank you for saving our lives. My apologies for answering you so rudely."

Thelin and his family dropped to their knees in front of the royalty that now graced their modest home.

"Arise, please," Roanan implored. "No apologies are necessary, and this is no time for formalities. The families of this region should not have to endure such violations. I am glad that we arrived in time, but I mourn the loss of your neighbors."

Roanan ensured the family was safe and he and Lasarion spent a few minutes with the two children, a young boy and girl named Madal and Galana. They left the family with a satchel of gold and silver coins–more than the family would typically earn in several years–as well as several of the bandit's horses. Roanan and Lasarion then built a pyre to dispose of the fallen criminals. As the blaze burned brightly, the two knights huddled together.

"This is not the first of these unprovoked attacks we have encountered lately," Roanan said.

"To be sure," Lasarion agreed. "What do you think it means? It has been many years since such villainy has been so open in its assaults. We have enjoyed a long period of peace.'

"I do not know for certain," Roanan said. "But I hope these events do not portend darker days ahead. Some say unrest stirs just beneath the surface. I do not know if I believe such predictions, but either way, we must remain vigilant."

CHAPTER 3
ANCIENT SECRETS
AMBRASIAN YEAR 1384

The two dark figures picked their way slowly through the thick undergrowth. They had left the marshes behind and now found themselves on firmer, higher ground, but the stench of rotting and dying vegetation still permeated the region. It was a grim and mostly forgotten corner of Ambrasian.

"This place stinks," the male said, hacking through the briar that stuck to both his clothing and his skin.

"After four days on the road without bathing," the female answered, "you don't smell so inviting yourself."

The male grunted. The two were covered in dark hooded robes, hidden from the view of prying eyes. They had nearly arrived at their destination, a secret location known only to a few, difficult to reach on a path with many twists, turns, and traps. Nevertheless, neither bore a map. The female had committed the path to memory and her single-minded focus had served her well.

The night sky here was cloud-covered and the air misty, making the darkness nearly complete. Yet the two travelled stealthily, moving as silently as possible and quickening their pace as the ground cleared. They found a series of weathered stone steps, cracked in some spots, crumbling to dust in others. They stepped carefully, as the continuing mist and dampness had given the steps an ice-like sheen. After a prolonged climb, they finally reached the summit.

There lay the ruins of a former stronghold, time slowing gnawing at it over the centuries toward its inevitable demise. Most of the roof had long collapsed and disappeared, and in various spots, the stone walls had given way. The forest surrounding it had re-claimed parts of the fort. The male visitor noted several locations where trees now literally grew out of the walls of the structure. Entropy was a universal constant.

The inside of the fortification was nearly as devastated. Stones lay scattered among the grounds. The remains of most of the buildings sat collapsed. Only one small structure remained mostly intact, crudely patched and repaired haphazardly. A dim light shone from one of the windows.

The two figures slipped through the ruins of the courtyard toward the building. Suddenly, out of the darkness, a half-dozen sentries moved from the shadows and blocked the path. The guards drew their swords that glistened in the dull light. The sentries were Drens, descended from the Dranaki but bastardized by those who sought to exploit them through the generations.

The male figure drew his own sword, but the female stopped him, outstretching her arm to calm his fury.

"I will tell you if we need your weapon," she said firmly and waited until her partner had returned his blade to its sheath.

The guards viewed the two travelers suspiciously.

"Identify yourselves," the nearest sentry commanded them sternly.

"We are the ones you expected," the female said calmly.

The sentry huffed in consternation.

"And I know that how?" he challenged. "You look like no more than vagrants to me."

"Elraith-Vy sent us here," the female continued deliberately. "He gave me his mark."

Suddenly, the female raised her hand. A jagged sun cut through with a spear glowed from her palm. The light was so bright that the sentry temporarily stepped back, shielding his eyes.

"What devilry is this?" asked one while the others muttered under their breath. But the lead sentry raised his hand to silence his companions. He now considered the visitors more carefully, eyeing them up and down.

"You have come to avenge the wrongs we have endured in both past ages and those that continue to this day?" he asked, more than a hint of skepticism in his voice.

The female nodded in assent.

"I have come to lead you to victory over your ancient nemesis, the Cadaren, and the others who stole your lands and your riches," the female answered. "I understand how you have been wronged."

The sentry turned suspiciously at the male, whose hand remained on the hilt of his sword, ready to draw it at a moment's notice.

"Him?" the sentry asked. "What good is he?"

"You need warriors," the female explained. "He is skilled with the sword and he will bring others to fight alongside us. You cannot defeat the Cadaren armies by yourself."

The sentry grunted, clearly less than impressed.

"He doesn't look like much," the Dren spit.

The male glared at the sentry angrily.

"I'll have your balls with one swing and your head with the next if you don't watch your sharp tongue," he scowled.

The sentry grasped his own sword more firmly.

"Would you now?" the sentry said defiantly. "That I'd like to see."

"Gladly," said the male drawing his sword once again. The two raised their weapons to attack.

"Stop," the female commanded. "No matter the species, all males seem to think with their smaller head. We are all on the same side, you cretins. It does no good to kill each other. That benefits only the Cadaren."

Her male companion and the sentry glared at her and then back at each other. They held their stare for a moment, then relaxed. A silent truce endured.

"That's better," the female said. "Now show me the path to the scrolls."

The sentry examined the two strangers once more, then seemed to reach a final decision.

"Follow me," he said.

The Dren led them to a dimly lit path around the building. Down a dark and narrow alleyway between two dilapidated buildings, they finally reached a stairway that led thirty steps down. There, two additional sentries stood guard at a landing protecting a thickly hewed door.

The lead sentry pulled out a key and slowly turned the aged tumblers on the iron lock. It gave way reluctantly, finally opening. The sentry removed the lock and the chains that held the door securely. He nodded to the guards, who put down their swords and helped to pull the door open.

It refused to give for a moment, then ultimately did so with great resistance. The door creaked and groaned as it slid slowly across the landing.

With the door open and set in place, the lead sentry pulled a torch off the wall and lit it, handing it to the female.

"You'll need this," he said. "Nothing permeates the darkness in the chamber."

The male and female entered the dark hall and proceeded down another twenty steps underground. The air cooled as the stone walls bordered a small inner chamber. In the middle of the room stood a vault perched on a stone slab. The mark on the female's hand glowed once more. She placed it on the center of the vault and the box slid open.

Inside lay a number of animal hides treated and turned into crude scrolls. The words inscribed on them were written in an ancient tongue, but the female after much study had mastered the language and was able to translate the words. She paused only twice to better understand the meaning.

"Maldur," the woman said with excitement, "the secret to our victory lay in my hands."

The male laughed and placed his hand on his sword.

"Do what you will with your crumbling texts and fancy words, Celidia," the male said. "I have been holding the secret to our victory in my hands for many days."

The Sorceress glared at her companion, then at the last moment unsharpened her tongue.

"You will get your chance to prove the might of your weapon," she finally said. "But we will need these to provide you with that opportunity."

Celidia slipped the scrolls under her robe and the two left the chamber. Shortly thereafter, they slipped from the compound without uttering another word and disappeared into the darkness. They had much to do.

Chapter 4
A View from the Sky
Quadrant Delphi,
Galactic Date 2142-07-41

The Galactic Class vessel Explorer suddenly emerged from the darkness and re-established itself in the space around the ship.

"Confirm location," Captain Tryllm Evenru said.

"Quadrant Delphi, Star 196732, just outside the local planetary system," the ship's artificial intelligence, nicknamed Kevo after its inventor, reported. "Target destination achieved."

"Set course for Planet Terra," the captain said. "Navigation speed."

"Course plotted and engaged," Kevo said without emotion. Evenru felt the ship accelerate to interplanetary speed as the Solaran Drive kicked in and moved the Explorer toward the inhabited world perched deep within this system.

The Explorer was an interstellar vessel from the planet Lux, located in a neighboring star system here in a part of the galaxy far closer to the galactic center than Earth. With a much denser concentration, the night sky was filled with a thousand times more stars than those planets on the outer rings. Lux, in fact, was so named because four suns were in close enough proximity that no part of the world was ever in complete darkness. At best, the inhabitants of Lux experienced a prolonged twilight that comprised their "nighttime" hours–and even then, night did not arrive every evening.

Despite their limited view of the surrounding universe, the citizens of Lux developed advanced technology that led to a rigorous space exploration program. After more than a century of travel within their own system, the universe of Lux expanded exponentially with the discovery of actual wormholes–until then only a theoretical construct by enthusiasts looking to make travel to distant worlds a viable possibility.

Developing spacecraft that could navigate a wormhole became the next challenge, and over time, the term "wormhole" on Lux transformed itself to "snakehole" to describe the ship design needed to survive the trip. As Lux engineers learned through many trials and errors, their craft needed an outer skin sturdy enough to survive the void of space, but flexible enough to navigate the twists and turns of the interstellar conduit–an exterior more akin to the skin of a snake than the soft outer layer of a worm.

Thus, the Explorer's design was much unlike the stereotypical imaginings of spacecrafts. Instead, it was a long, thin, tubular ship that could "wriggle" through the narrow confines of a snakehole by a series of flexible plates that made up the outer hull of the ship. The ability to travel beyond their own star system brought Lux into the fellowship of other planets who had previously achieved the same status. It was a fellowship that grew at every turn as more and more civilizations learned to move beyond their own terrestrial boundaries.

As that fellowship grew, it soon became obvious that standard protocols were needed to determine time and date, since each planet rotated and circled its home sun in its own unique pattern. In addition, the concept of identifying the year was typically based on some series of events long ago and specific to the development of intelligent life on each world. It was quickly determined that it was nearly impossible to gauge accurately the timing of galactic occurrences using local time systems all of which differed dramatically. Now, a galactic time construct governed the comings and goings of those who had learned to travel beyond their own solar system.

This was not the first visit of a Lux ship into this sector. A previous expedition had determined that the fourth planet orbiting this yellow-orange K star lied in what Earth scientists millions of light years away had dubbed "the Goldilock's zone"–an orbit that would generate temperatures conducive to the development of life, not too hot and not too cold. That would allow a planet with sufficient atmospheric pressure to support the development of liquid water, the universal elixir of life. Further investigation discovered that intelligent life had in fact developed on this planet and additional observation had been recommended. But subsequent scans of the region also had found an unexpected threat: a planet-killing asteroid was hurtling toward the planet, its projected path showing a direct, fatal hit. The Explorer had been dispatched to learn more of the planet and eliminate the threat of the giant space rock.

When flying through any planetary system, a ship had to be cautious of not only the various planets and their moons, but the various interplanetary debris remaining from the sloppy business of galactic expansion and planet-building. These zones of stray rocks and other leftover material most often were found at the edge of local galaxies. But the Explorer had mapped these risks carefully and the ship whisked through the system and settled into an orbit around the planet three days later.

Advances in artificial intelligence had significantly reduced the need for large crews. Still a contingent of about twenty Lux representing specialties such as science, anthropology, weapons, medical, engineering, and other essential functions worked to assemble as much information as possible. It was questionable whether even most of these crew members were necessary, but inherent suspicion of intelligent technology had proven to be a universal trait. The crew was there ostensibly to react should the ship's intelligence somehow fail.

"Let's review what we know about this planet," Captain Evenru said to Officer Jahrat Penra. Evenru knew Kevo could provide the same information, but he purposely worked to maintain interaction and challenge the fellow Lux members of his crew. Like others, he wanted to be prepared if the wonders of technology became less wondrous in a crucial situation.

"The planet's composition is atypical compared to other habitable worlds," Penra answered. "There is a single large land mass. The rest of the planet consists of one giant ocean, with only a few small islands reaching the surface. While the planet does not enjoy the four suns of

Lux, there is a second, M-class star close enough to appear to be a small satellite in the evening. The planet itself has a single orbiting moon of moderate size."

"What about the civilization?" Evenru pressed. "Tell me at what stage of development is the intelligent life on the planet. Pre-industrial, I presume?"

"Oh yes," Penra said. "The inhabitants call their world Ambrasian. Interestingly, there is quite a diversity of intelligent species. As best as we can determine from this distance, it appears there are at least five different and somewhat distinct biological entities with some levels of higher intellect. Quite frankly, a closer study could reveal additional species. However, because the various classifications of intelligent life have lived in relatively proximity without physical geographic barriers, there is much less racial diversity than in some cultures we have studied."

Penra read the analysis for a moment to better synthesize his findings.

"It appears Ambrasian is in what some anthropologists would classify as a Medieval period," the Lux officer said. "There is a significant level of construction and blacksmithing. The land is fertile for the most part and agriculture flourishes. From what I can gather, as is typical in technologically primitive societies, monarchies or similar structures dominate the form of government."

Penra smiled slyly.

"I should also report, Captain, that the universal species exists here on this planet as well," he said.

"Horses?" Evenru said.

"Affirmative," Penra confirmed. "Just as on every other planet we have identified that can support life, horses exist here. And in this stage of their development, they remain the main form of transportation."

Evenru's double eyelids–evolved by the Lux to help manage their sun-drenched landscape–blinked as he looked curiously at the planet on the ship's screens.

"In other words, it's not likely we'll see them in space for a thousand years or more," he chuckled.

"Not likely," Penra agreed, his smile creating lines on the dark-brown skin tanned by generations on a planet with no night. "However, I might add there is a strong belief in magic across all species on Ambrasian. Perhaps their magic is more powerful than we believe."

"Magic?" the captain said skeptically, allowing a chuckle to escape past his lips. "I daresay they would find this ship to be quite magical if they saw it. Magic is a convenient way to explain that which you don't understand. Don't worry, lad, I've been to many solar systems in my travels, and I've yet to find anything that qualifies as real magic. All the so-called magic that I've encountered has been nothing but the clever manipulation of those easily deceived."

Evenru paused and looked about the command center.

"Look at this ship," the Captain added. "Our magic lies in our science. We would all be great magicians on the surface of Ambrasian."

Penra was about to continue the conversation, but at that moment, weapons officer Samra Kalli entered the Explorer's command center, glancing only briefly at the image of the planet on the ship's main display screen.

"Captain," Officer Kalli reported firmly, turning back toward Evenru, "we have analyzed the current location of Asteroid X1-224."

She moved to a control panel and brought up a three-dimensional holographic display on a secondary screen.

"The asteroid is currently in proximity of the eighth planet of this system," Kalli explained matter-of-factly. "While that planet is not inhabited, destroying the object in that location could adversely affect the planet or one of its 26 moons. It would also entail added unnecessary risk to the mission. I recommend we delay our orders until the target is located in a more fortuitous position between planetary bodies."

Evenru studied the display, then glanced back at the image of the planet that dominated the command center.

"I think this planet is worth a bit more study," the captain concluded. "Keep me informed when a more appropriate window to accomplish our mission presents itself."

"So noted, captain," Kalli responded and left the room, the door whistling closed on her exit.

"Now," Evenru said, turned back to Penra, "let's see what else we can find out about the world of Ambrasian and its fondness for magic."

"Agreed," Penra replied. "Might I suggest we deploy a cadre of drones to provide a closer study of the inhabitants."

"Excellent suggestion," Evenru said. "Make sure they're cloaked. Let's not interfere with the natural development of the planet. You know what kind of paperwork that creates at Galactic Command. My ass would be on a grill until the inquiry was over."

Penra nodded and manipulated several controls.

"And remember to turn on the universal translator this time," the Captain chided him gently. "I'd like to understand what we're hearing."

Penra nodded, painfully recalling his oversight in the last star system.

"Cloaks confirmed and activated," he reported. "I have released the drones for observational purposes."

Chapter 5
The Death of Broden
Ambrasian Year 1385

The smell within the bedroom was distinctly identifiable, even densely obscured by scents and perfumes purposely used to mask the obvious. The King was dying.

"Peace is not as secure as it seems," Broden, the Red Knight and King of Chrysalis, told his son, Roanan. "Evil lurks where you least expect and it will not remain silent for long. There are those that will see opportunity in my death."

Roanan nodded. His father was slipping from his grasp, far too soon. Broden had ruled for nearly fifty years and was known as a kind and benevolent ruler. The King had lived a long and full life. But it was never enough time when a son was losing his father. Roanan was born later in the King's life to his second wife, Glynnis, who died in childbirth. The King's first wife, Maribella, grew sickly soon after their marriage but lingered for many years until she finally succumbed. As King, Broden could have cast her off for the good of the realm to secure an heir. But he was faithful and truly in love and stayed with her until the end. After the deaths of his two wives, Broden did not choose another. Instead, he doted on his son as he did his kingdom, training Roanan as best he could. Still, only two years past his twentieth birthday, the King-in-waiting already felt unsteady under the weight of the coming burden.

At his father's death, Roanan would assume the hereditary title of the Red Knight and be crowned King. He was young, too young in his mind for such a responsibility. Though tested in battle, he would need to win the love and trust of his people. It was a task for which he was not prepared and did not want. Maybe in a decade, but certainly not now. He was still learning his way in the world. But fate did not provide that option. Illness had struck Broden suddenly and death was certain. No healer in the realm thought otherwise. Wishing for additional time would not give the beloved King more life.

Already recognized as the finest warrior in Ambrasia, Roanan had become over time the main defender of Chrysalis as his father had grown older and ultimately when his health faltered. While he had already achieved the admiration of the citizenry, he felt far from ready or deserving to wear the crown. But he had little choice.

"The history of Ambrasian is a proud one," Broden continued, "and Chrysalis has always served as the defender of that heritage. Without our strength, the splendor of this land would be vulnerable."

Broden became silent. No further explanation was necessary. Roanan had been immersed in the history of Ambrasian since his childhood. He had learned about his kingdom and its role in the larger world from the instructors and elders who had shaped his education. Chrysalis was the westernmost kingdom on the continent of Ambrasian. The Darris River ran swiftly through the middle of the kingdom after finding its birth in the north and strengthened by many streams, springs, and other tributaries. Its waters fed the thirst of many of Chrysalis's citizens as well as the fertile ground around it. It eventually split, the main tributary bearing west toward the sea and capable of carrying tall ships, while the smaller and less-traveled eastern branch traversing the farmlands of Chrysalis. It was near this strategic nexus where the Hall of Chrysalis had been built.

The Kingdom of Chrysalis enjoyed natural protection on all of its boundaries. To the north, the Great Mountain Range cut across the hardened terrain of scarcely inhabited Isalis. To the east, the Ancient Great Forest stretched over much of Ambrasian. To the south, the Land of Mystery, an uninviting land avoided by all living beings, cast an unwelcome shadow. Bordering the Land of Mystery and Chrysalis lie the Sea of Dragons, so named for the serpents who once ruled the sea from the island of Carpal since the rising of the Sun–or so it was said. Though the dragons had not been seen in many years, their legacy remained.

To the west of Chrysalis lie the unending Seas unknown to the people of Ambrasian. The few who had ventured west either returned after tiring of navigating the choppy waters or ventured too far and were never heard from again. Many speculated as to what could be found beyond the Sea, but there was little first-hand knowledge to support or refute these claims. For now, the Sea remained an impenetrable barrier, transversed only to the length that ships did not lose sight of the land.

Beyond the eastern boundaries of Chrysalis lay the rest of the lands of Ambrasian. The southernmost kingdoms were the habitat of herders and mountain people. Short but stout of body and blessed with great strength, they called their lands Balinwald and Selin. Here, the native peoples grew to old ages–some as long as 125 years–and led a simple life in both the plains and hills of their lands. Their farms and their herds supported their needs, and they lived peacefully, avoiding confrontation and staying to themselves. They rarely involved themselves in the affairs of the greater continent of Ambrasian.

In the North lay the mostly unexplored wilderness of Isalis, an unforgiving region filled with jutting peaks and punishing terrain. That, at least, were the scant reports of those who had risked such a journey. Because few ventured to the northern lands, what was accepted as common knowledge was again comprised of much guesswork and speculation. True tales were scarce and written documents even scarcer. Of those legends, however, it was said that somewhere in the otherwise unexplored regions of this land lay the Realm of the Wizards. Some travelers claimed the Wizards were hidden in a mystical valley secretly tucked within the Northern Mountain Range, though no one could prove they had ever seen such a valley or knew how to find it. Also, deep in the midst of Isalis lay the lair of the ancient monster, Icyx, its cave far from the inhabited regions of the world. Icyx was another beast rarely seen by those living in Ambrasian, and the monster had become the fodder of childhood tales. Nor was it clear if Icyx–if the beast even existed–was the last of its kind, or a tribe which other races could not tell apart.

In the center of the world was Karmana, and in the center of this land was the Hall of Karmana. Here in the enchanted kingdom lived an eternal race of females, all fair and possessed with powers beyond the knowledge of the other races of Ambrasian. The magic of this land was strongest at its heart and there, Karmana enjoyed a never-ending spring. The residents of Karmana lived at peace with the animals of nature, which had become tame in this otherworldly domain.

Other lands fell within the formal boundaries of Karmana, though they only shared in the mysterious magic that emanated from the land to far lesser extents. The Elvii lands of Necinia stretched throughout the Great Forest, and the wood-dwelling Elvii possessed their own special abilities outside those of other Ambrasians. Rarely seen outside of their natural habitat and even less in recent years, the Elvii were yet another race subject to rampant speculation.

A southern region, Kar-Braenes, fell outside of the enchanted realm entirely, but had long ago pledged allegiance to the kingdom of Karmana. Many of the warriors who made up the defense of Karmana came from this region.

In the most Eastern region of Ambrasian, however, lay Damora, a land inhabited by the Drens. The Drens were descended from the Dranaki eons ago in the early days of the world. They were strong and fierce, and unwelcoming of others. They believed, rightly or wrongly, that the other races of Ambrasian had used and mistreated them and denied them their fair share of the bounty of the land. Over time, Damora became a closed land and few ventured within its boundaries. Once more, because of this isolation, little was known of the Drens or their land.

"Damora once again stirs," Broden said weakly, breaking the silence. "We have heard many reports of Drens once more congregating. An evil sign."

"But the Drens were soundly defeated long ago," Roanan protested. "Their numbers are but a fraction of what they once were. They haven't dared venture into the West since."

A shadow seemed to come over Broden's aged face.

"Do not underestimate your enemies, my son," the King continued. "You will be the fifty-sixth King of the Realm, covering a span of more than fifteen hundred years. We have tried–and failed–to eliminate the Drens and other enemies throughout that reign. Evil is more resilient than it appears. The Drens are not the only adversaries willing to rise up when the opportunity presents itself. The numbers of your enemies are always greater than you assume."

The Chrysalian king coughed violently but signaled his courtiers and healers away.

"I'm dying," he snapped at them. "There's nothing you can do about it now, None of your potions or medicines will delay my passing from this world, and I need to keep a clear head as long as possible."

The King concentrated once more on his son.

"I suspect there is more to this than just Drens finding their courage," Broden mused. "I believe there is an outside force at work here–and a malevolent one at that."

"But who?" Roanan asked. "I have not heard any such reports."

"I do not know who may rise up to face us," Broden answered. "And it will not be my charge to find out. But I fear it will create a great challenge for Ambrasian–and for you. Alas, the legacy I give to you will not be one of peace and tranquility."

"Father," Roanan said softly, "I fear you may see demons that don't exist."

"They exist and they are nearer than you believe," Broden assured his son softly but firmly. "You will find that a King must always be aware of the unseen danger that lurks in the shadows. You will hone that instinct over time and you will know when to be cautious when there appears that there is no justification to do so. You will learn there are times you cannot trust the peace and that the tranquility before you is nothing but an illusion."

Broden paused momentarily, a hint a sadness crossing his face.

"I am sorry this burden falls to you, my son," he said.

"Father, please," Roanan said. "I don't know if I am ready."

"You must be," the King said. "And you must find those you can trust in the most desperate times."

"Who can I trust?" Roanan implored.

Broden pursed his lips, searching his son's questioning eyes. He paused once again, summoning his thoughts.

"There are many true friends, and many that are less so," Broden said cryptically. "You will learn to recognize the difference. But you can always trust the Wizard."

"Tabeus?" Roanan asked skeptically. "The old man doesn't appear he would be much of an ally."

Roanan looked away in thought. He had experienced meetings with the Wizard, a frail being of interminable age, whose appearance was highlighted by a flowing beard, a dark gray loose-fitting robe, and an ornately carved staff topped with a myriad of unusual stones. The staff, of course, was no ordinary staff but one infused with the power of a Wizard–or so it was said. Tabeus had occasionally taken the time to instruct the young knight in some subject where he had a special interest, but those lessons were at the Wizard's whim and their occurrences unpredictable.

More often than not, a black bird he called Raven sat perched on the Wizard's shoulder. Recently, Roanan had seen Tabeus in consultation with his father frequently, and more often as Broden's health failed. Roanan occasionally glimpsed the Wizard studying the young knight carefully, but whatever thoughts the Wizard may have had were well hidden by his indecipherable visage. Tabeus had, however, found more occasion to counsel Roanan as this time of transition came closer to reality.

Roanan turned back to his father and found Broden smiling in spite of the pain that seared his failing body.

"You speak truly that Tabeus may appear old and unassuming, but he is far more formidable than at first glance," Broden said. "His wisdom comes from a thousand years of experiences. Tabeus hears the secret whisperings of the trees and the intrigues hidden behind the songs of birds–as well as powers neither you nor I fully understand. You will find him your closest and most valuable ally–and, in time I am sure, your friend."

"But father . . .," Roanan objected.

Broden held up his hand and paused his son.

"I have little time left," he interrupted his son. "I feel the wings of death circling around me waiting for my last breath."

Broden looked at Roanan intently, his voice again turning serious.

"One more thing you must remember," he said. "Above all, you must protect Karmana. Ambrasian thrives because of the power that emanates from its center. The Oracle of Karmana is far more vital than many suspect. Do not underestimate the importance of Karmana, even though its inhabitants may sometimes be somewhat haughty."

The king-in-waiting smiled.

"I remember," Roanan said. The young prince recalled in his mind his infrequent meetings with the mysterious females of their neighboring land. It was difficult not to be entranced by the inhabitant's physical beauty and inherent allure. It was just as difficult to not become maddeningly frustrated shortly thereafter by their ego and sense of self-importance. The females of Karmana were best endured in small doses.

"I see your sneer, though you try desperately to hide it," Broden chuckled. "Just because the females of Karmana do not swoon at the sight of you does not mean they are not worthy of your protection."

Roanan began to protest but thought better of it. His father could pass at any minute. No sense wasting it on a silly argument.

"I understand the importance of Karmana," Roanan ultimately answered, flatly.

"Karmin will show strength unimagined," Broden said, his voice starting to falter. "Though she may seem distant and unapproachable, you must remember the eternal queen's knowledge transcends that of mere mortals. Listen to her."

The king coughed violently spitting up blood.

"I can see the spirits of my ancestors descending upon me," Broden said cryptically. Roanan looked about the room but saw nothing. "I am sorry that one so young must enter into his heritage on the verge of crisis. But I leave Ambrasian in good hands."

"But father," Roanan objected once more. "All seems at peace despite your protestations."

For a moment, the lawlessness that Roanan battled in the farming regions of Chrysalis flashed through his mind. Perhaps his father was more correct than he was willing to concede.

"Do not let looks deceive you," Broden cautioned. "You will learn to see that which is not apparent at first glance. Soon, the storm will commence. You will be swept up in its fury, but you must battle to come out the other end. All of Ambrasian depends on your success. I know you will make me proud."

Roanan began to think these were the ramblings of a dying man, a great king whose specters and nightmares now haunted his final moments. But he remained quiet.

"You will be a fine King, my son," Broden croaked. "Balance authority with compassion and you will wear the crown of the Red Knight of Chrysalis well."

Broden paused, concentrating on his final thoughts.

"Do well," he said to his son quietly. "All my love."

"Father!" Roanan cried.

Broden left a faint smile form on his lips and slowly closed his eyes. Roanan rested his head on his father's now lifeless body. After a few minutes, he finally rose.

"Dammit," Roanan said. "I needed more time."

After a few moments, he recognized that wish was not to be, no matter how fervent his hopes.

"I will miss you and I will love you forever," Roanan whispered. "But now, you are free."

The son wept. In an instant, the young heir had become the Red Knight, King of Chrysalis.

•   •   •   •   •

The ensuing days and weeks were a blur of activity. King Broden was laid to rest in a traditional Chrysalian service, Broden's remains were entombed in an intricately carved stone sarcophagus, which was placed in the Crypt of the Kings alongside his ancestors located deep underground. As he said his farewell to his father, Roanan noted that he, one day, would be placed in the space next to him. It was a grim reminder of mortality for one so young.

Roanan put off his formal coronation, driving his courtiers to distraction and causing concern among his closest confidantes. Lasarion could sense the heavy weight on the Red Knight's heart.

"Roanan," Lasarion said to his cousin plaintively, "this land needs a leader to rally around. You cannot put off the formal ceremony forever."

"I am a warrior, my brother, not a king," Roanan argued.

"Now, you are both," Lasarion said. "You cannot avoid your destiny. None of us can take your place."

"So it seems," Roanan answered.

Lasarion, tall and ruggedly handsome with jet-black hair, stood eye-to-eye with his sandy-haired cousin. Just as nearly all Ambrasians, their skin color had a darkly tanned tone with a touch of blue. Lasarion was Roanan's elder by four years and a powerful knight in his own right. He was also his cousin's best friend, and Lasarion could tell better than anyone the inner struggle that faced Roanan. He was genuinely concerned with the outcome. He hoped Tabeus could talk sense into him.

The Wizard Tabeus was a trusted confidante of the Kings of Chrysalis for generations. Broden had entreated Roanan to turn toward the Wizard for counsel with good reason. Tabeus would occasionally disappear for long stretches but always returned when needed, as if some inner beacon summoned him. While his origins were unknown, so too was his age, though the deep lines in his hollow face suggested the Wizard had witnessed many eras and many battles, both in victory and defeat. His eyes, however, a deep ocean blue, crackled with life and infinite wisdom.

In reality, Tabeus was one of the most powerful of Wizards, despite his aged appearance. He had served the Kings of Chrysalis–albeit in his own way and in his own time–for more than twenty generations and had roamed Ambrasian far longer than that. What brethren he had long ago had grown disinterested in the affairs of the peoples of Ambrasian. However, Tabeus still believed those who roamed the land held a greater purpose and would serve whatever the future held in store.

As Roanan and Lasarion continued to speak, Tabeus slipped into the King's meeting room quietly before either ever realized.

"The burden of leadership is heavy," the Wizard said. "You need both a strong back and an even stronger mind to carry it comfortably."

Roanan and Lasarion pivoted quickly, surprised they had not heard the Wizard's entrance. On Tabeus' shoulder sat Raven, the small but powerfully built black bird that served as the Wizard's companion. Whatever its species, it was unknown to either of the two knights. While

Raven never appeared to leave Tabeus' side, it appeared to all to have no special qualities. Still, Roanan held the bird with some modicum of suspicion and believed it had more talents than it typically demonstrated. Nevertheless, he could find nothing to explain his feelings, so he remained silent on the matter.

"Tabeus," Roanan said, watching the Wizard walk casually about the room. "Is there something you need?"

"Me?" Tabeus smiled. "Not personally. But I believe the people of Chrysalis need a proper King, and in their eyes, they cannot have that without a proper coronation. Though I know you have avoided the ceremony with all the wiles you can muster, it is time you take the step expected of you. Not for you, Roanan, but for your Kingdom and for your people. While the ritual may not be critical to you, and all the pomp and circumstance an unwanted annoyance, it is an important symbol of transition and celebration for your people. And a King is hardly a King if he does not serve his subjects."

Roanan looked at Tabeus, perhaps only now fully understanding his value.

"My father said it would be hard to argue with you," he said. "I see that he was wise in his counsel."

Tabeus smiled knowingly.

"I can offer as much advice as you can bear to hear," the Wizard said. "Perhaps too much at times. But as King, it is your decision what to do with my words."

Roanan studied the ancient Wizard once more.

"On his deathbed, my father spoke of a coming crisis," the Red Knight said. "Did he speak to you about his concerns?"

"Alas, he did," Tabeus responded. "Even as his body betrayed him, your father had a keen mind. We had many talks about an unspecified coming danger. And though I concur that some unknown threat feels near, even I cannot tell from where our peril lurks or when it will strike."

The Wizard studied the young ruler.

"But in any event," Tabeus continued, "if Chrysalis is to deal with whatever threat looms in the future whether near or far, they need a proper King, one they have witnessed having the crown placed on his sometimes stubborn head."

Roanan looked at Tabeus with some shock, but the Wizard merely smirked.

"So my sage counsel to you," he said, "is to give the people what they need."

Roanan studied Tabeus for a moment longer then chuckled.

"If that is what they need," the Red Knight said, "we shall accommodate them."

Four days later, Roanan the Red Knight was crowned King of Chrysalis and defender of Ambrasian. While the ceremony was not as extravagant as earlier coronations, it was still attended by all the knights of Chrysalis, as well as Karmin, the Regent of Karmana and other dignitaries from neighboring lands. When the festivities concluded, Karmin invited many of the young knights to participate in the Annual Games of Karmana, scheduled to begin in the ensuing days. A number of them accepted her invitation, and Karmin led an unlikely parade across Chrysalis to the heart of Ambrasian.

•   •   •   •   •

Following the celebration of his coronation, Roanan's official duties as King awaited him. Some days later, Roanan approached his first formal day of Court with deep apprehension. Never before did he serve as the ultimate authority. Rather than feel empowered, he felt trapped. Roanan had watched and admired his father deftly navigate the various visitors and supplicants to the Hall of Chrysalis, a duty he continued to perform until only recently when his illness overwhelmed him. But the Red Knight would much rather protect his kingdom mounted on his horse, Alajar, and brandishing his sword than sitting on a throne hearing impassioned pleas, hopeful promises, and outrageous proposals.

Nevertheless, Roanan spent many hours listening to the entreaties of the citizens. Tabeus was by his side, providing counsel and encouragement. Roanan delegated a number of requests to others who served Chrysalis, settled several disputes, and demonstrated fairness and wisdom beyond his young years. Daylight was already beginning to ebb when the Red Knight finally had heard all petitions for the day.

"You did well," Tabeus assured him afterwards. "These pleas and disputes are never as easy as they may appear."

"How do I know I did the right thing?" Roanan asked plaintively. "What if a decision I made today was wrong, and an innocent person suffers because of it?"

The Wizard smiled, understanding the young monarch's concerns.

"No one can predict a person's actions or foretell the future," Tabeus said. "Not even a Wizard. You can only be true to yourself and do what you believe is just for the parties involved and best for Ambrasian. If you do that, I believe that your good deeds will far outpace your bad."

Roanan smiled in appreciation.

"I thought Wizards couldn't foretell the future?" he asked.

Tabeus nodded.

"On occasion, I allow myself to break the rules," he said. "If you always maintain a sense of justice, that will provide you with the guidance you need."

Roanan and the Wizard parted ways, and the Red Knight slipped through the crowded castle. He retired early that night, directing his evening meal to be delivered to his sleeping chambers. Roanan had discovered through first-hand experience that the mental demands imposed on a King were sometimes just as taxing as the physical expectations. He slept well and woke before sunrise.

As he did on most mornings, the Red Knight decided he needed some quiet time and fresh air before another day at court. He needed to feel the wind running through his hair in the solitude of an open field before facing the din of the crowds. He slipped into the stables and acknowledged those caring for the horses. Several riders offered to escort the King, but Roanan waved them off. He needed time to be alone. He mounted Alajar and rode alone into the open fields. The King felt most free during these times.

The sunrise was just emerging over the horizon. The sky was calm. Roanan urged Alajar on toward the Darris River. The tall, chestnut stallion needed little guidance and appeared to be enjoying the exhilaration of a run as much as his rider. Roanan breathed deeply, finally finding some inner peace away from the frantic demands of the castle.

But suddenly without warning, the weather began to turn against him. Thunder rumbled menacingly and lightning flickered crazily across the countryside. The skies turned dark and winds howled across the landscape. Within seconds, the rains came, a terrible deluge that swept across the glade in torrents. Trees arched under the ferocious gales, and the rain turned the fields into a muddy, unnavigable slop. The storm was more ferocious than any Roanan had ever seen.

Still, the storm grew even worse, and despite Roanan's best efforts, it blew him and Alajar toward the river. Roanan urged his horse to fight against the monsoon-like winds, but together their herculean attempt was no match for the anger of the elements. The rain pelted sideways from the sky, nearly blinding both Roanan and Alajar. The rider and his horse fought off exhaustion, but the unnatural storm continued unabated. Alajar galloped this way and that, and Roanan lost all sense of direction, unable to see or maintain his course.

As they approached the Darris River, Roanan could tell that the channel had overflowed its banks and its waters ran uncontrollably through the plains. The winds became even more fierce, hurtling Roanan and Alajar into the raging waters. Roanan was thrown from his horse, and separately, the two were sent spinning down the rampaging currents of the Darris River.

The Red Knight fought for as long as he could, but ultimately, he was overwhelmed by the surrounding elements. He was hurtled down the river fighting to stay afloat and alive.

Shortly thereafter, the storm abated as quickly as it came. But in those few moments, the newly crowned King of Chrysalis had utterly and completely disappeared from his kingdom.

• • • • •

When Roanan did not return and riders found no trace of him, the sounds of alarm spread across the Hall of Chrysalis. Tabeus and Lasarion were among the first to reach the glade by the river. The Wizard looked suspiciously at the site.

"This was no ordinary storm," Tabeus said. "Nor was it coincidental that it hit when the King was alone. I fear this is the work of dark forces and the peril predicted by Broden may already be upon us."

Just then, both the Wizard and Raven cocked their heads to the east.

"Alas," Tabeus said. "It has begun. Those who work against us have wasted no time in their assault."

The Wizard's brow furrowed deeply as he gazed into the distance.

CHAPTER 6
THE ORACLE OF KARMANA

Celidia gazed into the distance, then turned away in satisfaction. She had begun to unfurl her plan across Ambrasian.

"The Weathermaster has done his job well," Celidia said, sensing Roanan's peril. "Now is the time to act."

The Sorceress had fashioned a spell to hide the location of her and her co-conspirator, the knight Maldur. But in truth they were already deep within the heart of Karmana, prepared to execute their scheme.

Maldur, clad in his self-chosen black colors, put his hand on his sword.

"It's about time," he spit. "We have been stuck in this hovel too long."

"I am sorry our accommodations do not meet your approval," Celidia said mockingly. "They were chosen for stealth, not for comfort."

The Black Knight scowled.

"Let's get on with this," he finally said. "It is past time we settle our grievances."

"As you wish," the Sorceress said.

Celidia and Maldur stepped out of the nondescript building into the heart of Karmana. They carefully masked their appearance to avoid recognition, but also counted on the hustle and bustle around them to blend into the crowd. The Annual Games of Karmana were an elaborate, days-long event that attracted both competitors and spectators from throughout the West. The village around the Hall of Karmana was filled with visitors, the perfect setting for strangers with ill intent to move about unnoticed.

The highlight of the Games was a fierce competition among the young and aspiring knights of the lands of Ambrasian. Youthful warriors traveled from Chrysalis, Kar-Braenes and even the pastoral lands of Selin and Balinwald to earn recognition and renown. Karmin herself trained many of the young aspirants in the glorious fields that surrounded the Hall of Karmana. Though they competed with blunted instruments, the battles were vicious nonetheless – many injuries were inflicted due to the aggressiveness of the tourney.

The Games attracted huge crowds from across the land, as many of the inhabitants of Ambrasian found the spectacle to be an ideal time to find both entertainment and respite from their busy lives. Vendors lined the streets, and those visitors from more remote areas could purchase clothing and fabrics, food and household necessities, and even farm animals and equipment in the markets that sprung up spontaneously in the heart of Karmana.

While the Games provided an ideal venue for an annual pilgrimage, no one needed an excuse to visit the fair lands of Karmana. The eternal springtime enjoyed in the heart of Karmana blessed the surrounding countryside with magnificent beauty found nowhere else in Ambrasian. The trees rose high into the air, their leaves a hearty and vibrant collage of green and red. Flowers bloomed in many-colored beauty. The land was a carousel of color: red flowed into blue, blue into purple, purple into pink, pink into yellow. The lush green grass was cut with paths lined with stones that seemed carved out of the surrounding landscape. Food and crops could be grown year-round and yielded bountiful harvests. Karmana was a land infused with magic at every level.

The roots of Karmana's beauty were well-known across the land, shared by bard and bedtime stories alike. Nevertheless, visitors to the Games could hear any number of orators wax upon the legend, even more so if the listener deposited a coin or two in the bucket next to the speaker's platform.

"Long ago, when the peoples migrated throughout the lands of Ambrasian, a certain tribe came to the center of the land," one bard recited to a crowd of ten or more. "The country was fair beyond description, with groves of trees and exotic plants and flowers as far as the eye could behold. The air was fresh and gardens grew as nowhere else in the world. There was a magical quality about Karmana from the first, as if the land had been truly blessed from its genesis."

The bard was dressed in a simple brown tunic and short breeches and wore open-toed leather shoes with a wooden sole. His collection bucket– a crudely constructed affair cut from wood and tied together with string– held a handful of coins of coppers and base metals of varying value.

"Truth be told, even the people grew fairer to behold and in time were the most beautiful in Ambrasian," he continued. "Clearly, as you can see, I was not one of the chosen few."

His audience chuckled. The storyteller nodded in appreciation.

"By and by, however," the bard said, "a strange thing occurred as even this land holds its own inexplicable mysteries. While the lives of the females grew longer and longer to the point of immortality, the males not only remained mortal but saw their lives shortened and their strength sapped. It was soon discovered that the very power than enriches the females of this land is the same that dooms males should they tarry longer than they must. In the end, the males were forced to move outside the borders of Karmana's magic."

The bard cleared his throat.

"In time, the females of Karmana found themselves separated from the lives of transient males," he said, a hint of melancholy in his voice. "One hundred years or fewer is but a blink of an eye to an immortal. The gift of immortality–if a gift is truly what it is–comes at a price. The females soon discovered that if they left Karmana for any length of time, their immortality faded, at times quickly. Occasionally, one would age unnaturally fast and die, sometimes in a matter of only a few months or even weeks. Their lives had become intimately enmeshed with their homeland. Life itself emanated from Karmana."

The orator paused dramatically and looked about, catching the eye of each member of his audience. A group of Karmana natives heard the last part of the bard's tale and looked at each other skeptically and chuckled between themselves. That, however, did not deter the storyteller from continuing his tale.

"Perhaps the magic did not come so much from the land itself," he suggested, his conspiratorial tone capturing the full attention of his audience. "Many strange tales tell of some sort of talisman that is the key to Karmana's long-lived residents and magical powers. Few have ever seen the object, but it is said to be in the shape of a golden beast, or perhaps some ethereal spirit. Speculation runs rampant, but I have been told by reliable sources, the true secret of this powerful object . . ."

The audience twittered among themselves. Any suggestion of the magic that lie behind Karmana drew both rapt attention and wild speculation. The speaker continued to hushed tones.

"A golden horse, two stories high," he said, "locked deep in the bowels of an invisible mountain . . ."

The Sorceress and Maldur walked by the spectacle at that moment, and Celidia rolled her eyes.

"Idiots and morons," Celidia spat as she listened to the last part of the bard's tale. "He wouldn't know the Oracle if it hit him on his thick head and knocked him cold."

In reality, for all the power held by the Oracle and for as much as it guided Karmana's fate, only a chosen few truly knew its secrets. Its form and even its very existence was the subject of much debate and conjecture. Both bedtime stories and tavern discussions often led to the power of the magic behind Karmana.

The truth was just as spectacular as the supposition.

In the center of Karmana was the Oracle, held deeply and securely within the Hall of Karmana. The Oracle, constructed in times lost to Ambrasian history, held a great power that gave both the land and its people their eternal beauty. While the Oracle was more powerful in close proximity, its influence emanated across Karmana, though it weakened the further from its resting place in the Hall.

Despite its power, the Oracle could not corrupt. Only in the hands of evil could the Oracle be used for evil purposes. The power of the Oracle had helped keep Ambrasian free from tyranny throughout its history. Karmana and Chrysalis had formed an unbreakable bond to secure peace and relative prosperity across the Western lands.

Little did anyone know the imminent peril the Oracle and those it protected now faced.

•   •   •   •   •

As the morning burst into full glory, the young warriors assembled on Sarania Field to prove their valor, their courage, and their skill at arms. With knights and those aspiring to be knights displaying a multiplicity of colors across the field and the crowds assembling to watch the spirited competition, Karmin arose as she had done so for many generations and in a loud, clear voice proclaimed:

"Let the Games begin."

Bells rang and a huge cheer emanated from the gathering crowd as the competitors across the field raised their swords and lances. Soon thereafter, the contests began in earnest. Throughout the competition, warriors tested their skills and mettle in individual competition. Horses roared, swords clanged against each other, fighters toppled in defeat and others lifted their arms in victory. Reputations rose and fell. The Games had begun early in the morning and were expected to last much of the day. Spectators cheered and booed their favorites, shared food and drink, and were thoroughly enthralled by the event. Successful warriors gained a following as the day went on.

This day, however, the Annual Games also provided the perfect diversion for Celidia and Maldur's foul plans. No one took much notice to two drably clothed strangers moving through the crowds in the heart of Karmana. Few if any discerned the effort the pair took to conceal their faces. But beneath their unpretentious and secretive appearances lie two formidable personas. Celidia, a fallen member of the race of Karmana, exiled for crimes both small and large. It was said that Celidia led an ill-advised coup to overthrow Karmin and assume the leadership of the land. Her obsession with power was fully revealed, her efforts repelled, and she was cast out of Karmana. She fled into the east, to Damora, where she slowly built a partnership with the Drens and eventually found a fellow exile: the knight Maldur. How she did not age rapidly as the bard's tale suggested was a matter for speculation: perhaps the warning was wrong or at least exaggerated, or perhaps Celidia had counteracted such a dire end with some unknown dark arts.

Maldur was born of a prominent family from the northeastern edge of Chrysalis. He demonstrated his skill with a sword at an early age and was a renowned warrior. But whether it be by choice or some mental defect, Maldur displayed a propensity for ruthlessness and cruelty. He harassed and robbed farmers and traders needlessly, killing several in incidents which he claimed were in self-defense. Few believed him and his violence became more wanton. Finally, the House of the Red Knight interceded, driving Maldur from the kingdom and stripping him of both of his land and his colors. Maldur and his family did not go quietly and took up arms against the King. But while Maldur survived the skirmish, his brothers were slain in the battle and the family of Maldur decimated. He landed in Damora, embittered and vowing vengeance, adopting black as his mantle and re-emerging as the self-proclaimed Black Knight. No country acknowledged his claim.

Both of them embittered by the perceived wrongs that Ambrasian had inflicted, Celidia and Maldur formed a compact based on revenge and the uncontrollable urge for power. They found willing partners in the Drens who held ancient grudges against the other peoples of Ambrasian. The Drens were complemented by the remnants of fighters still loyal to Maldur, though the ill-advised battle against the Red Knight and Maldur's own viciousness had reduced those warriors to only a handful. Nevertheless, those soldiers were skilled and experienced fighters and they recruited others from the darkest corners of Ambrasian.

Now, Celidia and Maldur were ready to launch their retribution on those who, in their minds, had unfairly stripped them of their rightful legacies and destroyed their good names. But to accomplish their ambitious plan, they needed to reach the Hall of Karmana undetected.

"Keep moving," Celidia castigated Maldur, aggravated at his slower pace. "We're not here sightseeing."

Maldur picked up his pace to keep up with the Sorceress.

"I don't see the need to run through the crowd and draw attention to ourselves," he muttered.

"Imbecile," Celidia hissed. "Do you think I can walk through Karmana all day and not be recognized? I am the most notorious criminal in their history. I have been banned from this land for eternity. If one of them recognizes me, our quest will be finished before it even begins."

The Black Knight grunted, but quickened his pace nevertheless.

After a few more turns through the busy streets, Maldur and Celidia reached the majestic gardens that decorated the grounds that lay before the Hall of Karmana. They looked about, but most of the crowds had already converged onto Sarania Field for the Games or continued to shop at the various shops and stands throughout the town. Only two guards remained at the entrance, one a native female warrior, the other a male from Kar-Braenes in service to Karmana.

"As usual, Karmin is overconfident in her own perceived omnipotence," Celidia scoffed. "The location of the most powerful single force in Ambrasian is empty and hardly guarded. These two sentries have barely reached puberty."

The two waited as inconspicuously as possible until the area emptied of passersbys. Then, with no one within sight, they approached the two guards, who came to attention and blocked the entrance to the Hall.

"Halt," the female guard announced. Celidia and Maldur simultaneously pulled daggers tipped with poison from within their cloaks and hurled them in a well-practiced motion. The daggers caught both guards in the throat, and they dropped dead instantly. The two hurriedly dragged the bodies of the guards off to the side, crudely hiding them behind the trees and flora of the garden. The ruse would not last long, but hopefully long enough for them to accomplish their task.

"This is an undignified way for a knight to slay his foe," Maldur complained. "Hidden knives and poison. This is the business of swords."

Celidia looked at the Black Knight incredulously.

"Would you rather attract the attention of all of Karmana with a noisy and bloody battle directly in front of the Hall of Karmana?" she asked. "Patience! We have not completed our task here yet. You'll likely still get your chance to prove your manliness before we finish."

Maldur scowled but said nothing further.

Celidia moved toward the huge bronze gates that barred the entrance. She closed her eyes and chanted quietly, finally placing her hand on one of the gates. It held firm for a moment, then slipped open under the Sorceress' prodding.

"So predictable," the Sorceress muttered. "You would think Karmin would at least bother to make the spell more complex than that."

The two entered the inner chamber unnoticed. The Hall of Karmana was nearly deserted. Once inside, Maldur and Celidia proceeded cautiously, deliberately choosing a path to avoid any additional guards that may be stationed within the Hall. They moved slowly and carefully through the many corridors whose walls told the story of Karmana's history: its leaders and accomplishments shown by painting, statues and other great works of art. Each sound Maldur and Celidia heard was amplified tenfold by their ever-alert senses, and each time they froze briefly, waiting for the sound to pass. At one point, Maldur began to speak, but Celidia raised a finger and glowered at her companion viciously. The Black Knight reluctantly fell silent.

After a time that felt longer than it truly was, Maldur and Celidia approached the Room of the Oracle. It was located on one of the lower floors of the Hall, guarded day and night by two additional guards, one again a native female of Karmana and the second another young knight from Kar-Braenes. A magical incantation of great power sealed the doors which were brightly colored and followed a mystical sequential pattern. Colors flowed one into another until it was impossible to know where one hue started and another ended.

Celidia surveyed the scene, finding it exactly as she expected. After thousands of years, Karmana had settled into a routine that rarely changed.

"Just as it has been done for five hundred years," she muttered under her breath. "That will be her downfall."

Celidia cast a spell that distracted the sentries, allowing the two intruders to gain an advantageous position without being noticed.

The Black Knight moved quickly. Darting out from behind a thick marble pillar, he dropped his cloak and drew his sword. The weapon exploded through the air as Maldur moved toward one of the guards. Unable to avoid the sudden attack, the male guard felt the weapon pierce his chest, cutting deeply through bone and flesh.

The second guard had snapped back to attention and was more skilled than her counterpart. However, she was held another moment by the gaze of Celidia, long enough for Maldur to finish with the first guard. She finally recovered, and now faced the Black Knight, both of their swords ready to attack.

Their weapons flashed through the air meeting each other with a loud clang. The guard, much smaller and less experienced than the imposing Black Knight, lost her footing fleetingly but regained it quickly. Still, she was left to parry his constant attack, defending herself as best she could. Finally, both Maldur and the guard swung their swords nearly simultaneously, but the Black Knight's was a second faster and more true. The sentry fell in a heap.

"Satisfied now that your bloodletting has more than likely alerted all of Karmana to our scheme?" Celidia asked.

"Hurry," Maldur cried, turning back to the Sorceress. "We haven't much time."

The Sorceress glared at her companion petulantly.

"You should have thought of that before making such a racket," Celidia said. "Now you have to show some modicum of patience. You cannot hurry past ancient magic. It must be broken properly, or it will not be broken at all."

"If you do not work quickly," the Black Knight retorted, "we will be discovered and quickly surrounded. Then you can take all the time you want—while hanging from a scaffold."

Celidia frowned, glancing over to her accomplice.

"This chamber is much like your brain, Maldur," she responded. "Nearly impenetrable."

Maldur glared angrily, but the Sorceress failed to notice. At that moment, Celidia seemingly went into a deep trance. She remained silent for some time, remembering the exact words she had memorized from the texts preserved by the Drens for so many generations. She uttered a series of short phrases in the ancient tongue, putting careful emphasis where required. She repeated it, then again, and the doors swung open revealing the magnificent treasure within the inner chamber.

The Room of the Oracle was filled with gold, silver and precious jewels piled high along its glistening walls, as the most protected room in Karmana was also used to house the land's treasure. The chamber itself was constructed from rare metals with ornate scenes delicately etched into its walls. An unnatural glow filled the air, illuminating the room with no obvious source. In the middle of the room, by itself on a marble column protected by a crystal dome was the Oracle of Karmana.

The Oracle took the form of a miniature obelisk, and from it radiated a nearly blinding reddish-white haze which pulsated, growing stronger and weaker in short, irregular intervals.

Maldur and Celidia momentarily stood in awe at the sight before them. The power of the Oracle was hypnotizing for those who gazed upon it. Soon, however, the Black Knight and the Sorceress were shaken back to action by their goal and the knowledge they had little time to accomplish their task. Together, they moved toward the Oracle. In a flash, the sword of the Black Knight came crashing down, shattering the glass dome. Maldur reached out to pick up the Oracle but could not. No matter how much strength he exerted, the Oracle remained in place.

He looked at Celidia confusedly.

"It won't move," he said, his quandary deepening with each passing second.

"Dullard," Celidia answered. "Do you think you are stealing some bauble for your latest female conquest? The Oracle is the single most powerful force in all of Ambrasian. You don't just come in and snatch it like a grape off the vine."

The Sorceress shook her head in disgust.

"It's good you fight with your sword and not with your head," she muttered.

Celidia then moved Maldur aside and quietly whispered over the Oracle, again reciting in a tongue unknown to any living being. The Sorceress arose and looked at the Black Knight.

"Now watch this," she said.

The Sorceress easily lifted the Oracle from its resting place and muted its powerful glow. Celidia then slid it under the folds of her gown and turned toward the door.

"It is time for us to depart," she said. "Let's try not to draw any more attention to ourselves."

Celidia left the room with Maldur following in her footsteps. The two hurried through the Hall of Karmana, retracing their earlier steps. Somewhat to their surprise, Karmana had not yet awoken to its imminent peril. As the two burst from the Hall and into the sunlight hurriedly continuing their escape, Dainwirth Lir, a young knight from the southern kingdom of Balinwald, finally spotted them. Unnaturally tall and lanky for his people but slight of frame and strength, Dainwirth Lir had been defeated early in the Games and was heading dejectedly home.

No longer disguised, Maldur and Celidia were notorious and known widely across Ambrasian. After only a few moments, Dainwirth Lir recognized the pair. He quickly rushed at them with his horse, trying to deter them. Though he was unaware of their plot, Lir was sure they held nothing but evil intentions.

"Stop, in the name of all of Karmana," he cried, drawing his sword.

Maldur turned and looked at the young warrior with disdain.

"Another heroic jackass," the Black Knight muttered, bringing his sword up to an attack position. "We have no time for this."

In one quick notion, the Black Knight knocked Dainwirth Lir to the ground as he passed. As he fell, Lir's head bounced off the pathway below, rendering him unconscious. Maldur and Celidia adorned their robes once more, hurried into the main streets of the village and slipped back into the steady flow of passerbys. A short while later, they reached their horses hidden nearby. Within minutes of their theft, the Black Knight and the Sorceress galloped away from the center of Karmana toward the land of Damora leaving no trace of their whereabouts.

Meanwhile, ever so slowly across the center of Karmana, as Dainwirth Lir slowly regained his senses, the alarm was spreading throughout the land. Karmin sensed the peril first, but as the Oracle moved further and further away from the center of the realm, all the native females of Karmana began to feel its loss. Somewhere deep within their being, many of these eternal beings felt the stench of mortality for the first time in their lives. They rushed to the Hall, but far too late. Maldur and Celidia were already hurrying across the plains of eastern Karmana and were approaching the Sylil River.

Unlike any other point the recorded history of Ambrasian, the Immortal Land of Karmana now faced the prospect of Death.

CHAPTER 7
THE GREY KNIGHT

While Karmana was only starting to awaken to its peril, the full terror of the day had not yet been realized. For while the Oracle of Karmana was the jewel of Maldur and Celidia's plan, it was only one piece of the overall plot they had unleashed across all of Ambrasian. They had untethered terror and chaos across the land.

In the Elvii land of Necinia found deep within the Great Forest, a swath of destruction marred the ancient beauty. Trees were uprooted, stones overturned, and wanton annihilation marred the landscape. A number of Elvii lay grievously injured, and even a few lay dead. Much of the fair kingdom of the Elvii, whose homes blended seamlessly with the surrounding forest, was in shambles. The delicate balance the Elvii had achieved with nature through generations had been shattered. Wooden arches were torn in half, while grass-thatched roofs and stone paths were cloven and scattered.

The Elvii busied themselves tending to the dying and wounded and repairing the widespread damage that surrounded them. The mysterious race was little known and even less seen outside of their forest home, avoiding the greater society across Ambrasian. The Elvii were lithe and small, rarely rising to more than five feet in height. They were fair of face and hair, with a paler complexion than the other peoples of Ambrasian. Nimble and quick, the Elvii could move through the forest like the wind and only the most sharp-eared creatures of the land would hear their approach. The Elvii were skilled with the bow but were naturally peaceful and only used their skill in self-defense. Even the wild beasts did not need fear Elvii arrows for the Elvii ate no meat. Some went as far to say that the Elvii's nourishment was not natural to Ambrasian but had some magical quality about it. But this day, the Elvii had seen a terror not seen in many years and their collective psyche had been badly battered.

What could have inflicted such wanton destruction on such a peaceful folk hidden deep within the Great Forest?

"Icyx," Siora said with a mix of anger and sadness as he surveyed the damage with a group of fellow Elvii. The recognized leader of the Elvii had trouble comprehending the sudden turn of events. "The beast hasn't been seen for generations. What evil has befallen Ambrasian that he wreaks terror here? And to what purpose?"

The Elvii were not immortal as the women of Karmana, but they were long-lived, with life spans stretching into the hundreds of years. Yet they remained isolated, typically separating themselves from the heroics and follies of other races. Only rarely did they leave the confines of Necinia, and even then only briefly. Few of Ambrasian's inhabitants had even seen the Elvii. To some, they remained in the realm of bedtime stories and legends.

"You listen or the Elvii will steal you in the middle of the night," more than one mother had told her children. "Then they will cook you and eat you!"

Such admonitions were grossly unfair and impugned the reputation of the tranquil forest folk. But the Elvii were little concerned with the thoughts of those outside the woodland.

Nevertheless, the Elvii had proved valiant in the War of the Marshes many centuries ago and had remained friendly with the Wizards. Tabeus, especially, had formed a bond with the Elvii and their leader. The Wizard knew the Elvii, though generally pacifist in nature, would respond in times of crisis.

Benoa and Grilia, fellow elder Elvii, surveyed the scene with Siora.

"Why would the beast attack us?" Benoa asked aloud. "We posed no threat."

"I do not understand why this could have happened," Grilia echoed.

Siora looked at the two thoughtfully.

"Icyx did not leave Isalis without provocation," the eldest and wisest of the Elvii said. "Nor did he attack Necinia randomly. No, some power drove him to a madness that led to this act, and I fear we are not the only victims. I believe the whole of Ambrasian is under attack, and we are but a small part of a greater plan. I feel a series of tragic events that have uprooted our land. Some evil scheme is intent on despoiling all that it can."

As Siora and his two companions walked through the willful destruction of their ransacked habitat, they observed the Elvii already working to rebuild their villages. Those injured had their wounds tended, the few who perished trying to deter Icyx were given back to the soil of Ambrasian.

The Elvii had belatedly defended themselves when they realized that the beast had been driven to its frenzy by some malevolent force and their attempts to calm the creature failed. A few had fired arrows that hit their target, causing some injury but failing to inflict serious harm to Icyx. The beast's tough, nearly impenetrable outer skin prevented the Elvii arrows from causing any grievous wounds. Finally, driven away by a more and more furious Elvii counterattack, Icyx continued his rampage beyond the borders of Necinia. The Elvii, still reeling from the sudden and unprovoked attack, allowed Icyx to flee.

But despite the sudden terror and tragic loss, as the three Elvii walked, song permeated the forest. For even in times of distress, the Elvii celebrated life, and their voices were fair indeed.

For years uncounted we have toiled among these trees of green
In harmony and peace with those around us
Despite our troubles and our current travails
We will endure and prosper once again
We remember those we lost and it fills our hearts with sadness
But we move forward in hopes of better days to come . . .

"Evil has grown stronger while we have sat idle," Siora finally said, breaking the silence. "We have heard warnings in the wind, but too late. The old magic loses its potency. This land may not be safe much longer for the likes of the Elvii or their friends if this path continues unabated. Perhaps we have been mistaken in keeping our distance from the everyday affairs of Ambrasian."

The Elvii picked up the remnants of a broken wall. He pondered the recent chain of events.

"Broden is dead," Siora continued. "The knights of Ambrasian speak valiant words, but they are untested in the face of true adversity. Lands such as Selin and Balinwald show little resolve. Even we Elvii have withdrawn from the greater world. It is little wonder that evil has chosen now to strike."

"What will we do?" Benoa finally asked.

Siora pondered his options and then appeared to come to some internal decision.

"I must find Tabeus and learn how this threat has manifested itself across the land," he finally said. "We may no longer be able to avoid the dealings of our neighbors."

• • •

In Balinwald, the third part of Maldur and Celidia's sinister plan unfolded simultaneously in a well-orchestrated sequence of actions. The Black Knight and the Sorceress hoped to send Ambrasian into utter chaos and in that goal they achieved spectacular success. Brelex, the Grey Knight, a powerful ally of Maldur who coveted the throne of Balinwald for himself, was holding the King's castle under siege.

The southernmost land had lay in peace for generations, and though a few of its youth often joined in the games of Karmana, knighthood did not flourish in Balinwald. The land had assumed an agrarian lifestyle, and most natives were content to farm their land and tend to their herds. They had little appetite for combat, and their travel was typically limited to the markets in which they traded their harvest for other household needs.

Brelex came from a family that rejected such passivity. His great-grandfather had vied for the throne many years before, and though had had been defeated, the House of the Grey Knight never fully surrendered the quest. Simmering resentment passed through generations. Though his grandfather and father maintained an uneasy peace with those who ruled in the Hall of Balinwald, there was little warmth in the relationship. Open revolts had never occurred, but the threat always remained viable.

Brelex, however, was more impulsive and ambitious than his father and grandfather and had tired of the sleepy rule of King Sardenia, vigorous in his prime but now an elder ruler who could barely raise a sword, much less represent the House of the Blue Knight. Sardenia had aged and grown as sedentary as his people. The Grey Knight had grown weary of seeing his land and his people fade into perpetual somnolence.

Recruited into Celidia and Maldur's overall conspiracy and promised free rein over his own kingdom, Brelex had used the people's inertia and the fading of Sardenia's rule to his advantage and attacked an unprepared kingdom with a collection of warriors and soldiers corrupted to his purpose by promises of treasure and power. A troop of Drens sent by Celidia and the Black Knight from Damora joined him, though their swords were hardly needed as the Grey Knight encountered little resistance.

Brelex himself was a knight with no equal other than perhaps Roanan and Maldur. His appearance was unlike those of most of his Balinwald kin. While his countrymen rarely exceeded a height of five-feet nine-inches, Brelex towered a good six inches over that, with broad shoulders and a powerful build. He possessed great strength and his stamina was a thing of legend. It was said that after all others had tired the figure of the Grey Knight prowled the battlefield for many hours afterward. However, Brelex was feared rather than revered. Greed alone, it was said, drove the Grey Knight. Celidia's promises of wealth and a throne of his own easily played on that trait and his lust for power.

And so secretly, Brelex had crossed the marshes into Damora and there plotted with Maldur and Celidia, planning his attack and agreeing on a date to unleash his fury. Upon his return, he summoned his army, complementing his standing force with new recruits and a battalion of Drens. The Hall of the Grey Knight swelled with his followers. He promised his fighters both wealth and position, the leaders of his new order in a redefined world.

When Roanan was cast downstream and with Chrysalis in its own turmoil, the Grey Knight finally enacted his part of the master plan. With Celidia and Maldur penetrating the defenses around the Oracle, the Sorceress released the power of Icyx to further disrupt the land, hide their true intent, and distract the Elvii from the real evil at hand. Finally, Brelex took his assembled forces and marched on the Hall of Balinwald to challenge Sardenia. Despite clear rumblings across the kingdom of Brelex's movements, the king was ill-prepared for his inevitable attack. As a dread storm moves quickly through the night, Brelex's fighters easily overtook the King's vanguard and stormed the inner gates.

Brelex met little resistance even within the castle. The surprised defenders of the King were badly outnumbered and ill-prepared. They were easily swept away in the surge of the Grey Knight's offensive. Soon, the castle was ablaze, its occupants trapped and helpless.

Leaving the rest of the castle to his ravenous army, the Grey Knight summoned a small contingent of his closest fighters and headed toward the royal chambers. He met pockets of resistance, but Sardenia's soldiers were poorly prepared and overwhelmed. Brelex's fighters left a trail of bodies in their wake, and the Grey Knight set guards to make sure they would not be surprised from behind. Finally, Brelex and his remaining followers burst through the inner confines of the Castle and reached the conclave where Sardenia hid. He was guarded by four knights, the last of his defenses. They raised their swords, but Brelex and his companions hacked them down with little effort.

Finally, the Grey Knight faced the King of Balinwald. Sardenia, aged and gaunt in the best of times, now appeared even more frail and defenseless. The King backed into the corner, staring at Brelex fearfully. The Grey Knight stepped deliberately toward Sardenia.

"What do you want?" Sardenia asked, attempting to muster whatever authority his voice still possessed, but instead hearing it crack in fear.

"That's easy," Brelex said. "I want the crown on your head."

"That is not yours to take," Sardenia said as defiantly as he could.

"No?" Brelex chided. "If you don't give it willingly, I will take it by force."

The Grey Knight raised his sword, and in one powerful burst, beheaded the fallen King. Sardenia dropped in a heap. Brelex leaned over, casually plucked the crown off the head, whose eyes now stared lifelessly into the distance. The Grey Knight turned back toward the door.

"There is one more prize to be had," he muttered.

Brelex and his men stormed down the hall toward the chambers of Sardenia's daughter, Athena. Two last guards stood at the entrance, their swords drawn.

Brelex laughed mockingly.

"You are hopelessly outnumbered and your King is dead," he said. "Are you really going to be a martyr to a lost cause?"

The guards hesitated, then charged toward Brelex and his soldiers. The fight was brief and one of the Grey Knight's men killed. But ultimately, the guards fell.

Brelex moved forward and burst into the princess's chambers. Athena whirled to face him, firmly holding a thin knife. She was hardly the fearful maiden the Grey Knight might have expected.

Brelex merely laughed.

"A rare jewel," he said. "A princess whose beauty is matched only by her spirit."

Athena spit at the Grey Knight in response.

"Leave me be," Athena said bravely, "or I'll stab you through."

Brelex smirked.

"With that?" the Grey Knight laughed. "I will forgive your insolence considering the circumstances. You may accompany me either as my guest or as my prisoner. Your choice."

"I should die first," Athena responded.

"As you wish," Brelex laughed. He moved toward Athena, avoided her wild swing, and quickly forced the knife from the princess' hands with a series of deft moves. Then, the Grey Knight's men bound Athena's hand and feet, and Brelex himself picked the princess up and threw her over his shoulder. He and his solders worked their way back through the myriad of hallways and mounted their horses. Brelex roughly hoisted his prize over one of the horses and tied her fast. When finished, the Grey Knight and his forces departed the grounds.

Brelex had left the castle in ruins and the rulers of Balinwald dead. He was soon charging across the rocky terrain of the country to his own Hall on the Sylil River on the boundary of Damora. Balinwald belonged to the Grey Knight. The third part of Celidia and Maldur's plan was completed.

Further to the north, Maldur and Celidia had crossed the plains of Karmana at a lightning pace and reached the Watchtower on the boundary of Damora. The Watchtower had originally been built to guard the only natural path into Karmana from the East. The marshes lay to the south, and the Great Forest formed a nearly impenetrable barrier to the north of the Tower.

But the Watchtower had been virtually undefended during Ambrasian's time of tranquility and the threat of an attack by the Drens-thought to be scattered and greatly diminished-dismissed as unlikely. No one considered the possibility of outsiders rousing the forces of the East into action. But as turmoil enveloped Ambrasian, a troop of Drens easily overtook the Watchtower, slaying the few guards who remained. The Drens were savage and relentless in battle. Those in the West claimed their lust for blood and havoc was surpassed only by their lust for food. They ate monstrously, yet remained thin, their skeletons seeming to cling to their dank prickly skin.

Now that they had claimed the Watchtower, Celidia and Maldur had begun to remake it into their own fortress, an ideal location from which to launch further attacks and gather their forces from the East for battle. While the Watchtower lacked for material comforts, it served as a ready and sturdy base for warfare.

Celidia entered an inner chamber that she had claimed as the lair from which to launch her all-out attack on Ambrasian. Both large and secure, the chamber provided a strategic view of the west. No force could come upon the Watchtower unawares, yet the Sorceress could continue her work in privacy without constant interruption.

Celidia took the Oracle from beneath the folds of her gown and unwrapped it from its casing. The reddish-white glow flickered eerily off the ancient stone walls, and Celidia could feel herself already growing stronger and more powerful by its presence. She knew, however, that to exploit fully the power of the Oracle she would need to master its secrets and bend its strength to her will. That would take some time, but Celidia was confident in her own skills and the knowledge she had gained.

Maldur had stayed with the Drens momentarily, inspecting their progress and barking directions, then followed the Sorceress into the Watchtower, shaking his head in disgust.

"Those Drens are hopeless," the Black Knight mumbled. "Stubborn and thick-headed."

"You must be related," Celidia said. The Black Knight ignored the insult.

"And worse yet . . .," Maldur added.

"Worse?" the Sorceress asked mockingly.

" . . .they stink," Maldur said. "They smell like the swamp. They must never bathe."

"A small price to pay for all of Ambrasian," the Sorceress answered. "And where exactly do you expect all of them to wash? We have an army of thousands. I don't recall you bringing bathing facilities in your provisions."

The Sorceress looked intently at Maldur and turned more serious.

"Too long have we been scorned and cast aside," she said. "Do not fret over small inconveniences, Maldur. Our revenge draws near. Soon, Karmin and the rest of Karmana will know the power of Celidia."

"And the Black Knight," Maldur added.

"Yes, you too," the Sorceress mumbled begrudgingly.

Maldur walked around the room impatiently.

"In a few days, we will be strong enough to destroy all the armies of the west," he chuckled. "Brelex will arrive, and together our forces will be unbeatable."

Maldur paused.

"But even so, one thing disturbs me," he added.

"What's that?" Celidia asked.

"Despite the presence of the Oracle, I feel no different than before," Maldur observed.

"Perhaps you are too dense for it to have any effect," Celidia suggested.

"Perhaps your words are sharper than your spells," Maldur snapped.

The Sorceress shook her head in frustration.

"Patience, you oaf," Celidia said. "The Oracle works without you having to feel it. Its effect will be brought out in battle–when you slay Roanan, if he is ever seen again."

"Yes," Maldur finally agreed, "whoever leads the pitiful army of Chrysalis, Roanan or some poor substitute, I will slay him where he stands."

The Black Knight, satisfied, turned and left the room.

In truth, Maldur and Celidia had wreaked devastation across the land. In just a few short hours, Roanan had disappeared without a trace, leaving Chrysalis in disarray. The theft of the Oracle had sundered the ancient balance of Karmana. The Elvii lands of Necinia had suffered through a deadly rampage, and the kingdom of Balinwald had fallen. Ambrasian teetered on the brink.

CHAPTER 8
MISSION DELAYED,
GALACTIC DATE 2142-08-02

Aboard the Explorer, the turn of events on the surface of the planets had been wholly unexpected. Captain Evenru and Office Penra stood stunned as they watched the violent upheaval occur across Ambrasian. What appeared at first to be a planet in a relatively standard phase of development now faced a societal turmoil of catastrophic proportions. The officer finally turned back at Evenru.

"Captain," he said, "it appears we have arrived at the outbreak of a war."

"You think?" the captain said sarcastically. "A world war for all intents and purposes."

"From a broad perspective, the conflict seems to be a classic conflict of good versus evil," Penra observed.

Evenru looked at the officer thoughtfully.

"Never assume," the captain said. "Remember, the victors always write history. The vanquished become the villains. History is inevitably a one-sided affair. There's little objectivity in most accounts."

"A universal truth," Penra agreed.

Kevo was about to offer the perspective of Artificial Intelligence, but it paused when the Command Center doors whistled open.

"Captain," Officer Kalli said as she entered the command deck, "the asteroid has cleared the outer planet and is in open space. We can proceed with our mission at any time."

Evenru checked the ship's screens that charted the path of the potential planet killer. He then glanced back at the images of the drama occurring on the planet. His mind was conflicted.

"How much time before the asteroid enters critical space?" the Captain finally asked.

Approximately 42 galactic days," Kalli reported, quickly double-checking her calculations.

"Exactly 42.472 days," Kevo interrupted.

Evenru stared at the command console, started to say something, then thought better of it.

"That gives us some time," he said, "and it appears we are witnessing a critical juncture in the history of this planet. I think we can take some period to continue our observations and record the sequence of events so this planet can be fully documented for future missions."

Kalli considered the options and nodded her assent.

"I agree we have a significant window before we need to take action," she said.

Officer Penra walked up to join the conversation.

"Captain," he said, "we have witnessed some unusual anomalies on the planet. The storm that swept the King of Chrysalis away appeared to come out of nowhere with no antecedent weather pattern that could account for such an event. And I have no rational explanation of why the so-called Oracle has such power. It's like the laws of science do not apply here."

The ship's AI suddenly came to life, lights flashing angrily across the console.

"Impossible," Kevo interjected with emphasis. "The laws of science always apply to every situation. To suggest otherwise is illogical."

Had they not known better, the Lux crew could have sworn that Kevo had more than a hint of irritation in his voice. Evenru sighed.

"I'm sure there's a sound scientific explanation," the Captain said, calming the AI and assuring his crew. "Besides, we haven't really seen any magical powers emanating from this so-called Oracle. It glows, but there are many substances across the universe that can do that with no help from magic. Simple chemical reactions can create the same effect."

Evenru stared back at the multiple screens and holographic images in the Command Center transmitting back the various views gathered by the drones spread across the planet.

"We'll learn more about the planet and its people in the coming days," he concluded. "Let's see if this crisis on the planet resolves itself–with or without magic."

The crew was sure Kevo grunted.

"I will redouble my analysis of the planet and its inhabitants," the ship's AI said curtly.

Evenru sat back into the command chair, somewhat bemused at the turn of events.

"Assume your normal stations," he said.

The Explorer continued its geosynchronous orbit around the suddenly much more interesting world of Ambrasian. The ship's crew continued to collect data that would eventually be shared with all known intergalactic travelers.

CHAPTER 9
THE CAVE OF INNAIS

Sometime later that morning after the terrible storm had driven him far off his chosen path, Roanan awoke. He was lying by a creek on the grass under an Elex, a hardwood tree with thick bark and long, drooping branches. The storm had passed and bright sunshine warmed his still wet body and clothing. Alajar grazed nearby, shaken but apparently uninjured.

Roanan slowly stood, his body bruised and swollen. Water dripped from his red and grey clothing. The Red Knight was hardly the image of a warrior King as he moved stiffly through the meadow. He first checked his trusted steed. Alajar suffered from some scratches, but Roanan confirmed that he had escaped serious harm.

We were lucky, Roanan thought. *Or protected. But I have never seen the likes of such a storm.*

Roanan carefully surveyed the surrounding scene. The waterway behind him bore no resemblance to the mighty Darris, and the Red Knight presumed his path had somehow taken him well off the course of the well-travelled river. The forest stretched endlessly in every direction and another small stream skipped over the rocks nearby. The sun had risen over the tops of the trees and glistened between the branches. Its heat was drying the morning dew and birds began singing as they crept out of their shelter. The Red Knight had no idea where he was or how far he had been driven away from Chrysalis. He suspected foul play in such a sudden and violent storm and feared what was occurring in his absence.

"There's some evil intent at work here," Roanan muttered. "My father was right. I should have taken his words more seriously. Things are gravely astray. I must return to Chrysalis as quickly as possible."

But where exactly is Chrysalis, he wondered. *Perhaps more importantly, where am I? I do not recognize this place.*

The Red Knight peered across the landscape. Hills lie in the distance and he committed to reaching higher ground in order to help determine his location. He proceeded across the meadow, only to see a sudden movement among the trees ahead of him. Somehow, despite his travails in the river, his sword was still sheathed to his body, and he quickly drew it, assuming a defensive posture. Examining his surroundings closely, he saw nothing but the dense forest before him. He took several more steps, but again sensed the motion before him. He moved slowly, reaching the tree line, then carefully and intensely searching in the thick underbrush. Again, he saw nothing.

Advancing once more, Roanan found an elex tree blocking his path. Stepping around it, he saw yet another in his path, and glancing about he found they now surrounded him. The trees circled him in a wide arch, leaving no passage.

"Now what treachery is this?" the Red Knight scowled. "Has even the ground and the trees turned against me?'

Roanan rode to all his Kingly height, but a telling bead of perspiration glided down his forehead.

"I am Roanan, the Red Knight, King of Chrysalis," he proclaimed in a commanding voice. "Speak, or I shall sever your limbs from your trunks one by one and leave you to whither and rot."

Even Roanan sensed the irony of threatening a cadre of trees.

This is ridiculous, he thought. *I am being held captive by a collection of timber.*

The trees for their part swayed gently in the wind, seemingly unimpressed. After a few seconds, the tree nearest Roanan laughed in a low, smoky voice.

"Do not waste your time," it bellowed. "Before your sword would inflict one blow, we will have changed into the very air it swings through."

Roanan was undeterred.

"Explain yourself," the Red Knight demanded. "I am in no mood for riddles."

The tree appeared to grow taller and closed in on Roanan.

"I speak no riddles," it rumbled. "I am Phelin, leader of my people. We are the Reomites. We can assume the shape of the beings or elements about us, and we do so effortlessly and instantly. This is our land, which we call Arminan, a land on which you have trespassed. So it is you who should explain yourself, supposed Red Knight from Chrysalis."

Roanan examined Phelin more carefully.

"Arminan?" he asked. "I have never heard of such a land, and I have traveled Ambrasian from east to west and north to south."

"To you," Phelin continued, "it is known as the Land of Mystery."

"The Land of Mystery?" Roanan said uncertainly. "It is said no one ever enters here, for those who do never return."

Phelin laughed wickedly.

"You Cadaren learn well," he said. "Too bad you did not heed those warnings!"

Roanan assumed a look of contriteness.

"A storm the power of which I have never seen before swept me many miles," he explained. "I was unaware of my direction, nor could I have changed it if I did. I finished my journey here. It was not by design."

Phelin remained coldly silent.

"Surely, there is some compassion in your hearts," the Red Knight continued. "I implore you to lead me out of your kingdom. It is not a place to which I expect to return, and I fear some great evil is afoot that brought me here."

"Compassion?" Phelin shot back. "If Cadarens would only show some of the compassion of which they so glibly speak. Many of your kind have entered the Land of Mystery. No one has left and for good reason. Vile, disrespectful of other life forms, dangerous and violent. They have learned their lesson, and you will suffer the same fate. There is no escape!"

Roanan's face hardened. He did not take well to threats.

"I am not so certain of that as you," he said angrily.

In one swift motion, the Red Knight brought his sword forward, and the blade thundered through the air toward Phelin. And yet, there was no contact. The weapon passed harmlessly through the slight breeze. The tree—Phelin—had vanished as had the rest of the Reomites. Roanan searched to the left and the right and finally above him. He saw a flock of bluish-green birds, each only six inches long, of the kind that had flitted about and sang throughout the morning.

One of the birds flew down and sat on the branch of a nearby elex.

"As I said before," Phelin chirped, "it is useless to attack. You have but a single hope. There is only one way out of the land of Arminan. You must find the true shape and identity of the Reomites. Should you do that, we will lead you out of our kingdom and become your ally in time of need. In not, you must resign yourself to your fate."

Roanan held back the fury building within him.

"Exactly where will I find the solution to this latest riddle of yours?" the Red Knight asked.

The bird flew off, and the flock followed him.

"The answer," Phelin answered, his voice trailing off, "can be found in the Cave of Innais."

The bird then stopped and turned toward Roanan.

"Do not tarry," he warned. "We will return when the sun rises once more to see if you have succeeded in your quest."

The bird laughed.

"But do not be too optimistic, Red Knight of Chrysalis," he continued. "When morning comes, if you have not discovered our identity, you are doomed to wander the rest of your life in a land where there is no escape. Be prepared—the time we allow will make little difference."

Suddenly, the flock pivoted abruptly and flew away rapidly.

"Wait," Roanan cried. "Where can I find this Cave of Innais?"

But Phelin and the rest of the Reomites disappeared into the distance without an answer.

"Dammit," Roanan swore as he watched his adversary fly out of sight. The Red Knight slammed the tip of his sword into the ground. He was the King of Chrysalis, but at this moment, he felt completely powerless. He could not summon aid, and his own considerable strength appeared to have little worth in this strange and mysterious land.

The Red Knight surveyed the vicinity once again. His bruises and aches from his journey down the river throbbed once more. The Cave of

Innais? He had never heard of such a place, nor had a clue in which direction to begin his search. Roanan was still even too puzzled to consider his next action. Who were the Reomites and why were they only found here in Arminan? Why was there no record of their existence in the chronicles of Ambrasian?

Roanan pondered these questions but standing alone in the ever-changing midst of an unknown land, had no answers. He knew, however, that he had to begin his search. Whatever the truth of his situation, there were many tales of those lost in the Land of Mystery. Every minute was critical. Roanan mounted Alajar and urged him on, beginning his desperate search for an escape to this accursed land, or barring that, the mysterious Cave of Innais.

But he found neither. Roanan rode for hours, yet the forest proved to be a giant maze, full of false paths and dead ends. More times than not, he finished in the same spot he had started. The sun seemingly danced in the sky while the landmarks appeared to move and rearrange at will. The trees and undergrowth shifted imperceptibly. Roanan found it impossible to maintain any sense of direction. Paths that Roanan took disappeared before his eyes. After an arduous and frustrating search that left both him and Alajar exhausted, the Red Knight found himself back in the very spot where this same excursion had begun. He dismounted Alajar, and in his distress suddenly felt a great drowsiness overcome him though it was only late afternoon. He tried to fight through the surrender of his body to this urge, to no avail. Soon despite his best efforts otherwise, Roanan laid down in the lush grass nearby and fell into a deep sleep.

●   ●   ●   ●

Many miles away, the Wizard Tabeus had sensed what had unfolded. Tabeus had much to do in multiple venues and little time to accomplish what he must but returning Roanan to his rightful place was clearly his most important task. Had he not been grappling with how to respond to the series of events, Tabeus might have admired the execution of such a daring plan. But there was no time for that as utter chaos had suddenly enveloped Ambrasian.

In the case of Roanan, in fact, there was little the Wizard could do. The Land of Mystery contained many strange powers, limiting even the abilities of a Wizard. Assuming he arrived in Arminan in time, there was no assurance Tabeus could navigate the tumultuous landscape any more effectively than Roanan. For whatever reason, the countryside did not respond well to conventional magic. Roanan had to do most of the work by himself. Tabeus could only provide some direction.

So the Wizard had cast the Red Knight into a deep sleep and sent to him a dream. To Roanan, it seemed almost real as he slept unmoving through the long afternoon. The message was undoubtedly authentic, as it painted a path through the maze that would–with some luck and ingenuity–lead Roanan to the entrance of the Cave of Innais. Roanan had the clue he needed. He would have to do the rest on his own. Tabeus had done what he could.

• • • • •

Later that afternoon, Roanan awoke with a start. His body and mind were now refreshed. He noticed the sun, raging in the radiant sky, was well into its slow descent across the horizon.

"How long have I slept?" the Red Knight asked aloud. "Such precious time lost."

But now, for the first time since he washed ashore, the Red Knight was clear in the path he must follow. Roanan vaguely recalled the dream he had as he slept, though the memory of its content was elusive. The dream had etched its critical message into the Red Knight's mind. Roanan rose swiftly and called for Alajar, who galloped through a grove of trees by the stream. The Red Knight mounted his chestnut steed and immediately drove his horse into the forest. His destination now showed itself in his mind, but he had little time to tarry.

Negotiating the path proved more difficult than the Red Knight imagined. Roanan's route was long and winding, tangled with underbrush throughout his travels. He rode as briskly as he could, rarely resting and then only for a few brief moments. Several times, he was forced to change directions as the paths wandered aimlessly or stopped suddenly, with a dark impenetrable forest ahead. But each time the land attempted to confuse Roanan, the path in his mind became clearer and he forged on unfazed, continuing to follow the vision that he had been shown. He knew he was on the correct path. The land was rising as he approached the hills, stones and rocks became more prevalent and slowly the forest diminished. Nothing escaped the discerning eye of the Red Knight, and the land's tricks now became a transparent ruse.

Dusk quickly turned to nightfall, but Roanan continued to ride onward. He had no time to wait for the light of the next day. Alajar galloped on, hurtling into the strangely silent dingy night. No moonlight illuminated the path.

Yet another bit of mischief, Roanan thought. *It should nearly be a full moon and the NightSun should also be bright in the sky. This land of Arminan and its inhabitants are quite the tricksters.*

It was an inky dark night through whichever trail the Red Knight travelled. As darkness enveloped the land, the animals became unnaturally quiet and even the streams lapping over the rocks seemed somehow muffled. A forest that usually came alive with the sounds of its nocturnal inhabitants stood quiet as a grave. Roanan, steely with resolve, refused to be unnerved. As the long night passed by, Roanan traveled tirelessly, finding energy for both him and his steed as he sailed through the forest. He left even the stars behind.

The first rays of sun were peeking over the distant hills. The Red Knight glanced in the distance toward his destination and hurried Alajar onward. The Reomites could not be far behind. The cave had to be close by somewhere. But could Roanan find it in time?

Time went on. Roanan came to a fork in the path. The search had now become a race, and one false step meant certain defeat. The Red Knight thought he heard voices rising deep in the thick forest, gradually increasing in volume and coming closer. He looked down the trails. One was strewn with stones, while the other disappeared quickly into the thick underbrush. Roanan turned Alajar to the right and drove him down the stony path, hurdling a large rock that blocked the trail.

The Red Knight rode even more swiftly, hurried on by the now imminent arrival of the Reomites. Soon, the forest cleared. Roanan had found his destination. The Cave of Innais sat on a small incline, huge weather-worn boulders sprayed erratically about its entrance. Roanan intuitively recognized the scene immediately though he knew not how—but he had seen it before in Tabeus' dream. The Red Knight approached the opening cautiously, finally dismounting Alajar, leaving him at the bottom of the ridge. Roanan began his ascent, stepping carefully. Suddenly, a carnivorous shrub snapped at his ankle.

Roanan jumped back.

"What damnable abomination is this?" he roared angrily. "This land is full of the work spawned by some demon's hands."

The Red Knight drew his sword, quickly defoliating the shrub and cutting it to pieces. But as Roanan turned, he saw more shrubs encircling him. They were waist high and of humble appearance, yet their green leaves were as sharp as the most feared weapon of war. The shrubs moved quickly and aggressively over the barren earth near the cave. The Red Knight's sword lashed through the air again and again, but the shrubs kept coming, their numbers swelling. Despite his best efforts, the weary Roanan could barely stay even with his tireless attackers. One shrub slashed the Red Knight from behind, catching him off guard. Roanan held back a cry of anguished pain as the shrub dug its fiery spikes into his back. The warrior began to lose his grip, his footing becoming less sure. Falling would mean sure doom . . .

But suddenly, Roanan felt the pressure ease from his back. He again gripped his sword firmly and swept it into the middle of the shrubs, which fell lifeless before him. Clear liquid oozed from their severed appendages. The Red Knight turned to face to the attacker behind him, but Alajar had caught the shrub by surprise. The horse had dragged it off his master and was now stamping the helpless attacker into the ground.

"You are a most faithful companion," Roanan cried to Alajar. The horse seemed to nod in response.

The rest of the shrubs sensed the renewed fury of the Red Knight and quickly scattered. Roanan again turned toward the entrance of the Cave of Innais. The voices behind him were becoming louder and more distinct.

Roanan stood before the imposing entrance of the cavern. The opening was eight feet high and six feet wide, seemingly carved out of the very stone surrounding it. With one long deep breath, the Red

Knight slipped into the cave. Adjusting to the darkness, Roanan scanned the interior of the cave. Mammoth in proportions, the cavern was totally empty.

Roanan searched frantically, running from wall to wall, looking for what he could have missed. A secret compartment? A hidden door? Another room? The Red Knight combed every inch of the cave yet discovered nothing. Not even a pebble lay on the floor.

"Nothing," Roanan said in disgust. "Absolutely nothing. They came here before me and removed whatever it was. I should have known I could not trust them."

Angrily, the Red Knight left the cave empty-handed. His eyes once more adjusted to the daylight, and he cursed aloud. For the first time, Roanan felt the sting of the wounds he had suffered in his recent skirmish. He picked up a stone nearby and threw it to the ground in anger. Roanan watched the small explosion of dirt caused by the impact of the stone. Then, he rubbed his eyes and looked more closely. On a nearby boulder of some size, there appeared to be scratching etched into the rock. Roanan ran to the stone, examining it carefully. Suddenly, his anger dissipated and a feeling of elation replaced it. For it was not random scratching in the rock, but instead, an inscription. The Red Knight read it slowly once more:

All shapes for the shape of one
But for all the shape of none

Roanan leapt to his feet, the frustration and anxiety of the last day finally relieved. Now he understood. He ran down the hill and in a few deft movements was on Alajar riding back in the direction he came. It was time to meet head on the Reomites once more.

He did not have to go far. Soon, a wall of water came rampaging down a normally tranquil stream, licking the top of the bank and splashing violently against the trees and stones by the brook's side. Roanan watched in amazement as the eddy rose into the air, leaving the stream, defying gravity and spinning in a whirlwind. A flash of light crackled across the sky, forcing the Red Knight to cover his eyes. A cold wind now blew, and a chill came over his entire body. The gale seemed to swirl around Roanan in a circular rotation, howling through the leaves, filling every crevice behind each stone and boulder. When

Roanan looked about once more, he was in front of him a whole herd of unknown animals he had seen occasionally on his journey. They were about two feet tall when standing on their hind legs but preferred to scurry about on all fours. They had oversized teeth, short brown fur and an abnormally large, bushy tail.

"We have returned," Phelin announced, an air of haughtiness in his voice.

"And quite impressively," Roanan nodded.

Phelin bowed with some exaggeration.

"We have allowed you the allotted time to discover our identity," he said scornfully. "Have you succeeded?"

"I believe I have," Roanan said matter-of-factly.

Phelin appeared momentarily shaken, but quickly regained his composure.

"What is your answer then, Red Knight from Chrysalis?" his voice taking on a challenging tone.

Roanan eyed Phelin with steely eyes.

"It is really quite simple," Roanan explained straightforwardly. "You are nothing but parasites, existing off the forms of whatever is around you."

The Red Knight paused and pointed back toward the boulder in front of the Cave of Innais.

"'All shapes for the shape of one, but for all the shape of none,'" Roanan recited. "A riddle not so clever as all that. You can assume any shape you want, Phelin, either living or not. But you cannot assume your own shape, for you do not have a true form. That is why the cave is completely empty, isn't it?"

Phelin stood shocked and silent. The rest of the Reomites were also absolutely hushed, some dropping their heads in despair. Finally, Phelin shook his head in defeat.

"If nothing would exist around you, then neither would the Reomites," Roanan said. "I suppose that's true of every race, but your existence takes that to the ultimate extreme. The whole of your being rests in the forms and the shapes around you."

Roanan paused, an air of triumph in his voice. It was now the Red Knight who stood with an air of victory.

"Have I answered your challenge?" the Red Knight asked.

Phelin hesitated, then spoke softly in measured words.

"Truly you have, Red Knight of Chrysalis," he said. "You have discovered our ancient secret. There is but one thing you have overlooked. There is one shape that we can never assume–and that is the shape of a Cadaren."

Roanan looked puzzled.

"Why is that?" he asked. "What keeps you from assuming my shape?"

"Because we dare not take the shape of those who can bring an end to our existence," Phelin explained, "and it is the Cadaren who can destroy us."

"More riddles?" Roanan challenged. "Don't you ever stop with your puzzles?"

"This is no game," Phelin persisted. "Many years ago, we were cursed by a Cadaren in whom ancient magic still coursed through his veins. It was written that any Cadaren who comes to know the secret of the Reomites will have dominion over them. It is a curse that has remained with us. That is why we have never allowed one of your kind to leave our land–for fear that if a Cadaren ever gained control over us, we would surely be doomed to destruction. Arminan was our haven against utter destruction. But now, after many millennia of safety, you have discovered us."

The Red Knight studied the suddenly humbled Phelin closely.

"Why did you allow any time at all for one to discover your secret if the price was so grave?" Roanan continued to probe.

The Reomite leader paused.

"The curse continues," Phelin said, "that one day, ultimately, our secret would be revealed. But if we attempted to forestall that day by eliminating our threats immediately, we would surely be destroyed that much sooner. Arminan would rot with the stench of our own corruption, and our very lives emanate from this land. If we would leave if for more than a short time, we would perish. Thus, Red Knight from Chrysalis, we had to allow you time and risk our existence. You have fulfilled the curse. Now, we are at your mercy and servitude."

Roanan smiled, his tone now becoming more conciliatory.

"You have nothing to fear from me," the Red Knight assured Phelin. "What you speak of is tyranny, something the House of the Red Knight of Chrysalis has stood against for many generations. I have no plans to destroy you, nor to rule over you. We shall not trespass into Arminan, and the Reomites may live freely as they always have provided you no longer imprison the peaceful peoples of Ambrasian who may wander here by accident."

Roanan paused, studying the Reomites once more.

"I do have one demand of you, however," he said.

Phelin held his breath.

"I need you to lead me out of your land with all speed," the Red Knight finally said. "I fear the same mischief that brought me to your land has far greater evil purposes elsewhere and that Ambrasian may be in more dire peril than we realize."

The Reomites breathed an audible sigh of relief.

"We are most grateful," Phelin said. "We will lead you back to the path to your kingdom immediately. You are indeed the wisest of Cadaren, Red Knight from Chrysalis, and we shall be forever in your debt. Be assured, in your hour of greatest need, the Reomites will serve as your ally."

"If that is in fact the case," Roanan said, "then I will surely call you friend."

Roanan accepted the offer of the Reomites and the journey back to Chrysalis commenced. The Reomites transformed themselves into a beautiful and swift herd of white deer-like creatures and led him and Alajar to the edge of the Land of Mystery.

"Before you depart," Phelin added solemnly, we have a gift for you."

"A gift?" Roanan said in surprise. "That is entirely unexpected."

"Unexpected perhaps," Phelin answered. "But well deserved. In fact, this is less a gift than it is returning something which is rightfully yours. We believe you are the true owner of this possession that we have protected for many years. We have waited centuries to return it to whom it belonged."

Two Reomites brought an ancient case forward and laid it at the feet of the Red Knight. Roanan knelt and inspected the battered relic of another era, constructed long ago in Ambrasian's past. Despite its age and condition, it retained much of its original splendor. The case was decorated with precious jewels and inlaid with gold. But the greatest shock came when Roanan found inscribed near the case's latch the seal of the House of the Red Knight.

"What is this?" Roanan asked as he opened the case in wonder.

The Red Knight carefully unwrapped the contents inside. As the silken cover dropped away, it revealed a brilliantly glowing battle sword of the finest craftsmanship. Roanan stepped back in awe. The sturdy handle was studded with deep red rubies, and the glint-edged weapon was constructed of the finest metal, both sharper and stronger than any he had ever seen. Picking the sword up, the Red Knight swung it slowly through the air and found it perfectly balanced, easily handled yet obviously powerful. The sun shone brightly off the finely polished metal.

"There is only one sword that fits this description," Roanan finally said.

"You are quite correct," Phelin agreed. "This is Infernus, the hereditary sword of the House of the Red Knight."

"I thought this sword was merely a myth," Roanan said. "Chrysalian history is filled with tales of great feats accomplished by my ancestors with Infernus. But the sword vanished many centuries ago. It has been passed off as a legend."

"Infernus is hardly a legend," Phelin said. "It is real. It was stolen from Carleanis, the King of Chrysalis, twenty-two generations ago. Carleanis was in a battle with Outsiders from the South. By then, Carleanis was aged, but insisted still on leading his army. The Chrysalian forces drove the Outsiders back, but Carleanis perished in the prolonged conflict. He fought bravely, but warriors younger and stronger finally overran him. One of the Outsiders ransacked his body and stole Infernus before his guards could reach him. But that thief made the error of entering Arminan. Needless to say, he never left. We have kept watch over this sword since then. But you are its true and rightful owner, and your actions have proven you are a worthy heir. I can think of none more deserving to bear this blade."

"Phelin," Roanan said. "You have my deepest gratitude. I am in your debt."

"Nay," the Reomite answered. "Our debt to you is one we can never repay."

Roanan smiled and raised Infernus high into the air.

"It is said that this sword was crafted by the predecessors to the Elvii and instilled with the most powerful of the old magic," the Red Knight said.

"That we cannot confirm or deny," Phelin said. "We have had little dealings with those outside of our boundaries. But as I understand it, that is the legend that is told."

The Red Knight nodded to his benefactor, mounted Alajar once more, and sped toward the distant land of Chrysalis.

•   •   •   •   •

As Tabeus led a small contingent of Chrysalian knights over the countryside and approached the boundaries of Arminan, Tabeus sensed the resolution of this crisis approvingly.

"He has learned well," the Wizard said. "He makes allies from enemies and grows both stronger and wiser."

Quickly, Tabeus turned.

"Come Raven, we have much to do," he said. "We have reached a crisis point in our history. We must return Roanan to Chrysalis so we can begin to plan our counterattack. I need to be in Chrysalis, in Necinia, and in Isalis all at once, but even a Wizard cannot accomplish that. However, we must do our best."

"Can I help?" Raven asked.

The Wizard looked at the bird carefully, pondering the possibilities.

"Now that you suggest it," he said, a plan formulating in his head, "perhaps you can."

CHAPTER 10
A LAND IN CHAOS

Roanan quickly departed the veil surrounding the Land of Mystery and urged Alajar to gallop with all possible speed toward Chrysalis. He soon reached a rendezvous point with Tabeus and his companions. The reunion, however, was hardly joyous. After Tabeus heard the Red Knight's own tale, the Wizard wasted no time in relating the evil that had befallen Ambrasian: the theft of the Oracle, the plundering of Necinia, and now ominous tales and rumors coming from Balinwald.

"The sudden storm that drove you to Arminan was more than happenstance," Tabeus concluded. "This was a well-planned and executed attack designed to create havoc across Ambrasian. I fear your challenges have only just begun."

The Red Knight was stunned. Roanan took a few seconds to consider how the world of Ambrasian had been thrown into chaos in such a short time. How things had changed in less that two days. Finally, he looked again at Tabeus.

"It appears that my reign will not be one of peace," the Red Knight said with more than a hint of regret. "This was not the legacy for which I hoped, but it is the destiny that my father foretold.'

"Alas," Tabeus said, "few of us have the luxury of choosing our own path. More often, our destiny is thrust upon us. Yours, it appears, will be decided by the sword, for better or for worse."

Roanan sighed and considered his options, then seemed to come to some sudden resolve.

"We waste our time here," the Red Knight finally said. "There is much to be done, and seemingly no time to accomplish it. We have many miles to cover to return to Chrysalis."

Tabeus nodded in approval.

"I will join you shortly," the Wizard said. "I have a task I must complete before I journey back to Chrysalis. I will be there shortly."

Roanan opened his mouth to object, but Tabeus held his gaze.

"Lasarion has done his best to steady the kingdom and begin the preparations for war at the same time," the Wizard continued. "But in times such as these, only a true King can bring his people to achieve the impossible. I have vowed to aid you in whatever way I can, and right now, that promise takes me on a different path. In time, all will be revealed and you will understand. I have already sent Raven off on yet another assignment. But we will both return."

Tabeus shook his head in consternation, while at the same time Roanan wondered what task the Wizard could send a bird to complete.

"Even a Wizard cannot be in multiple places at one, though at the moment that would be most advantageous," Tabeus said ruefully, then turned back to the young King. "Go now and reclaim your kingdom. The time to defend Ambrasian is at hand, whether or not you are ready. You are now called to prepare your army for battle."

Tabeus turned his white stallion, Ghost, toward the east, and in a few minutes, he had ridden out of sight. Roanan studied those that remained with him, recognizing Toranis as one of the young knights of Chrysalis.

"Your highness," Toranis said, "I am sorry your more senior knights, Halmar and Lasarion, could not be here, but the Hall of Chrysalis has been in upheaval since you disappeared. And now, with the loss of the Oracle . . ."

Roanan raised his hand and waited for Toranis to pause.

"I take no offense," the Red Knight said. "As a matter of fact, I am happy to once again see a familiar face. It appears that we must get home with all haste."

"I agree," Toranis said. "Are you fit to ride?"

"Let's find out," Roanan said, and spurring Alajar on, rocketed north toward the Hall of Chrysalis. Toranis glanced at his companions, urged his own horse onward, and hurried forward to catch up to the blur that was the Red Knight.

•   •   •

Tabeus and Siora met in a peaceful glade on the border of Chrysalis and Karmana, if any place in Ambrasian could be described as peaceful in this suddenly tumultuous time. However, the region was remote enough to be safe–for the moment–and a natural meeting point for the Wizard and the Elvii leader. Under normal circumstances, the Wizard's journey would have taken two days or more. But in the desperation of the moment, Tabeus and Ghost moved across the countryside with incredible speed, appearing to be nothing but a passing shadow as he sped to his destination.

The Elvii also had the ability to move with astonishing quickness, and though Siora was naturally uncomfortable outside his native forest world, necessity drove him to this meeting. A small band of fellow Elvii accompanied him, and they were already waiting in the shadows when Tabeus arrived at their designated rendezvous point.

Siora stepped out quietly from between the trees to meet the Wizard.

"It is not the same Ambrasian as it was when the world was young and the palette was yet to be painted," Siora said.

"Nothing remains the same," Tabeus answered. "All things change, some for the better, some for worse. The old withers, and the new is born. So it has always been and will be in the future."

Siora shook his head slowly and looked absently in the distance. After a moment, the Elvii again looked at Tabeus.

"What evil has been unleashed on the land?" he asked. "Has our age passed us so quickly when we were not looking?"

Tabeus looked at his friend with all seriousness.

"I counsel you to stay strong," Tabeus urged. "We have known each other too long for me to believe you have lost all hope. The power of Chrysalis has been reborn in a young king. He may yet surprise you."

"And if he fails?" Siora persisted. "He is young and untested. He seems no more than a young pup at first glance."

"If he fails, then the land as we know it will perish," Tabeus conceded. "And we will perish with it. However, I believe that Roanan will prove stronger and more resilient than you imagine. We must provide whatever assistance we can to ensure he succeeds in this quest. We must act quickly. Roanan will need all the aid he can muster."

Siora considered Tabeus' words for many long minutes. Finally, he returned the gaze of the Wizard.

"The Elvii will be with you," Siora said. "I do not know if that will be enough against the forces that have gathered against us. They are impressive and they have struck quickly and decisively."

"We will need all the allies we can muster," Tabeus said. "I am hopeful some will emerge that as of now we cannot even identify."

Siora looked at the Wizard skeptically.

"You are more optimistic than I," the Elvii admitted.

"I have no choice," Tabeus answered. "I will not admit defeat. I cannot afford a moment of despair."

Siora nodded but remained silent.

"Return to Necinia and prepare your people," Tabeus advised. "The coming storm is not far off. I am needed in Chrysalis as quickly as Ghost can take me."

Siora walked up to the horse and touched him gently.

"Maybe the speed of the Elvii hasten your journey," Siora said.

Tabeus nodded, again mounted Ghost and disappeared in an instant.

•   •   •   •   •

By day's end, even the peril of the moment could not hold back Roanan's exhaustion from the constant activity of the past two days and nights. The party reluctantly stopped for rest late into the night and slept fitfully for a few hours. The Red Knight awakened early and his party resumed their journey before daybreak.

By mid-morning, the Red Knight returned to the outskirts of the Hall of Chrysalis, and as he and his fellow knights rushed through the village built around the castle, the news of his return spread quickly. Even moving at top speed, Roanan could not outrun the announcement of his arrival to the Hall. It appeared every tree, every bird, and every blade of grass looked for some small glimmer of hope in this desperate time. It arrived in the form of the young and newly crowned King of Chrysalis. The Red Knight came galloping through the Gate House into the Castle Courtyard and quickly dismounted, greeting Lasarion at the entrance of the Great Hall. The two cousins embraced fondly.

"We are fortunate you have returned safely," Lasarion said earnestly. "Many here feared the worst."

Roanan smiled reassuringly.

"I am still in one piece, no worse for wear," the Red Knight answered, "but the same cannot be said of Ambrasian."

Lasarion nodded, recognizing the weight of the circumstances.

"I have begun to assemble our knights and sent out a call across Chrysalis for warriors," Lasarion said. "Forgive me if I have overstepped my authority, but the situation appeared dire."

Roanan placed his hand on Lasarion's shoulder.

"You are my family, and my most trusted knight," he said. "You have done exactly what I would have, and you have taken steps to protect our kingdom and our world. You never have to apologize for doing what is right. I am in your debt."

Lasarion nodded. He glanced back toward the Hall.

"The rest of the council is assembled inside," Lasarion said. "Unfortunately, we have no time for homecoming parties."

"True enough," Roanan agreed. "Let us get started. Time is short and our enemy has a significant head start."

Lasarion glanced about the crowd.

"Is the Wizard not with you?" the knight asked.

"Tabeus said he had another task of urgent importance," Roanan explained. "I don't know what could be more urgent than commencing a War Council in this critical time, but he rode off to the East as if his horse had wings. He said he would return as quickly as possible."

Lasarion looked at Roanan quizzically. The Red Knight shrugged.

"You know as well as I the whims of Wizards are hard to predict," he said.

Roanan and Lasarion entered his Council's chambers, a large room deep within the Hall of Chrysalis. Animal hides and banners decorated the stone walls, providing both decoration and comfort in colder weather. With the warmth of late spring permeating the air, no fire was needed in the immense hearth.

In the center of the room sat a long rectangular table carved from a fine dark wood and ornately decorated. Upholstered chairs were positioned on either side and at both ends. The High Council consisted of Roanan's uncle, Arkala, the treasurer of Chrysalis; Rabezil, the conscience of the Council; Machi, the Council's agricultural expert; Tarkea, the head of ships; Barkan, the head of merchants and trade; and Laedelus, the overseer of the armory. Halmar, though technically not a member of the Council, had also joined the gathering as the most respected senior knight of the realm.

Roanan needed the support and advice from the Elders of Chrysalis. Though he was the King and could order the Council members to do what was needed, the many monarchs who had ruled under the banner of the Red Knight had learned that building consensus and creating a general agreement ultimately generated more loyalty and more proficient results. Roanan had learned this lesson early from his father, and today was to be his first test.

The Red Knight stood before the assembly of the High Council, and together as a group, they carefully detailed all that had happened in Karmana and Necinia and the dire rumors emanating from Balinwald. The assembly frequently interrupted each other with questions and comments, trying to confirm or deny the many rumors that had reached the ears of the Elders. All within the room still reeled from the sudden change of fortune throughout the land.

"And so," the Red Knight concluded, "we have no choice. We have been thrust into battle and must defend not only our own land but all of Ambrasian from its plight."

But Rabezil arose and protested.

"We proclaim to be a peaceful race but are thrown constantly into the horrors of battle," he said. "Why must we mimic our adversaries, falling to the depths of violence for solutions? Surely, has no one considered negotiation or compromise? Must we just immediately thrust ourselves into a war, whose outcome is far from certain? Live to fight again and shed as much blood as possible? Have we turned to the life of wild animals, staking our claims by who is the strongest? It is the same story as always and a tired story as well. I too am tired. Very tired."

The Red Knight sighed and sat down, gazing thoughtfully past the High Council for a moment. Then he looked directly at his challenger.

"No one abhors violence more than I, Rabezil," Roanan answered. "I had hoped my rule would be one of peace. There are few just wars. Most are fought over greed, jealousy, or other less than honorable desires. They are fought for treasure, for power, for fanaticism, or even for love. But when evil arises and our way of life is threatened, war is just and battle is inevitable . . ."

Roanan paused, and as he did so, the doors of the chamber burst open. Standing in the doorway stood Tabeus. The Wizard had whisked himself through Chrysalis in an unfathomably short amount of time and made a timely and dramatic entrance.

"There are times when war is necessary to preserve the goodness of all peoples," Tabeus continued Roanan's thoughts. The Wizard walked grandly into the room, holding the gaze of each member of the High Council intently. "There are times when the just must ultimately fight to maintain the peace.

"No one rushes into war blindly or with false hopes," Tabeus said. "There is no certainty in battle, and for those who have shed blood on the battlefield, little glory. But there are times when those races who value righteousness are given no choice."

The Wizard looked about the room.

"One day," he continued, "there must be a time when all wars must cease, when the destructive power of our weapons will become a far greater risk than the power of the peoples of Ambrasian, greater even than that of a Wizard. In that time, we must grow in wisdom, or face destruction at our own hands."

Tabeus turned directly at Rabezil and looked at him sternly.

"Today, however, the world is merely an infant and its inhabitants but children," he said. "This is an era of barbarism, where the sword speaks mightily, and words speak not at all. But this will pass, in time, as will the age where magic walks freely through Ambrasian. As surely as you and your world will one day pass away, these things too shall perish.

Neither you nor I have control over the currents of time. We control only our own destiny and the immediate future."

Tabeus' tone grew even more urgent and forceful.

"Listen now, Elders of Chrysalis. We must seize this chance or die in disgrace," he said. "Our fight against evil may be forgotten in a thousand years, washed away in the sea of time. But what is our legacy if we go to our deaths with evil running rampant? Can we allow oppression to rule our land and destroy our heritage? Can we allow future generations to suffer because we chose to do nothing? Nay, I say. In times such as these, peace is merely an illusion. Though no swords are raised in anger, there is no peace, for the minds of men are shackled and their freedom stripped away. Are those that oppose the call to arms to be called peacekeepers?

"No," Tabeus concluded. "They are cowards. Rabezil, will you force me to call you a coward?"

Rabezil remained silent. The Wizard broke his gaze and again surveyed all the members of the Council.

"There have been many victims already," Tabeus said. "We will learn of more each day. Maldur and Celidia will unleash an unparalleled reign of terror across Ambrasian if they are victorious. We must oppose such tyranny with our last breath."

He turned toward the door and as he did so, a disheveled figure who nevertheless held himself up as proudly as possible, entered the room. He was badly wounded, but his determination was firm.

"This is Gandrion, a loyal knight of Balinwald," the Wizard proclaimed. "I found him on the road trying to reach the Hall of Chrysalis. He was near death, and I have done all I could to give him enough strength to complete his journey. I do not know how much longer he can stand. His wounds are beyond even my skill."

Gandrion appeared to summon what strength remained.

"Brelex attacked the Hall of Balinwald and killed the King," he said, his voice breaking.

"Our worst fears realized," Roanan said. "Sardenia is dead?"

"He is," Gandrion confirmed. "The Grey Knight's army overwhelmed our forces. He slayed our King and took the Princess Athena captive.

Balinwald has fallen. I escaped after we lost all and came to you as our last hope."

The Red Knight came to Gandrion and helped him to a nearby chair.

"Do not lose hope, my friend," he said. "The enemy has not yet felt our full fury."

Tabeus turned to Roanan.

"Then we must not tarry," the Wizard warned. "Our adversary grows stronger each day and their trespasses more grievous. Even since I last spoke to you, a new evil has befallen us."

"What new evil is left?" the Red Knight asked.

"Maldur and Celidia have sent their Drens into Karmana, where they burn, loot and kill all in their path," Tabeus said. "They are not content with the Oracle. They will not rest until they have destroyed us all."

Now, Arkala broke the silence of the High Council. The thin, white-haired Elder rose, shaking his head slowly.

"How can the Oracle, the very symbol of Ambrasia's strength, be turned to such evil," the Elder asked. "No one ever thought such a violation was possible."

"You speak truly," the Wizard answered. "That the Oracle be incorruptible was the original intent. But along with others, I suspected that some unknown degradation had occurred during its creation and that evil forces would some day attempt to unlock that secret. As we have seen, those fears have become a reality."

Arkala shook his head sadly, the weight of his many years clearly visible on his face.

"Karmana violated and helpless, Balinwald in the hands of the enemy, with Chrysalis lying in wait as the next victim to this plague," he said quietly but forcefully. "Rue that I have lived long enough to see such dark days. No, this is a scenario I cannot accept. We must fight. How weak we would look if we let this misery run rampant unopposed. My King–my blood–this is a test: a test of ours and future worlds. Will the powers of good rule us or the powers of evil? Will our nature be benevolent, or be corrupted to selfishness and the love of power? Go in haste, Red Knight of Chrysalis, but not in hate. Destroy this evil, but do not turn to evil yourself. Power is a tempting maiden, and it must not lure us. It is a fine line we tread. Do not overstep it."

The remainder of the High Council nodded their assent. Rabezil remained quiet. He could not condone violence, but even he could offer no alternative.

"We will do only what is necessary," the Red Knight assured them, raising Infernus from its scabbard. "But this evil must perish and we must restore Ambrasian to order, no matter the cost."

Roanan placed his sword back into its sheath and returned to the head of the thick oaken table. The Red Knight quickly turned to the many tasks at hand.

"Machi," he began, "I need stores to sustain an army and I need them quickly. Five days, no longer."

"That will hard press our supplies," the Elder said, "but it will be done."

"Tarkea," Roanan continued, "our ships must be ready to sail."

"Preparations have already begun," the Head of Ships reported.

"Arkala," the Red Knight continued, "our knights and warriors will need to be compensated."

"Yes, your highness," the Head of the Treasury affirmed. "We are developing the needed resources."

The Red Knight continued his preparations.

"Laedelus," he said, "empty the armory and commission tradesmen to produce more weaponry. Blacksmiths and leather craftsmen, whatever we need."

"Consider it done," Laedelus confirmed. "We have already sent out the call to every skilled artisan in the land."

"Barkan," Roanan now turned to the final member of the Council, "Horses, medical supplies, supply wagons, tents, and all else required."

"We will be prepared," Barkan confirmed.

Roanan turned toward Halmar and Lasarion.

"In five days, when we have assembled all we can in such a short time, we march," Roanan said. "I know there is much to do and not enough time to accomplish these tasks. But we can wait no longer. We must prepare as quickly as possible. You must aid in ensuring our soldiers are ready for battle."

The knights nodded their assent.

"We will follow you wherever you lead," Halmar said.

Roanan then turned to Rabezil.

"Rabezil," he said, "I commission you with the most difficult task of all. If we fail, if Maldur and Celidia succeed despite our best efforts, Chrysalis and the rest of Ambrasian will be helpless. In that event, you must find a way to save as many of our people and as much of our heritage as possible."

"But how?" Rabezil protested. "How will we be kept from overwhelmed?"

"I do not know," Roanan answered earnestly. "Any way you can."

Roanan adjourned the conference and the High Council left the room. The healers of Chrysalis came to tend to Gandrion. They took him away to their chambers, exchanging grim looks and dire thoughts. They held little hope for their patient.

Left alone in the large ornate room was the Red Knight and the Wizard. Tabeus looked unnaturally frail. He placed his hand on the King's shoulder.

"I am proud of you," the Wizard said. "The role of the leader suits you. We need your confidence and your strength. We have a hard path ahead of us."

"My friend," Roanan said softly, "let us hope we can travel the path successfully and return home victoriously."

CHAPTER 11
THE WATCHTOWER

In the Hall of the Grey Knight, Brelex now held Athena captive. The Grey Knight was whipping his growing rebel army into readiness and would begin the march to the Watchtower in the morning. The union of his forces with those of Maldur's would surely create a formidable army, one that Roanan would be hard-pressed to match. In addition, while Brelex had plotted and schemed with Maldur and Celidia for some time, developing their tactics and building their forces, Roanan and his allies would need to assemble his army and develop their plan of attack on the run. Brelex and his confederates had both superior numbers and the advantage of a well-executed surprise attack.

Victory is certain, the Grey Knight thought. *All of Ambrasian will soon be in my grasp.*

Brelex sat in the main chamber of his castle, pondering the ease with which his plan had been achieved so far. He was, for all intents and purposes, the King of Balinwald. No one would challenge his claim now that he had slain Sardenia and scuttled his castle. But he had greater ambitions and hunger than the rule of a sleepy land dismissed as subservient to the glittering jewels of Karmana and Chrysalis.

"Bring me the girl," he finally ordered his guards.

A few minutes later, Athena was escorted against her will to Brelex. The princess had been treated well – so far. She had been provided with a comfortable room, the chance to bathe, and even a walk in the courtyard. But there was little question she remained a prisoner. She was heavily guarded at every moment and her actions carefully watched and reported back to the Grey Knight. She refused to reciprocate any kindness shown to her.

At first, Athena did not understand the gracious treatment. But after hearing enough whispers and poorly camouflaged innuendoes, Athena realized her horror was far from completed. Brelex, the Grey Knight, wanted the princess to consent to becoming his bride and renouncing her father, solidifying Brelex's reign of terror and providing further legitimacy to his claim of the crown. As the undisputed King of Balinwald, Brelex reasoned, he could far more easily extend his claim across Ambrasian.

Two sentries led Athena to the chamber where Brelex waited impatiently on a lush chair he fashioned as his throne. When they entered the chamber, they released the princess' arms and stood on guard by the door. Brelex looked at them and with a nod of his head, ordered them to leave the room.

"Your forefathers brazenly stole the crown from my ancestors many generations ago," the Grey Knight said angrily. "I am reclaiming what was taken from my family. But my marriage to you will dispel any doubts of my true inheritance."

The princess looked at Brelex with both disdain and incredulity.

"Never," Athena answered. "Never will I marry a snake such as you. Your claim to the throne rests on the murder of my father. Now, you want me to sanction your villainy. How dare you. Are you insane?"

"I would think twice if I were you before you reject me," Brelex said lustfully.

The princess looked at her vile captor with hatred.

"That will be twice more than you ever think, Brelex," Athena answered.

"That's His Highness, King Brelex, the Grey Knight, to you," he said.

Athena spit at him.

"Only a jackal in disguise," she answered.

Brelex smiled.

"You have a sharp tongue – for a prisoner," he said. "No matter. We will have much more time together when the defenses of Karmana and Chrysalis are crushed."

Brelex arose from his chair and approached her, grabbing her by the arm. He began dragging her toward a side room off the main chamber.

"Perhaps it's time for a taste of what my future bride will offer," he growled.

"Let me go!" Athena screamed desperately. "I will never give myself to you."

"Ha!" Brelex said. "It's time you entertain me before I go to war. If you don't do so willingly, I will take what a want."

The Grey Knight pushed Athena into the small room, tearing off her dress. He closed the door behind him.

•   •   •   •   •

Some time later, Brelex exited the room, leaving Athena rumpled and broken on the bed behind him. He closed and locked the door and again summoned his guards.

"Do not let her escape," he said then looked at the guards threateningly. "But anyone touches her and I will kill him myself. And trust me, it will be slow and painful. She's mine alone."

The guards nodded in understanding. They had seen the Grey Knight's cruelty first-hand and knew better than defy his orders.

"Take her back to her cell," the Grey Knight said. "Don't provide her the kindnesses we have offered to her so far. Perhaps a truer understanding of the life of a prisoner will give her a better appreciation of my charms."

Brelex left the chamber. It was soon time to march to the Watchtower. But before he left, the Grey Knight turned, glancing back at the guards.

"If by some incredibly lucky blow I do not return," he said, "kill her."

The guards acknowledged the Grey Knight's order and Brelex left. The rumble of an army on the march soon permeated the building and the surrounding area.

•   •   •   •   •

Since their arrival at the Watchtower, Maldur and Celidia had worked to secure the fortress and prepare for the battle to come. A mix of Drens and Maldur's forces that had followed him in this revolt worked to strengthen the battlements, add to the supply of armaments, and build defensive positions.

Because the Watchtower was originally designed to defend the West from the infiltration of Drens and others from the East, many of the ramparts and other features designed for defense faced the wrong direction for Maldur and Celidia's ambitions. The Black Knight ordered the Drens to improvise as much as possible, building temporary ramparts and modifying sections of the castle to launch offensive weapons against their foe. The re-fittings would not likely survive for any duration in a prolonged battle, but they were designed to inflict early damage and demoralize their foes. Maldur knew that ultimately, the fight would have to be won on the ground, soldier against soldier.

Maldur and Celidia stood gazing from a window high above the field in front of them.

"An ingenious plan, Celidia," Maldur smirked. "Using the Weathermaster to send a storm to cast Roanan into the Land of Mystery and sending Chrysalis into chaos, then unleashing the beast through Necinia so those annoying Elvii could not interfere, having Brelex overthrow Sardenia, and using Karmin's neglect and obsession with her silly games to take the Oracle–Ambrasian is in chaos overnight and we are on the brink of victory. They know not which way to turn."

"I know," the Sorceress said smugly. "That's why I'm here. To think and plot and ensure our victory."

Maldur considered the circumstances further.

"I still don't understand how you freed the Oracle from its enchantments," the Black Knight said. "It has always been said that its defenses were impenetrable."

Celidia smirked with self-satisfaction. She moved across the room, her midnight purple robes flowing freely.

"So it was believed," the Sorceress said. "But as hard as it may be to fathom, the Drens held the secret to freeing the Oracle from the clutches of Karmin and the rest of her pompous minions. The scrolls we retrieved on our journey to the hidden stronghold held many secrets and were most helpful. They were written shortly after the very creation of the Oracle. It took time to translate all the nuances from the archaic tongue, but their ancient treasure served us well."

"The Drens were helpful?" the Black Knight asked in surprise. "Those old scraps we found guarded by that ragged band of supposed soldiers held the secret to capturing the Oracle? I can hardly believe they held information more valuable than the location of their next meal."

"You would be surprised," Celidia said. "They hold grudges from time immemorial, perhaps older than any others on our world. At one time, they lived freely throughout Ambrasian. But the Elvii and the peoples of Karmana, Chrysalis, and the other western Kingdoms hunted them and drove them to the east, to Damora."

Celidia glanced back toward the Drens' home, a land that seemed dark and forbidding even to her.

"Damora was an ill-fit for any long-term prosperity," Celidia said. "Swamp land and marshes, or rocky terrain that proved barren for farming. It is little wonder the Drens turned more vicious as time went on."

"They stink, that is for certain," Maldur commented.

"You likely do not smell all that pleasing to them," the Sorceress commented. "Regular bathing is not a high priority in time of warfare."

Maldur grunted, conceding the point.

"All this still does not explain how the Drens helped unlocked access to the Oracle in the first place," the Black Knight said. "Even the brightest of them seem ill-prepared for that."

The Sorceress looked up into the sky and shook her head.

"Patience, you oaf," Celidia said. "I am trying to explain. The ancestors of the current Drens–much wiser than the vermin that now wander outside–had enough foresight to preserve valuable ancient documents handed down through hundreds of generations. Legend had it that these documents contained secrets to the Oracle of which even Karmin was unaware."

Celidia paused, this time nodding her head toward the scrolls that sat on a table in the corner of the room.

"It took me many years wandering through Damora to track down the origins of these tales," the Sorceress said. "While you were learning to fight your foes on the battlefield, I was searching for the true key to our success."

Maldur looked at Celidia scornfully.

"I have not yet found a better method of defeating my enemies outside of hacking them in half," the Black Knight said proudly.

"You wouldn't," Celidia said. "And you will get your chance to prove the importance of your skills in battle. But your prowess with the sword would do no good if I had not freed the Oracle from its captors in Karmana."

Maldur growled but remained silent.

"As it turned out, the Drens had valuable information that was protected and guarded to this day," the Sorceress said. "Those were the scrolls we retrieved that night. Those documents revealed the Oracle had been secretly corrupted during its creation and that, in the right hands and with the right spells, could be turned to do one's will."

The Black Knight looked at his accomplice in surprise.

"Corrupted?" Maldur said. "That is a surprise! As it happens, the Oracle was not so invulnerable as Karmin supposed?"

"Absolutely not," Celidia said. "In fact, its weakness was unknown to most in Ambrasian. The Wizards may have suspected but had no firm proof. Yet our journey into Damora was fruitful, for I learned that if I unlocked the secret of freeing the Oracle from the grasp of those pretentious females of Karmana, I could use it for those of us who have been oppressed and cast aside. Even after I found the secrets, it took much time and study to decode the proper language and sequence to activate the hidden code, but finally, I accomplished my goal."

Celidia smirked in self-satisfaction.

"Yet even with the power of the Oracle unlocked, I cannot defeat an army by myself," the Sorceress said. "I still needed skilled forces to defeat Roanan and Karmin. Thus, our alliance with the Drens and our further partnership with Brelex."

"Ha!" Maldur said triumphantly. "Even with all your spells and hobgoblins, you admit you still required my strength and skill in battle."

Celidia sighed.

"Yes, even you are necessary for us to build a new Ambrasian that extracts proper vengeance on our oppressors," she acknowledged.

"Let's make Ambrasian great again!" the Black Knight proclaimed haughtily.

Celidia shook her head.

"Just do your job when the opportunity arrives," she said and turned back to unlocking the power of the Oracle."

•　　　•　　　•　　　•　　　•

A short time later, Dren lieutenant Izuburu-Gy scampered into the room, spitting on the rough- hewn stone floor. He was larger and more powerfully built than most of his kind, his face scarred from previous battles.

"The first raid has begun," he muttered, saliva dripping down his cheek. "Hell fire on Karmana. It is long past time we gain some measure of revenge on those who stole our lands and treated us as nothing but scum."

The Black Knight smiled in satisfaction, then turned his nose away from the Dren.

"Good work, slime," he said. "Send out the next group of marauders. Tell them to pillage and burn and leave all behind them to waste. I care not what destruction and atrocities they leave in their path."

Maldur looked at the Dren again.

"And tell them to send their stench to Karmin," the Black Knight added.

"And tell them," Celidia quickly added, "to tell Karmin that the stench is from Maldur."

Maldur turned angrily toward the Sorceress.

"And from Celidia as well, of course," she added, smiling slyly.

Izuburu-Gy grunted and left the room, satisfied with his orders.

"That should hasten Roanan's preparations," the Sorceress said. "Let us make sure he has as little time as possible to prepare for this battle. We don't want him to think we will wait until his army is fully prepared to fight. We must press the urgency of the issue. We must give him no choice but to attack before he is fully ready."

Celidia smirked.

"We have been plotting this for years," she said. "I only want to give Roanan a few short days to respond."

She laughed heartily, but Maldur remained unsatisfied.

"We have the advantage now," he argued. "Why not just gather our forces and charge across the land with our entire army, taking them unprepared?"

"What?" Celidia scoffed incredulously. "Run our troops across Ambrasian, having to haul food and supplies and other necessities? And then, as Roanan's forces scatter, chase them across the land for years eliminating each threat? Fool! We have fortified the Watchtower, we have built defensive positions, and our forces are prepared and rested. Let them come to us, because we compel them to do so. We will eliminate our entire opposition in one strike and Ambrasian will be ours."

Celidia walked across the room and unsheathed the Oracle. The space filled with an unearthly glow and she raised it into the air allowing its power to flow into her. She moved toward the window and looked high into the heavens, searching for some object unseen, her eyes blazing.

"Exactly what are you doing now?" Maldur asked. "Praying to whatever god would have you?"

"No," Celidia answered. "I am greeting the watchers who have no business here. Let them feel my presence. They don't appreciate the power I wield."

The Black Knight looked at the Sorceress with no comprehension of what she had just said. He finally shook his head.

"I am going to check on the progress of our army," he said.

Celidia did not respond, ignoring Maldur as left the room. She continued to look intently into the sky.

Chapter 12
Orbital Aberrations,
Galactic Date 2142-08-05

The Explorer maintained a steady orbit above Ambrasian. The crew noted the frenetic activity around Chrysalis as Roanan and his allies tried desperately to assemble an army to battle Maldur and Brelex. They speculated about the nature of the Reomites but concluded that enough chameoleon-like races existed throughout the universe to explain this extreme and in many ways unique example. Kevo generated hundreds of examples of shape- and color-shifting species that existed throughout the known galaxy.

A separate drone spotted Celidia gazing out of the window of the Watchtower toward the sky. Her singular concentration soon caught the attention of the Explorer's crew.

What is she looking at? Captain Evenru wondered.

Suddenly, an unseen force jolted the ship. Warning lights flashed across the Command Center.

"Kevo, what was that?" Evenru asked urgently.

"Unknown, Captain," the ship's AI responded. "Analyzing now."

Evenru got up from the captain's seat and studied the orbital screens in the Command Center carefully. The readings he reviewed began to concern him.

"Kevo," he said, "what exactly is happening?"

"Our orbit is beginning to decay," Kevo reported. "Making necessary adjustments now."

"How is that possible?" he asked. "I thought you had calculated all the atmospheric variables."

"Affirmative, captain," Kevo reported. "That is indeed the case. As is normal protocol, I considered 983 variables that could have impacted our flight path and accounted for each scenario."

"Is this variable number 984?" Evenru asked with a smirk. From the corner of his eye, the Captain could see a satisfied smile cross the face of Celidia.

"I am still analyzing the aberrant factors," Kevo said, ignoring Evenru's attempt at humor. "But apparently, some planetary force was not easily identifiable in my initial scan."

Evenru smiled, wondering if aritificial intelligence could feel frustration.

"Are you telling me you did not take into account the power of the Oracle?" he asked.

"That is illogical," Kevo answered, as indignantly as AI was capable. "I have thoroughly analyzed this so-called magical Oracle. It is nothing but a collection of minerals, precious and semi-precious stones, and other organic elements. There is absolutely nothing supernatural or magical about it."

Evenru frowned, his eye still on the ship's control panel.

"And yet, we're losing orbit right after Celidia looked our way," the Captain challenged.

"Purely coincidental," Kevo argued. "A female on the surface on the planet cannot affect the orbit of a galactic cruiser of which she has no knowledge by merely looking up into the sky."

"Hmm," Evenru said. "And yet, I wonder ..."

Alarms continued to go off throughout the ship. The situation became more urgent as the Explorer's loss of altitude persisted and it began to slip dangerously close to Ambrasian's atmosphere. The temperature in some of the more vulnerable areas of the ship started to rise as the ship's climate controls became seriously taxed. The Explorer's hull began to register stress beyond acceptable limits. Kevo compensated where possible, but more and more of the AI's resources were focused on stabilizing the ship's orbit.

Evenru's level of concern suddenly deepened.

"Coincidence or not, Kevo," Evenru finally said, "you need to pull us out of this trajectory or we'll be meeting Celidia firsthand."

"That is what I am attempting to do," Kevo reported. "Some systems are not responding as anticipated. I am attempting to use alternate pathways to countervail the current course."

"I'd move more quickly if I were you," Evenru said. "It's getting a little toasty in here."

"I am working at maximum capacity," Kevo answered. "I will engage our reserves to boost my speed of response."

The doors to the Command Center whistled open and Penra and Kalli arrived showing serious concern. Meanwhile Officer Galeni, the ship's operations chief, began pinging the Captain in panic.

"Captain," Galeni said, "the ship can't take much more of this. We're coming into the atmosphere too flat and the gravitational controls are not set for re-entry."

The Captain could hear the seriousness in Galeni's voice.

"Understood," Evenru said then turned his attention back to Kevo. "Perhaps you might consider using our directional thrusters to aid in getting us back into a normal orbit?"

"Engaging the thrusters at this point will likely result in significant damage to their assembly," Kevo objected.

"Better to damage the thrusters than destroy the ship and kill the entire crew, don't you think?" Evenru argued, growing more agitated.

Kevo took a beat to respond.

"Agreed," the AI finally said.

"Then, do it!" the Captain commanded.

Kevo complied instantly. The ship groaned and lurched, and at first the trajectory did not change. But in a few more seconds, the Explorer began to once again gain altitude. Several new emergency lights flashed as the ship pulled itself out of danger. A few tense minutes later, the ship settled comfortably above the atmosphere, reestablishing its geosynchronous orbit.

"Maintain orbit," Evenru ordered. "And try to keep it here it this time."

Evenru was sure he could hear Kevo curse softly. Perhaps it was his imagination. Nevertheless, the Captain smiled. But at that moment, Officer Galeni entered the command center.

"Captain . . ."

Evenru held up his six-digit hand.

"Let me guess," he said. "The thrusters sustained damage during our ascent."

Galeni looked at the captain suspiciously.

"That would be correct," he confirmed. "Overheated the propulsion systems. I'm going to need several days to repair them."

Evenru looked at his crew members, then at the screen showing the various planning sessions, military raids and other troop movements on the planet below.

"It certainly seems like something is trying to keep us here for better or for worse," the Captain concluded. "Still, I think there's enough research possibilities to keep us occupied here for a bit longer. You can commence repairs and keep me informed of your progress."

Galeni nodded curtly and left the Command Center. Evenru then looked over at the array of controls.

"Besides," he added, "Kevo has to determine how a harmless stone and a powerless female on the planet's surface nearly turned us into an inferno. I will be anxious to hear his explanation."

The AI remained silent, its analytical capabilities still attempting to make sense of the recent turn of events.

Evenru once again sat down in the Captain's chair and considered the situation.

"We have some time while the thrusters are being refitted," he concluded. "This planet and its inhabitants are certainly full of surprises. Let's continue our research while repairs are taking place. It appears we'll be viewing an all-out war in the next few days."

He looked over at Penra and Kalli.

"We need as much information as we can gather about all the wizards, sorceresses, and magical swords, oracles, and other beings and objects that seem to pop up every time we look," the captain said. "We've already had one surprise we didn't need. I don't want to encounter another. Assign as much analytical power we can afford to understand what is below us on this very unusual world."

Chapter 13
The White Castle

The Elvii had driven Icyx from Necinia, but only before the beast crazed from Celidia's enchantments had wreaked havoc throughout the land. However, whether by choice or ill luck, the Elvii could not subdue the beast. Icyx escaped, disappearing into the north injured but not killed and still in an unnaturally provoked state.

The Elvii had no appetite to pursue the beast nor the motivation to do so. They did not seek revenge on a creature driven mad by outside forces. In addition, the destruction and injury across Necinia had left the Elvii with more urgent matters now that the threat had passed.

For all intents and purposes, Icyx had vanished into the wild once again.

To the northeast, however, hidden in the mountains and all but forgotten by everyone but the most long-lived in Ambrasian sat the city-state of Regala. The inhabitants were distant cousins of the residents of Karmana and remained a female-dominated society. But unlike Karmana, the residents of Regala counted both males and females and while long-lived, Regalans were hardly immortal.

The Regalans had migrated north many generations ago, as the differences in their lifestyle and life spans distanced them from their Karmana sisters. And with the land wilder and less forgiving in those early days of Ambrasian, they retreated into the hills and established their walled city on the side of a mountain, the alabaster-colored stone soon earning it the name of The White Castle.

The Regalans were enterprising and inventive, and over the years, Regala became surprisingly self-sustaining, using geothermal heat to warm elaborate greenhouses, building aqueducts to provide water, and growing food and raising herds on the rocky hills around their protected abode with remarkable efficiency. With their hidden city-state difficult to reach and harder to find, and with little need for any goods from the outside, Regala became more and more isolated from the rest of Ambrasian. Ultimately, they chose secrecy and isolation as a way of life and to most of Ambrasian, disappeared from the pages of history.

Regala had no queen–nor king, for that matter. While not quite a democracy, the Regent of Regala was chosen more or less by popular assent. In recent years, that title had been bestowed on Vandelyise, a woman of not quite middle age who came from a prominent Regalan family. Vandelyise had shown both wisdom and compassion, and Regala continued to flourish under her stewardship.

But while Regala was isolated and difficult to reach, it was not impossible to do so–especially for a frenzied beast capable of traversing even the most difficult of landscapes. As Icyx rampaged throughout the countryside, it did so without destination or direction. By unlucky happenstance, the beast came across the paths that led to Regala, though it would likely have failed to do so had it been searching for them.

Into the peaceful and secretive state charged a frenzied Icyx, injured by the Elvii's many arrows and still in a maddened state from Celidia's spell. Icyx towered over eight feet high and was massively built. Brownish-white fur covered the creature and it stood upright. No one had ever come close enough to the beast to determine its sex, nor did most of those who had encountered it give much consideration to the question.

Icyx's hands and feet were almost cartoonishly oversized, and the beast could easily lift a normal-sized Ambrasian with one arm. Icyx's mouth dominated the creature's face and was filled with knife-like fangs. Its ears and nose were hardly discernible, small and almost entirely covered by thick, curly fur. Icyx's eyes protruded from their sockets and were large and inky black. As the monster moved closer, its grunts were mixed with piercing screams, high-pitched and frightening. If the creature spoke any sort of language, it was not one that any other race on the land could understand.

But its cries gained the attention of the sentries guarding the city-state's fortifications. Icyx was spotted a short distance from Regala and the citizens were quickly put on alert. They hoped the beast would skirt their city and continue on its way to some unknown destination further north. But it was not to be. Icyx's path brought it directly toward the great wall of Regala.

As the creature scaled the mountain and climbed the ivory walls, battle cries and horns warning of danger coursed through the city's streets. Male and female warriors took positions on the wall's bastions to defend their home against the approaching terror. Icyx hurled rocks and pounded on the base of the ramparts as it tried to tear apart the obstacle before it. The creature was far more deft at scaling the impressive wall than the Regalans anticipated and it was quickly reaching a point of being a legitimate threat.

Regalan warriors were skilled with both the bow and the long spear. Archers set their sight on the beast as it continued up the wall, which now appeared to be no more than a minor deterrent. The captain of the regiment commanded his archers to pull back their bows for a defensive volley.

Suddenly, a voice pierced through the battlements.

"Hold!" said a voice, countermanding the captain.

The Regalan warriors looked up and saw Vandelyise at the top of the spire.

"Calm the beast and bring it to the central chambers," the steward said. "I sense there is a tale here to be discovered. By killing it, we may never judge the importance of the events that brought the creature to our city."

The captain of the guard momentarily cast a skeptical look at Vandelyise but retracted it immediately when she returned it with an icy stare. The Regent was certain of her path forward and was not to be dissuaded.

"Gaudia," the captain said to Regala's best archer, "do as she says."

The captain looked back once to the steward once again.

"And don't miss," the captain added.

The archer glanced at his captain momentarily.

To whom do you think you are speaking? she thought. *I never miss.*

Gaudia then removed the arrow from her bow and replaced it with another held in a special pouch in her quiver. She dipped the exquisitely sharpened arrow in a liquid from a flask she pulled from the folds of her uniform and looked back down over the wall. Aiming carefully, she fired truly; the arrow pierced the skin just above Icyx's shoulder.

Icyx initially became angrier and redoubled its efforts to mount the wall. But no more than a minute or two later, the beast's movements slowed and grew more and more sluggish. The Regalans watched carefully as Icyx's fury dwindled and a short while later became fully extinguished. The powerful tranquilizer had quelled even a beast the size of Icyx and it now lay unconscious against the wall.

"Sleeping like a baby," Gaudia finally said. "Though a very large baby, truth be told."

The warriors next to her grunted.

"Now we have to drag that enormous baby up here and through the city," one muttered.

Over the many generations of their solitude, the Regalans had become masters in the healing arts and had developed innate abilities to communicate with animals and other species. While Icyx represented an unknown species and a creature much larger than those Regalans were typically used to dealing, there was far less fear than what might have occurred in a different land. With more than some effort, they retrieved the beast through an ingenious set-up of ropes and pulleys, brought it to the city-state's gates, and carried to Vandelyise's chamber.

Icyx lay in the large room to which Vandelyise had tasked the most skilled healers in Regala who now tended to the wounds of the beast's body and mind. The room was filled with the scent of various herbs, roots, and concoctions and mixtures developed over the centuries. Icyx was kept in a sedated state, but nevertheless, a half-dozen of Regala's fiercest warriors stood guard and the creature was securely bound by its arms and legs, as well as across the waist and around its neck.

Vandelyise herself probed the mind of Icyx to learn how the beast had taken a wayward path to Regala. She saw a series of images confused and conflated by the madness that had overtaken the creature. But the

Regalan steward slowly calmed Icyx's thoughts, cut through the beast's confusion and madness, and eventually, a clearer picture of its path and the events surrounding its rampage became far clearer. Vandelyise saw the machinations of Celidia through the fog of the beasts's brain, and as she saw the larger picture, Vandelyise became more and more distressed. She soon realized that the initial danger that Regala had averted was inconsequential compared to the greater threat to all of Ambrasian.

Finally, she tore herself away from Icyx and considered what she had just learned.

"I must consult the Glass," she concluded and swept herself quickly from the chamber.

The Glass was held in a room known only to the Council that guided Regala and those who guarded and protected its secrets. The Glass had not been used in generations as the city-state and its people became more and more independent and self-sufficient. In fact, no one in living memory could recall the last time anyone had gazed into its depths.

But the Glass remained the one link Regala had to the rest of Ambrasian in time of need. The Glass reached across the mountains of Isalis and the plains of Karmana to provide a communications portal to Regala's distant cousins.

Vandelyise entered the secret room, bolting the doors securely behind her. She removed the deep royal burgundy cloth that covered the Glass, folding it and laying it neatly to the side. She sat down, looked ruefully at the object and then, tentatively at first, laid her hands on the surface of the Glass.

At once, the object glowed and as Vandelyise grasped the orb more confidently, the illumination became more intense. After several minutes, the flow from the Glass assumed a bluish cast. Vandelyise waiting patiently for a figure to respond to her outreach.

Finally, the image of Karmin's distressed face slowly appeared within the Glass. Karmin focused sharply as the view of Vandelyise appeared.

"I apologize for the delay," Karmin said. "I am pressed on all sides with urgent matters."

Vandelyise nodded.

"I understand," she said patiently.

"I am Karmin and I represent the land of Karmana," the face in the Glass finally said. "To whom do I speak?"

"I am Vandelyise, the Regent of Regala," the Regalan answered.

"Regala?" Karmin mused. "It has been many passages of mortal lives since word has emerged from the distant mountains. I sense it is not a coincidence that you contact us in these most desperate of times."

"As fate would have it, that is true," Vandelyise responded. "We hold the beast Icyx and from his mind I have gleaned at least some of the evil that has befallen Ambrasian."

"Some I am sure," Karmin replied, "but certainly not all."

"Agreed," Vandelyise said. "However, I sense great malevolence across the land, so I come to the Glass representing the peoples of Regala for the first time in many, many years."

Karmin studied Vandelyise for a moment.

"Your instincts are true and your concern most valid," she responded. "In the blink of an eye, Ambrasian has been thrust into the most desperate times."

Karmin then recounted the terrors of the past days and the uncertain future that Ambrasian now faced as quickly and as factually as she could muster. Even Vandelyise was stunned by the theft of the Oracle and the potential ramifications of Celidia and Maldur's actions. She covered her mouth with her hands in shock.

"As you can see," Karmin concluded, "if Celidia achieves victory, even your hidden enclave will no longer serve as a safe haven. The peace we have all enjoyed has been disrupted in barely more than a heartbeat."

Vandelyise considered the possibilities. While Regala was well concealed, it was clearly not undiscoverable as Icyx had most recently proven. And if Icyx had found their location, it was possible–even likely–that Celidia had already gained that knowledge as well. While the White Castle was a sturdy fortress, it was not impenetrable if forced to repel an army at full strength.

"I will speak to my Council immediately," the regent said.

"Do so quickly," Karmin implored with perhaps too much of an air of haughtiness. "Now is not the time for speeches."

"We have not been isolated so long that we do not recognize the urgency of the situation," Vandelyise said, firmly but with compassion.

"I will call our Council at once. We have much to do in a short amount of time."

"My apologies if I sounded as though I questioned your resolve," Karmin said. "These are difficult times, to say the least."

"I understand," the Regent said. "I take no offense."

"What will you do with the beast?" Karmin asked.

Vandelyise paused for a moment as though pondering the question.

"Leave that to me," she finally said. "Icyx, at least, will no longer concern you or your allies."

Karmin nodded in understanding.

"Be well, Regent Vandelyise," she said, "until we meet again."

"Until we meet again," Vandelyise repeated.

Vandelyise took her hands from The Glass and the image of Karmin faded away. She replaced the cloth once more and left the secret room, securing it again behind her. She pondered her next move for several moments, then committed herself to a course of action.

"I must call the Council to order," she said to herself. "Then, I must go the beast once more. I must reach even deeper inside the mind of Icyx."

The Regent of Regala rushed through the hallways as she formulated her priorities. Her country, however small, could no longer remain isolated from the rest of the world. The centuries of seclusion had ended.

CHAPTER 14
PREPARING FOR WAR

The Darris River flowed from the Lake of the Red Jewel in the far north of Chrysalis' borders. The lake was named based on an ancient tale, true or not, of a visit by Rolyn, the first King of Chrysalis, who discovered a red gem in the shallow waters of the lake. Seeing it as a sign, the jewel and its color became an integral part of the sigil of the line. Thus, the House of the Red Knight was born.

The Darris River cut the Western Kingdom in half. Located on the river's banks near the Hall of Chrysalis was the King's Grove, perhaps the most beautiful garden in all of Ambrasian, though the peoples of Karmana would disagree. Within the grove sat the Eternal Tree, whose huge trunk and soaring height had prompted awe and wonder throughout generations. It was legend that Rolyn had planted the Eternal Tree and that the tree would flourish for as long as the line of the Red Knight survived. When the line ended, so would the tree wither and finally die.

The Hall of Chrysalis stood majestically on a hill beyond the Grove, overlooking the glade below. The scene could nearly match even Karmana in its wonder and its splendor. The outer walls of the castle rose proudly through the air, its smooth, grey stones shining brilliantly in the sunlight. Within the outer wall stood an inner wall, a defensive design built to fend off an attack. The inside of the Hall was multi-tiered, with an open middle court surrounded by many chambers.

The inner walls of the castle were made of thick stone but were finely polished and elegantly finished. Spiral stairways ran throughout the complex, and each room had its own level. In this design, one had to climb at least three steps to move from any one room to another.

In the lower chambers of the Hall of Chrysalis, the gardeners of the King's Grove perfected their craft. Unlike the gardens of Karmana, which flourished naturally and mostly unattended, the Grove of Chrysalis was carefully cultivated. The caretakers of the Grove meticulously raised and bred exotic new breeds of flora and spent their lives sculpting, crafting and expanding the Grove even further.

In normal circumstances, the Hall of Chrysalis and its surroundings provided a tranquil haven and a regal setting to conduct the business of the realm. The beauty of the castle and its surroundings had awed many visitors.

But these were not normal circumstances. With threats at each turn, the urgent and desperate mission of Roanan and his allies had turned the castle into a non-stop buzz of activity. While Chrysalis had a standing army to provide for defense of the kingdom, the immediate danger was far too severe for the relatively small force. The call to war had gone out to all corners of the land, and now every able-bodied soul was responding.

Knights from the esteemed houses of Chrysalis, warriors from past service, and even farmers bearing nothing but pitchforks from across the land migrated toward the Hall to prepare for battle. While the great majority of those were male, a fair number of females also heeded the cry for action. Soon, not only the castle but the village surrounding the Hall of Chrysalis was overflowing, tents and other ramshackle temporary quarters dotting the surrounding countryside.

The fighters were followed by a bevy of vendors, suppliers, and others: farmers with smoked meats and fresh fruit and vegetables; stable masters who ensured horses were rested, groomed and fed; blacksmiths sharpening swords and lances and forging new weaponry day and night, their hot fires burning incessantly.Wagons were repaired and stocked. Couriers ran constantly to Karmana and back, bringing news of Dren raids moving even further west, and of the Elvii gathering their forces. Siora had sent troops of Elves to impede the relentless drive of the Drens, but even the marksmen of the Elvi had difficulty containing the enemy. The Drens stayed far from the borders of the Great Forest, forcing the

Elvii out of the comfort of the trees to have any effect. Plus, the Drens had mastered a form of guerilla warfare, sending multiple small bands in various directions to wreak havoc and move quickly from target to target, keeping the Elvii stretched thin and guessing where to defend.

Couriers had also brought word that the young warriors from the Games had banded together, and under Karmin's tutelage, were now preparing to join Roanan's army. Tabeus scoffed at Karmin "teaching anyone to fight."

"What is she using to teach them?" he wondered. "She has never brandished a sword in her life, and that life has stretched many centuries."

But Roanan cautioned the Wizard not to judge Karmin too harshly.

"In times such as these," the Red Knight said, "we can refuse no aid that is offered."

Tabeus nodded in agreement, but still privately wondered at the type of tutelage Karmin could offer.

Roanan frequently walked through the gathering crowds, assessing the strength and preparation of his gathering army. On one occasion, amid the din of preparation, Roanan watched in amazement as a thin Cadaren with long, stringy brown hair dressed in ragged, baggy green and red clothes walked through the crowd singing merrily. As the singer's appearance became more distinct, so did the words of his tune.

Once a soldier fought in battle
Was as strong as twenty cattle
But he couldn't tell a donkey from a horse
He was very brave and strong
But his brain deserved remorse . . .

The Cadaren casually walked up to Roanan and bowed low, causing the Red Knight's guards to prepare to defend their king. Roanan held up his hand to stop them and studied the man carefully.

"Tell me," the Red Knight said after watching the cartoonish figure with some amusement. "What is your name?"

"I am Mendelheimer the Minstrel," the man replied, "at your service."

"A minstrel?" Roanan asked incredulously. "I would expect a better song from a bard."

'I am known far and wide as the world's worst minstrel,"
Mendelheimer replied matter-of-factly. "And I am honored to offer my
services to you my Lord, King of Chrysalis."

Roanan laughed, a much-needed respite in these tense times.

"And what possible service can you offer as we go to battle?" the Red
Knight asked. "I know of no enemy yet who has been killed by a song,
though I suspect yours may come close."

"I would like to offer whatever aid I can provide in defeating Maldur,
who possesses no sense of humor," Mendelheimer explained. "I am not
much skilled with sword or lance, but perhaps I could keep the troops
entertained and later chronicle the exploits of their battle in song."

The Red Knight studied the scraggly individual before him more
closely.

"I have little faith in you as either a songwriter or historian," Roanan
replied light-heartedly. "But I accept your offer nevertheless. After your
songs, the thought of battle should not seem so harsh. And I am not one
to turn down assistance sincerely offered. I have learned there are those
who have a larger role to play than I might imagine."

Roanan surveyed the nearby scene.

"I see you have no horse," the Red Knight said. "Need I find you a
ride?"

"Thank you, my Lord," the minstrel responded, "but I do indeed have
a horse. He is a bit headstrong, however."

The minstrel turned and looked around the corner.

"Preston!" he shouted.

A brown, overweight horse walked lazily toward Mendelheimer.

"Preston?" Roanan asked.

"Yes, my horse," the minstrel acknowledged.

Roanan laughed again. After a struggle, Mendelheimer finally
mounted Preston.

"Malcontent," the minstrel muttered.

The Red Knight shook his head.

"Perhaps now would be a good time to introduce yourself to the
troops," the king said, "while you improve your riding skills."

Mendelheimer bowed, turned toward a nearby group of soldiers, and
again began to sing.

A cow stood in the pasture
In the grass by the stable
And as she stood grazing
The soldiers came blazing
They burned down the village
And then began to pillage
Moo moo Moo moo
Pity the plight of the cow
Moo moo Moo moo

"Minstrel," Roanan complained, "that is even worse than your previous effort. You will need to work on both your riding and your music."

"As you command," Mendelheimer replied and broke into yet another tune.

•   •   •   •   •

In a quiet corner of the Hall of Chrysalis as twilight approached, Tabeus watched as a small black figure flew toward him. The Wizard studied the flight of the bird carefully.

"The Weathermaster seemed amiable enough," Raven finally chirped as he landed on Tabeus' shoulder after his return. "Not very talkative, though. All he was concerned about was wind currents, temperatures, and humidity."

Tabeus stroked the bird lightly, smiling at his consternation.

"The Weathermaster was never a major concern, Raven," the Wizard said. "He is not inherently evil. He merely operates on his whim, and Celidia used whatever wiles and spells she could to coax him into sending a sudden storm. I'm glad we could show him how he was duped."

Tabeus ran his hand slowly down his white beard.

"Perhaps it worked out for the best after all," Tabeus said. "Roanan has gained an ally in the Reomites, one whose power may be underestimated by the enemy. And perhaps, more importantly, he has gained confidence. He is growing into his role as a king. That is good. We need strong leadership in these troubled times."

Raven looked about his surroundings before changing the subject.

"I found no sign of Icyx, however," the bird added. "I don't know how such a large creature could go unnoticed. None to whom I spoke had spotted the beast."

The Wizard chuckled.

"We need not worry about Icyx," Tabeus assured the bird. "It is in good hands and I trust it will no longer be a threat to us."

Raven cocked his head and looked at Tabeus with his unblinking black eyes.

"That is good to hear," Raven said. "I was afraid it might think I was a tasty snack."

Tabeus peered upward toward his companion.

"You would hardly be worth the effort," the Wizard laughed. "In any event, Icyx is no longer of any use to Celidia and she has forgotten about the creature. I hope we can use that arrogance to our advantage."

Raven looked about. If a bird could show skepticism, Raven did just that.

"We need that and much more for us to be victorious," the bird concluded.

Tabeus nodded in agreement but remained silent.

• • • • •

The Red Knight had decreed that his forces would leave Chrysalis in five days in the meeting with the High Council, and Roanan drove all to meet that proclamation. It was an aggressive but necessary goal. Any delay would give the forces allied against him an even greater foothold and Ambrasian was already suffering grievous injury far and wide.

In that time of preparation, Roanan spent many hours in conference with Tabeus, Halmar, Toranis and the members of the Council. When not in planning for battle, the Red Knight visited with his troops, trained with Alajar, and worked endlessly trying to form a bond with his forces. He practiced with young warriors, improving their fighting techniques. During these tense days, Roanan demonstrated his abilities as a leader of an army and a kingdom. He led by both example and directive, demanding respect by his very presence. He well knew that he was leading many of these young soldiers to their deaths. He looked about at these eager warriors, some of whom would never return to see their families or their loved ones again. With his unique blend of authority, friendship and leadership, Roanan truly embodied the role of Red Knight, King of Chrysalis.

In times of solitude, the Red Knight tried to find rest in the King's Grove. There, oftentimes, he would discover Tabeus roaming among the trees and flora deep in thought. On the eve of the departure, Roanan once again came across the Wizard there, and together, the young King and the ageless Wizard strove slowly to the Eternal Tree.

Finally, the Red Knight stood next to the ancient bark and studied it carefully, running his finger carefully over a segment of the trunk. It was a tree as no other in Ambrasian. The trunk stood five feet in circumference and seventy feet high. Its greenish-blue leaves were long and pointed and grew thick and lush.

"This is the tree of my ancestors," Roanan said. "It was planted when Ambrasian was young and untroubled."

"Yes," Tabeus noted. "Rolyn planted it many, many generations ago, or so it is said. By the time I traveled among the lands Ambrasian, the tree was already tall and strong."

"How long will it survive?" Roanan pondered. "It is said it will last as long as the line of the Red Knight. Will it still stand next week? Or next month?"

"No one can say," Tabeus admitted. "But today, it is strong and healthy and it has survived many challenges during its history."

"What of our chances?" the Red Knight persisted. "Can we defeat our enemy?"

Tabeus paused, softly touching a leaf on the tree.

"We are vastly outnumbered," the Wizard said. "Maldur and Celidia have built an impressive army. They have planned for many moons and have caught us flat-footed and ill-prepared. They have recruited a powerful ally in Brelex. They patiently waited for our most vulnerable moment. But we are not blinded by overwhelming greed, and those who have fought or served under your father are more disciplined and better trained. The Drens are vicious but difficult to keep in control."

"We must hope for the best," the Red Knight said summoning what hope he could, "and fight our way into history."

Roanan clasped the Wizard's hand, then walked away.

Later that night, the Red Knight and his closest knights reviewed the plan they would set in motion. The Red Knight's forces would embark on a two-pronged path. The major portion of the troops would follow Roanan across Chrysalis back into Karmana. There, they would join with the Elvii and the young knights trained by Karmin, and then ride on to meet Maldur and Brelex's forces on the battlefield, most likely in eastern Karmana near the Watchtower and its borders. Even Roanan assumed they could not coax their opponent from the well-stocked and fortified area around the Watchtower. With Roanan would ride Halmar as his second-in-command, Toranis, and Tabeus, when he was not away in other preparations.

Dainwirth Lir, the young knight who had confronted Maldur and Brelex and survived, had been sent to Chrysalis by Karmin to provide what information he could provide. After listening to Lir's tale, Roanan decided–to much protest–that the young knight would be one of the leaders of the cadre of warriors training at the Hall of Karmana. Lir was young and untried and generally considered weak. But Roanan persevered.

"Dainwirth Lir has much to prove, and I believe it is his fate," the Red Knight said, "for better or for worse, to prove it here. In times of peril, he may show hidden strength."

Roanan would lead a force of about six thousand. Lasarion would lead another thousand across a different course. Lasarion would board the ships of Chrysalis and sail into the Sea of Dragons, around Selin to the eastern coast of Balinwald. There, he would re-take the Hall of Balinwald by surprise and free Athena from the Grey Knight's murderous henchmen. Lasarion would then travel along the Sylil River, hopefully picking up additional warriors along the way before finally meeting Roanan in battle at the Watchtower.

Splitting their forces this way came with inherent risks. What if Lasarion's forces were delayed, and they did not reach the battle in time? What if Maldur and Brelex's combined forces too easily and too quickly cut through Roanan's army? On the other hand, the Red Knight argued that leaving Balinwald in Brelex's hands provided an easy escape for the Black Knight and the Grey Knight, and even if victorious, Roanan would need to spend weeks or perhaps months and years chasing down their opponents and freeing that land. Finally, the need to recruit more soldiers along the way to help even the field was deemed critical to success.

The Red Knight's forces, as of now, totaled seven thousand soldiers. Karmin's warriors and the Elvii would add perhaps two thousand additional troops with luck.

Tabeus shook his head.

"Maldur has assembled ten thousand Drens or more with additional soldiers arriving daily," the Wizard said. "Brelex will add at least five thousand more of his soldiers and bandits."

"They will outnumber us nearly two to one or worse," Roanan said ruefully. "We can only hope that the populace of Balinwald recognizes their danger and joins our efforts. Without them, we have no reinforcements on which to call. We can only hope to persevere."

The night had grown dark by the time the conference finally dispersed.

"It is time to rest," the Red Knight said. "It may be many days before we can slumber peacefully once more."

•　　•　　•　　•　　•

Mendelheimer "entertained" the assembling army throughout the preparations, much to their chagrin. The minstrel continued both his songs and his fights with Preston, keeping the mood as light as possible in these dire times. Periodically, if Mendelheimer was riding Preston, the horse would halt suddenly and nearly hurl the minstrel from the saddle or run off the path or roadway toward the wilderness. It was a wonder that Mendelheimer remained in one piece.

The minstrel's music was rarely inspired and barely palatable. However, like a bad joke, Mendelheimer's act slowly grew on the company in spite of themselves. As the assembled peoples prepared to march, the minstrel belched his songs throughout the region.

In times of trouble
There once was a man
Who looked like a frog
And walked like a clam
He wasn't much help
And wasn't too brave
When the soldiers came by
He gave them a wave
He did have two daughters
Who weren't very cute
They sat in a tree
And sometimes did hoot
The point of this tale
If you must guess
Is a minstrel knows little
And sometimes much less . . .

"That's terrible," Dainwirth Lir cried at one point as the minstrel wandered among the army, listening to Mendelheimer's nearly non-stop collection of mismatched songs, stories, and anecdotes.

Roanan laughed. In some odd way, he appreciated the minstrel's efforts to lighten the darkened mood.

"That's one of his better ones," he said sarcastically as he moved through the camp. "At least it rhymes–almost."

No matter what criticism or catcalls may come his way, Mendelheimer was undeterred. But as he warmed up for the next song, he heard another voice cut him short.

"Well now, here's a likely party," the gravelly-voiced newcomer said. "What could I interest you in? Genuine dragon scales, just two chrysalians. Elvii amulets, a steal at six chrysalians. Healing potions, Dren detectors, daggers easily hidden . . . you name it, I have it. Or I know where to get it!"

From a distance, Roanan surveyed the scruffy, jovial Cadaren, who was approaching the nearby group. He was of average height, but not of weight. Layers of flesh overlapped each other. He had thinning, bird's nest, brown hair, a stubble-filled face untended for at least a week, and a prominent moustache. His clothes were loose fitting and dirty, and in them he resembled a large tent. Behind him was a ramshackle wagon overloaded with goods and materials, mostly junk and merchandise with claimed magical qualities but mostly useless.

"Who are you?" the Red Knight asked as he approached the stranger.

"I am Theopolis Fenton Ruck IV, trader and merchant," the bushy Cadaren said. "Can I interest you in any of my goods? They're of the finest quality, guaranteed."

Roanan glanced at the wagon and shook his head. The Red Knight allowed himself a slight smile.

"Do you know who I am?" Roanan asked.

"Well, sir, off-hand..." Ruck paused and squinted his eyes. "My eyesight isn't what it used to be, but now that I mention it, you do look familiar."

"I am Roanan, the Red Knight, King of Chrysalis," the King finally informed the mountebank.

The trader's eyes brightened.

"Ahh, yes, yes, now that you mention it, I recognize you," he said. "Well for you, I have a special deal fit for a King!"

Dainwirth Lir had been standing nearby, and he now leapt in front of Roanan, obviously offended.

"That is Your Highness to you!" the young knight said, then turned to the Red Knight.

"My apologies for the miscreant's behavior," Dainwirth Lir said angrily. "He would sell his mother for the right price if he hasn't already!"

Rather than be offended, Roanan appeared to be enjoying the light-hearted diversion.

"No harm done," the Red Knight assured Lir.

Nevertheless, the merchant bowed before the King in an exaggerated fashion.

"My apologies for my lack of proper etiquette," Ruck said. "I am but a humble trader attempting to earn an honest living, and I am not familiar with the finer details of the courts of Kings."

Roanan indicated that Ruck should rise, but Lir was not satisfied.

"Honest?" Lir asked suspiciously. "I think not. I doubt you've had an honest transaction in your entire life."

Ruck looked at Lir carefully.

"Didn't I meet you two towns back?" Ruck started. "I'm sure I sold you ..."

"What?" Lir said in shock, cutting off the trader. "I have never ..."

"Just kidding," Ruck mumbled. "You obviously do not appreciate sarcasm."

Lir looked back at Roanan.

"Your Highness," Lir started, "will you allow such insolence from this–this junk dealer? I will be glad to give him a well-deserved thrashing."

The Red Knight laughed and glanced at Mendelheimer. Then he looked back at Dainwirth Lir and winked.

"We seem to have developed a habit of collecting misfits," Roanan said. "Leave him be. He is a harmless trader eking out what I suspect is a meager living."

"Harmless?" Ruck feigned insult. "Nay, I protest. I'm a killer when provoked."

Now it was Mendelheimer's turn to laugh.

"Come now," the minstrel said, "the only people to whom you and I are dangerous are ourselves. If they gave both of us a sword, we would be lucky if the worst we did was stab ourselves in the rear end."

The merchant sized up the minstrel quickly.

"Who is this indigent?" Theopolis Fenton Ruck IV protested.

"Oh Theopolis," Mendelheimer said, "Your brain is a sieve. Drinking too much mead again, I presume?"

Ruck looked again and thought for a moment.

"Mendelheimer?" he finally asked.

The Red Knight spun quickly toward the minstrel.

"You know this scoundrel?" he asked.

"My Lord," Mendelheimer said, "we scoundrels seem to keep the same company. We have run across each other many times in our travels. In fact, I believe he sold me Preston."

The Red Knight roared heartily and turned back toward the Hall of Chrysalis.

"While I appreciate the entertainment you have provided, I will now leave you two to your reunion," Roanan said. "I have far too many preparations to make and not enough time to accomplish them."

Dainwirth Lir looked back and forth suspiciously at Mendelheimer and Ruck, then turned to follow Roanan. The two headed back toward the castle while the minstrel and the merchant were left to consider each other.

"I don't remember inviting you," the minstrel said.

"Ha!" Ruck said. "I don't recall you ever learning to swing a sword either."

"Well, here we both are," Mendelheimer concluded. "and it appears we are going to both be part of history, whatever that may be."

"War is what we're talking about," Ruck said. "And war is always good for business!"

•   •   •   •   •

At the Watchtower, the Black Knight considered the progress recently reported by Izuburu-Gy. For the moment, he was quite pleased.

"The raids have them on the run," Maldur said triumphantly. "A quarter of Karmana is already ours. Our enemies cower before us."

The Sorceress was less impressed.

"A quarter is not enough," Celidia hissed, "unless we talk of what is inside your head. Then, a quarter brain would be an improvement."

Maldur thought about a retort for a moment, then let it slip away.

"Brelex's army has been spotted by our scouts," he said. "He will be here within the day."

"That is excellent news," Celidia said, the Sorceress' mood brightening. "Soon we will be at full strength. We will draw Roanan and his quest for so-called justice right into our trap."

Just then, a ruckus broke out in the field before the Watchtower. Maldur and Celidia moved quickly to the window, to see the Drens arguing and fighting among themselves.

"Perhaps you should get your brothers under control," Celidia said.

"Brothers?" Maldur objected. "Those smelly slime have eaten everything in sight and they are still nothing but skin and bones."

"I'm sure you can whip them into shape," Celidia assured him. "You speak their language."

Maldur began to protest, but Celidia turned away and looked into the distance.

"Look," she said, pointing to a cloud of dust in the distance and the dark shadow behind it, "Brelex's army arrives sooner than expected."

"Finally," Maldur said. "I have real warriors with which to work."

"I'm glad that you are happy," Celidia finally said. "Now leave me to my own commission. I still have much to accomplish before Roanan and his army arrives."

CHAPTER 15
THE FLIGHT TO WAR

It's off to war we go
It's off to war we go
Heigh-ho and pack your swords
It's off to war we go . . .

The day of the departure finally arrived. Chrysalis was a bustle of activity, and even Mendelheimer's hapless songs were drowned in the ongoing din. Slowly, the knights, warriors, soldiers, and commoners that comprised Roanan's hurriedly thrown-together army collected in the wide road that lay in front of the Hall of Chrysalis.

Still, barked commands could be heard up and down the line from a cacophony of voices.

"This horse must be re-shoed . . ."

"We need more stores in this wagon . . ."

"Lines of five, lines of five . . ."

"Where are the Draconian knights? They must bring up this flank . . ."

"This bow is bent and will not do . . ."

"Magical elixirs, guaranteed," Theopolis Fenton Ruck IV suddenly bellowed as he reached the lines. "Healing salves, Elvii-forged swords, priced to sell, don't regret leaving Chrysalis without it . . ."

The trader had experienced a record three days, scurrying back and forth across the fields of Chrysalis peddling all varieties of questionable paraphernalia possible. Amulets and treasure maps, alleged Elvii relics and magical potions of every ilk–anything that would sell for a handsome profit Theopolis Fenton Ruck IV dealt. By the morning that the marching lines formed, the trader was known to nearly everyone in Roanan's army and his coin sack was quite heavy by any measure.

In the Hall of Chrysalis, Roanan and Lasarion stood facing each other. The two greatest knights in Chrysalis, the King and his cousin and most trusted companion, were acutely aware this could be their last meeting if their plans went awry. It was only with luck and good fortune they would meet again.

"Your mission is perilous," the Red Knight said. "I can trust it only to someone such as you."

"My charge is no less dangerous than your own, my King," Lasarion answered. "You will face the crux of Maldur and Brelex's armies head on."

Roanan smiled, considering the untold dangers that each would face.

"We are outnumbered, but we will not be out-fought. Be brave, but cautious as necessary," the Red Knight advised. "But most of all, be resourceful. No plan is ever perfect, and it is impossible to guess what pitfalls you may face along the way."

Lasarion embraced Roanan warmly.

"I will see you again on the battlefield," Lasarion said. "And we will ride back together in triumph."

"Let us hope so," Roanan answered.

"The ships await us," Lasarion said. "We must depart."

The Red Knight nodded. Lasarion turned and left the room. Roanan strapped Infernus securely to his waist, and in a moment, he too departed the Hall of Chrysalis.

Will I ever see my home again? He wondered.

As the Red Knight exited the chambers, Galena, the last of Balinwald's king's guard, hobbled once more from the castle.

"Rescue the princess," he pleaded. "It was my sworn duty, and I have failed. Please restore my honor."

The knight tried to speak once more, but his voice trailed off.

"Rest now," Roanan said reassuringly. "We have not forgotten Balinwald's plight. You did all you could. Your honor as a knight has never been in question."

Galena nodded and slowly returned to his chambers in the Hall. He would never see the light of day again.

Roanan finally reached his troops and in short order took his place at the head of his warriors, sitting proudly atop Alajar. To his right side was Tabeus on Ghost with Raven on the Wizard's shoulder. To his left was Halmar, Toranis and Dainwirth Lir. Surrounding the party was the King's Guard, a group of soldiers charged with defending the Red Knight at the cost of their lives.

Roanan nodded and ceremoniously drew Infernus and raised it high into the air. Quickly, he brought it forward. Then, urging Alajar on, Roanan moved forward. The long march had begun.

•   •   •   •   •

At the same time that Roanan and the bulk of the army began their march across Ambrasian, Lasarion had filled four tall ships with a thousand solders and enough supplies for their journey. The ships were built for speed and would slice swiftly through the water with favorable winds.

In short order, the navigators set their courses, and the hired oarsmen thrust forward. Ever so slowly, the ships creaked and groaned and eased themselves into the currents of the sea. The ships carried Lasarion and his men into the Sea of Dragons, heading south with the coastline visible in the distance.

Lasarion leaned against the rails on the starboard bow watching the ship cut through the sea. Dakar, a young knight who had gained Lasarion's favor in previous missions, soon joined him. A skilled fighter, Dakar was also curious and always willing to learn.

"It is told," Dakar said, "that fiery beasts roam the sea around Carpal and that the name of the Sea of Dragons is well earned."

Lasarion looked at the youthful knight calmly.

"In olden times, they did so freely, or at least that is what the legends say," Lasarion acknowledged. "But I have not heard of a dragon sighting in many years. To be sure, some men believe they have left Ambrasian never to return."

"Driven away by warriors of Chrysalis?" Dakar pressed. "Children's stories tell of such feats."

Lasarion laughed and peered across the endless waters.

"Hardly," the knight finally said. "Our spears and arrows were ineffective when pitted against the fury of a dragon. One can only speculate on why they left. Perhaps it was the work of the Wizards. Or perhaps all the tales of dragons were as much imagination as reality."

Dakar nodded and looked out to the sea. Lasarion remained in thought for a few seconds, then walked away.

"It will be a long and dangerous journey," he said, looking back at the young warrior. "Let us hope we return. Perhaps then we can go together in search of dragons."

•　　•　　•　　•　　•

"Secure the fortress over here with more stone!" Maldur barked. "That ditch needs to be twice that depth! No, you idiots, the water goes over here! Over here!"

The Black Knight stormed into the Watchtower, whose defenses continued to be fortified even further. While the fort had been left in some disrepair in recent years, the Drens had strengthened both the Watchtower and its surroundings to a far greater level than ever before, despite the Black Knight's complaints.

"Imbeciles," he cried, "you must watch everything they do, or they do wrong it–or not at all."

Celidia stood calmly listening to the Black Knight's rant, a refrain oft repeated over the past several days.

"Perhaps you expect too much of them, Maldur," she said. "They do not have six hands."

"They are nothing but a bunch of beasts," he complained. "It is good they fight better than they think."

The Sorceress laughed, though not as hard as she would have liked.

"The same has been said of their leader," she said.

The Black Knight scowled, but at that moment, Brelex entered the room. The Grey Knight puffed impatiently.

"I grow tired of waiting, Maldur," the Grey Knight said. "Where is Roanan? I am in need of a good fight. The sooner the pompous Red Knight falls, the faster we can depart this wretched place and claim our true legacy."

"They are coming," Maldur assured him. "Patience. It is a good thing he has not yet arrived. The Drens think of nothing but food and blood. We are not nearly ready for battle."

"That is your problem, Maldur, not mine," Brelex answered. "My men have been ready to fight since we arrived. We are a finely honed and battle-tested army."

"Your men are ready?" Maldur asked mockingly. "They have done nothing but eat, drink and whore."

"What are you saying?" Brelex asked threateningly.

"I'm saying I haven't seen your men lift one shovel, move one stone, or cut one log since they arrived," the Black Knight said.

Brelex rose angrily, but the two warriors were separated at that moment by Celidia.

"Fighting between us is not only unnecessary, but counter-productive," she reproached sternly as she came between them. "Remember, we are working for a common cause. It makes no sense battling each other over such trivialities."

"Yes," Brelex said unconvinced. "But this waiting serves no purpose other than to make my warriors less sharp. I say we march now and claim our victory that much sooner."

The Sorceress groaned in obvious aggravation. She thought she had already put this argument to rest.

"Oh no," she said disgustedly. "You are ossified from the neck up as well. How can I get into your blundering heads that we are stronger here than in the open field?"

The two knights cursed under their breaths.

"Then I wish Roanan and his pitiful army would hurry up and arrive," Brelex concluded.

"He will, he will," Celidia concluded. "His so-called honor leaves him no choice. Now go and prepare your troops."

At that moment, the Black Knight turned and looked outside. He saw three Drens moving a catapult under a tree.

"No!" he shouted. "That does not belong there, you idiots!"

Maldur rose from the room. Brelex laughed and followed.

"I shall see what nonsense these Drens are up to myself," the Grey Knight laughed.

They left Celidia alone, shaking her head. She turned and moved toward another chamber of the Watchtower.

"Let us hope they do not get into a battle of wits with Roanan," she muttered. "We would be unarmed."

· · · · ·

Roanan's forces followed the Road to Karmana as it cut through the center of Chrysalis. It was a wide, well-tended and much-traveled road, allowing the army to expedite the first leg of their journey. They soon reached the border, and on the second day of the march, entered the magical land.

A good number of the Red Knight's six thousand warriors had rarely seen the land of Karmana and for many, it was the first time they had ventured from their home in Chrysalis. While it was true that many of those that had been knighted had attended the Annual Games in their youth, even they now saw Karmana with new eyes. Previously, full of vigor and searching for glory, the knights had allowed much of the enchanted land's beauty to escape them. Afterward, the demands of everyday life, challenges elsewhere, and the sheer mystique and legends of the land kept most travelers at a distance. Outside of the knights, others that had joined Roanan's efforts–who in truth comprised most of the Red Knight's army — had never had the wherewithal to travel such distances away from the families. So now, in these days of desperation, these young and noble fighters, both male and female, were appreciating the full beauty of Karmana for the first time.

And it was undeniably beautiful. The Dren raids had not yet reached the western half of the land, and the gardens and forests grew wildly and lushly. The greens were rich and resonant, and the rest of the myriad of colors of an eternal spring were vibrant and multi-faceted and dazzled all who looked upon them.

In this part of Karmana, at least, there remained the illusion of peace, one last respite of solitude before the stench of the battle that lay before them. Dainwirth Lir rode in awe through the gardens. Mendelheimer pranced merrily about, entertaining the troops, though not to the delight of all.

"The minstrel sings like a sick frog," Halmar complained, and that was as kind an opinion the veteran knight had of the bard.

"And that is on a good day," the grizzled soldier added.

But despite the relative calm, at least one observer of Karmana grew uneasy. And as his disquiet increased, Roanan noticed the Wizard's concern.

"You seem troubled, my friend," the Red Knight said, riding up to Tabeus' side. "The battle lies inevitably before us. We cannot let it worry us now."

The Wizard continued to look to the left and the right.

"It is not just the battle that concerns me," Tabeus answered. "It is much more than that. It is Karmana itself."

"Karmana?" Roanan said in surprise. "Do not worry, Tabeus. We will fight until our last breath to drive out the Drens. Look around you. Here, Karmana is as beautiful as ever."

"At first glance, yes," Tabeus seemed to agree. "But notice. A dying flower by the side of the road, a tree with dead limbs, a small creek reduced to a mere trickle . . ."

By this time, Halmar had rode up to the two and had listened to Tabeus' last observations.

"But Wizard," the knight protested, "these are all natural events. There is nothing unusual here."

Tabeus looked about once more, then eyed Halmar directly.

"In any other part of Ambrasian, yes," the Wizard explained patiently. "But not in Karmana. Karmana is an undying land. Not only its people, but in fact all other living things within it are immortal as well. Flowers do not die here. They cannot. They have everlasting life."

"Then how is it that they show signs of dying now?" Roanan asked.

"The Oracle has more power than even you realize," Tabeus said. "The Oracle lies at the center of all life in Karmana. With the Oracle in evil hands, all that is good begins to decay and will eventually die. And that death is not limited to merely Karmana. That death will spread throughout Ambrasian, and all that is just will become extinct."

Roanan looked at Tabeus deep in thought.

"I think I am beginning to understand fully the powers of the Oracle," Roanan said.

"It is good that you do," the Wizard responded. "You then realize that we cannot fail, even against impossible odds."

Roanan nodded, considering the consequences of failure. With heavy thoughts, the party rode on silently.

•   •   •   •   •

Day turned to night and Roanan's army encamped in the open fields of Karmana. Even though this region of Ambrasian was still considered safe, and they had seen no sign of a Dren raid in the vicinity, the Red Knight posted sentries that alternated throughout the evening. None spotted any sign of enemy activity.

Just before dawn, the army was called to attention by the morning reveille, and by the first hints of daylight, the forces were ready to once again continue the march to the Hall of Karmana. Roanan planned on reaching their destination by the end of the day, a pace that would require an aggressive advance. But the Red Knight knew that each moment was critical in this quest.

It was a quiet, gloomy day, unusually overcast and grey for Karmana. Tabeus noticed and seemed solemnly pre-occupied, wandering far afield from the rest of the columns. Mendelheimer sang incessantly.

> *Across the plains of Mizeldee*
> *There was a man of power*
> *But every time he saw a spider*
> *In a corner he did cower . . .*

But it was of no use. Even the minstrel's songs were flat and lifeless. Mendelheimer eventually fell silent as well and Preston slowly lost ground falling behind much of the procession. The minstrel spent much of the day trying to urge his horse to keep up with the rest of the army.

Near mid-day, with the Wizard nowhere to be seen, Dainwirth Lir took advantage of Tabeus' absence and approached Roanan. The Red Knight watched the young warrior carefully as he rode quietly toward him.

"Something troubles you, Lir," he said.

"Of a sort," Lir admitted. "I wonder why we must shed so much blood when a Wizard as powerful as Tabeus could likely dispose of the enemy single-handedly."

"I think you both overestimate the power of a Wizard and underestimate the strength of our enemy," Roanan said. "Maldur and Brelex have assembled an army that is singularly powerful, beyond the ability of even a Wizard to defeat. And even if Tabeus had such power, he could not use it without unleashing dire and unintended consequences."

"Why is that?" Lir challenged. "I don not understand."

"Wizards cannot kill," Roanan explained. "The Wizards have a unique relationship with the natural order of Ambrasian. Only the Wizards themselves understand it fully. A Wizard is only partly of this world. Whence they came, they will not tell. Some say from lands far to the west across the endless waters. Others say from the impenetrable mountains of the North. But I say they have come from a place not found on a navigator's map. I cannot say exactly where . . ."

Roanan paused momentarily.

"However, no matter their origin," the Red Knight continued, "in Ambrasian, they cannot kill anymore than they can become a King. For this is not their world to rule. Surely, they provide aid and advice to a cause they deem good and just. But they cannot create that cause, or it will become their master. Those Wizards who in the past have overstepped their role have come invariably to suffer unfortunate and unexpected ends."

Roanan paused, letting Lir reflect on what he just said. Then the Red Knight continued.

"It may be true that we see only a hint of the Wizard's true powers, for they are powerful indeed," Roanan said. "Who knows, perhaps with a wave of their hand, they could wash us away in the sea of time. No one can say for certain. But this much is true: power can easily be turned to evil and that is why Wizards never use their gifts or capture a throne. Power would consume them and the unknown well from which they draw their strength would swallow them. They would be set to flames by the very magic they betrayed, left to wander in the nether world and beyond. I cannot explain it fully and Tabeus will provide no clues. On that subject, he is singularly quiet no matter how many times you ask. Thus, my explanation though incomplete must suffice."

Dainwirth Lir remained quiet for a moment.

"I suppose," he finally said thoughtfully, "that such strength is a double-edged sword. The Wizard must be frustrated he cannot use his powers to correct such evil in Ambrasian."

"It is not his fight," Roanan said. "It is ours. Tabeus aids us whenever he can. His dreams, his visions, his advice, and his subtle displays of magic all are designed for our benefit. Perhaps he will provide more important help in the battle to come. For though he cannot use his magic in the fight, he can use his wizardry against Celidia if she calls upon the power of the Oracle. If that be the case, Tabeus is free to summon all his strength to fight magic used against our quest."

The Red Knight and Dainwirth Lir continued to ride side by side. Well before the sun set, the army approached the Hall of Karmana. In the plain before them, the glittering edifice dwarfed the small towns surrounding it. The gardens sprawled opulently, again apparently naturally and unattended. Still, now that his senses had been sharpened by Tabeus, the Red Knight once more noticed signs of deterioration. A tree had been hewn in two by a stray bolt of lightning and dead limbs lay in the grassy meadow. A small bird lie dying by a still pond. Knowing hat time was precious, Roanan spurred Alajar on toward their destination.

As the Hall of Karmana came even closer, Tabeus finally rejoined Roanan. But something untold and desperate had occurred along the way. The frail body of the Wizard shook violently and was covered with beads of sweat. He seemed exhausted, ready to collapse. It appeared that only Ghost kept the horse and his rider moving forward. Raven watched his master with concern.

The Red Knight rushed up to the Wizard and called two nearby soldiers to aid Tabeus in staying on his horse. Roanan took a cloth and wiped Tabeus' forehead.

"Tabeus," he asked worriedly, "what happened? Are you all right?"

The Wizard looked up at Roanan. His eyes were glazed and distant, his voice strained.

"I will recover," he whispered, "as will Lasarion and his men."

"Lasarion?" Roanan gasped. "Tabeus, what . . ."

The Wizard lifted his handed and interrupted the Red Knight.

"They have seen the mouth of the abyss and survived," Tabeus finally said. "But we have barely averted disaster. Evil is far more prevalent and its reach much greater than we anticipated."

The Wizard slumped downward and lost consciousness. Roanan looked toward the Hall of Karmana in desperation.

CHAPTER 16
THE BATTLE OF SUDDEN FLAME

A thousand soldiers left the calm shores of Chrysalis under the command of Lasarion, the first cousin of the King in the line of the Red Knight. They were carried in four tall ships of war, finely built, well-stocked and secured. The ships sailed proudly, passing through the soft waves of the Sea of Dragons, as they began their desperate journey. They knew their voyage would end in conflict, but little did they know the fray would reach them much sooner than expected.

No sooner had Lasarion left Chrysalis, however, then evil and dark forces reawakened in the Sea. The disturbance stretched far across the waters to the Island of Carpal, a full one hundred miles beyond the Ambrasian shoreline. The men of Chrysalis had long heard legends of great and powerful dragons that roamed these waters, but few if any had actually been seen in contemporary times, and nearly all of those present-day sightings were held in question. Many believed the tales of dragons were nothing more than folklore and fairy tales, cautionary tales to scare children into better behavior. For most of the warriors on this quest, dragons were the least of their concerns.

In earlier days, however, the story was far different. Dragons, it was said, roamed Ambrasian freely, plundering towns and hoarding great riches. Great battles had been fought to defend the populace, though few dragons had been slain. In most cases, those attacked counted themselves lucky if the dragon had somehow been driven off before finishing its work. However, nearly all believed the dragons had left long ago. Still, those tales of yore still spawned fear among the common folk, and the ancients had named the Sea on which Lasarion now sailed after the powerful beasts.

Carpal was a rocky mountainous island nearly devoid of life or vegetation. In the days of the Red Knight's ancestors, the island was rumored to be rife with dragons, a spawning ground for the foul beasts of the air, but no one who set sail to verify such tales ever returned. Though few Cadaren could face the dragon and survive, the number of beasts dwindled over time until they were relegated in this day to the role of myth.

Even still, the people of Ambrasian did not explore the lands of Carpal even after the dragons disappeared, for the island was barren, and those that journeyed there found no trace of the dragons' alleged treasure. And thus, those brave or reckless explorers returned to the mainland disappointed and let the island be. No signs of dragons were to be found. Seafarers dismissed such tales with laughter and sailed the ocean around Carpal with impunity.

Little then, did Lasarion or the rest of his crew know that one dragon still remained, an ancient and most powerful worm. The dragon's name was Ravager, and it had slept for many, many years deep within the bowels of the mountain in the center of the island. But now, it had been re-awakened, whether by coincidence or more likely by the spread of evil throughout the land. Could it be that Celidia's powers stretched even so far as the mountain caverns that housed the dragon? While it could not be said for sure either way, such a scenario seemed most likely.

Ravager was the greatest of all the ancient dragons. It was a full hundred and fifty feet long and of great mass and weight. Its body was covered with dark green, impenetrable scales hardened even more by uncountable years of its existence. Only a small portion of the underbelly was left exposed and vulnerable, where the dragon's lungs inhaled great quantities of air to feed its internal fire and whose rhythmic pulsing prevented any scales from adhering. The dragon had also been wounded there many years before, a wound that had never fully healed.

Ravager's tail was a powerful appendage on its own, forty feet long, and its wings spanned over fifty feet in both directions. Ravager was a fire breather, and his flames could easily smote entire villages in minutes. Its long, thin tongue slithered from its mouth menacingly.

But many in the days where the beast flew freely thought the dragon's eyes most fearsome, deep-set with black pupils, the mysteries of the ages swimming within them. Bloodshot were the supposed whites of Ravager's eyes though he had been asleep for many years. The dragon was both sinister and wise. The dragon's eyes could hold the weaker wills of the peoples of Ambrasian under their control, driving them mad, or leading them to their deaths. Ravager was truly a force with which to be reckoned.

And now, in times already full of peril and uncertainty, that force once again stirred. The dragon's eyes slowly opened and its fire lit the long-dark cavern.

"Who has so rudely awakened me from my restful sleep?" the beast rasped as he languidly looked across the cavern, his vision pierced through the darkness.

Hidden deep within the mountain, Ravager's lair lay secret even from the most adventurous of Cadaren who had searched the island. Here in reality was the legendary treasure of the dragons, hoarded by Ravager many years before. Diamonds and rare gems of all kind sparkled throughout the lair, but the gold that lined the floor and chambers of the cave dwarfed those by a thousand-fold or more. Ravager held the treasures of entire kingdoms within the cave, more gold than in the vaults of Karmana or the King's Treasury in Chrysalis.

However, it was not merely for Ravager's love of treasure that the dragon amassed these riches, though the beast surely coveted and fiercely protect his gold. But the hoard served a much more basic, primitive purpose. The dragon's huge and jagged body was slippery with its secretions, which without protection would burn the earth beneath its great weight. Only gold could withstand the destructive power of the dragon's body for long periods. Thus, the gold served as the dragon's bed, a cushion from the scorched earth beneath it.

Now, however, the eyes of the dragon drifted left to right and back again. The fire, once nearly extinguished by the ripples of time, began to re-ignite and again burn brightly within the beast. The great worm stretched sluggishly, its powerful limbs moved creakily, and the hot breath of the dragon filled the now glimmering cavern. The very mountain seemed to quake with the awakening of the beast within.

The dragon sniffed suspiciously, his eyes peering through the dark into the distance beyond. A spark of recognition swept through the brain of the beast, a flash of anger coursing through every fiber of the dragon's body. He recognized the smell of Cadaren.

"I have slept for far too long," Ravager observed. "These specks have emboldened themselves and now trespass in my Sea freely and without fear. They will pay for such insolence."

Deliberately, Ravager arose and with a great cry that shook the very stone foundation of the cavern, slowly lifted himself up and then, in one sudden movement, swooped gracefully from the hidden cavern, drove upwards, and emerged from the mountain into the splendor of the day. It encircled the Island of Carpal, once, twice, and yet a third time, spewing great trails of flame along its path as the open air now fed its internal furnace once again. Turning in the sky, Ravager climbed above the clouds, and the terrible sight of the dragon was beholden above the seas of Ambrasian for the first time in many generations.

Woe to those who cross my path, Ravager thought as it sped across the waters below. *I have debts to collect and bodies to char. There are a great many payments are past due.*

·   ·   ·   ·   ·

Two days into their journey, Lasarion and his troops drove through the Sea of Dragons toward their destination. The winds had been advantageous, and they sped toward their destination in favorable time.

Perhaps, Lasarion thought, *our journey will find good fortune after all.*

Once more, Dakar, the young knight, approached Lasarion. The commander of the mission spotted him coming toward him.

"I fear we will find no dragons for you to see today," Lasarion laughed. "The sea is calm and the winds work in our favor. But be glad. You will have enough to battle without the dragons you seek."

Dakar smiled, looking about the surrounding sea.

"I will gladly do without them," the young knight said. "I suspect we will have fight enough when we land."

"I believe your words to be true," Lasarion agreed. "By the end of this journey, we will likely see enough battle for a lifetime."

And still the four ships of war sailed on farther into the sea. They arched their sails in a southwesterly direction, and the still beneficial wind sped them past Selin's shores and toward the southern coast of Balinwald. Lasarion's army began to anticipate the days and hours until they went ashore and began their march toward battle.

But some time later, unexpectedly, the waters grew restless, and the wind swirled. Lasarion grew concerned as the temperatures dropped and the high cumulus clouds turned grey. The sun became hidden, and the day turned strangely dark and ominous. The sailors braced their ships for the onslaught of a storm. But an old, wrinkled sea veteran came onto the deck, looked up, and shook his head.

"This is no storm," he said ominously. "I have read about such events in the ancient texts. This is the coming of the dragon."

And the old Cadaren limped below, disappearing once again into the bowels of the ship.

Lasarion, too, grew more skeptical of the storm gathering around them.

"Something is seriously awry here," he proclaimed. "This is like no storm I have ever seen."

Lasarion watched the gathering maelstrom more carefully, his level of concern rising as the seas became more disturbed.

Across the sea far in the distance, the mountain of Carpal belched thick smoke and rumbled deeply, coming back to life after so many years. The bowels of Ambrasian trembled, and the sky grew even darker. The warriors on the ships of war looked collectively in the direction of the tremors. They saw a somber-red sky before them, and it grew closer and closer with each passing second.

The warriors stared at the scene as though they were held in some trance. The sky above them turned from red to nearly pitch black, with sudden sharp flashes of lightning flaring down toward the ships. The seas swirled violently, rocking the sides of the crafts with foamy white waves.

Lasarion was the first to tear his eyes away from the ominous sight.

"It cannot be," he whispered and quickly moved about the ship, shaking his soldiers to attention. Lasarion ordered the marksmen to be brought to the upper decks of the ships and all available shields be placed as armor around the ships' most vulnerable areas. Lasarion knew it was but a small gesture. The Chrysalian ships were made of fine timber and were imposing ships in nearly all situations. But if this was one of the dragons of legend come back to life, the ships' strength was laughable when pit against the fire of the beast.

As if on some morbid cue, the blackish clouds above the ships parted, and through them, Ravager swooped down in all its might and fury. Its outstretched body soared ominously over the ships beneath it and cast a long shadow upon the sea. Ravager left out a fearsome cry, more terrible than any sound in all of Ambrasian. Even the most courageous of Lasarion's soldiers cringed. Fright overwhelmed others, and some cast themselves into the sea, while others ran madly about the ship's deck. Slowly, order was restored, and Lasarion ordered the bowmen to fire when ready. Ravager breathed a long stream of flames through the air but was well outside the range of the archer's arrows.

Once again, fear spread over the ships, yet this time the soldiers held their ground. Ravager flew into the clouds, turned and sped toward the first ship with unbridled fury. Lasarion and the rest of the army in the other ships could only stand and watch the ensuing scene. The dragon's flight pierced the air and the serpent rapidly approached the ship. The bowmen stayed firm in the face of Ravager's rage. Some fired, but their arrows bounced harmlessly off the dragon's well-protected body. The gaze of the dragon's eye caught others, and in their madness, they threw themselves into the volatile waters below.

Lasarion watched the scene with increasing dismay. He screamed loudly across the din.

"Avoid the dragon's eyes," he instructed. "Do not look into its eyes."

His message spread rapidly throughout the ships, but it was an order difficult to heed, for the dragon itself was drawing the eyes of the soldiers toward it. Captains tried again and again to divert the gaze of their soldiers, but the dragon's mind exerted a near overwhelming power on the resolve of its foes.

Ravager continued to rush toward the first ship and pulled up at the last second. The dragon opened its mouth slowly, foul juices dripping from its jaws. A burst of flames engulfed the ship, setting its sails ablaze. The navigators tried closing the canvasses in an attempt to extinguish the fires, while others doused the flaming materials with buckets of water. Thick, billowing smoke encircled the ship, but the fire, at least temporarily, was under control.

The dragon, however, was hardly done.

Fools, Ravager mused to himself, *thinking they can survive an encounter with the oldest, wisest, and greatest dragon of the land. Has the world gone mad in my absence? They will learn to fear me once more.*

Ravager sailed high into the sky and again hurtled toward the beleaguered ship. Once more, the bowmen fired, but to no avail. Ravager breathed a great burst of fire, which overwhelmed the mast of the ship, sending plumes of smoke high into the air. Now the ship blazed uncontrollably and was rocking wildly in the disturbed sea. Many of the warriors jumped from the flames, not from madness this time, but for the sake of survival.

The smell of the burning ship and the human flesh of those trapped aboard it filled the surrounding seas. Now, the terror of death was imminent and a feeling of desperation became ever more pervasive. Even Lasarion was quiet, at a loss as to how to stop the dragon. Rescue operations were performed to save the fallen soldiers as their burning ship illuminated the darkened sky. Rescue boats were loosened into the water from each of the ships and ropes were hurled from every direction.

The dragon is preparing to attack again, Lasarion thought, *and I have no way to defend us. If we are doomed, so too is Ambrasian.*

Now Ravager turned gracefully but frightfully once again and eyed the second ship. The bowmen prepared for the dragon's onslaught. Arrows whistled through the air. Once more, however, they fell harmlessly off Ravager's outer crust. The dragon breathed its hot fire on the ship. This time, the protective armor caught much of the flame, keeping the ship secure. From this initial blast, however, nearly all the armor was incinerated, laying bare the ships for Ravager's next attack.

Lasarion now rushed about the ship, trying to keep his own men calm, while his inner apprehension continued to fester. He turned a corner, spying the dragon in the distance. The Great Worm had again peeked above the clouds and cried in a long, cold rage.

Suddenly, the old Cadaren who had initially recognized the coming of the dragon appeared from a dark hole leading to the lower levels of the ship. Silently but firmly, he motioned Lasarion to come forward. The Chrysalian commander hesitated, but the old Cadaren became more animated and limped hurriedly down the steps.

"I am in the middle of a battle with a dragon," Lasarion said angrily. "I have no time to follow you on some folly."

"A battle you will lose if you do not accompany me," the stranger said firmly. "I assure you this is no fool's errand."

Driven by some inner knowledge that even he could not identify, Lasarion followed reluctantly, straining his eyes in the dark hallway. The old man scurried down a long corridor, into a musky room. He moved quickly to a dust-covered box in a corner, apparently long forgotten. He picked it up gingerly and held it as though it was some lost and valued treasure.

"There is only one way to defeat the dragon's breath," he said deliberately.

Lasarion squinted in the dim light.

"Who are you?" he asked. "I don't recognize you."

"That need not concern you now," he said. "Is it not enough that I am here?"

Then, the old Cadaren seemed to acquiesce, as if he felt the need of showing some proof of his claim.

"I have been sent by Tabeus to watch for an occasion such as this," he explained.

"How do I know you speak the truth?" Lasarion demanded.

"Do you have a choice?" the old Cadaren challenged. "The dragon has destroyed one ship already and will destroy the second in a matter of moments. Your remaining two ships will not survive the hour without aid. How will you stop him?"

Lasarion shrugged hopelessly. The old Cadaren, apparently content with this small victory, continued.

"You must close the eye of the dragon," he advised.

"Every one of my marksmen have tried," Lasarion protested. "They have all failed."

"In this box," the old Cadaren continued seemingly oblivious to Lasarion's interruptions, "contains a single arrow. The Elvii forged it when Ambrasian was young and magic was strong. It is the last of its kind. It is the only arrow the power of the Worm will not divert."

Lasarion took the box and opened it. A silver arrow with a gold tip shined brightly in the dim room.

"The arrow must penetrate the eye of the dragon," the old Cadaren continued. "Only then will the Worm expose itself to danger. The dragon is not protected in a small spot just below its long neck, at the top of its underbelly. It is the spot where the dragon fully absorbs the air that feeds it fire, and its scales do not adhere to its body. It was further weakened many years ago by a stray arrow that pierced but did not kill the dragon. That wound has never fully healed."

Again, Lasarion protested.

"This arrow, even if successful, will blind only one eye," he said. "The dragon can hold one's will with either eye."

"This is true," the old Cadaren said. "But it will give you a few seconds of diversion. The dragon's hold will be broken so that the Worm can concentrate its power into the remaining eye. But I warn you, its left eye is more powerful. Your chances will be greater if you disable the Worm there."

Lasarion still appeared skeptical.

"What will prevent me from falling under the power of the dragon as I take aim?" he asked.

The old Cadaren nodded and disappeared into the darkness for a moment. He returned, holding a visor framed in silver of a design Lasarion had never seen. He handed it to the knight.

"Wear this," he said. "It will offer protection long enough to complete your task."

The knight still held some doubt but had no alternative to defeating his foe. He finally nodded to the old Cadaren.

"Let us hope this works," he said.

Lasarion took the arrow and the visor and hurried back toward the top of the ship. By the time Lasarion reached sunlight, the second ship was now burning brightly and was being swallowed by the turbulent seas. More knights and warriors thrashed wildly in the waves, searching for an object with which to grasp. Some found stray logs ripped from the plundered ships and claimed them with a desperate passion.

Now the dragon flew high into the air once again and turned toward the third ship. Lasarion rushed toward Dakar, who stood transfixed on the sight.

"Get a bow for me and for yourself," Lasarion ordered, "and gather the best bowmen we have. I will be waiting."

Dakar shook himself out of his daze and stared at Lasarion.

"Bowmen?" he asked. "So far, they have proven useless."

"We have but one chance," Lasarion explained urgently. "We must now hunt the dragon ourselves. Now go . . ."

Dakar nodded stupidly and ran as quickly as his legs could carry to fulfill his leader's orders.

At the same time, Lasarion directed that his own ship be brought closer to the companion ship that Ravager was now preparing to attack. The chief navigator looked at Lasarion with obvious bewilderment.

"Begging your pardon, sir," but shouldn't we move away from the beast?" the navigator questioned.

Lasarion looked at him icily.

"You heard what I said," he commanded. "We do not run away from a fight. We need to save our comrades if we can. Now move, quickly."

"Aye sir," the navigator said. Reluctantly, the oarsmen turned the ship toward that of their battered colleagues.

Ravager now flung itself toward the third ship, spraying it with hot mists of fire. But the ship held firm. The bowmen and Dakar returned to Lasarion, who stationed them on the side of the ship closest to the dragon.

"Get the dragon's attention," Lasarion ordered, speaking loudly and clearly so there was no mistake in his direction. "When it turns toward us, I will blind it. Then, you have a few short seconds to hit the soft spot of the beast. It is just below the worm's neck, a vulnerable area on its underbelly. Understand?"

The bowmen nodded. Lasarion turned toward Dakar.

"The dragon hunt you yearned for is upon us, young knight," he said.

Dakar glanced at the beast.

"Let us hope we survive to tell about it," he said.

Lasarion grasped Dakar's hand, held it for a moment, then took his position.

The dragon sailed into the distance until he became a mere speck in the sky, then whirled around again and began moving rapidly toward its prey once more. Frantically, Lasarion urged his own ship onward. When they had come into the range of the dragon, Lasarion ordered his bowmen to fire. They did so, just as Ravager prepared to release its next debilitating burst of flames. The arrows dropped off the Great Worm causing no damage. But Ravager turned from its target and faced its new adversary angrily.

Who dare challenge the great Ravager? the ancient Worm thought. *I will show them how their bravery is nothing but madness. Fools, all of them! Let them burn in the scalding fire of the dragon.*

The Cadaren on Lasarion's ship momentarily cringed, but the Chrysalian knight held them firm. All avoided the eyes of the dragon with the entirety of their will. But still Ravager drew some into their unfathomable depths, and its gaze cast the weak into fits of hysteria and madness.

Ravager hurtled toward the ship, peppering it with its hot breath. Lasarion slipped on the protective visor fully over his eyes, took the precious arrow from its container, cocked it in his bow and awaited the shot. Dakar stood near him, along with the rest of the bowmen, waiting for their captain to act. But in the dragon's first pass, it provided no clear opportunity to shoot.

Across Lasarion's ship, sailors and warriors alike scurried to extinguish the scattered fires. Ravager had not yet hit the ship with full force, and many of the protective shields lay intact. Despite this, flames burst intermittently throughout the vessel.

"I have only one shot," Lasarion whispered to himself. "Be patient."

I hope the ship can stay in one piece long enough to fire truly, the knight thought to himself.

Lasarion was occasionally prone to impetuousness and had to control his emotions and actions. Here, however, he realized acting a split second too soon would be catastrophic.

The dragon turned and thrust its great body toward the ship once more. His outspread wings cast a long shadow on the besieged craft. The waves rocked the vessel ferociously. Again, the beast passed beyond Lasarion's range, sending a great burst of flames that cut a wide swath of destruction through the ship. Several bowmen lost their balance as the support beams gave way and were plunged into the hungry sea. The fire was rampant now, its spread barely checked by the heaving, sweating, desperate Cadaren crew. Beads of perspiration ran down Lasarion's rugged face. His brown hair hung limply, the spray of the sea hanging from it stickily.

Nearly half the ship was decimated by flames. The shields had melted under the heat of the dragon's breath. Much of the crew worked desperately to douse the fires. If Lasarion failed to find a clear shot on this pass, there would be no other chances. The ship, the army, and the war for Ambrasian would all be lost. Dakar watched his captain intently, his blonde flash of hair illuminated by the flames behind him.

Now to finish these insolent specks, Ravager thought. *Have you felt the full fury of my wrath? It is time you do!*

The dragon pushed its massive frame toward the beleaguered ship, gaining speed as it came closer. The Great Worm now flew directly toward Lasarion, its tail skimming the sea beneath it. The beast opened its mouth wide, its tongue slithering out from the dark hollow behind the dragon's imposing jaw. Its eyes fixed themselves on its prey. Quickly, the distance between the dragon and the ship grew less and less.

Lasarion now took his bow and drew back the magical arrow, fixing his target.

The left eye is more powerful, he thought to himself. *Aim for the left.*

He drew his head up and his eye met the eye of the dragon.

For a long second, Lasarion felt the power of the dragon attempt to enter into his very being. The visor's protection held, but Ravager persisted and slowly, Lasarion saw the soul of the beast. It was ancient, yes, and dark, full of unfathomable knowledge but corrupted by centuries of unbridled greed and hate. Hate, that was the key. Anger and hatred of all things living, a furious, illogical, psychopathic, blinding hate and wish for death . . .

Lasarion heard a buzzing in his ear and suddenly the fury of the dragon was expelled, and the Chrysalian captain was pulled from the vortex toward which his mind was drifting. Still, he gazed into the eye of the dragon. But while the Worm's essence lay bare and powerful forces attacked Lasarion's psyche, the knight remained protected. In fact, the Wizard Tabeus, far across Ambrasian, now exerted all of his power holding firm the will of Lasarion against the fury of the dragon. Even for the Wizard, it was a task of great effort. But in these precious moments, Lasarion understood that the power of the dragon lay in its victim. Fear killed. The unknown brought fear. Fear destroyed the mind. Ravager was an ancient, unknown, all-consuming hate.

Revitalized by the efforts of the Wizard, Lasarion raised the bow once more, taking point blank aim at his target. The dragon breathed its hot gust of fire. Now Lasarion's moment was at hand.

Lasarion cocked the arrow and fired. As if watching in slow motion, he saw the arrow whistle through the air. The dragon's eye expressed rage at first, then dismay, and finally, just before the arrow pierced the left eye, the very fear it sought to instill. The arrow was swallowed up in the well of darkness, and Ravager pulled up, screaming in a deafening, horrifying cry. In the midst of the chaos, Lasarion turned to his bowmen.

"Now!" he shouted above the din. "Shoot now!"

The bowmen fired. Their shots still missed. But Dakar pulled his arrow back, released it, and his shot rang true, landing squarely and deeply in the heart of Ravager's soft underbelly. Boiling, venomous blood spewed from the fresh wound, and then, the old wound beneath it ripped itself open anew. Now, dragon blood poured uncontrollably out of the worm as its life's essence drained into the seas beneath it.

Ravager kicked wildly, somersaulting through the sky as pain and mortality creased through its massive frame. Finally, the Great Worm cried aloud once again, gazed haughtily at its conqueror and fell into the sea, sinking instantly as the Sea became a boiling cauldron. From the distance, the volcano of Carpal erupted with all of its fury, spewing ash and molten rock throughout the surrounding waters. In the violent explosion, Ravager's treasure was buried forever, deep within the underworld of Ambrasian.

Lasarion slumped to his knees, drained from the inner journey into the depths that few experience and survive. His soldiers were equally exhausted. Still, the captain found enough energy to raise himself up and rouse his warriors to secure the ships, douse the remaining fires, and attend to the injured. Time was now of the essence if the mission was to be salvaged.

The task appeared hopeless. All the ships were crippled to some degree. Two were destroyed, their smoke-filled hulls half-immersed in the waters that were only now beginning to calm. Lasarion's ship was severely damaged, the scent of burnt wood permeating the air. How long it would remain seaworthy remained a pressing question. The last ship was less mutilated, but still needed repair. And even then, it was woefully inadequate to carry all of Lasarion's men.

The old Cadaren had mysteriously vanished. Despite a rigorous search of both ships and the surrounding waters, Lasarion could find no sign of the veteran sailor who had provided the means to defeat Ravager.

Did he die in the battle? Lasarion wondered, *or was he never here?*

For now, the knight had no time to further consider the possibilities. The seas had finally calmed, the clouds had dispersed, and the sun shined once again. The violent and malevolent winds ceased. Light radiated across the beaten, battered ships. Lasarion's soldiers were sluggish, drunken with exhaustion from the efforts of the last hour. Worse, the battle had driven the fleet far off their path and now Lasarion sailed in unknown waters. Their compasses and other directional instrumentation had been smashed and shattered in the battle with Ravager. Lasarion ordered his solders to patch the ships as best they could and hope they would remain afloat until the army reached land. Without instrumentation, the crippled ships travelled nearly blind, navigating through the Sea of Dragons using the movements of the sun as their only guide. Lasarion ordered the ships to travel due east, hoping the shoreline would be reached as soon as possible.

For a day and a night, the ships wandered, searching for a path to follow. At dawn of the next day, the navigators peered into the distance, and in the amber horizon, spotted land. The ships sped forward with new-found life. By midday, the battered vessels, battling their death throes and further punished by the elements of the sea, had reached land with one last, great effort. Much of Lasarion's ship literally crumbled as the army docked as close to the shore as possible.

The army filed out of the ships onto the canoes and eventually collapsed on the soft white crystal sand of the unknown beach. There they rested, preparing to march the next day. Lasarion posted guards and surveyed the scene, wondering where they had landed. Unknown to both him and his army, they had reached the land of Selin.

CHAPTER 17
BIOLOGICAL PERMUTATIONS, GALACTIC DATE 2143-08-08

The Explorer continued to maintain a stable orbit above Ambrasian, with no further aftereffects from whatever had temporarily disabled the ship earlier. Kevo continued its data analysis from the incident in search of a reasonable explanation of a cause, to no avail. If the AI was feeling the binary equivalent of frustration, it would hardly admit as much to the Lux crew members.

For their part, the crew continued to monitor the activities on the planet below, but the most recent events had confounded them to a degree not considered possible.

"Dragons?" Evenru said incredulously. "I thought our scientists had dispelled the notion that dragons had ever existed anywhere in the known universe. 'Biologically impossible' is the term I recall. I've heard complex explanations of how a flying animal that breathes plumes of flames is a nonviable life form possibility."

The Captain of the Explorer studied the view screens that showed the carcass of Ravager disappearing below the waves. What remained of Lasarion's army scrambled to find safety, eventually drifting to the shores of Selin.

"But here we are," Evenru said. "Real live biologically impossible dragons."

Kevo continued to process the data being received from the planet, at first not commenting on Evenru's remarks. The planet below continued to challenge the Lux's knowledge of both the known galaxy and its understanding of scientific principles.

"I am still analyzing the phenomenon," the ship's AI finally responded flatly. "I have not yet reached a conclusion, but I am studying 2,187 alternative explanations."

Penra entered the Command Center studying the holographic images recorded from the drones.

"Ambrasian continues to surprise," the officer said. "The biological diversity of intelligent species was already unique, but a dragon . . ."

Penra shook his head.

"There is no accounting for such a thing," he concluded. "Breathes fire and all, just as the legends say. Who would have thought that was possible?"

Evenru walked back and forth across the Command Center. He wasn't sure what to make of the planet below him that defied science at every turn.

We are technologically more advanced in every way, the captain thought. *Yet Ambrasian presents a new world of both wonder and danger. Are we as safe as we believe?*

"There doesn't seem to be many things that we can account for on this world," he said. "Don't the damn laws of physics apply here?"

"The laws of physics are immutable," Kevo answered without emotion.

"Well, apparently someone forgot to tell them that down there," Evenru said. "Because every time I look, the immutable laws of physics are being immuted. Can someone explain that to me?"

The Command Center was silent except for the soft whirs and hums of the ship's AI working furiously to make sense of the data it was receiving from the planet.

Evenru had stopped waiting for an answer, knowing that his fellow crew members and even Kevo were at a loss to explain what theoretically was impossible. The Captain took a few minutes to continue to watch the various images transmitted by the drones that now covered most of the conflict occurring on the ground.

Warfare was a rare phenomenon on an intergalactic scope and Evenru had learned most of what he knew through the study of history. But the signs of conflict on the planet below were clear.

This will be a violent and bloody affair, he thought. *Barbaric, but we cannot interfere. The inhabitants of this planet must chart their own course.*

Evenru finally turned back toward Penra.

"I think we need to collect as much data as possible," he said. "Our scientists can figure it out when we return to Lux."

The Captain then turned his attention to the AI.

"Kevo, maintain orbit," he said. "And gather as much information as your memory drives can hold."

CHAPTER 18
THIEF IN THE NIGHT

Roanan and two other knights rode as quickly as Tabeus' condition would allow toward the Hall of Karmana, Raven keeping pace in the air above them. As the Wizard's disposition had become more urgent, the Red Knight was quickly reminded of a simple truth: no matter how desperate the situation, there was no quick way to move an army of thousands and the needed provisions from one location to the next.

Roanan ultimately decided to go ahead of his army with all possible speed, leaving Halmar, Toranis, and Dainwirth Lir to lead the forces the rest of the way. Even then, the Red Knight could not go as quickly as he would have preferred, since Tabeus' fragility limited his progress. In a time that tested even the patience of the tactical young King, however, he finally reached his destination.

There, Roanan found a chamber for Tabeus and helped him onto the soft bed within. The Wizard still suffered greatly from whatever had weakened him on the road and the Red Knight's concern was palpable. He sent for Karmin herself, and within a few minutes, the Regent of Karmana burst into the room. Acknowledging Roanan only momentarily, she moved directly to the side of the Wizard, speaking softly in a tongue unknown to the Red Knight and helping Tabeus drink a few sips of a clear fluid in a small flask she pulled from a hidden fold of her gown. The subtle lines on Karmin's face belied her concern.

Roanan and Karmin stayed by the Wizard's side, watching him intently. As the rest of the Red Knight's army arrived and pitched camp in the countryside outside the center of Karmana, the two still remained with Tabeus. The Wizard drifted in and out of a fitful sleep, his body jolting on several occasions as he seemed to re-live some excruciating event.

"He will recover," Karmin finally said to the Red Knight, "though he has experienced a traumatic event of which even I cannot guess."

Roanan studied his friend and ally carefully.

"I don't understand how that is possible," he said. "We encountered no enemies and had no confrontations on our journey. He mentioned Lasarion, but how he could know what happened in the sea many leagues away I cannot fathom."

"Whatever occurred," Karmin responded, "stretched the Wizard's skills beyond time and space. I suspect we will discover the truth shortly."

Slowly, after spending a restless night recovering, the Wizard grew stronger and finally sat up, gathering his wits.

"I am glad to see you have come back to us," Karmin said. "I was quite concerned for your well-being."

Tabeus looked back and forth at Karmin and Roanan.

"The healing powers of Karmana and its Regent have proven true," the Wizard acknowledged, "even in its diminished state."

"Diminished am I?" Karmin said with a sly smile. "You do not appear to be working at full vigor either, Wizard."

Karmin and Tabeus acknowledged each other, but Roanan was well aware there was more than a bit of competitive tension between the two. Each recognized the value and the skills of their companion, even if they could barely tolerate the other for any length of time.

"This is no time for my two most powerful allies to quarrel over such pettiness as we face such peril," Roanan interjected as diplomatically as he could.

Tabeus nodded in agreement.

"This young king is wise beyond his years," Tabeus said. "We will postpone such discussions until brighter days."

"The Wizard speaks the truth," Karmin agreed, then turned her attention to Roanan.

"Tabeus," the Red Knight said in due time, "what happened?"

"A disaster we never seriously considered," Tabeus said. "The ancient dragon of Carpal awoke."

"Ravager?" Roanan said incredulously. "I thought him long dead and gone."

Tabeus nodded.

"That was the popular opinion," the Wizard agreed, "though I have often suspected that belief may have been overly optimistic."

Tabeus arose and slowly paced across the room.

"I knew of the risk, but I thought it remote," the Wizard continued. "Clearly, however, the tentacles of our opponents have spread even further than we had suspected. On our journey, I felt an evil arise, an evil whose presence I had not felt in many, many generations."

"So the dragons have never left Ambrasian after all," Roanan stated, more than a hint of wonder still in his voice.

Tabeus stroked Raven, who sat on the table by his side.

"No, they have never completely left," Tabeus said. "A few still remain, far across the seas. One day, more may return. But Ravager has slept until now right here on the edge of Ambrasian."

"Ravager did not awaken at this moment by happenstance," Karmin interjected. "This is further evidence that Celidia is mastering the powers of the Oracle."

Tabeus nodded in agreement.

"What of Lasarion?" Roanan asked desperately. "Did he survive?"

"The normal cycle of events in Ambrasian has been disrupted," Tabeus said calmly. "Evil spreads quickly without protection. As Karmin said, Ravager, the oldest and most powerful of dragons, was awakened under Celidia's influence. The Great Worm burst from its hidden chamber and attacked Lasarion's ships with little warning. He has lost several hundred men and his fleet has been disabled. But thanks to his skill as a leader, he lives as does much of his army."

"Few have escaped the dragon at all," Roanan observed. "We could have easily lost the entire force."

"Quite true," Tabeus agreed. "Not only did he escape, but Lasarion slayed the Great Worm as well. Lasarion himself blinded Ravager temporarily with a shot deserving of an Elvii marksman. That gave his men enough time to find the Worm's weakness."

Roanan beamed with pride at his cousin's success.

"I knew he was a great warrior," the Red Knight said. "But few in history have held the mantle of dragon slayer."

But Roanan's thoughts soon turned to the greater mission and the status of the surviving forces.

"But where are they now?" the Red Knight asked with concern. "Floating helplessly on the Sea of Dragons?"

"No," answered the Wizard reassuringly. "They have found a path to Selin and will land there safely in short order."

"Selin?" Roanan asked with a glint of worry.

"Yes," the Wizard said calmly. "And if all works as I hope, the intentions of evil may yet turn to our good fortune."

Karmin and Roanan looked at Tabeus, but the Wizard in his own way offered no additional explanation. Finally, Karmin broke the silence.

"We are lucky that Lasarion survived the battle with the dragon," she said. "A defeat would have been catastrophic."

The Wizard looked at Karmin with a hint of bemusement.

"Luck was not all that was involved," Tabeus protested. "He did not enter the sea unprotected. But even so, much credit must go to Lasarion. He is inarguably a fine knight, Roanan. Loyal to a fault and a fierce, determined, and skilled warrior. He has been given his orders, and it is achieving them that drives him on against all odds. He will not let down his King."

Still, Karmin remained dour.

"The dragon was awakened because the Oracle has been lost," she said ruefully. "The entire world of Ambrasian is out of balance. Evil spreads rampantly, out of control. Things long thought exiled find new life. I do not know how long we can maintain our resolve . . ."

The immortal Regent of Karmana fell silent.

"Do not fear," the Red Knight answered. "the issue is not yet settled. Much still needs to unfold. Our enemies have not yet felt our wrath.'

Karmin forced a hopeful smile.

"Let us hope we can turn aside the oncoming storm, for it is a storm whose strength we have never seen before," she said, turned and left the room.

•   •   •   •   •

Karmana was now a vortex to which all activity was drawn. With the immediate crisis of Tabeus' condition resolved, Karmin now took the time to lead Roanan to the young warriors whose training–however brief — she had supervised. The Red Knight met the more than five hundred aspiring knights and gave a cursory inspection of their readiness, then moved on to a group which fascinated him even more: the Elvii.

Roanan had heard much of the creatures of the forest but had rarely set his eyes on one. The Necinians had not ventured en masse from the Great Forest in many years, but now over one thousand greeted the Red Knight. The current crisis and the attack on their own land had helped the Elvii overcome their reluctance to interfere with the affairs of the Cadaren and travelled to the Hall of Karmin to prepare for battle. By now, Tabeus had recovered enough to join Roanan and Karmin.

"My friend," the Wizard said to Siora," we encounter each other once again."

"You had my word," the Elvii leader responded. "We share a common enemy."

Siora turned and faced the Red Knight.

"King of Chrysalis," the Elvii said, "we meet at last. Many tales have reached my ears."

"I have heard many plaudits of you and the Elvii as well," the Red Knight responded. "I am fortunate to have such an ally."

"Let us hope our combined forces are enough to achieve victory," Siora said.

"Agreed," Roanan said. "A formidable challenge lay ahead of us. I believe, however, that righteousness and justice will prevail."

"I hope your words are true," Siora said. "Unfortunately, in my time, I have often seen justice perish at the sharp end of a sword."

Roanan nodded in understanding.

"It is our mission to ensure that does not happen here," the Red Knight said.

"Then let us work together toward victory," Siora said as the two leaders forged a common bond.

That evening, Karmin held a great feast for the combined forces. The magnificent banquet hall was enormous, holding more than two thousand solders. The walls were ivory white with high tapered and marbled supports. Multi-tiered, stained glass lined the hall and hundred of servers, both male and female, their loyalty sworn to Karmin, served the bountiful feast. The feast overflowed into the meadow outside of the hall, and servers brought food and drink for those who waited there.

The banquet was a melodious cacophony of voices. Song rang freely, and outward gaiety hid the inner peril of their imminent challenge. With Tabeus sat Roanan, Karmin, Siora, and the friends the Red Knight had grown to trust in this desperate journey: Halmar, Toranis, Dainwirth Lir, and yes, even Mendelheimer. The Wizard, the Red Knight, the Elvii leader and Karmin remained huddled during much of the festivities. Through the discussions, Roanan discovered an inkling of Elvii customs and traditions. But the four talked far more of their common enemy and the oncoming battle.

As the meal approached its conclusion, the attendees were not quite ready to disperse. Perhaps many realized this would be their last bit of respite before the battle ahead. For whatever reason, the great majority of the attendees lingered in the magnificent Hall, holding on as long as they could to friends and the world as they knew it.

"Sing us a song," the crowd finally cried to the minstrel. And Mendelheimer obliged with no further urging.

It came upon a windswept hare
That glorious carrot of old
But when that hare did see the gift
He said it had too much mold . . .

On Mendelheimer painfully continued through a series of fractured rhymes and tortured metaphors, somewhat off-key and hardly melodious. When he finally finished, he was greeted with a mixed scattering of applause, catcalls, whistles and obscene gestures and suggestions. The minstrel bowed, greatly exaggerating his actions. The party's attendants laughed nervously.

Still, amid the surrounding frivolity, the leaders of Karmana's defense sat huddled, deep in conversation. Ripples of worry danced upon their foreheads. They knew well that the oncoming storm would soon sweep aside the lightness of the evening.

Sometime later, the planning and related discussions waned. For the first time that evening, Roanan separated himself from the crowd and stood alone in thought. Dainwirth Lir saw a dark figure from the corner of his eye lurking near the Red Knight. Lir whirled around quickly, but saw it was only a server. The figure came a bit too close for the comfort of the King's guards standing nearby and was turned away. Dainwirth Lir looked elsewhere, but at the last moment, something drew his eyes back toward the figure. Why, he wondered, could he not see the person's face? And there was something suspicious in his movements. But still he could not be sure . . .

"What's the matter?" Toranis finally asked, noting the diverted attention of the young knight.

It must be the lighting, Lir speculated to himself. He turned toward the Chrysalian knight with whom he had become fast friends.

"Nothing," he answered. "The battle plays tricks with my mind. Everyone looks like the enemy."

"I know what you mean," Toranis agreed.

Still, Lir glanced toward the corner of the room once more. He thought he saw the dark figure disappear into the shadows but couldn't say for sure. Uneasy fears and irrational conclusions danced through the young knight's head. Driven by these doubts, Lir got up and followed the figure into the darkness.

"What are you doing?" Toranis asked, bewildered.

"I don't know," Lir said. "There's something in the eyes that doesn't look right . . ."

The young knight continued his pursuit.

Something in whose eyes? Toranis wondered. *What is Lir talking about?*

Confused and worried about his young friend, Toranis decided to follow Lir. Halmar, one of Roanan's most tested and finest knights, noticed the strange movements of the young warrior as well with growing concern.

"The young sometimes notice minor signs of danger that the older miss," the knight mused. "Or sometimes, they jump to unwarranted conclusions. But in either case, they often rush into situations with youthful impatience. I need to make sure they stay out of trouble. We cannot afford to lose them on the eve of our march."

And for those and other unsaid reasons, he rose from across the room and followed the two.

Best I keep my eye on them, whatever the circumstance, he concluded.

The general activity in the banquet hall continued unabated and Roanan eventually rejoined his council with Tabeus, Karmin and Siora, unaware of the strange behavior of his knights. In fact, only a few noted the departure of the three. Tabeus and Karmin were among those who took a momentary interest, but though the unusual behavior made them uneasy, both let the incident pass without comment as their attention was quickly drawn to other seemingly more important matters.

And so, the three warriors drifted into the dark night that had descended upon Karmana. Karmin had posted guards throughout the Hall and the village and few thought the enemy would be so daring as to penetrate deeply within the gathering. But despite these precautions, this group of Roanan's most trusted allies had detected something perverse and following their instincts, quickly disappeared from view.

•   •   •   •   •

The level of preparation at the Watchtower had increased geometrically since Brelex's army had arrived. Drens ran about in scattershot fashion, building walls, tearing them down and rebuilding them in a different location as they tried to follow Maldur's frantic orders. Brelex, half amused and half frustrated, instructed his men to dig ambush ditches and cover them with leaf-filled branches and dried wood. They did so, though the location of each was often unbeknownst to the Black Knight as he focused on activities elsewhere.

The Grey Knight's men finished and moved to another site. Maldur strolled around the corner of the Watchtower, just after the workers left. Stalking proudly amid the chaos, the Black Knight walked briskly to inspect the work of a group of Drens, looking into the distance rather than watching the surroundings where he was walking. He laid one step on one of the traps and fell six feet into the ditch.

"What in blazing hell is this?" Maldur screeched in anger from the bottom of the pit.

The Grey Knight reached the edge of the trench first. As he looked down at his disheveled ally, Brelex was laughing so hard that he almost fell in himself.

"I had my men dig these ditches to catch Roanan's valiant fools," he chuckled.

"Well, you at least caught a fool," Celidia muttered as she came from the Watchtower to view the cause of the commotion. Her gown glistened in the hot sun and she seemed to have grown in both power and strength.

"Maldur," the Sorceress said, peering down on him, "you look absolutely ridiculous."

"I was not the one stupid enough to dig a ditch right in the middle of the main path," the Black Knight growled angrily.

"Of course not," Celidia scoffed. "Why build a trap on the path the enemy is most likely to walk? Much better to build it in a location where no one is expected to be ensnared."

The Sorceress shook her head in disbelief.

"On the other hand," she added, "you were the one stupid enough to fall into it."

Celidia finally showed mock concern.

"Are you hurt?" she asked with only a modicum of sincerity. "What do you hit?"

"My head," Maldur answered.

Celidia sighed.

"We are fortunate," she said. "Nothing important."

The Black Knight tried unsuccessfully to extract himself from the trap.

"How do I get out of here?" Maldur finally asked.

"I don't know," the Sorceress chuckled. "Maybe we should let you in there and keep you out of trouble until it's time for battle. We can throw food down for you when you're hungry."

The Black Knight growled once again, cursing all those peering down at him. The Sorceress finally looked at the gathering crowd about her.

"Get him out," Celidia finally relented. "We have much to discuss. Roanan has reached the Hall of Karmin and Lasarion has slayed my beautiful dragon. Soon we will have the combat for which we have prepared and for which you all yearn."

"Finally," Brelex roared gloriously. "My bones ache for battle."

"Speaking of aches," Celidia interjected. "Someone make sure Maldur has not actually been injured. We need him in one piece."

The Sorceress whirled around and returned to the Watchtower. Brelex shrugged and look at Maldur, still in the pit.

"Get me out of here," the Black Knight bellowed.

· · · · ·

Dainwirth Lir continued his pursuit of the mysterious figure through the dark streets of the village entrenched around the Hall of Karmana. The homes were elegant, made by the finest craftsmen and reflected the beauty of both the culture and country of the land. But Lir was sure there was something untoward here. Behind Lir followed Toranis, and farther back, Halmar, a strange caravan with each not knowing he was being followed by the other.

Lir moved south until he was about a mile from the Hall of Karmana. There, he was sure the person he pursued stealthily entered a small, well-lit tavern, one of the few resting places in the land. But on this night, the inn was crowded, pregnant with soldiers and other visitors that had travelled here from across Ambrasian.

Dainwirth Lir entered the tavern a few moments later and was greeted by a sudden barrage of light, the smell of food and drink, and a cacophony of voices. Little room remained to move about the inn. Above the din, however, Lir heard a familiar sound.

"Amulets and double-edged swords," the voice cried. "Priced to sell, satisfaction guaranteed. Everything you need and more for battle! You'll be sorry if you don't take advantage of these bargains."

Lir worked his way steadily through the crowd until he faced the grimy, rag-covered, and sweaty character of Theopolis Fenton Ruck IV.

"What are you doing here?" Lir asked. "You followed us to Karmana?"

"The chance of a lifetime," Ruck exclaimed. "Why, I could retire with what I'm making on this trip. How could I pass up such a rare opportunity?"

"Scoundrel," Lir muttered and shook his head. "Taking advantage of hardship and fear."

The knight returned to the matter at hand.

"No matter," Lir said as he turned to pass by the trader, "I haven't time to argue."

The young knight searched the tavern but could not spot his prey.

"Perhaps I can help," the unscrupulous trader chimed in, thinking he could somehow profit from the transaction.

Dainwirth Lir whirled around.

"How can you help?" he asked. "I am not here to buy any of your merchandise."

Theopolis Fenton Ruck IV smiled deviously.

"I deal in more than just goods," the trader said. "You search for someone, that's plain enough, Who knows the wanderings of strangers better than an upstanding merchant?"

"Upstanding?" Lir protested, then forced himself to hold his tongue.

The scum may be right, he thought. *He might have seen something.*

"You may actually be able to help," Lir said more calmly. "I do search for someone, though I know not who."

Ruck smiled knowingly.

"Well now," he said, "in that case, I know just the thing. You should look over there."

The trader pointed into the far right corner of the tavern where a comely young female Cadaren sat seductively waiting for a guest.

The suggestion outraged Lir.

"You. . .you . . .," he sputtered angrily. The knight forcibly composed himself.

"This is not for what I search," he spit, the agitation clear in his voice. "I followed someone here, a dark figure. He was at the banquet and his movements and appearance seemed suspicious."

"Why didn't you say so?" Ruck asked. "A spy sent by Brelex."

"A spy?" Lir blurted in shock. "A spy? How do you know he's a spy?"

"A merchant learns to watch and listen," Ruck explained. "His coloring and his accent clearly identified him as someone from Balinwald. He carried weapons which he tried to hide, but not well. And he asked far too many questions about King Roanan's army."

Lir interrupted the trader abruptly.

Where did he go, you fool?" the knight asked.

"Out the back," Ruck said, "just as you came in."

Dainwirth Lir didn't wait for the merchant to finish. He spun toward the door, pushing aside the tavern's patrons abruptly. As he burst through to the outside, the knight ran smack into Toranis entering the tavern from the other direction. The two collided and went sprawling, the heavy thud of armed soldiers bouncing off the ground.

Lir shook his head and crawled back to his feet awkwardly. Toranis slowly picked himself up from the ground outside.

"What are you doing?" Toranis screeched. "You nearly ran me over."

"No time," Lir responded. "There's a spy. He was at the banquet. He's getting away."

"Which way did he go?" Toranis asked.

"He was seen leaving out the back," Lir puffed. "Let's go. We need to find him."

Dainwirth Lir and Toranis turned and ran in the direction that the spy had been seen leaving. Through the dimly lit paths they rushed, searching for the mysterious figure that had so far eluded them. Lir and Toranis struggled through the darkness for some time, their initial fury blunted by despair and finally fatigue. At the moment of surrender, however, the two young warriors heard voices in the distance, subdued and secretive.

Dainwirth Lir rushed forward, but Toranis held him back. Lir turned to protest, but the more experienced knight motioned him to be silent, knowing they needed time to assess and weigh the strength of the opposition. With Toranis leading the way for the first time, the two warriors found their way to a thick swath of trees, which hid their presence. Slowly, they crept through the darkness, the voices they heard growing louder though still unclear. Finally, they came to the edge of a clearing and inched themselves to a vantage point where they could view their prey. Together, they rose, parting the underbrush and saw their adversaries.

"Drens!" Dainwirth Lir gasped softly, and he was correct. Eight of the foul creatures had permeated the heart of Karmana itself and now stood in a semicircle around the dark figure of the mysterious spy. Drens normally did not ride, as few horses would yield to them. But all manner of wild beasts surrounded these creatures, which must have been tamed by some vile magic to hold them. And now, even the shroud cast over the spy dissipated as he pulled his dark cloak down to his shoulders. Lir recognized him as a prospective knight that had taken part in the Annual Games. So, he thought, spies have been at work here for far longer than we had been aware. Their opposition had been working tirelessly as their plans carefully unfolded across the land.

Though Toranis and Dainwirth Lir had tried to be as quiet as possible, the Drens have keen hearing. Lir's earlier proclamation of the discovery and the rustling of the two knights through the underbrush had attracted attention, and two Drens previously unseen had found their way behind the two young warriors. At the last moment, the knights recognized their peril. Toranis turned and pushed himself and Dainwirth Lir out of the path of the Dren's sword. The two young knights drew their own weapons as the rest of the Drens and the spy were alerted to their discovery. Now Toranis and Lir were encircled by eleven enemies and were further hampered by the surrounding darkness. The dull, luminescent green eyes of the Drens and the sharp dint of swords were reflected in the half-moon that rose high above Ambrasian, and the dull brightness of the NightSun.

Toranis knew that he and Lir had little hope against such odds, and the Drens were moving in on them quickly. The two warriors stood back-to-back, their swords moving defensively, angling against each opponent.

"We may not survive this," Toranis whispered, "but we will make them remember us."

"May we honor the names of our family," Lir said. "You have been a good friend."

Toranis nodded and quickly avoided the jab of a Dren's sword. But the Drens moved ever closer, and their quick thrusts were becoming more frequent and less distant.

One of the foul creatures ventured too close too soon, and with one mighty swing Toranis took off its arm. The Dren backed away, clutching its shoulder, cursing in foul shrieks in his native tongue. But Dainwirth Lir fared less well and was already bleeding from his leg and shoulder.

The two young warriors showed courage and strength but were too outnumbered and inexperienced to last much longer. For though these Drens were not the most skilled fighters, they compensated for their lack of technique with sheer strength, viciousness, and relentlessness. In addition, they appeared to withstand any number of wounds without effect. The Drens had been hunters for many generations and they were, if anything, efficient killing machines.

The fighting became more furious, and with each passing moment, Lir and Toranis lost ground. The latter, more polished, continued to fare better than the young knight from the Games. But even Toranis was hard pressed to ward off the number of attackers around him, who now became more daring and more aggressive.

However, at the moment when both Toranis and Lir finally despaired, a figure parted the underbrush and emerged into the clearing. A mighty knight entered the fray with lightning speed. The powerful fighter hewed down three Drens with his sword and they dropped headless in his path before they rightly knew the danger they faced. With renewed vigor, Toranis and Lir both struck down the confused Drens closest to them, and Halmar made quick work of the rest.

The spy that Lir initially pursued escaped into the forest, but Lir and Toranis pursued him quickly. Dainwirth Lir reached him first and tackled him at the forest's edge. But when Toranis helped turn the villain around, the spy was already dead. He had a small vial in his hand, the poison which it held having killed him instantly.

"What devilry is this?" Dainwirth Lir asked in frustration.

"The work of Celidia," Toranis said, answering Lir's inquiry. "As her magic becomes stronger, she gains the ability to drive those around her mad and bends them to her will. The vial was likely meant for our King, but this spy was turned away before he could come too close. Obviously, if he should be captured, Celidia did not want this one to divulge any information."

Dainwirth Lir shook his head and turned away, walking ten yards away from the dead body. It was too much for the young knight to take. Lir was learning much about war firsthand.

Halmar walked up to Toranis purposely and looked him over quickly.

"Are you injured?" he asked.

"Not badly," Toranis answered. "But Lir has wounds that need to be attended to quickly."

"You are fortunate I saw you two leave the banquet," the elder knight said. "I thought you might get yourselves into more trouble that you could handle. It's good that my instincts told me to follow you."

"How did you know?" Toranis asked.

Halmar shrugged, inspecting the two knights further.

"Something didn't feel right," he said. "The scent of war is unique and has its own perils. We all need to be doubly aware of any possible threat."

"We owe you our lives," Toranis said thankfully.

"Some credit," Halmar said, "goes to the trader back at the tavern. He told me where you were headed."

Lir had re-joined his fellow knights, and Halmar's remark brough Lir back into the conversation.

"I owe my life to that . . that . . .," he said.

Lir shook his head again and grumbled incoherently.

"I think I'd rather be dead than be in the debt of that thief," he concluded.

"You almost were," Halmar said. "And you were equally lucky with your encounter with the Black Knight. You have already used up two of your lives. Do not tempt fate too often."

•　　•　　•

News of the encounter and the incursion of Celidia's spies spread quickly through the Hall of Karmana. When details of the plot reached the ear of Karmin, her dismay was obvious. Roanan reassured her, however, that anything Celidia could have learned from the spy would not further endanger their already desperate mission.

"She already has the advantage," the Red Knight said. "This spy, even if he managed to get the Sorceress any information, served only to verify what she already knew."

Tabeus agreed, but privately remained concerned how easily a spy had penetrated into the very heart of the Hall of Karmana and had come within a few feet of Roanan.

"Have we learned nothing from the loss of the Oracle?" he muttered.

Despite the concern, Halmar's feat was duly recognized and celebrated, as was Dainwirth Lir's detection, Toranis' bravery, and even Theopolis Ruck's part in the whole affair, much to the chagrin of Mendelheimer and Lir.

"War hero my big toe," the minstrel said. "I will not be composing a song about such a scoundrel."

Shortly thereafter, the Red Knight turned to Karmin and then Tabeus.

"Our mission grows more dire with each passing day," he said. "The Drens become braver and more daring while our own troops become restless. It is time we commence with our march to battle and see this to the end."

•   •   •   •   •

Pierisonie was a member of the race of the females of Karmana, but one with her own unique sense of individuality. Unlike most of her sisters who rarely left the protected realm and even then only for short periods of time, Pierisonie traveled freely throughout Ambrasian, wandering through the lands of Chrysalis, Balinwald, Selin, and even Isalis throughout her life – only the fearsome world of Damora was beyond her adventures. Her journeys sometimes encompassed months and even years at a time.

Because Pierisonie had been outside of power of the Oracle for long periods, unlike other women of Karmana, she had shown graceful signs of age. Her appearance was that of a middle-aged female, still beautiful but with lines of wisdom etched subtly on her face. Looking carefully, one might catch a wisp of grey in her reddish-blonde hair.

It was perhaps not surprising then that Pierisonie was the Karmana female who first felt the effects of the loss of the Oracle. Allowing the aging process to impact her for such long interludes throughout her life had weakened her ability to withstand its loss. And now, for whatever reason, with the Oracle unprotected and in Celidia's hands, the many years Pierisonie had spent wandering Ambrasian attacked her body with a vengeance. Perhaps the Sorceress' evil intent created some especially virulent effect on those most vulnerable, but whatever the circumstance, Pierisonie aged with dreadful acceleration shortly after the Oracle was whisked from Karmana.

The most powerful healers of Karmana did all possible to slow Pierisonie's turmoil, but to no avail. Karmin herself had come to her sister's side, but even she could not impact Pierisonie's fate.

"I am sorry I can not do more," Karmin finally said, a tear running down her cheek. "Look over us if you can."

Pierisonie smiled, her eyes showing assent.

"I regret nothing I have done or any decision I have made," she whispered, her voice strained. "I have lived a full life. Hopefully, the rest of my sisters will avoid my fate."

Several days later, Pierisonie now lay in her bed appearing unfathomably old and frail, blinded with her mind gone. The healers did what they could to make her comfortable, but they watched helplessly as Pierisonie's life force finally left her body. It was the first death of old age that Karmana's residents had recorded in many centuries. Celidia's war had come home.

CHAPTER 19
THE CONVERSION

Shortly after reaching the shoreline, Lasarion was able to determine their location. It did not take long for what remained of Lasarion's force to attract attention. Local farmers, herders and fishermen looked upon the army from afar with trepidation fearing an unprovoked invasion. It took some time for Lasarion to finally get close enough to any of the local residents to speak to them, but when he finally did, he assured them that his army was not intended to savage their land. He and his warriors had arrived here only after their disastrous encounter with Ravager. Even still, his appearance was met with skepticism and fear.

Where the wayward army had landed soon became obvious to even the most casual observer. Only in Selin did the people of Ambrasian resemble those who now surrounded him. The people were short—not much taller than five feet–but were broad-shouldered and powerful. They had rust-colored hair and their bodies were thickly matted. Broad noses were accented by eyes set far apart. But despite their lumbering appearance, the Selinites were surprisingly quick on their feet and moved as hunters, silently and watchfully. Their clothes blended with their environment, which were predominantly green and brown. The Selinites were peaceful, slow to anger and slower still to action. But now, Lasarion needed their aid and needed it quickly. Whether he could gain their trust and resolve remained to be seen.

Lasarion assembled what remained of his forces. It was a ragged collection, with most surviving only with the now stiffened and torn clothing on their backs and what weapons they carried with them.

Supplies had been salvaged from those ships that had made it to shore, but many of the stores had been damaged during the battle with the dragon. Worse, the fleet had never been equipped for a long trek across country. The original plan was to land as deeply in Balinwald as possible, reclaim the territory savaged by Brelex, then make a mad dash toward the Watchtower. The few wagons and horses that had survived the bruising battle in the Sea of Dragons were hardly sufficient for whatever new course Lasarion would decide.

Once the army had sufficiently recovered to move as a force once again, Lasarion marched across the countryside of Selin. Dakar served as his first lieutenant. Only a few additional horses and wagons could be purchased from the wary country herders–those were used to transport the additional supplies from the ship, and the wounded who could not march. The rest of Lasarion's army traveled on foot. The knight also procured what food and medical supplies he could to supplement those he had saved.

Lasarion's troops moved in a direct easterly course, in search of the Hall of Selin. Selin, separated from the rest of Ambrasian by the Land of Mystery, the Sea of Dragons, and the near equally solitary land of Balinwald, had mostly lost contact with the rest of the peoples of Ambrasian. Through the years, the Selinites had become isolated and had cut off nearly all ties with others. And thus, the peoples of Ambrasian had cast a solitary aura around the land. The castle of the King had become known as the Lost Hall, for few had visited or even set eyes on it in living memory. Now, Lasarion and his forces had become the first outsiders to step on Selin's soil in many years, and their arrival and ensuing march sparked suspicion among the local residents. Word spread quickly of the foreign army that had landed on the shore and was now proceeding toward the King's castle.

Selin's land was less than inviting. Mostly by luck, Lasarion had landed on one of the few navigable beaches. Most of the coastline was comprised of sheer, rocky cliffs and rough terrain. The countryside was similar. The land was hilly and rocky, much of it difficult to farm. Despite its ominous appearance, Selin was far from arid. Trees grew well, if not as lushly as in the Great Forest, and a high bluegrass-type of plant was abundant, making the land ideal for grazing. Thus, many Selinites became herders of various animals that helped feed and clothe the land's residents.

For an entire day, Lasarion drove his forces through the open land and the few small villages that dotted Selin, purchasing additional supplies from those willing to deal with a foreign force. The army was another half-day from the Hall of Selin and the uncertain greeting that awaited them from King Sorick. Just as few outsiders had ventured into Selin, even fewer had come face-to-face with Sorick, who had ruled the land for at least the last fifty years and had a peculiar reputation.

"How do you think they will greet us at the Hall of Selin?" Dakar asked Lasarion with a hint of nervousness in his voice after hearing many of the rumors along the way.

"Hopefully, as friends," the knight answered. "We cannot let the chirping birds who tell all sorts of half-truths color our expectations."

Early in his reign, Sorick was a powerful yet obstinate King. He continued the policies of his ancestors and had, for the most part, kept Selin isolated from the rest of Ambrasian. Yet the country prospered under Sorick's firm hand adapting their agrarian ways to take the most advantage of their land. But now, in the twilight of the King's rule, much of that strength had been sapped, and the country showed signs of neglect. What had once been a bastion of proud individualism among the people had declined to one of unfounded suspicion and apathy. Even the land was less prosperous, and Lasarion's drive through the countryside was both dreary and disheartening.

After setting a sparse camp for the evening, Lasarion awoke his army at dawn and urged his weary forces toward the Hall of Selin with all possible speed. Six hours into that day's journey, Lasarion stood on a slight hill overlooking the village that encircled Selin's castle. Before him lie a grassy, open field two miles long. Lasarion's men refreshed themselves at a nearby stream and began the last leg of their march.

Lasarion brought his forces just outside the village and ordered them to stand down and make camp. The knight knew he could hardly march an army to the gates of the Hall of Selin and request Sorick's aid. It would do no good to appear to threaten an already suspicious and distrusting monarch. This would take some agile act of diplomacy, an effort that

Lasarion hardly had time to achieve. But try he must for he had no other choice.

He took Dakar and five others and approached the castle on foot. The village's inhabitants followed Lasarion and his party suspiciously from a distance, watching their every move. To most of them, Lasarion and him companions were the first foreigners the Selinites had ever seen. At their passing, many residents cowered into the shadows, but still kept an ever-vigilant eye on the strange party, some holding sturdy cooking pans as their weapon of choice should the strangers for some reason decide to attack.

After a short walk that seemed much longer, Lasarion strode to the gates of the Hall of Selin and greeted the two sentries. The knight could see more soldiers behind the castle's gates should the conversation not go well.

"We come in peace," the Chrysalian knight said. "We mean no harm."

The older guard eyed Lasarion skeptically, inspecting him from head to toe.

"From Chrysalis, eh?" he said scornfully. His black hair was flecked with more than a bit of grey. "You can tell by the accent. It's been a long time since one of yours trespassed where they did not belong. And I notice you brought an army with you. That hardly looks peaceful to me."

"We are in a desperate situation," Lasarion continued calmly. "Ravager, the ancient beast of the sea, attacked us with all its fury. Our ships barely made it to shore."

"Humph," the guard shrugged. "A likely story–supposedly attacked by a worm that hasn't been seen in a millennium. If it were up to me . . ."

The sentry stopped in mid-sentence when he saw Lasarion's stern face growing angrier with each passing second. The two stared at each other until the knight finally had enough. He had neither the time nor the patience for such insolence.

"Unless your name is King Sorick and you are guarding the castle gates in disguise, it is not up to you," Lasarion said, finally losing his patience. "We come to see the King, not a pompous, tart-tongued gatekeeper."

The guard's face flushed and began to respond, but at that moment, the ancient gates slowly creaked open, and a dark figure emerged from the shadows. The individual was dressed in loose-fitting robes and wore a dark hood about its head.

"The King will see you," the person said with a commanding voice and again disappeared behind the gates.

Lasarion gave the guard one last glance and the sentry reluctantly stepped aside, though he continued to eye the Chrysalian knight suspiciously. Lasarion motioned Dakar to follow him and left the rest of the company outside. He quickly stepped through the gates, squinting in the dim light and finally spotting the figure far ahead. He rushed to catch up and soon had reached the lithe guide.

"The King is old," whispered the guide. "Be patient, but firm."

Lasarion looked more closely at the unlikely escort but was told no more.

$$\bullet \qquad \bullet \qquad \bullet \qquad \bullet \qquad \bullet$$

Lasarion and Dakar followed the guide through the long corridors of the Hall of Selin and ultimately into the chamber of the King. Along the way, guards stood at attention, all well armed, should anyone threaten their liege. Lasarion noted that most were well past their prime fighting years. The guide finally led the two knights to the innermost chamber. The room appeared majestic at first glance: plush carpets were strewn across the floor and ornate tapestry decorated the walls. But closer inspection showed the decay of Selin had reached even here. The carpets were threadbare in spots and moisture had caused the walls and ceilings to peel badly. Mold had eaten at the tapestries and the entire room felt dank and uninviting. Only half the torches were lit.

The guide led Lasarion and Dakar even deeper within the chamber. There, the attendant stopped. Within the shadows, the Chrysalian warrior discerned a frail, near emaciated figure clothed in ill-fitting robes with a tarnished crown sitting precariously on his head. King Sorick leaned heavily on the armrest of his throne, itself showing as much age as the person sitting upon it. Sorick appeared a caricature of a mighty leader.

Lasarion looked back at the guide and saw the figure removing the robe from its head. The knight began to once again turn back toward the

King, then quickly redoubled back. Their mysterious escort turned out to be a beautiful young woman, taller and more slender than the average Selinite. Lasarion looked at her quizzically.

"I am Alexandra," the woman matter-of-factly. "The king's granddaughter."

Lasarion was momentarily torn between the woman at which he now gazed and the impatient shuffling of the decrepit old King. Finally, the knight turned deliberately toward Sorick.

"Your highness, I am Lasarion, a knight of Chrysalis and the representative and cousin of Roanan, the Red Knight, our own King," he said. "Though I know relations between our two lands have been limited in recent years, I assure you we mean no harm. Our mission is urgent and our plight desperate.'

"Your sight desperate?" the King asked quizzically, cocking a hand to his ear.

"Plight," Lasarion corrected, emphasizing the word. He cast a sideways glance toward Dakar.

"If we fail in our quest," the knight continued, "even your own kingdom will be imperiled, for great evil has befallen Ambrasian."

"Ah yes, Ambrasia," the king said wistfully, "I remember her well."

Lasarion looked both hopeless and confused. How could this doting old man–hard of hearing and his mind mottled by age — rule a kingdom, he wondered. He again turned toward Dakar, but at the same time, Alexandra stepped forward.

"Let me try," she said quietly. "My grandfather is old and stubborn, but perhaps not so helpless as he appears. He hears my voice even when he is deaf to the sound of others."

Lasarion considered his options. He had little choice but to agree to Alexandra's proposal. The young Cadaren led Lasarion and Dakar out of the room and into the wide corridor where Lasarion noted elaborate spider webs decorating the corners of the walls and ceilings. From there, the knight wound his way through the hallways once again, and slowly, the Chrysalian warrior left the slumbering castle, with little hope of any forthcoming aid.

"Be patient," Alexandra counseled. "Perhaps I can be more persuasive."

"You must try," Lasarion said joylessly. "Your grandfather must look beyond his ills, for great evil lurks nearby. If he delays too long, all may be meaningless."

"I understand our peril," Alexandra said. "Your tale reached the castle long before your army. But I am your only chance to move my grandfather to action. Trust me."

Lasarion nodded and he and Dakar left the castle.

What choice do I have? The knight wondered.

A short while later, the two knights joined the remainder of their forces. They offered little cheer. They remained there the rest of the day and a night, Lasarion well aware of the risk of waiting for an answer that may never come. He debated taking up the march once again, determined to reach the battle in time with whatever forces he could offer.

Meanwhile, many rumors and tales reached Lasarion's ears during this restless time. Many concerned Alexandra, the strange and mysterious hooded maiden who was Lasarion's only link to the king. The Chrysalian warrior learned that few from Selin had ever seen the King's granddaughter, mostly because the overprotective King had rarely allowed her to venture from the castle. Her parents had died when she was a child in a tragic fire, the princess saved only because she was spending the night with her doting grandmother. The King and his Queen had raised Alexandra to adulthood, but when Sorick's wife died unexpectedly a number of years earlier, the multiple tragedies Sorick had endured had finally extinguished the light from the King's eyes. Alexandra reached adulthood in a cold, loveless castle with only the wisp of the former King as her companion.

Many believed this was the point in time when Selin began to fade as both the King and his kingdom passed into neglect. In any event, whether Sorick and his land were inextricably linked or not, there was little doubt that the country had suffered and was but a shadow of its former self.

Despite all the tragedy that had befallen her in her short life, Alexandra still held dreams of a fair and prosperous Selin. Sorick, however, slowly slipping into old age and even dementia, remained stubborn and retained his power jealously. He viewed any who approached him with proposals to better the land with near paranoid suspicion. Only slowly, with great skill and relying on the trust the King placed in his granddaughter, did Alexandra wield her subtle influence. Meanwhile, the people of Selin, misty-eyed with fond remembrances of a youthful and invigorated King, had followed Sorick's path into decay.

None of these tales lent much hope to Lasarion's quest. With hope of aid beginning to fail, the knight sifted through his options. He could leave Selin without Sorick's aid, but his army was battered from the battle with Ravager and in desperate need of supplies and reinforcements. Without additional support, it was doubtful his forces would successfully free even Balinwald much less reach the battle at the Watchtower. Lasarion could also try to join Roanan directly in Karmana. But that would entail travelling through the Land of Mystery, and despite the Red Knight's recent journey, there was still great reluctance to enter the unknown terrain of that land. Even if they took that risk, it was doubtful he could navigate an army through Arminan–a land of woods and rocky hills with no established roads and even few paths–in time to join the battle. Even if he somehow succeeded, his weary, hungry, and poorly armed troops would be of little help. Or Lasarion could return to Chrysalis, but what purpose would that serve? Would he then wait to be overwhelmed by Maldur and Brelex's victorious army as they rampaged through Ambrasian? No, that course would serve no one but the enemy. In truth, the knight seemed to have no viable alternative. Lasarion could only hope Alexandra could find the key to reaching her grandfather.

The initial news Lasarion eventually received from the Hall of Selin did not raise his spirits. Alexandra sent word that though her grandfather finally understood their plight, he was reluctant to act. The citizenry of Selin echoed their King's feelings.

"Why should we fight another's battle?" they said. "We have done well enough caring for ourselves."

Enough of these doubts reached Lasarion's ear that he tried to make his case directly to the citizenry.

"Without your aid, this will become your battle as well as ours," Lasarion tried to reason with the town elders. "This land of which you are so proud will be overwhelmed, and you will no longer have even the chance to fend for yourselves. Maldur and Brelex will not be satisfied with Karmana and Balinwald. They will not stop until they reach the shores of the western sea."

But his pleas were to no avail and his entreaties fell on deaf ears. The population of Selin and their King held firm, and Lasarion again studied his unsatisfactory options. The knight well knew that the desperate quest upon which all the forces of good depended upon was in imminent danger of failure. In desperation, he now seriously considered beginning his march without Selin's assistance.

Serendipity, however, can sometimes be a greater ally than even the most persuasive arguments.

Perhaps Lasarion and Alexandra would have never roused the sleepy population or their sleepier King. But the forces of evil sometimes are blinded by greed and overplay their hand–or play it too quickly and recklessly. And so it was with the Drens, who impatiently overran the boundaries of Balinwald and burst into Selin before the time was ripe. The force, it was said, burned farms, seized herds, and killed the peaceful residents who offered little resistance. As news of this invasion spread quickly across the populace, the reaction of the citizenry of Selin was near instantaneous. Lasarion's quest, on the brink of being dashed and the fall of Ambrasian becoming more certain by the hour, received new life. The immediate peril of Maldur, Brelex and the Drens suddenly awakened the apathetic Selinites.

Suddenly, the cry, "Drens have attacked Selin!" rang throughout the land as though the threat had never presented itself before. In fact, only a small band of the enemy had wandered across the border of Balinwald and savaged the farmlands. But the atrocity of the thought, the sheer deed of wreaking havoc on a pacifist people, many of whom were related to each other, stirred the sleeping population to action. No longer were the Selinites sedentary. Now, Lasarion had to advocate no longer. Instead, he was forced to calm and organize the maddening crowds engorging his camp and volunteering for battle.

Within an hour of the report of the Drens' attack, Alexandra rushed into Lasarion's camp herself.

"My father's mind is open," she said excitedly.

"It appears the people's minds have opened as well," he observed. "My forces have been doubled and my food and medical supplies overflow."

"Wonderful," Alexandra proclaimed. "Then soon it is time for us to depart."

"Us?" Lasarion observed. "I don't recall that conversation."

Alexandra smiled knowingly.

"If you're going to tell me that war is an affair of males only, then save your breath, knight of Chrysalis," she admonished. The princess rose tall and proud. "The warriors of Selin will ride only under the colors of their King. You must choose between Sorick or myself."

Lasarion allowed his mouth to drop open as he considered a response. Then he shook his head gruffly.

"I doubt the old man can even mount a horse any longer," he muttered so quietly he hoped Alexandra could not hear the quip. Then he looked toward the King's granddaughter.

"Well, I hope you can at least handle a sword," he said.

Alexandra beamed with a broad smile.

"Probably better than most of your soldiers," she responded.

Lasarion was now the one to smile, allowing himself to admire Alexandra's beauty for a long second despite the urgency of their quest. He thought for a moment that she returned the gesture.

* * * * *

The next day, Lasarion was ready to depart and head toward Balinwald. The knight knew he had lost much time, and meeting Roanan would take miraculous speed. But his rejuvenated troops offset that grim knowledge. Nearly two thousand Selenites had joined Alexandra in bolstering the once ragged force. Lasarion only hoped he would be in time.

Lasarion rode to the castle of Sorick and greeted the emaciated king one last time.

"Your highness," the knight said as he bowed low. "We are off to war."

"Off to more?" the king asked quizzically. "More what?"

"War!" Lasarion said more firmly, the slightest irritation creeping into his voice. "Battle."

"Cattle?" the king asked. "I thought you were fighting Drens."

Lasarion's face turned a bright crimson, but before the knight could prove just how unstatesmanlike a frustrated soldier could be, Alexandra stepped forward and intercepted his vitriolic words.

"Grandfather," she said, "It is time I must go. Be strong. I will return as quickly as possible."

Sorick nodded placidly and held Alexandra weakly as the princess threw her arms around him. She quickly broke off and left the castle. Sorick sat silently, a single tear escaping his eye.

"Be sure no harm comes to her," the frail King pleaded to Lasarion.

The Chrysalian knight looked at the King with a mix of surprise and pity and nodded in assent.

"I will do all I can to return her safely," Lasarion said, "though in truth, we now take a perilous path."

The King nodded in understanding. Suddenly, Sorick seemed much more regal than the warrior had ever felt possible.

Lasarion turned and joined Alexandra. They re-mounted their horses and rode from the castle, not looking back. They joined the procession of warriors and began the long march, first to Balinwald and then to the Watchtower. Time was critical and the threat grew ever stronger. There would be no time to reflect until much later.

Chapter 20
Demons of the Mind

The day after the feast and the discovery of Celidia's spy, the main force of Roanan's army made their final preparations for their march to battle. But as the eve of their departure drew long and darkness fell, Tabeus still felt a great evil that lurked far too near.

Something is terribly askew, the Wizard thought to himself. *I have not felt such vitriol in many years. This somehow extends beyond Maldur and Celidia. But how can that be?*

The feeling did not subside, so following his Wizard's instincts, the ancient wanderer left the silent vigils and strategy sessions and quietly disappeared into the night. No one saw the grey and bent Wizard follow his lonely and mysterious search.

Indeed, Roanan was in the company of Siora and the Elvii and had discovered a brief solitude from the maelstrom that swirled around him. The Red Knight reveled in the Elvii's songs, customs and traditions. Intentionally isolated, roaming the Great Forest at will, the Elvii had formed an intimate bond with nature and a unique culture of their own. Only the most desperate of circumstances had driven them from their homes to the brink of battle.

"We are a different species," Siora said to the King of Chrysalis. "In you, however, I find qualities lacking in most of the race of the Cadaren."

"Good qualities, I hope," Roanan quipped. "And I must add, the race of Elvii is not so strange and peculiar as legend and bedtime stories have made them out to be."

Now it was Siora's turn to laugh.

"Yes," he agreed, "legends are like that. Most are one part truth and many parts imagination. The storyteller fills in the unknown with the most audacious tale that can be mustered. Passed down through generations, the stories become more and more distorted. I am sure we would not recognize ourselves in many of these accounts."

Siora paused, looking into the nearby fire.

"Be it that we could become acquainted in happier times," the Elvii leader said, a hint of regret in his voice.

"Do not lose that hope," the Red Knight replied. "When all this is over and if we are indeed victorious, if you will have me, I will travel to Necinia – if someone will show me the way and the path is not camouflaged by the mischievous Elvii."

Roanan and Siora again shared a chuckle.

"You will always be welcome," Siora said. "Perhaps even I will wander into Chrysalis. I hear the Castle of the King is as beautiful as those of Karmana."

"Perhaps even more so," Roanan said. "Of course, one should not say such a thing near Karmin and my opinion may be somewhat biased."

"As it should be," Siora responded. "As is mine. I think it is wise if we keep our biased opinions to ourselves."

Roanan and the Elvii agreed with a smile.

The night had grown long as the two leaders continued to relate their tales and fears. Stars lit the night sky and the creatures of the night pierced the air with their cries. The NightSun shone brighter than any other star. Roanan and Siora fell silent as they watched the embers of their fire slowly become enveloped in the crackling flames.

Almost indiscernibly, Infernus began to faintly glow in the Red Knight's sheath. At first, Roanan didn't notice. But Siora did, and as the sword brew brighter, the concern on the wise Elvii's face grew more noticeable. Finally, the Red Knight followed his companion's eyes to the strange sight of the ancient sword.

"What is this?' the Red Knight asked. "Infernus has never done this before."

"Not that you have seen," Siora said ominously. "It has not done so for many a generation. That it glows now can only bring evil tidings."

"More Drens nearby?" the Red Knight asked suspiciously.

"Nay," Siora shook his head. "Even Drens would not cause this. This must be much worse than simple Drens."

"Worse than Drens?" Roanan exclaimed. "What could be worse than Drens?"

"I do not know," the worried Elvii answered. "But I feel we must find out soon. I sense great danger is in our midst."

•　　•　　•　　•　　•

Tabeus continued his journey, leaving the flickering lights of the night camps and the Hall of Karmana far behind and wandering purposely into the dark countryside. A great distance he walked through paths rarely travelled, many long forgotten. Even the Elvii had left these trails unexplored. Finally, the bent wizard came to a low cavern, overgrown with strange weeds – an unfamiliar sight in the beautiful land of Karmana. The Wizard noted the sweet smell of the forest had turned to a foul, rotting stench.

Nothing about this scene belongs here, the Wizard thought. *This is unnatural even in these dire times.*

Tabeus now moved slowly, choosing his path carefully, his senses becoming more alert with each passing moment. Something was terribly wrong, something that even the Wizard had never encountered in his long stay in Ambrasian.

Raven had stayed near his companion, either perched on his usual spot on the Wizard's shoulder or flying nearby. But now, even the bird sensed something astray. It lifted itself in the air without Tabeus noticing and backtracked with all possible speed. Raven sensed that whatever danger lurked nearby, it could only be confronted with aid – a reality that even Tabeus did not consider.

The Wizard was totally focused – perhaps unnaturally so -- on what lie before him. Tabeus finally ducked into the small cavern and strained his eyes. It was no use; blackness overwhelmed the area. The Wizard raised his hand and a brilliant glow emanated from an intricate crystal ring that adorned his index finger. The glow illuminated the room, but the Wizard saw only smooth damp walls and a winding path leading into the darkness of the cavern's depths.

"I feel a great evil here," the Wizard mused. "But where is it? What could it be? There is nothing to see, but I sense there is something here I must find."

Tabeus continued down the loosely hewn path, turning this way and that, stooping in spots where the walls dropped too low. Finally, the Wizard found himself in a wide room with high ceilings and walls. Tabeus now realized he had travelled far underground, further than even he had originally imagined.

For the first time, he realized that Raven had disappeared. Tabeus looked at his empty shoulder curiously for a moment, then once more peered about the open space.

"Whoever or whatever you are," the Wizard shouted into the abyss, "reveal yourself! I command you!"

The Wizard watched in sudden shock and amazement as the light emanating from his ring dimmed, flickered, and then finally extinguished itself.

"What is this?" Tabeus asked.

Echoes of laughter bounced off the stone walls of the cavern.

"This is your doom, you pitiful so-called Wizard, a doom long in coming," a voice hissed scornfully.

Tabeus, surprised, glanced throughout the room. He saw nothing but blackness. The Wizard raised his staff and uttered a command, to no avail. The tip of the staff flickered for a moment, then the light was smothered. Suddenly, tiny twinkling lights flashed everywhere throughout the room, temporarily blinding the Wizard with their sudden brightness.

"Who are you?" Tabeus demanded. "Why does my magic have no effect in this evil place?"

Voices cackled ominously throughout the room.

"Your magic?" one voice mocked. "Hocus Pocus and simple tricks worthy of a child. Hardly worthy of being called magic."

The voice became more ominous and was joined by others until the volume in the room reached a near ear-splitting pitch.

"We are the First Born of Ambrasian," Tabeus heard, "conceived when the fires still raged and when the land had still not formed to its fashion."

The voices boomed across the room.

"The first born were the Elvii," Tabeus objected.

"No!" the voices cried angrily. "The cursed Elvii claim to have come first, but they came later. There were others before the Elvii–the Dranaki, our distant kin, who you so easily forget and subverted to the Drens today. But the Elvii brought their vicious light. They banished us from our rightful land of Ambrasian, and we have hidden in the depths ever since."

Tabeus searched the room quizzically.

"The First Born," the Wizard mused. "Yes, I now remember the legends I heard long ago. They are told in the tales of the Elvii–of an evil, voracious race fouler than anyone in Ambrasian could imagine. It took all the power and magic the land could muster to turn back the threat. And after the peoples of Ambrasian had succeeded, what was left of the magic of the land was substantially weakened."

The voices hissed at Tabeus' telling and their tone became more ominous.

"You recall your version of history well, Wizard, though its truth has been perverted by those who drove us from our rightful home," the voices said mockingly. "The magic you now practice is only a shadow of the original power that coursed through the land. And after so many years, we have finally renewed ourselves. Only one thing remained in our path."

"The Oracle," Tabeus said knowingly, beginning to put together the pieces of this latest puzzle.

"Correct, Wizard, you are not so dull-witted after all," the voices said. "The Oracle is the most powerful remnant of that early magic. It is the Oracle–and that sanctimonious Karmin–that has kept us confined. But now, the Oracle has been freed and unbound and is in the hands of our allies. We have been re-awakened, and though we are still weak in our re-birth, we could still easily tempt you into our lair."

"Now that you have me, what do you intend?" Tabeus asked scornfully. "As you have pointed out, I am but a lowly wizard, only one of thousands that come to oppose your supposed friends."

"We are not fooled by your false humility," the voices said contemptuously. "While your magic has no effect on us, you are the most formidable of our enemies. Even if your allies are victorious in the field, they cannot secure the Oracle from Celidia without your puny powers. Now we have done our part, and our role will become much greater as our powers return and blossom to their former glory. Ultimately, even Celidia and her cohorts will bend to our will. In the meantime, this will become your prison, where your magic is impotent and your influence made nil."

The Wizard looked carefully around the cave.

"How long do you think you can keep me?" Tabeus asked.

The voices laughed triumphantly, a long, hearty, and sickening bellow.

"Forever, Wizard," Tabeus' adversaries said, the words echoing about the room. "Here you will remain, your power fading, not quite death but not quite life, until the end of your days."

Then, just as suddenly as they appeared, the lights vanished and Tabeus was left in utter blackness.

•   •   •   •   •

Infernus continued to glow, growing steadily brighter and more ominous. Roanan and Siora were both worried and confused. For the Red Knight, this event was both strange and inexplicable. For the Elvii, the occurrence was just as improbable, and his guide was nothing but vague and mysterious allusions in ancient Elvii songs. Yet Siora had lived long enough to know that his instinct rarely failed him, and the Elvii was certain that imminent peril was nearby.

Together, the two leaders agreed to find Tabeus and seek his wisdom. Surely, the Wizard would understand the turn of events. They soon discovered, however, that the Wizard was nowhere to be found. Roanan and Siora rushed from camp to camp and fire to fire with increasing urgency. At first, the two leaders found the Wizard's absence strange on the eve of the last march. But as their search continued and grew no more successful, the initial perplexity turned to a sense of dread and foreboding.

"I don't understand where Tabeus could be," Roanan said in frustration. "He was with us earlier. This seems like an inopportune time to disappear."

The Elvii turned toward the Red Knight with deep concern etched on his fair face.

"King of Chrysalis," Siora said. "I see now that we have searched for our friend, the Wizard, in the wrong place. Your sword tells of a danger greater than even I imagined. I fear that Tabeus now faces foes even more powerful than he–and he desperately needs our aid."

"Tabeus in need of our aid?" Roanan asked in disbelief. "That is hard to fathom."

Siora merely nodded. The Elvii moved toward his horse and quickly told Roanan of the legends of the First Born and the tales of great evil.

"I fear that somehow these foul beings have entrapped Tabeus," Siora said. "Only the First Born would be powerful enough to stir the light within Infernus."

"How have the First Born been re-awakened after all these generations?" Roanan began, then quickly realized the answer. The Elvii studied his companion's face as the answer crystallized in his mind.

"The loss of the Oracle," the Red Knight concluded.

Siora nodded in agreement.

"Truly, not all have forgotten the First Born," the Elvii said. "Celidia has dug deep into the dark recesses of Ambrasian's history to unleash her plan."

"Then we must hurry and undo her latest scheme," Roanan agreed, mounting Alajar.

"Agreed," Siora said solemnly. "Though it's not clear where we should go, or when we get there, what even we can do."

* * *

Roanan and Siora rode their steeds through Karmana, using only the growing intensity of Infernus' glow as their guide. Alajar took the lead as Roanan's horse raced as the wind through the countryside of this suddenly beleaguered land. As the Red Knight and his ally rushed to the aid of the Wizard, Tabeus once again faced his imprisoners.

"You cannot hold me here, you ancient carriers of evil," Tabeus proclaimed defiantly. "Your time is past. Your pestilence has been vanquished."

Once more, laughter bounced from one wall of the cavern to the next.

"Try to escape," the voices mocked. "Use your potions, your spells, and your incantations if you dare. Your magic is useless here. We will re-emerge into the new Ambrasian as powerful as in our glorious past while you rot here for the rest of time."

In truth, Tabeus already recognized his powerlessness and there was little bite to his valiant words. He could feel his power sapped and all he had tried thus far had been in vain. Still, the Wizard retained one hope.

"My friends will have begun the search for me," Tabeus proclaimed. "My absence will be soon noticed."

"Will it?" the voices howled in derision. "Let them come! What can they do to save you? They can join you as our prisoners and we can help secure our inevitable victory that much easily."

The thought chilled Tabeus to the bone. Even the Wizard wondered what any of his friends and allies could do. And what would become of Ambrasian if Roanan, Siora, or even Karmin became captive? All would be lost. Still, the Wizard thought, Siora was an Elvii. Perhaps he would recognize the signs and know how to combat the First Born. Tabeus shook his head. It was a slim hope, and the Wizard felt himself growing weaker.

·　　·　　·　　·　　·

Roanan and Siora's confidence they could find their companion waned as they picked their way through the broken and uneven path. The night had grown long, and both rode near exhaustion, using only Infernus' glow and their steely reserve to continue their journey and find their lost friend. Alajar breathed heavily. Infernus continued to glow brighter and brighter. The sword vibrated with the tremendous energy within it. But even so, as Roanan and Siora reached a point in the path where the trail split in multiple directions, there was no certainty that any direction was the correct one.

Roanan glanced at Siora, the burning in his eyes hiding the fatigue of his body.

"Where now?" he asked. "The sword doesn't tell us whether to turn left or right."

At that moment, Raven flew through the trees directly toward Roanan and hovered just a few feet from the Red Knight. The bird cawed loudly multiple times until he gained the attention of the riders, constantly turning its small body toward the direction it had come.

"Raven," Roanan said with understanding. "Have you come as our guide?"

The bird cawed again, seemingly confirming the King's question.

"If anyone knows the location of the Tabeus," the Red Knight said, "it's the bird."

Siora nodded, paying close attention to the movements of Raven.

"Through those trees to the right," the Elvii pointed. "I can feel evil in this place. Now I see how the trees grow dark and menacing, a sight unseen in Karmana before these bleak days."

The path was unsteady at best and overgrown to nearly impassable at worst. Roanan and Siora finally were forced to dismount and proceed on foot with Raven at their side. Through the dim light, the two nobles struggled to find their way through the underbrush. Slowly, gradually, they discovered the same cavern as the one Tabeus found hours before.

"There it is," Siora said. "Your sword and the bird have led us true."

"How do you know?" Roanan asked, studying the Elvii carefully through the dim light.

"I know," Siora said confidently. "An Elvii has senses other beings lack. We can smell the stench of evil. Besides, look at the bird, trembling in fear."

Raven now flew nervously back and forth, apparently too afraid to move forward.

Roanan surveyed the scene before him.

"If this is indeed our destiny," the Red Knight said grimly, "how can we succeed if even Tabeus is powerless against this foe?"

"I am not certain," Siora admitted. "But I have faith that our search will not end in vain."

Roanan nodded and moved forward.

"Then let us go and face this ancient threat," he said with resolve.

The Red Knight and the Elvii leader slowly proceeded to the opening of the cavern. They cautiously explored the surrounding undergrowth, but at first found no enemies, no signs of recent activity. Then, Roanan discovered a small piece of fabric torn from Tabeus' robe. He picked it up and examined it closely, turning to Siora knowingly.

"This is undoubtedly the way," he whispered. "Whatever has befallen the Wizard lies in front of us."

Slowly, Roanan and Siora entered the low slit in the earth. Siora ran his hand along his own sword, which now glowed with nearly the intensity of Infernus. Unknowingly, Roanan and Siora mirrored Tabeus' earlier steps. Gradually, they heard voices in the distance and could discern dim lights flickering. This led the two to increase their speed, slicing the gap more quickly to their apparent destination.

After a few minutes that seemed much longer than that, Roanan and Siora came to the lip of the wide room. In an instant, the two were briefly overwhelmed with the sight of Tabeus sprawled weakly in a corner of the room, the flashing lights growing brighter and more ominous all around the Wizard with each passing moment. The light from Siora's sword was suddenly extinguished.

"Behold!" Siora cried. "Truly these are the masters of darkness–the First Born."

The voices laughed, turning their attention toward the Roanan and Siora.

"Look who has joined us — an Elvii! Dare one who condemned us to this fate enter our domain?" the voices said angrily. "Death to the Elvii!"

There was a breath's pause.

"And a Cadaren," the voices said more curiously. "The weakest of all creatures in Ambrasian. How stupid and arrogant that such an insect confronts us in an attempt to rescue this decrepit Wizard. They obviously have learned nothing in our long absence."

The voices laughed uproariously in a mocking tone.

Roanan looked indignant, but as he turned to Siora, he saw the Elvii leader stricken to the ground by a bolt of energy originating in the lights of the First Born.

"Siora," the Red Knight cried. But he found it impossible to move toward his ally and friend.

The Elvii forced his gaze toward Roanan, his face sculpted in pain.

"Roanan," he gasped hoarsely. "You hold our only hope."

Then, a new bolt of pain enveloped the Elvii, and he fell to the ground in agony, unable to speak.

Roanan looked to Tabeus in desperation. But the Wizard was too weak to respond and merely gazed at the Red Knight with diminishing hope. The King stood frozen for a moment, his two strongest allies reduced to helplessness on either side of him.

Now the lights circled around Roanan, but at the last moment, seemed to hesitate and retreat.

I was the hope, the Red Knight considered Siora's words. *How was I. . .no, not I . . . I hold the hope. . .*

Of course, he realized suddenly. It was the same reason he himself has remained untouched to this point, the same power that had defeated the First Born initially so many millennia ago. It was the force that had led them on this perilous trail: Infernus. The legendary sword had been forged by the master craftsmen of olden days and instilled with the power of the magic of the earliest times. Infernus was infused with the same potency that created the Oracle. Both were remnants of the days before the banishment of the First Born. Today, it was the only path to overcoming this ancient adversary. The First Born has not accounted for its inopportune reappearance.

Roanan, the Red Knight, King of Chrysalis, once more raised the legendary sword Infernus. It suddenly pulsated with power, lighting up the darkened cavern with a brilliant burst of light. The lights of the First Born seemed to diminish and a collective cry of anguish echoed through the chamber. With newfound strength, the Red Knight grasped the sword with both arms, and Infernus exploded with a brilliant light that engulfed the cavern, temporarily blinding all who were near. Through every crevice and crack, the magic of old was reawakened, Roanan advanced toward the Wizard, and with blinding speed and power, swung Infernus mightily over and over through the throng of the First Born. Hewing through the mass with great bursts, his foes exploded one by one and seemed drawn to the sword against their will. Infernus sliced through the First Born without mercy or pity. In mere minutes, Roanan and Infernus had put to an end, finally and completely, to the threat of the First Born, who had not yet achieved full strength and had no ability to defend themselves against the fury they now unexpectantly faced.

Finally, Roanan had vanquished his foes. All was silent. Light seeped through the crevices once again. Siora and Tabeus slowly sat up, their strength and power slowly returning to their bodies. Suddenly, the three allies turned toward the sound of footsteps moving toward the chamber. An impressive figure appeared in the opening to the cave: Karmin stood majestically over the scene of victory.

"The threat has passed," she said. "You have done well."

The Red Knight turned toward the Regent of Karmana with some surprise.

"How did you find us?" Roanan asked. "As far as I knew, only myself and Siora were aware of this threat."

"Perhaps that is true," Karmin answered, "but your mad dash throughout the camps searching for the Wizard generated more than a few concerns. Word eventually reached me, and I surmised enough of the peril that I hurried here with all speed."

Karmin surveyed the scene more closely.

"But my presence earlier would not have aided our cause," she concluded. "Only Roanan had the weapon to defeat the First Born. He rose to the occasion and defeated our common enemy."

Roanan raised his hand.

"Our greatest task still lies ahead," the Red Knight said. "And we must hasten our return to camp. We can delay our march no longer. All manner of evil is rising against us."

Siora nodded in agreement.

"Roanan speaks the truth," the Elvii said. "This is only the beginning of our confrontations with the forces aligned against us."

Thus, with Roanan and Karmin giving aid to the Wizard and the Elvii, the company returned to camp and put this prelude to battle behind them. There was no time to look back.

•　　•　　•　　•　　•

Across Karmana, Maldur paced nervously through the Watchtower. The Black Knight muttered unintelligibly under his breath, kicking garbage out of his path and impatiently looking out the windows checking on the progress of the troops.

At that moment, Celidia walked stiffly into the room.

"What's the matter, Maldur?" she asked curtly. "You're beginning to sound like a Dren."

The Sorceress paused.

"And smell like one, too," she added.

Maldur grunted miserably.

"Nothing smells that bad," he said.

Shortly thereafter, Brelex entered the room.

"Can you two stop bickering?" the Grey Knight said. "We have a war to fight and the day of battle comes ever closer."

Celidia looked at the Black Knight, then at the Grey Knight.

"Male Cadaren," she spit and stomped from the room. "I have real work to do. You two keep yourself busy playing with your armies. Your battle will arrive soon enough. I hope your swords match your boasts."

CHAPTER 21
GALACTIC COMMAND,
GALACTIC DATE 2142-08-11

While the Explorer continued to monitor and analyze the often hard-to-believe and even harder-to-explain events on the planet Ambrasian, Captain Evenru grew more and more frustrated with the technical glitches the surveillance continued to experience.

"What do you mean, we lost contact with the drone as it entered the cave?" Evenru asked Officer Penru with more than a strong hint of frustration. "How is that possible?"

"There must have been an unidentified malfunction," the officer explained. "We are still running diagnostics. This is highly unusual."

Evenru grunted disgustedly.

"What exactly are the First Born they were discussing?" the Captain asked. "And how is it possible that they disabled our drone? Why are we experiencing one unexplainable malfunction after another?"

Evenru glanced at the screen at Penru's workstation. The data did not help clarify the many occurrences that defied science as the Lux knew it. The captain's patience had been tested with demonstrations of "magic," a perfectly healthy female dying of accelerated aging before their very eyes, and a supposedly ancient race of natives wreaking havoc among the living.

"We aren't blaming this on magic, are we?" the Captain smirked.

"Captain . . ." Kevo began.

Evenru cut off the AI.

"I'm kidding," he said, then paused momentarily. "I think."

The captain and rest of the crew continued to watch the strange happenings on the planet below them. Nothing in their highly technological world had prepared them for the seemingly inexplicable activities occurring in this otherwise primitive culture. Ambrasian was one surprise after another, defying both logic and classification.

Officer Kalli entered the Command Center.

"Captain," she reported, "Galactic Command has sent us an interspace communication. They are inquiring regarding our delay in completing our mission. They have another assignment for the ship. There has been an incident at Tannhauser Gate."

Evenru gave an audible sigh.

"There's always another assignment waiting," he huffed. "Somehow, they never seem to run out of them. There's been trouble at Tannhauser Gate ever since the initial replicants were created. Where's Deckard when you need him?"

Evenru sighed, reviewing the monitoring screens once more and glancing down at the summary reports thus far.

"Tell Galactic Command that we are still completing repairs to the ship and that we will notify them when we are ready to leave orbit," the Captain said.

"Captain?" Kalli asked skeptically. "Repairs were completed yesterday."

Evenru glanced sternly at the officer.

"Do you need me to repeat the order for you?" he challenged. "I'm told that the repairs were more extensive than first expected and that additional diagnostic testing will be required to ensure the ship can safely navigate a snakehole before we proceed."

Kalli looked quizzically at the Captain for a moment, then a hint of recognition crossed her face.

"Understood, sir," Kalli answered. "I will transmit the message. I will inform Galactic Command that we will update them with our status when the ship is prepared to leave orbit. I recall now that we noted some unusual fluctuations in Solaren Drive accelerator chamber. We should run additional tests."

"Excellent, Officer Kalli," Evenru said. "Tell them exactly that."

The monitors in the Command Center showed Roanan and Karmin aiding Siora and Tabeus in leaving the cave. Raven was perched on the Wizard's shoulder once more, showing more than a bit of concern.

"Whoever or whatever the First Born were," Evenru said, "they apparently did not fare well. And that bird is much more interesting that at first appears."

Evenru watched carefully as the Red Knight led his two companions back through the path they had travelled to the cave. Siora mounted his own ride, while Roanan helped Tabeus mount Alajar and rode with the Wizard. Karmin rode her own steed, seeming to recite some protective incantation before urging her horse forward. Together, the four Ambrasians began their journey back to the Hall of Karmana, where their army rested, counting down toward their march to war.

"Make sure that disabled drone gets back here in one piece," the Captain instructed the crew. "Then, someone needs to take it apart and figure out why it failed."

CHAPTER 22
THE MARCH CONTINUES

In the end, the final battle march toward the Watchtower was delayed only a few hours by the struggle with the First Born, and few knew how close their quest had come to disaster before it had fully started. Roanan led the long rows of soldiers, flanked by Tabeus and Siora, both renewed in strength and spirit.

Near the front of the determined procession rode Halmar, Toranis and Dainwirth Lir. To their left and their right came a collection of Chrysalian knights and soldiers, Elvii, citizens who had joined the army, and a collection of younger warriors and aspiring knights, some of whom had been trained by Karmin. Only about a quarter of the army rode on horseback, since few citizens had horses ready to ride into battle and Elvii preferred to travel on foot. The supply wagons brought up the rear of the march, with a contingent of riders experienced and skilled in battle protecting the wagons from a surprise attack.

At first sight, it was an impressive array of soldiers and weaponry. But Tabeus and Roanan both knew they were overwhelmingly outnumbered by Maldur's Drens and Brelex's army, a host that swelled each day. In addition, much of the Red Knight's army was young, raw, and poorly trained. The regular army of Chrysalis has been supplemented by all manner of fighters with various levels of experience and skill, and with the need to act expeditiously, there was little time for training. There was no telling how they would react to battle where glory gave way to the reality of blood and severed limbs. With the power of the Oracle now imprisoned by the forces of evil, the outcome of this desperate fight was far from certain. In fact, to any objective observer, the most likely resolution appeared grim.

Karmin watched the host in silence as it marched past the Hall of Karmana. Roanan diverted Alajar toward her. Despite her best efforts to appear confident, the concern held by the Regent of Karmana was clear.

"You leave on a mission more critical than any crisis we have encountered in many millennia," she finally said. "I wish only that I could provide more aid."

Roanan nodded in understanding.

"This is a battle that must be decided by a sword's edge," the Red Knight said. "One day, perhaps, things will be different and we may resolve conflicts in a more peaceful manner. But Ambrasian has not advanced to that level of civility and we must meet on the battlefield to defend what is right."

Karmin nodded and Roanan returned to his place in the front of his army. The force began its march in earnest. The rows of soldiers slowly left the beauty of the Hall of Karmana and drifted into the East. Karmin watched with a mix of sorrow and pride as they slowly disappeared into the distance.

The army passed Sarania Field and crossed the Lorimen River. Karmana had built a stunningly elegant bridge across the river, but it took some time to take thousands of soldiers across the structure. The Red Knight understood the delay, but still he fretted about the time lost that could not be recovered.

Once the force crossed the river, the army reached full speed, Roanan led them northeast, on a path that would eventually bring them toward the edge the Great Forest and Malinas Lake. The procession was orderly, dignified and subdued, but accomplished with all possible speed. A sense of mission permeated through the army, as well as knowledge of a duty that, though desperate, was necessary to accomplish somehow, some way.

As expected, Mendelheimer was the only exception to the solemnity of the march, starting near the front of the army but slowly falling back, his antics and the characteristically sluggish Preston responsible for his less than rapid pace. At the very least, the minstrel elucidated a few chuckles along the way.

In the lead, Roanan rode closely by Tabeus. In his short reign, Roanan had grown much closer to the Wizard, in part by the necessity of the circumstances but also because the Red Knight truly valued Tabeus' wisdom, freely shared.

"We have gone through much just to come this far," the Red Knight said. "Yet our greatest challenge still lies before us."

"That is surely true," Tabeus agreed. "Our spirit must remain strong. But I wonder, my friend, Roanan, King of Chrysalis, descended from the legendary line of the Red Knight, if you have seen how much you yourself have grown?"

"Me?" Roanan asked in surprised. "I've been a bit occupied by the issues at hand. I've hardly had time to assess my own standing."

"I am sure you have had little time for introspection," the Wizard concurred, understanding the bias for action in a young king. "But grown you have whether or not you realize it. When this quest was thrust upon you, you were still a young king, unsure of your ability to lead or make decisions. But now, in a very short time, you have assumed your rightful role. You are undoubtedly a king, fierce in battle, thoughtful of your subjects, and respected by your peers. Never lose those qualities."

Roanan nodded, accepting the Wizard's assessment with humility.

"I appreciate your confidence and your kind words," Roanan said. "With your guidance, I will retain those traits you admire. Yet all these qualities will mean little if we fail in our quest."

"Without question," Tabeus said. "But those skills have already provided what little hope we have. You have forged an army and bonded friendships where you could have found new enemies. You have maintained hope when all looked bleak. And you have learned to trust your instincts in times of crisis. We must make use of all these strengths— and more—for us to defeat Maldur, Celidia and Brelex."

Roanan again acknowledged his appreciation for the Wizard's observations and once more they continued on their quest. It would be several days before his forces would be in striking distance of the Watchtower. The Red Knight thought of all that had happened and then looked even further back on happier days. He remembered carefree days when his father was King. He was a young prince and Ambrasian was at peace. The Red Knight recalled Tabeus' unexpected visits, unannounced but always welcome, who taught the future monarch much of the world and the role of knights and rulers. Roanan may not have understood the purpose of many of the Wizard's eclectic lessons as a child, but they had become far clearer during recent events. Those past days now seemed so long ago, far removed from his present course.

It was perhaps only now as the Red Knight led his forces toward battle that Roanan fully came to appreciate those lessons. It was the shared knowledge of his father and the Wizard that most shaped the life of Roanan. Perhaps, the Red Knight thought, they had prepared him with this mission in mind, knowing that the peaceful facade of Ambrasian would likely be torn apart by the gathering evil. How could they have known this day would come?

He wondered. Was this, then, his destiny: to rule over a war-torn land, a soldier on foreign soil, spilling the blood of an uncounted enemy, only to die in a hopeless struggle? Or to survive this test and heal Ambrasian of the wounds it had grievously suffered? No matter who emerged victorious in this struggle, the world as Roanan knew it would be forever changed. If only he could return to happier, more peaceful days.

Or would he? Now, those days now smacked of false security. Given the choice, would he elect to return to the subservient, hesitant, immature prince he used to be not that long ago, or remain the dedicated leader of men he had become? No, the Red Knight concluded, he could not return to the past. His destiny lay before him, in the present, and with any luck, into the future. At the very least, he had the ability to help shape what lay ahead.

Still the company moved on, making steady progress through northeastern Karmana, charting a course along the entangled masses of the Great Forest. Only the Elvii dared to make their way into the Forest, a natural habitat to their ancient race. Through the trees and underbrush they made their march, barely visible to the rest of Roanan's army, but moving at a speed at which the other members of Roanan's forces marveled.

The force finally camped at dusk. Though the camp was quickly made, Roanan tried to make it as comfortable as possible. After he posted adequate sentries to protect against a surprise attack, the soldiers lit fires and roasted fresh meat for a hearty meal. The Red

Knight knew his warriors had to be both rested and fed to face an enemy the likes of which had been assembled by Maldur and Brelex.

Following the evening meal, Mendelheimer approached the Red Knight, Tabeus, and the trusted knights charged with leading the attack. The minstrel held a large scroll as he settled in front of his audience.

"Minstrel?" Roanan asked quizzically. "You have business with me?"

"As a matter of fact, I do," Mendelheimer said robustly. "I have been working studiously on the History of the Great War of the Oracle and I would like to share my opening chapters . . ."

"Chapters, you say?" Roanan interrupted. "How many chapters have you written?"

"Only twenty-three, my lord," the minstrel replied, "with many more to come!"

Roanan glanced over to his companions. Tabeus smirked in amusement while Halmar growled in disgust. The rest of the party seemed to not quite know what to make of Mendelheimer's proclamation.

"Let me share with you some of my work so far," the minstrel continued, unraveling the long scroll without waiting for an answer.

"Heretofore and forthwith, below is the true and accurate account of the exploits and travails of King Roanan the famed Red Knight of Chrysalis, Siora the leader of the wondrous and mysterious race of the Elvii, and the knights and soldiers who so bravely assumed the mantle to defend Ambrasian from the vile forces of evil. The chronicler of this treatise is the much renowned and wise muse Mendelheimer, who heroically risked his own life and well-being by accompanying King Roanan's army on this perilous quest to share truly this tale for future generations . . ."

Halmar had already heard enough, and the grizzled knight stood up and left to find a more accommodating haven. The minstrel droned on in turgid prose for significantly longer, making sure to glorify his own questionable contributions wherever possible. Finally, Roanan signaled he had heard enough.

"I appreciate all of your hard word, minstrel," the Red Knight said dubiously, "but I will be more interested in hearing about our exploits after we return home victorious."

Mendelheimer bowed, re-rolled his scrolled, and disappeared into the night.

Roanan and Tabeus sat by a small fire and watched the flames shoot wildly into the air. Eventually, the fire consumed itself until it became nothing but glowing embers muted by the soft night and the gentle breeze. Both the Red Knight and the Wizard were silent, contemplating the cascade of activity that surrounded them. Youthful enthusiasm permeated the camp. Tabeus grimly chuckled to himself. Soon, the Wizard thought, those cries of ebullience would turn to the tears of real battle. War has a sobering effect. These young fighters so enthusiastic now would face a sudden–and for many deadly–reality. The ferocity of actual warfare with sharpened blades and spilled blood would dull the bravado of even the most exuberant fighters.

The night passed. Finally, the Red Knight laid down and drifted into a much needed but fitful sleep. As he did so, he heard Mendelheimer off in the distance:

Once there was a boy
With his family's prized cow
He ran into a trader
Who majestically did bow
The trader got the horse
The boy got three beans
And a bridge in Isalis . . .

The loud groans of those nearby followed the song.

Halmar is probably cursing a blue streak, the Red Knight thought, smiling at the notion.

Roanan nodded off, sleeping as best he could throughout the night. Suddenly, however, he awoke to screams, battle cries, and the sounds of angry swords. The Red Knight quickly unsheathed Infernus and found Tabeus outside his tent.

"What happened?" Roanan asked.

The Wizard turned, his outline illuminated by the moonlight and the fires in the distance.

"Drens," he said.

"As we feared," Roanan said.

Tabeus nodded.

"To no one's surprise, they attacked by night," the Wizard affirmed. "Not to defeat us. The raiding party was far too small for that. But to weaken us in both body and spirit."

"Damn them," the Red Knight said with indignation. "That will not happen."

"No," Tabeus agreed, "but it confirms we must always be on guard."

In an instant, Roanan bounded past the Wizard and as quickly as an animal in flight burst toward the scene of the disturbance.

But it was an unnecessary effort. As Tabeus was about to tell him, Roanan discovered the Drens had quickly been repelled. But it had not come without a price: eight warriors had been killed and several others injured. Of the small squadron of Drens, ten had been slain initially, with the rest retreating into the darkness of night after their surprise attack. But to the dozen Drens that had slipped into the Great Forest during their escape, they met a quick death at the sharp tip of Elvii arrows.

Roanan helped to restore order, re-doubling the guards around the perimeter. The Red Knight moved silently about the camp, listening to the scattered and somewhat contradictory reports of the Dren attack. Despite the Drens' ability to move stealthily through the night, the sentries had sensed something lurking near the camp at the last moment and called for aid just in time to thwart the attack. Roanan kneeled quietly by the bodies of each of his fallen warriors. Some were Roanan's own, from Chrysalis. Others were citizen volunteers or the young fighters trained by Karmin. All had fallen in defense of a way of life they had cherished. Roanan did not know any of the dead personally, yet he felt a close kinship with each one. After he was finished, Roanan walked into the night alone. A single tear ran down his face.

Much more blood will fall before the end of this commission, the Red Knight thought grimly. *For those, there will be no victory no matter the outcome.*

●　　●　　●　　●　　●

In the morning before continuing the march, Roanan called together all his closest allies. Among them were Tabeus and Siora, as well as Dainwirth Lir, Toranis and Halmar. Mendelheimer joined the contingent, uninvited.

"We approach our destiny," Roanan began, "and the stakes become higher. As the events of last night show, we must be on guard at every moment. Despite our long odds, we will find some way to overcome this increasing evil."

Tabeus surveyed the group.

"We must do so quickly because we have no time to spare," the Wizard added. "Our enemy grows stronger each day and takes more and more liberties with the land and its people. At the same time, Celidia becomes closer and closer to mastering the power of Oracle. If she succeeds, Ambrasian faces a long night ahead."

It took few words to motivate Lir and Toranis into a frenzy. They were already shaken and vengeful from the night before, ready to battle at a moment's notice.

"Curse on those filthy, damnable Drens," Toranis cried. "They will pay from their deeds of last night. Bring them on, a score at a time!"

"A score!" Lir agreed. Then the young knight began to count and looked worriedly at Toranis. "A score?"

Finally, the veteran knight, Halmar, cooled down his more impetuous comrades.

"Young fools," Halmar proclaimed. "Have you learned nothing from your journey? If your ability to fight matched your blind enthusiasm, we could take on Maldur's army alone. As it is, I must spend my time keeping you two out of trouble."

"Soon," Tabeus added, "there will be enough trouble to keep all of us fully occupied. Let us not wish for the battle to come to us too soon. It will arrive in due time and none of us will be the same, for better or for worse."

The remainder of the party remained silent absorbing the sober warnings. Eventually, Mendelheimer could remain silent no longer. The minstrel bolted into the middle of the small group, swinging his arms furiously.

"Enough of this chatter," the minstrel chirped. "Let us get on with it. I will even help!"

The rest of the council stared at Mendelheimer incredulously.

"You?" Roanan finally laughed. "What will you do? Sing them to death?"

Halmar shook his head.

"Another foolish idiot," the veteran knight said. "With our luck, the Drens will be tone deaf."

After a hasty preparation, Roanan's army broke camp and renewed its march. The day passed quietly, with no signs of Drens or other enemy forces. Still, the Red Knight was troubled. Now, even he could see without searching that Karmana was indeed fading. The plants and trees still grew plush. But the iridescent glow, the splendor unique to that magically gifted land, was merely a shadow of its normal self. As memories fade and their tones become less lustrous, so now suffered Karmana's immortal land. The spectre of death had invaded paradise. Karmana was only now first experiencing the sad and savage ravages of mortality.

Near the end of the long arduous day, the Red Knight turned away slightly from the borders of the Great Forest and maintained an easterly course. Roanan was bringing his army south of Malinas Lake. In this way, they would have to cross the Sylil River. Doing otherwise, however, would cost at least two, and perhaps three, additional days of travel, and the Red Knight well remembered Tabeus' warning of the ever-increasing strength of the opposition. Once across the river, the Great Forest would again bend toward the Watchtower, allowing Siora's Elvii to join the battle within their natural habitat.

It was then that the Red Knight's army found graphic evidence of their enemy's ruthlessness. They happened across the remains of a small hamlet, now burned to the ground, what was left of the small homes charred and still smoking. The bodies of the village's residents lay strewn across the ground, some mutilated beyond recognition. It was clear they had little chance against the ferocious Dren raid.

Roanan stopped the army and dismounted Alajar. He walked through the village somberly, shaking his head in disbelief. Several of his companions followed him.

"Why would anyone do this?" Dainwirth Lir asked incredulously.

"For sport," Halmar answered. "To satisfy these beasts' lust for blood."

Tabeus surveyed the scene.

"That," the Wizard agreed, "and to aggravate us to reckless action. They will do what they can to make us both angry and desperate."

The Red Knight stopped and took one last look at the scene.

"We will avenge this horror," he vowed. He ordered the bodies to be placed on a pyre and once it was lit, he once again returned to the head of his force.

Roanan maintained a brisk pace until dusk. He camped his force on a hill overlooking a grassy plain. Only a few trees interrupted the landscape, and whatever farmers lived there had abandoned a land so close to the ominous shadow of Maldur and Celidia. It provided the army with a broad view of the valley, a good defensive position should the Drens attempt yet another late-night raid. Roanan was intent on taking every possible precaution.

Not all were pleased with the army's accommodations. The Elvii grew restless in this near tree-less terrain, unaccustomed to living outside the Great Forest for long periods. But their hatred of Maldur and the evil that had befallen Ambrasian helped them overcome their discomfort, and they remained resolute. Still, Siora showed concern.

"Be calm, my brothers, fairest and eldest race of Ambrasian," he said in a tranquil tone. "The future of the land we have helped to build may depend upon a single battle. It is a cruel joke of fate, but a joke we cannot take lightly."

Siora felt the presence of Tabeus by his side.

"Patience, my friends, remain calm of heart but alert of mind," the Wizard whispered. "The trees may be your faithful companions, but before you return to them, you must ensure their safety and the well-being of all living things in this land."

The Wizard raised his staff and muttered words in an unknown tongue. The staff glowed softly, and a serenity appeared to descend upon the Elvii. As quiet settled over the camp, Tabeus disappeared into the night.

Mendelheimer, meanwhile, had joined Roanan and those closest to him near the sparse fire they had built in the open field. Though even the most dull-witted of the Drens could easily spot them, Roanan did not want his army to be too obvious in the dark night. The half-moon and NightSun were both clouded over, so even the smallest of fires blazed in the blackened landscape.

"Would you care for a song, your highness?" the minstrel said. "I've composed several dozen."

The Red Knight smirked.

"I'm sure you have," he said. "But my ears are not ready for such an onslaught tonight. Perhaps when we are victorious, you can sing loudly and proudly."

Mendelheimer bowed.

"As you wish," he said and turned, wandering back among the troops. In short order, Roanan could hear the minstrel's off-key voice singing among the camp.

"We can only be grateful that we are not his audience," Siora said.

Roanan smiled despite the circumstances.

"Of that we can be sure," the King agreed. "Though I still believe that somehow the minstrel has a role to play in our quest beyond his grating voice. I cannot imagine what that might be, but I must heed that thought."

Siora nodded in agreement.

"I understand how you feel," the Elvii said. "Sometimes a leader must go by that unseen directive, no matter how little sense it makes."

Siora paused for a moment.

"Though if the minstrel strays too close to Halmar, your knight may remove his tongue," he added.

Roanan and Siora shared a chuckle.

The two leaders slowly became silent, the weight of imminent battle bearing more and more on their thoughts. In the shadows of the night, a lone figure, unseen by Roanan's sentries, watched the busy camp until the moon rose high and its light broke through the dispersing clouds. Then as quietly as a shadow, the figure disappeared into the night as silently as it had appeared.

There was nothing quiet at the Watchtower. The Drens implemented their defenses with crashes and rattles, collisions and constant racket. The confusion soon frayed the nerves of the Black Knight, already on edge with the scent of battle so near.

"These nitwits are the clumsiest oafs I've ever seen," Maldur said. "By thunder, they're so loud it's impossible to think around here."

Celidia laughed. The Sorceress had found resources in her own mind that blocked out the hubbub around her.

"Seeing that thinking is a skill you rarely use," she cracked, "that should have no effect you."

"This racket doesn't bother you?" Maldur roared defiantly.

"I can think perfectly fine," the Sorceress said. "And right now I think you should go out and keep an eye on your brothers."

At that moment, the Dren Lieutenant Izuburu-Gy came strutting into the chambers.

"The patrol has returned and has raided Roanan's camp," the Dren captain hissed, licking his lips slowly. "They claim the Red Knight's forces total no more than 8,000. I can barely wait to taste the sweet flavor of their blood. It has been some time since I've feasted on fresh Cadaren."

"Good work," the Black Knight said dismissively. "You will get the chance to satiate your appetite for blood, weasel. If your reports are correct, we will fight in two days' time."

The Dren spit, much to Maldur's disgust.

"Of course my reports are correct," Izuburu-Gy said. "I can nearly smell the enemy myself. Their stench carries far."

The Dren laughed maliciously and bared his sharp fangs. With a combination of disdain and anticipation, Izuburu-Gy turned in a cat-like motion and deliberately left the room.

"They do smell awful," Celidia finally admitted. "He should be the last to talk about a stench."

"I told you," Maldur said.

"But it is no worse that being with you constantly," the Sorceress added.

Maldur quickly scowled at Celidia but made no comment.

Outside, Brelex stood alone, peering intently into the horizon. The Grey Knight had no desire for small talk or insignificant discussions and certainly had no time for the Drens. They were necessary to achieve victory in battle, but nothing more. Brelex had but a single focus. As a hunter stalks his prey, now too did Brelex await the arrival of Roanan's forces. The taste of power lay just beyond his reach.

CHAPTER 23
THE EMANCIPATION OF BALINWALD

While Lasarion and Alexandra had formed a bond based on something more than necessity, the rest of the army was built on an uneasy alliance. Lasarion's forces viewed the soldiers from Selin with skepticism, wondering how long the initial fervor would last. In any case, the combined legion began their march across Selin toward Balinwald. It was not the most impressive of military companies. Lasarion's own brigade had never fully recovered from Ravager's attack, and the Selinites were hardly trained warriors. But it was a well-stocked force of some size and Lasarion now felt he had at least a chance to help win this war.

As expected, some Selinite troops posed a problem soon after the march began. In the aftermath of the Dren attack, emotions had run high and support for Lasarion's cause was overwhelming. But now, as the public outcry waned since the Drens had not sustained their assault, the resolve of the Selinites grew less sturdy. A few had already abandoned the march, dropping off the trail never to be seen again. The wavering worried Lasarion. The contingent was too loosely knit and capricious to be a dependable well-honed force. The Chrysalian knight wondered if he could keep this untrained mass together at all, and if so, whether they would cower at the first hint of battle. Lasarion began to think he was little better off than before.

Alexandra had learned much of Lasarion in the last few days and had an almost uncanny ability to know what was on his mind. The knight was both disturbed and strangely pleased by this and was slowly warming to the ebullient Selinite princess. There was no denying that Lasarion found Alexandra beautiful and enjoyed her company. But the circumstances did not allow Lasarion to think of romance and the Chrysalian knight worked diligently to stay focused on the task at hand.

Despite his conflicted feelings, Lasarion felt some sense of relief as he saw Alexandra approach him during a short respite in the march. She rode a silver-grey mare and sat proudly and confidently, her long auburn hair flowing freely in the soft breeze. Her sword hung at waist, and she wore a belt with various packets, the contents of which were unknown even to Lasarion. The Chrysalian knight saw at once a vision of two worlds: a majestic princess and a ferocious warrior.

As Lasarion considered this dichotomy silently, the voice of Alexandra returned him to his more immediate concerns.

"I know what you are thinking," the princess said.

The knight blushed then regained his composure.

"Really?" he finally said. "What is that exactly?"

Alexandra reached Lasarion, stopping just a bit too closely for the knight's comfort.

"You don't think our army has the heart and determination to follow you into battle," she finally said.

Lasarion was relieved that Alexandra had chosen this tact and focused on the subject at hand.

"To battle?" Lasarion finally asked cynically. "I doubt they will follow me through the day. Their hatred of the Drens has diminished since their initial fury. They are too soft to be soldiers–they prefer the comfort of a warm fire and a strong roof above their heads."

Alexandra looked at her companion studiously.

"Don't we all?" Alexandra asked defiantly. "Perhaps you are right. But do not fear my brave knight from Chrysalis. My people will follow me wherever I lead them. And I will follow you into the battle of our lives."

Lasarion smiled wryly.

"We have far to go," he said. "Your trust will be tested more than you likely imagine along our path. I am not even yet sure how we will arrive on time."

"Then we must maintain a quick pace," Alexandra said with determination. "I will rouse the troops. You will have no trouble."

The princess paused and looked intently at Lasarion, then turned to fulfill her promise.

Shortly thereafter, Dakar came through the shadows, leading his horse. Lasarion was not sure how long he had been there but looked at him suspiciously.

"Don't say a word," Lasarion said.

"I wasn't going to say a thing," Dakar answered. Not expecting a response, the young warrior laughed as he led his horse to where the march line was forming.

·   ·   ·   ·   ·

Lasarion gave the appearance of a grizzled warrior, but Alexandra saw through the facade to see the tender heart he so carefully protected. As the pace to Balinwald quickened, however, Lasarion buried all his tenderness deep within himself. Now, he was the consummate knight and warrior, and he was on a mission where he could not fail. He knew that his King was in all likelihood far outnumbered and desperate for his aid. And he knew that nothing short of a miracle would bring his army to aid Roanan in time.

Knowing that, Lasarion drove to create that miracle. Though the attraction between Lasarion and Alexandra continued to lie just below the surface, the knight maintained his singular purpose. If by some chance this fated quest would somehow succeed, there would be time enough later to consider the princess. But first, Roanan's force must be bolstered and Ambrasian saved. The armies of Maldur and Brelex must be driven back and defeated. Until then, nothing else mattered.

Thus, Lasarion crossed Selin at an incredible pace, moving as a shadow across the land. The farm folk of Selin marveled at the speed of the advancing force, while the Selinite soldiers struggled to maintain the pace the Chrysalian army had discovered in the strength of their leader. To be sure, Alexandra had dispelled any doubts about the Selinite's resolve and the members no longer questioned their actions. But most of Lasarion's men were much better trained and had overcome the greatest of adversities. Now, they thought only of the peril of their King, their comrades, and their families.

Lasarion picked a course directly northeast. There was no reason to travel to the Hall of Balinwald, which Brelex had left abandoned and in near ruins. Instead, Lasarion would cross both Selin and Balinwald and intercept the forces Brelex had left behind at his own castle, the Hall of the Grey Knight. His goal was to not only overrun Brelex's stronghold but also to free Princess Athena, the last remaining member of King Sardenia's direct bloodline.

From there, he would turn north and move with all speed to the Watchtower on the border of Karmana and Damora. It was a course dictated not only by expediency but also by necessity. To turn north too soon would lead the army into the unknown trails of the Land of Mystery. The clearest and most travelled roads lay in the path that Lasarion had chosen.

And thus, in a day's time, Lasarion crossed the plains of Selin and pierced deeply into the rocky terrain of Balinwald. Reluctantly, he paused for the night. Driven by some stronger will, the knight was prepared to travel without rest. But not all who rode with him had his fortitude. Both his army and the horses that served them displayed signs of weariness and it forced him to camp for the night.

Well into the night, Lasarion still maintained a silent watch of the path before him. The clear skies painted an ominous view of Balinwald's sometimes unforgiving landscape. The land was sharply etched with hills as the ground rose, higher and higher toward the south. Eventually, the mountains of Balinwald dominated the land. Bat Lasarion had studied the land well and would not travel close to that difficult range that had limited passages.

Vegetation was not as lush as the awe-inspiring gardens of Karmana, but neither was the land barren. It consisted mostly of evergreens and short grass, and the sturdier and more resilient of the plants. This at least would benefit Lasarion's desperate charge. There were few forests and little thick brush that would work to deter his army. The path to the Hall of Brelex was relatively clear, if still a significant distance.

But Lasarion was looking far beyond that. As Dakar and Alexandra joined him on the darkened ridge, the Chrysalian knight held up his finger knowingly to keep them silent. He looked far afield toward an unseen plain.

"I can hear them," he said quietly, almost in a whisper. "I can hear Roanan and Tabeus seeking my aid. Their message travels on the wings of the night wind. I cannot let them down."

•　　•　　•　　•　　•

At dawn, Lasarion's cobbled-together army was once again on the move as they knight urged them forward. As before, they travelled across the landscape like a raging storm, a single force speeding toward their destiny. Lasarion would fulfill his duty or die trying.

By mid-day, scouts from the small force Brelex had left behind had spotted Lasarion and his army rampaging toward the castle. By mid-afternoon, the combined army from Chrysalis and Balinwald were poised to attack the lightly defended Hall of the Grey Knight. Brelex had never considered that Chrysalis would split its army and commit part of its forces to defend Balinwald. Thus, he had left his own lands and his recently conquered country vulnerable. Now, Lasarion was positioned to punish Brelex for that oversight.

Alexandra barely had time to reach Lasarion and touched his hand softly.

"Good luck," she whispered and again dropped behind him.

In the next instant, Lasarion rushed the castle, his army following him into battle. The scouts who had spotted him far in the distance had returned and sounded the alarm, but the small militia Brelex left behind were far outnumbered. Lasarion's rampaging forces drove into the stronghold, sweeping wave upon wave onto the Hall of the Grey Knight.

Though Brelex's forces had barred the entry to the hall and posted archers on the walls, the small militia could offer only token resistance. Lasarion's archers outnumbered those defending the castle by ten to one, and the wave of arrows quickly dispersed the soldiers on the battlements. With the outer walls of the castle undefended, Lasarion's fighters scaled the walls and opened the doors from the inside, dispersing with the need for a battering ram.

The castle exposed, Lasarion's forces stormed through the grounds. There was little more bloodshed, as most of Brelex's forces had either fallen already or hastened their escape. The few who remained–seeing they were far outnumbered–surrendered immediately. But even so, Lasarion was unsatisfied. There was no sign of Athena, the princess of Balinwald and daughter of Sardenia. The knight searched every crevice of the castle and tore through the dank dungeons below. He was frustrated at every turn.

"Where could she be?" he cursed. "She could not have disappeared."

Lasarion considered the possibility that the princess had already been killed and her body disposed of in whatever manner was most expedient. But as ruthless and Brelex could be, the Grey Knight was even more ambitious. Lasarion calculated that Athena was worth more to Brelex alive than otherwise, at least until he could consolidate his power. Thus, the knight continued his search through the castle.

Finally, Lasarion discovered a small cell deep below the castle which seemed to have been recently occupied. Further inspection bore out the knight's guess: this was surely where the princess had been held captive. Clothing and scraps of writing material confirmed this. But Athena apparently had had no time to leave a message, for there was no clue of her fate. The cell, in fact, was in disarray and showed signs of a recent and hasty exit.

"Find her!" Lasarion ordered, and his soldiers dispersed from the castle.

Lasarion's troops dutifully searched the nearby village house by house. They found a few members of Brelex's army, hiding pathetically. But the villagers, poorly treated and the victims of theft and even worse atrocities, were overjoyed at the arrival of a friendly force. They quickly helped ferret out Brelex's runaway soldiers. Once exposed, a few stood to fight, but most quickly surrendered.

Several of the townspeople, however, reported seeing a small band of soldiers riding in a great hurry through the streets shortly before Lasarion's attack. After much questioning and sifting through information, Lasarion discovered that a woman–most likely the princess–had travelled with them, apparently against her will. How many were there, the knight wondered. He heard as few as two, as many as fifteen or twenty. Finally, he had determined there were no more than six or seven based on the most reliable witnesses.

They have escaped, Lasarion thought. *Damn them.*

But where had they gone? Lasarion took Dakar–and Alexandra after she insisted on accompanying the search–and a small ensemble of his strongest and fastest warriors and followed in the general direction taken by the bandit soldiers. The trail, however, had grown cold. There was no sign of the soldiers and no sign of the princess. Precious few clues offered even a general direction to follow.

Soon, Lasarion grew impatient. With the glint of battle behind him and his emotional level now subdued, his mind now turned toward Roanan and his embattled troops far to the north. Too much time had already been wasted. Even if they left this instant, Lasarion's army had little or no hope of arriving in time. He hardly had time to go in search of a missing princess, no matter how dire her plight. If they arrived at the Watchtower too late, the battle would already be decided. If Roanan was already defeated, Lasarion's army would be alone and hopelessly outnumbered. As important as it was to save Athena, more critical priorities now gnawed at Lasarion's mind.

Suddenly, Lasarion turned from the path, reversed course and rode back toward the Hall of Balinwald. After a moment's hesitation, his companions joined him. Instinctively, they knew their leader's course.

"Where are you going?" Alexandra yelled at the top of her voice.

"To Roanan," Lasarion answered back. "He needs me. He needs us."

"But what about the Princess?" Alexandra asked.

"If we are victorious, we will come back for her," Lasarion said. "If we are not, it won't matter."

· · · · ·

And thus, Lasarion returned with all speed to the Hall of the Grey Knight and began to re-assemble his army for a frantic charge to the Watchtower. It was not an easy task. The troops had been widely dispersed, and many were running down the remnants of Brelex's militia, battling some while imprisoning most.

Slowly, much too slowly for Lasarion's satisfaction, the coalition again merged. But it was an arduous process and preparations took the rest of the day. The survivors of Brelex's forces were effectively jailed and provisions for the army were replenished. Lasarion chose a small group of soldiers to maintain and defend the Hall of the Grey Knight and guard the prisoners–a militia much the same size as Brelex had originally cast. Lasarion was reluctant to spare even that many soldiers, but finally conceded its necessity.

Ultimately, Lasarion was forced to remain at the Hall of Brelex for the night, determined to begin his march at earliest light. His concern made rest elusive. Every moment of delay seemed a greater assurance of defeat at the hands of the enemy. Finally, as the night grew late, Alexandra found him pacing nervously. It took some time to harness his attention, but she succeeded at last.

"You know," she said to Lasarion, torn between determination and desperation, "we'll never reach your friends charging across the countryside, no matter how early we leave or quickly we ride."

"We must try," Lasarion said curtly. "There is no other way."

The knight turned away. But Alexandra made a determined effort to match his pace, following him along the veranda.

"Yes," she said, "there is another path."

The knight stopped suddenly and whirled toward Alexandra. The action caught her by such surprise that she took a quick step backward.

"What do you mean?" Lasarion asked sharply. "I know of no other alternative."

"Few know of the way I speak," Alexandra said mysteriously. She saw Lasarion's brow squint in anger, and she talked quickly. "I have watched Balinwald closely these recent years. Some of us have not been so asleep as you presume. My own spies have foreseen the rise of Brelex. I knew that eventually, somehow, my own land must become involved, or perish. I spoke the truth when I said that few know of this path. My loyal friends stumbled upon it only by accident, and we have kept our discovery secret, for we knew that one day we might use it to our advantage. Little did I know that this would be the time."

Alexandra paused, studying Lasarion carefully.

"Will you trust me?" she asked. "It is but a little way from our original course. I will show you, and you can make your own decision."

Lasarion paused, looking far into the distance toward the battlefield to the north. This was a critical juncture, one that could make the difference between victory and defeat.

"You have proven yourself true many times, and I have come to trust your judgement," Lasarion said. "In all honesty, I have little choice. If what you say is accurate, it is perhaps our only chance to reach Roanan in time. I will follow where you lead."

Alexandra's eye twinkled and a wry smile crossed her face.

"Trusting a female in time of war?" she laughed. "Perhaps there is hope for you after all. In the morning, we must move quickly."

Lasarion agreed. Alexandra left shortly thereafter. The knight wasn't sure if he was more comforted or not.

At dawn's first light, the troops were poised for their last hurdle. The army's enthusiasm was drunk with its victory and even the soldiers from Selin showed renewed enthusiasm. Still, the march between the Hall of the Grey Knight and the Watchtower was daunting. Few knew of the conversation between Lasarion and Alexandra the prior evening and were still expecting a long and arduous march.

Lasarion, however, knew acutely that according to Roanan's original plan, the Red Knight's army would attack the Watchtower at daybreak the following day. Following the traditional path, Lasarion would arrive, two possibly three days too late unless the fight had somehow been delayed, which seemed unlikely. He could only hope Alexandra's alternate path was as promising as she suggested.

Recognizing the realities of the situation, Lasarion's psyche was battered with uncertainty. While he had achieved a small victory at the Hall of the Grey Knight, the prospects for the true battle appeared far more grim. Even with Lasarion's forces, Chrysalis' army was greatly outnumbered. But without them, and without the surprise attack from the flank and rear to hem in Maldur's army, Roanan would be exposed to the full fury of the enemy. Though the Red Knight's army would fight bravely, sheer numbers would pose a battle in which even Roanan would be hard-pressed to succeed. Defeat was inevitable unless Lasarion would somehow achieve the impossible. All depended on Alexandra.

At that moment, the Balinwald princess rode up to Lasarion.

"Are we ready to march?" she asked the knight.

"We are in your hands," Lasarion responded.

Alexandra spurred her horse forward. Once they left the grounds of the Hall of the Grey Knight, she turned the army east and a bit south. At this, Lasarion balked immediately.

"This is the wrong direction entirely," he objected.

"Trust me, I said," Alexandra implored. "I know where I am going."

She paused momentarily, watching Lasarion's facial expressions as he mulled his options.

"I trust you," he finally said. The knight motioned his forces forward.

The army quickened its pace and sped through the wooded countryside of Balinwald. Birds sang softly in languages long forgotten by mortal beings. The sun began to rise into the western sky, and brilliant sunlight would soon drape the landscape once again. But by that time, all traces of Lasarion's army were gone, and no one could say for certain the direction they travelled. Some claimed it was the work of Wizards, but other, less foolish folk, knew that a Wizard's magic could not so blatantly interfere in the works of the peoples of Ambrasian. Still, the disappearance of Lasarion's army would be the topic of much speculation and many stories for years to come.

Far to the north, Roanan's army began their last day's march toward the Watchtower. They would have one more day of relative peace before they would clash with the enemy and soak the battlefield in red. Balinwald was free, but it would remain so only if a far greater peril could be conquered.

CHAPTER 24
CALM BEFORE THE STORM

Roanan's army broke camp early. They moved quickly at first, but by mid-day their pace had slowed considerably as they crossed the Sylil River. The river was a beautiful, lazily flowing waterway that poured from Malinas Lake and flowed south through the eastern borderlands of Karmana. Despite its tranquil appearance, the river ran both wide and deep, and it took significant time for an army the size of Roanan's to cross it.

There was a palpable fear that the Drens or Maldur himself would attack while the force was in such a vulnerable position. Out of caution, Roanan arranged the archers from both the Elvii and his own army along the banks to protect the crossing forces from a surprise attack. But there was no sign of the enemy army and the danger passed without incident.

They are confident in their position, the Red Knight thought. *They believe they have an overwhelming force we cannot match. And they may be right.*

Once across the river, Roanan's army continued their march throughout the day with renewed speed and vigor, hearing not a whisper in the surrounding countryside. Maldur seemed to have finally corralled the unruly Drens and now waited in his stronghold at the Watchtower. Even the Red Knight recognized the strategic advantage held by Maldur and Brelex. While his army had to march across an open field to meet the enemy, their opponent could wait in a fortified position, rested and able to attack them with arrows and catapults well before Roanan's force could even begin an assault.

There is no alternative, the Red Knight thought. *We are walking directly into their lair just as they have planned and there is absolutely nothing we can do to change that.*

Throughout the march, many of the soldiers took this chance to admire momentarily the surrounding countryside. Despite outward confidence, the men knew well that this could in fact be their last look at the landscape of Ambrasian. And though this was quite a distance from the heart and magic of the Hall of Karmana and somewhat dulled by the loss of the Oracle, it was still Karmana and beauty, for the most part, ran rampant. Even so, just as the passing soldiers may have been lulled by the pastoral scenes, evidence of recent Dren raids would become apparent. For every picturesque view, a scorched farmhouse or a destroyed village would provide a sober counterpoint.

Finally, as the sun began to fade and Roanan's army approached their destination, the force camped for the night on the eastern edge of Malinas Lake. Fires were built and flickered crazily in the still night. Only a short distance away, perhaps only a march of a bit more than an hour, lay the overwhelming horde of Maldur and Brelex in the Watchtower.

"Close enough to smell them," Halmar muttered. "And smell them I do."

A heavy guard was posted, though it seemed by now as if Maldur's forces appeared content for the battle to come to them. Still, the entire army slept uneasily and prepared to rise and fight at a moment's notice. Nearly all rested uncomfortably still in their battle gear with their weapons within reach. They would not allow themselves to be caught unprepared by a nighttime attack.

Slowly, as the camp settled into a tenuous slumber, a select few assembled around one of the campfires. They comprised the leaders of this desperate expedition. For many minutes, no one spoke. Siora, the lithe, Elvii figure was the first to break the silence.

"We Elvii have had little contact with Drens except for the recent skirmishes with them," he said. "Are they the cowards they seem to be, slinking about in the night, or do they stand and fight in a true battle?"

"For all their faults," Tabeus answered, "they are ferocious and relentless warriors. They will not back down and will not surrender. Their intensity will challenge even the Elvii."

Raven shivered as he sat on the Wizard's shoulder. The bird cocked his head to one side, as if listening to something far in the distance.

"The Drens will fight until they no longer stir," the Wizard continued. "But they have one weakness. They lack clear peripheral vision. Attack them from the side whenever possible."

Halmar grunted, undoubtedly wondering how such as task would be easily accomplished on the battlefield.

"Of that," the veteran knight said, "our warriors have been told."

The Wizard nodded but raised his hand in caution.

"Yes," Tabeus said, "but it is not as easily accomplished as you may think. The Drens are exceedingly quick on their feet and they swing their swords with vigor. Our soldiers must not underestimate their ability."

Siora and Halmar indicated their understanding. Roanan turned toward the Wizard.

"And what of Maldur, Tabeus?" the Red Knight said. "How powerful will he be, now that Celidia is in possession of the Oracle?"

"He shall be as strong as any knight in Ambrasian," the Wizard answered. "You will need all your skill, strength, and cunning to defeat him."

"Will I be able to?" Roanan pressed. "He was a powerful foe even before the Oracle."

Tabeus remained silent for an agonizing moment.

"That is a difficult question to answer," the Wizard finally said. "The Oracle has strange and mysterious powers. Even I cannot foretell how powerful they will make the Black Knight or even if it will affect him at all. Will the Oracle make him too powerful for any force that comes against him?"

Tabeus paused, the agony of uncertainty coursing across his ancient features.

"I just do not know," the Wizard finally admitted. "That will not be revealed until you meet him sword to sword."

The Red Knight sat pensively, pondering his task.

"There is no choice," he said thoughtfully. "I must find a way to defeat him."

Slowly, Roanan looked across the campfire. He spotted young Dainwirth Lir and smiled wryly.

"Lir, you too have a nearly impossible task," the Red Knight said. "Brelex's soldiers are experienced and well-trained. And you have only your young soldiers and a small troop of Chrysalian warriors to withstand his army. The rest of us will have our hands full of Drens."

Dainwirth Lir acknowledged the Red Knight with the optimism only had by youth.

"We shall hold them until you can aid us," Lir said. "We will not fail you."

At that moment, Mendelheimer strolled by.

"Enough of these grim thoughts," he sang. "It is time for song and dance. If this is to be our last night, it should at least be a happy one."

Halmar rose abruptly, staring at the minstrel with disgust.

"How dare you interrupt such serious discussions . . .," the knight began.

The Red Knight raised his hand, stood and walked over to Halmar and placed a hand on the knight's broad shoulders.

"No, the minstrel is right," Roanan said. "We cannot go into battle with heavy hearts. We have planned as much as possible. With blessings and luck, we shall be victorious against all odds."

Then, the Red Knight turned to Mendelheimer.

"But I shall skip your song, Minstrel," he said. "Your horse can sing better than you."

Mendelheimer bowed deeply.

"This may be true, your majesty," the minstrel answered. "But he has not my good looks."

Roanan laughed and walked away. Quickly, Halmar joined him.

"Your looks are no better than your music," Halmar told the minstrel. "I think I will also pass on your so-called entertainment as well."

The knight spit out the last words.

"Critics," Mendelheimer muttered. "Always critics."

Roanan and Halmar walked along for a long time, both silent in the quiet night.

"I have not known you as well or as long as I would like," the Red Knight told his companion, "and tomorrow we go into battle together, with no assurance that either of us will return."

Roanan looked into the night for a moment.

"I am sorry now that we have had such little time to learn of each other," he continued. "I feel that we are much alike. Both of us have some higher calling that dominates our lives. Neither can live for himself, for that is not good enough nor what the time demands. We must uphold our duty and must stand for what we believe is right. We must be the defenders of our values. We must fight so that others may live freely."

Halmar smiled, acknowledging the King for his kind words.

"Your liege, too, am sorry that we have not known each other better," he said. "But I have watched you grown into adulthood and now assumed your role as our King, I believe you have been called to greatness. There is no one else I would rather follow into battle."

Halmar paused for a moment.

"We will find time to know each other more after tomorrow," he concluded.

"Yes," the Red Knight agreed. "After tomorrow, we must set about making many things right."

●　　　●　　　●　　　●　　　●

It had grown deep into the night, the blackness pierced by a glowing moon now just less than half, a less bright NightSun, and brilliant and luminous stars across the sky. The air was cool but fresh, and only the singing of the Malinas, a small reddish bird unique to this area of Karmana, broke the peaceful quiet. The Red Knight and Halmar parted paths, and Roanan left his band of warriors behind as he walked alone toward the lake hidden behind a thicket of trees.

The King's path alarmed several of Roanan's nearby guards, but the Red Knight drew Infernus and assured them he would be safe. He allowed that they remain nearby in case aid was necessary.

"I suspect you'll hear if I need you," he assured them.

The lake was as calm as the night, a paradise surrounded by a world under siege. The water was bluish-green and rippled only slightly. An unseen fish splashed further from the shore. Roanan walked along the lake slowly, his weary mind and body temporarily renewed by the unspoiled nature around him. He sat down on the grassy, damp earth and looked up at the stars. He momentarily wished that he could return to the carefree life of a child where the stars were his companions and the darkness full of harmless mystery. He yearned this were all over, but he knew it was only the beginning.

An insect flew by, flickering a greenish-tinted light. Roanan heard the voices of his followers in the distance but paid little attention. He picked up a stone that fit comfortably in his hand and stared at it for a brief moment. He raised his arm and threw the stone in a sharp straight line. It hit the lake, causing a splash then another and finally another. A drop of water landed on the dry chapped lips of the Red Knight. The impact of the stone made the water ripple crazily, tiny armies battering at impregnable lands. Roanan watched the battle for as long as it lasted, then slowly turned away.

As he did so, a figure emerged from the shadows and sang softly in a melodious voice:

March on toy soldiers
You've come to meet your destiny
Forget your old lovers
The best of you will hold the key;
From the west and from the east
The knights will come to claim their prize
To slay the evil beast
And tear off the liar's disguise

Your love and your life
And everything around you
May hinge on the battle
That now stands before you
You've got to give your best
You've got no time to rest
You have to keep on pushing on
No one knows the fallen fawn

March on hopeful soldiers
Life's greatest prize just may be won
Prove you're the greater
Don't turn in fear and start to run;
Send a message to your land
You've gone for glory and for fame
The end is now near at hand
In this world's most dangerous game

March on weary soldiers
The battle grows so long and hard
Your dreams are far distant
Your hopes once so high are now scarred;
Soon the battle must begin
The burden falls on me and you
We cannot fail here
And we have so very much to do

Roanan rubbed his eyes and peered through the dark night. He could hardly believe his eyes.

"Mendelheimer?" he finally asked. "Is that you?"

"The one and only, my Lord," the minstrel answered. "As far as I am aware, I am the only minstrel who has displayed the courage to accompany you."

"You also display a talent unknown before now," the Red Knight said. "Why do you not always sing like this?"

Mendelheimer bowed greatfully.

"Thank you, my Lord," the minstrel said humbly. "To answer your question, I found I can be more effective as a buffoon than as a serious bard. In that way, I can keep the minds of those in peril off their troubles. In your case, however, I thought a more thoughtful tune would be more appropriate."

"You are certainly a finer minstrel than is given credit for," Roanan said. "It is too bad Halmar could not have heard your latest work."

The Red Knight smiled approvingly.

"Perhaps you will be a worthy historian after all," he added.

"Do not give me too much praise," the minstrel said. "It has taken me the entire journey to compose this song . . .

"And," he finally added. "Preston helped."

•   •   •   •   •

Only a short distance away, the activity at the Watchtower suddenly showed more urgency. Brelex rushed into the central chamber and quickly found Maldur and Celidia.

"Our spies have returned," the Grey Knight announced. "Roanan's army has camped on the edge of Malinas Lake. We do battle tomorrow–finally!"

"Tomorrow?" Maldur screamed. "These idiots are not nearly ready."

"Quiet, Maldur," Celidia demanded. "You are the only idiot who is not ready. We have been waiting for this moment for many days. You and your soldiers have done nothing but whine because I have insisted we wait for the battle to come to us. Now it is here and we will fight just as we planned."

The Sorceress turned back to Brelex purposely.

"How many are there?" she asked.

The Grey Knight smiled.

"Our spies say there are not more than eight or nine thousand warriors," he answered.

The Sorceress glanced at Maldur, a satisfied smile crossing her face.

"You see, we have then outnumbered more than two-to-one," she said. "Even you should have no trouble achieving victory on the battlefield."

Maldur looked outside at the great assemblage of soldiers now were in the final preparations for battle.

"Yes," Maldur agreed. "Perhaps the great Roanan has finally blundered, coming into battle unprepared, outnumbered, and overconfident. Well, this will be his last mistake."

"Just be sure you are not the one to blunder," Celidia muttered.

"Have you no faith in me?" Maldur asked, raising his eye toward the Sorceress.

Celidia looked at Maldur, shrugged her shoulders, and walked away.

"On the battlefield, I have seen enough of your skill and your strength to know you are a formidable warrior," she said as she paused momentarily. "Still, it is good we have the Oracle. Despite our apparent advantage, I want every edge available to assure our absolute and unquestioned victory."

Celidia turned and left the room. She left Brelex and Maldur looking at each other.

"Come," Brelex finally said. "Let us go over our battle plan one last time. Let us make sure we crush Roanan and his brave fools at every turn."

•   •   •   •   •

It was some time before Roanan returned to the main camp. Mendelheimer had left the Red Knight gazing out onto the lake, quiet in the solemn night.

Roanan slipped back among the troops mostly unnoticed. As he did so, he heard the minstrel weave a tune to an attentive audience around one of the larger fires. The Red Knight moved into the shadows and listened to Mendelheimer's tale.

As a stormy twilight turns to dusk
I search among the sky
For stars that glisten and those that hope
And wonder why they pass me by

For many years I wandered
Through strange and distant lands
Found beyond one's reason
And life's everyday demands

I went in search of music
That is played behind the moon
And though I never captured it
I learned to play its tune

And in this mystic world of mine
Reality was lost
Any need or longing felt
Suppressed at any cost

And then the veil was shattered
And the sun rebuked the blind
And from this joyful clamor were cast
The demons of the mind

Mendelheimer gazed into the distance at the wistful peacefulness of Malinas Lake as he completed his tune. His listeners sat silently watching the dying embers of the night fire. War cries echoed in the distance. Tomorrow would bring a crimson morning, but tonight was one of anxious contemplation.

Mendelheimer looked across his attentive audience.

"There is a tale that goes with that song," the minstrel said. "Many years ago before the bards of Ambrasian recorded the events of history, it is said there was a young knight that was known as Rolyn Searcher.

"The story continues that Rolyn was cursed by an aggrieved spell caster," the minstrel continued. "In fact, Rolyn was truly heir to a fledgling kingdom but had been cast out by a powerful hex that would not allow him to claim his rightful destiny. It was said further that Rolyn could not again claim that kingdom until he overcame great suffering and discovered something essential to his own being. Thus, Rolyn became known as the Searcher.

"And so it was. Rolyn Searcher walked the early terrain of Ambrasian from east to west and back again for many years. In that time, he was accosted by bandits that foraged ruthlessly through the lawless hills and was scorned by townspeople in the plains who held the dark traveler in suspicion. Unwelcome wherever he went. Rolyn Searcher lived the life of a fugitive and an outcast.

"However," Mendelheimer said with dramatic flair and emphasis, "the physical suffering of Rolyn Searcher did not match the torture of his mind. Stripped of both heritage and kingdom, the Searcher went alone into a wide land that neither knew him nor acknowledged him. And in that land, Rolyn searched for friendship and for love. In friendship, Rolyn Searcher, at times, succeeded. For though it came slowly, and though he was often scorned and beaten, Rolyn Searcher won loyal companions who recognized his integrity despite his dark appearance. But love came grudgingly, and here, Rolyn Searcher failed in all quests. Indeed, here was what Rolyn had lost, that which was essential to his being: the Searcher had lost the ability to love and be loved."

Mendelheimer paused and looked across his audience, who now watched and listened in rapt attention.

"And it seemed that Rolyn Searcher's quest was without hope and that he was bound to continue his quest forever on," the minstrel said.

"In contemplation, Rolyn Searcher walked among the Great Forest one night–the Forest was much vaster in those days than it is today. Through the dim light, Rolyn Searcher barely saw the figures descending upon him and reacted too late. The forest bandits had struck once again.

"Beaten and bleeding, Rolyn Searcher stumbled blindly through the trees. Near exhaustion, he saw a small cottage and, oblivious to any possible danger, used the last remnants of energy to struggle to the door and fell hard against it. It was there he collapsed and lost consciousness.

"Much later, Rolyn Searcher awoke among soft sheets, his wounds dressed and bound. He opened his eyes and met the caring gaze of a beautiful maiden. 'Who . . ?' he stammered.

"The maiden pressed her finger to Rolyn's lips and hushed him to be quiet. 'My name is Terayslie,' she said. 'But that can wait. You are gravely wounded and need to heal. Rest now and get well.'

"And Rolyn Searcher looked at the beautiful face of this woman who had risked her life in the middle of the night to save him, and saw softness and warmth, gentleness and compassion. He trusted her without question.

"In the ensuing days of his recovery," Mendelheimer continued, "Rolyn Searcher came to know well the fair maiden Terayslie. She was without question the most generous and thoughtful of all creatures. Compassionate in both body and spirit, Terayslie gave to Rolyn the ability to feel emotions he had not felt in many years. In truth, he discovered that which he had lost long ago: the ability to love.

"But though Terayslie did feel affection for Rolyn, she was reluctant to return his feelings. For her heart was torn between the new love of Rolyn and that of an old love from a man named Derikan. Though she had lost Derikan long ago, he had mortally wounded her heart, and it was more than Rolyn could overcome. Though Derikan was self-serving and had hurt Terayslie often, the ties that bind are surely strong and strange.

"And thus, Rolyn Searcher left the cottage of Terayslie and wandered the forest once again. At his weakest moments, he wept openly, for it seemed that he was doomed to see his salvation but never be able to achieve it. And Rolyn found Terayslie unique among all the maidens of Ambrasian.

"Time passed, but Rolyn found he could not dismiss Terayslie so easily. So he went in search of an answer to his quest. First, he travelled to the provincial King and asked to borrow great riches to win a fair maiden. The King knew of Rolyn and his plight, but said, 'Rolyn, you are young and idealistic, strong and talented. One day, all of Ambrasia will heed your call. But you must learn that wealth alone will not replace that which comes from within yourself. You must win your true love in another way.'

"Rolyn went next to a wizard and asked for a spell to win Terayslie's heart. But the wizard replied, 'Young knight, a wizard must not dabble in the strange and subtle emotions of the peoples of Ambrasian. A spell will not win your love's heart truly and forever. Love must be given openly and freely and must be earned. You must win trust, understanding, and affection by your actions. You must share all of yourself with the one whom you truly love. That love will be greater than any spell that even the most powerful of wizards can weave.'

"Finally, Rolyn went to a bard and asked him to compose a song that would win Terayslie. But the bard merely laughed. 'You cannot win love with a song,' he replied, 'and the words must come from your own heart. You cannot force your love upon her, nor force if from her through guilt or deception.'"

Mendelheimer paused to allow the lessons of his tale to simmer in the minds of his audience.

'Though empty-handed, Rolyn Searcher eventually returned to the cottage of Terayslie. And in the time that followed, Rolyn learned much of himself. 'Terayslie,' he said one day, 'I come with no gifts to woo you, no spells to enchant you, and no songs to capture your heart. I bring to you only myself. But I have learned that may count for more than any gift I could produce. For I have found that love must flow from within and only from there find its true form. I swear on my honor, my knighthood, and my kingdom to stand by you until my last breath if you will have me."

"And Terayslie slowly felt the barriers she had built collapse and came to love and accept Rolyn Searcher. And eventually, with the curse lifted, Rolyn became complete once again. And he returned to his kingdom and, together with his queen, grew his land the greatest in all of Ambrasian. And that land became known as Chrysalis, the guardian of the West. Rolyn became the first true King of the Western Land."

All were quiet for a moment. The Wizard looked up first.

"Thus are the stuff of legends made," Tabeus said, "and so began the land of Chrysalis and the line of Kings who rule to this day. Well told, minstrel."

Mendelheimer bowed, acknowledging the Wizard's compliment.

"But there also lies an important lesson," Tabeus continued, "for love and war are much the same. Remember, the mastery and control of both must come deep within each of us. Tomorrow, we go into battle, and we must reach into ourselves for strength previously unknown. It may be our greatest hope for victory."

•　　•　　•　　•　　•

Later that night, with the embers of the fire slowly dying, Roanan and Tabeus sat alone. The rest of the Red Knight's cabinet of war leaders had already retired to their own camp.

"The minstrel really is an accomplished artist," the Red Knight chuckled. "Who would have thought it possible?"

The Wizard seemed unsurprised.

"I always suspected there was more to him than appeared," he said. "Heroes arise in the strangest of forms in times of peril."

Roanan studied the Wizard, his lined face illuminated by the fire.

"Yes," Roanan agreed. "But I am afraid Mendelheimer's music and tales will be of little help tomorrow. The Drens are not likely to be impressed by either. What we need more is the arrival of Lasarion and his army. And of that, you have said little."

"I am afraid we cannot count on their assistance," Tabeus admitted. "Lasarion has undergone a great many perils of his own, but of late even I am blind to his fate. I have heard he has freed Balinwald, but whether he has found the princess and what path he has followed thereafter, I cannot say. Even Raven has been unable to discover any news. It is most curious, but I cannot judge whether his path is for good or for ill."

The Red Knight considered the disturbing but not unexpected news. He looked dolefully to the south, wondering where his cousin may be and what fate he had encountered.

"Then we will have to fight without him," Roanan said firmly with renewed resolve. "We will do what we can. I doubt Maldur and Brelex will wait to start their attack for their arrival."

"We may fail," Tabeus said. "We are significantly outnumbered and they hold a superior position."

"That is all true," the Red Knight said. "Yet we have no choice but to fight and hope that the justice of our cause will be enough to prevail. I, for one, am ready for Maldur."

Tabeus studied the young king intently.

"You will have to face him," the Wizard said. "You are the only one in Ambrasian with even a chance of defeating him. But do not underestimate your foe–with the presence of the Oracle, he is likely far stronger than before. He will be a most formidable foe."

Roanan knew this was true.

"Then I will have to be as my ancestor, Rolyn," he concluded, "and find the strength to match him within myself."

Tabeus finally forced himself to smile.

"I am certain that you have more strength than either you or I know," the Wizard assured him. "But now, it is time to get what rest we can. The morning will come quickly."

It was a cold, tense night and long, passing as slowly as a leaf falls to the ground. Roanan's army slept fitfully, their weapons in hand, as they remained a breath away from the enemy. Throughout the night, guards from both camps peered through the darkness suspiciously. Each sound made them jump and redouble their patrols. The soldiers felt a mix of anticipation and fear, the promise of glory and the terror of death just beyond their fingertips. For some, the next day would bring heroic acts, courageous battles, and daring risks. For others, all that awaited was a fiery death on a blood-ridden field. The destiny of Ambrasian was at stake. But would it be a day of triumph for good or for evil? Even the Wizard could not tell, for it was not their task to decide the affairs of the peoples of the land. Throughout Ambrasian, forces stirred. But it was here, on the fields before the Watchtower, that legends would be born or dreams would perish. Tabeus did not rest this night. He sat silently beside the sleeping body of the Red Knight, Raven on his shoulder, wondering whether he had done all he could.

And whether that would be enough.

Tomorrow will tell, the Wizard thought.

Chapter 25
Question of Right,
Galactic Date 2142-08-14

The crew of the Explorer continued to watch the developing series of events on the planet's surface with greater and greater concern as the moment of the battle came closer. Three-dimensional holographs in the Command Center showed the shifting armies coming closer and closer to actual combat. As the tensions on the ground boiled toward the inevitable conflict, the mood among the ship's crew shifted to a darker tone.

At the precipice of so much death and destruction, second thoughts were unavoidable. Some of the crew felt like voyeurs preparing to watch a vile carnage they had no right to view. Others wondered if the policy of non-interference should be discarded. Many of the crew members had never been exposed to the bloody barbarism they were about to view. Their stomachs churned at the thought of the wanton violence on the horizon.

"Captain," Officer Penra said, "what if the forces of Maldur, Brelex, and Celidia are victorious? What will become of this planet? Who knows what horrors the natives will endure? We may see an all-out genocide."

Captain Evenru sighed. While he understood Penra's concern and sympathized with his viewpoint, he had little leeway in his charter as captain.

"The Galactic Command policy of not directly interfering with developing cultures has no exceptions," he sighed. "No matter the circumstances. You are well aware of that."

Penra could recite the non-interference order word for word, just as every officer that was part of Galactic Command.

"But Captain, these are extraordinary circumstances," the officer argued. "Thousands will die in the battle. Not only families, but entire species may be destroyed. And if Roanan's army is defeated . . ."

Penra left the thought go unfinished.

Evenru considered the situation once again. The Captain admitted to himself the situation on the ground would turn cruel and merciless at daybreak. The battlefield would be soaked not only with blood, but the shattered limbs, broken bodies, and the entrails of the combatants.

But against that, the Captain weighed the risks of interference. How would a medieval culture be uprooted by the sudden entry of advanced technology? And while on the surface the sides of good and evil appeared clear, would that opinion withstand the lens of history? What if the reign of Roanan became just as cruel and tyrannical as that of his opponents? History across multiple worlds was littered with the tales of seemingly benign leaders turning savage and barbarous.

Not to mention that both he as Captain and his entire crew would be brought up on charges. They not only would lose their commissions, but likely would end up in a detention center as well, their reputations and legacies destroyed. It would tarnish the reputation of the planet Lux across the galaxy.

Evenru sighed deeply and continued to monitor the various transmissions of the ship's drones.

"Maintain current course and continue observation only," he said. "We have no orders that would permit direct interference."

Kevo, who had remained silent during the discussion, responded immediately.

"Wise choice, Captain," the AI said.

Evenru grunted in resignation.

"I wonder," he said.

CHAPTER 26
THE BATTLE OF THE ORACLE

Trumpets greeted the morning as it awoke in the east. Rain threatened in the distance. The air was pungent. Both armies now came face to face with the moment of the inevitable conflict.

Roanan's troops stirred early, and with quiet determination, prepared for the battle to come. In the pre-dawn hours of this fateful day, the Red Knight moved from camp to camp, saying little but telling a tale of hope and destiny, sorrow and triumph, with only his eyes.

What little there was that still needed to be said was done so. But the knights, the warriors and the common soldiers who made up Roanan's army had not traveled this distance without knowledge of their mission or their desperate odds. Their words were one of hope, with promises of reunions and shared holidays to come. What inner dread any soldier felt was left unsaid.

Soon, the first rays of the sun broke through the ominous clouds, dispersing the threat from above and blistering the landscape for the conflict below. Soon thereafter, Roanan returned to Tabeus' side.

"We have come far, my friend," the Red Knight said, "and we have endured much. Now we have arrived at our destiny. Is this where our story ends, or begins?"

"The answer to that question eludes even a Wizard," Tabeus said wryly. "Today is an affair primarily between the peoples of Ambrasian. Even the Oracle does not lie at the heart of this battle. This day will decide if this land will follow the light or the dark. My magic will mean little this day–it is a mere seed in a long field of wheat."

"Your presence has already meant much," Roanan assured him. "Let's hope we can prevail today and maintain the light into the future."

Around them, preparations continued. The army slowly congregated into divisions and within those into its lines of battle. The sound and the smell of the nearby enemy pierced the air as the war cries drifted over the plain.

Roanan rode Alajar briskly among the troops, organizing, cajoling, encouraging. Satisfied, he returned once again to Tabeus, who sat silently with Raven perched on his shoulder. The Red Knight looked at the bird strangely for a moment, for Raven appeared to be peering far to the south. But matters more critical soon demanded Roanan's immediate attention.

Concerns both grave and trivial danced through Roanan's mind. A few minutes later, Roanan approached the Wizard again.

"Where," he asked, "is that confounded minstrel of ours?"

Tabeus smiled, the first bit of respite he allowed himself that morning.

"You are need of a song at this moment?" the Wizard chuckled. "Do not be concerned. He will be along presently. He could not awaken his horse this morning."

"Tabeus, when we return to Chrysalis, I shall offer the minstrel a home," Roanan said. "Despite his antics, we owe Mendelheimer a great debt."

"When we return?" the Wizard asked with a raised eyebrow.

"When we return," Roanan repeated with conviction. "We must and we will. There can be no other outcome."

The Wizard smiled, pleased at the Red Knight's optimism.

"If the minstrel gives you such confidence, his worth is far greater than it at first appears," Tabeus noted.

At that instant, a bedraggled Mendelheimer rode up alongside the king and the Wizard, his horse clearly moving reluctantly.

"I am certain that Preston is part mule," the minstrel said, not bothering to greet the two.

The Red Knight laughed.

"Or perhaps a very intelligent horse," Roanan noted. "He appears to want to avoid battle at all costs."

"Do not laugh so easily," Tabeus interjected. "Horses are often quite wise–perhaps more so than their masters."

"Speaking of that," Roanan added as he examined the minstrel up and down, "do you think even a minstrel should go into battle without a sword?"

"I do not own one, my Lord," Mendelheimer answered. "And I doubt I could use one properly if I did."

"How will you stop an oncoming Dren?" the Red Knight asked. "With a song?"

The minstrel shrugged.

"I could try, my Lord."

"Drens do not appreciate music," Roanan answered. "Especially during battle."

So despite Mendelheimer's protestations, Roanan ordered the minstrel be fitted with a sword and a hauberk to provide at least some modicum of protection. When he was handed the sword, however, he nearly staggered underneath its weight. As he swung the weapon unsteadily through the air, even Mendelheimer realized the hopelessness of his ever staving off an attack.

"Does this come with an owner's manual?" the minstrel finally asked.

Halmar rode by just in time to see the minstrel examining the sword curiously.

"The sharp ends sticks out," he shouted through his gruff laughter.

Mendelheimer bowed, nearly stabbing himself in the foot in the process.

Meanwhile, the Drens' ruckus had grown louder and nearer, and the Red Knight's army knew the combined forces of Maldur and Brelex would soon bear down on them as an angry mob in full fury. Roanan gathered his closest friends once more: Tabeus, Halmar, Dainwirth Lir, Toranis, the Elvii Siora–and the minstrel. He barked last-minute instructions as the army swirled into action, wishing each other hope and good fortune. The Red Knight clasped the hand of each of these close friends, held it for a second, and then joined the dispersing forces. The horses of the knights' cavalry reared in anticipation. The dust grew thick.

Roanan's forces knew their positions. The Red Knight himself would lead the bulk of his troops against the main force of Maldur and the

Drens. With him would go the brunt of the Chrysalian warriors, along with Tabeus and Toranis. Halmar and Dainwirth Lir would take the rest of the soldiers, and together with the young forces trained by Karmin, face Brelex's seasoned army. Hopefully, they would hold them long enough until Roanan could dispatch aid. With Roanan's host straddling the edge of the Great Forest as closely as possible, Siora's Elvii would move through the cover of the trees, using their natural habitat to help neutralize the far greater numbers of the Black Knight's and Brelex's forces.

As a wheel turns slowly, then gradually picks up speed, now did Roanan's army move toward the plain before the Watchtower. The avalanche of soldiers gathered momentum as it progressed, becoming a mass of rolling thunder, unstoppable and undeterred.

It was not long before the two sides caught sight of each other. Their vision was hazy at first, clouds of dirt and dust obscuring the indeterminable masses. Slowly, the sight became clearer as lines of foot soldiers and cavalry on horseback rushed angrily toward each other, the eyes of each warrior filled with disdain and resolve. Each side strained to measure their foe. Trumpets blared, soldiers shouted, swords were drawn. The earth shook violently beneath the feet and the hooves of the furious masses. The speed of the approaching armies grew even greater as they closed on each other, and the plain became a swirling cacophony of confusion, sounds blending into one another until they became indistinguishable. Some warriors saw destiny before them. Others, for the first time, only saw their fear. In either case, there was no turning back.

Roanan glanced at Tabeus for the last time before battle.

"This is why you and I were placed on Ambrasian," he said. "Whatever our fate, our legacy is written today on this battlefield."

The Wizard smiled and gave him an understanding nod. Roanan raised Infernus and spurred Alajar on to one last death-defying charge.

"I will never understand the mortals of Ambrasian," Tabeus said to Raven. "They feel most alive at the very moment when their lives hang by the merest thread."

"I noticed that as well," the bird observed. "I have heard worms feel much the same way just before we snatch them."

"Quite an inappropriate analogy, don't you think?" the Wizard asked.

"Perhaps," Raven acknowledged.

Just before the two armies clashed, Maldur ordered the archers and the Drens operating the catapults on the ramparts of the Watchtower to fire at will at Roanan's oncoming forces. A combination of Drens and soldiers from Brelex's army filled the skies with arrows that crossed over their own army and over the plain between the forces, finding their marks as members of Roanan's army fell. Brelex's archers were far more effective than those of the Drens, who were more comfortable with swords and axes than bows. Still, enough hit their marks.

The Drens however, had covered the stones launched from the catapults with a flammable substance and sent fiery boulders into the fray. Roanan's own archers and the Elvii returned fire, and soon the skies were filled with deadly projectiles flying in every direction. Still, the armies trudged on, moving closer and closer.

In a dance of seeming slow motion, the two armies finally met. Lir and Halmar's forces led the charge, meeting Brelex's forces with conviction. Then the Drens poured into battle with Roanan, disordered but ferocious and were met with fierce resistance by the army of the Red Knight.

The sound of metal filled the battlefield. Sword clashed against sword, shield against shield. Armor was pierced, flesh torn. For those foot soldiers protected only by leather armor, their blood soon stained the tortured earth beneath them a deep reddish brown. Those on horseback drove through the masses as hard as they could, but many Cadaren and Drens were toppled. Dust swirled, choking off the air. Cries of pain died in mid-scream, hewn bodies fell and were mercilessly trampled. Many who had never seen a battle before today became ill at the carnage.

Warriors fought until exhaustion, then summoned more strength to continue. Their swords flashed and met in a field of confusion, with hundreds of companions and enemies fighting and falling all around them. Solders soon discovered there was no glory on the battlefield, merely a fight for survival.

Roanan urged Alajar on, and the horse carried the Red Knight into battle. With lightning blows, Roanan wielded Infernus as a weapon of terror, killing three Drens at a time, the last its head toppling from its body with one swift, clean strike.

The fight continued, both soldier and Dren dropping, the ground slick with a sickly and ominous growing pool of blood. The sun again retreated behind a thick grey cloud layer. One more, the skies threatened to burst open. Silently, Mendelheimer watched the slaughter safely from a rise beyond the battlefield. He could not write a word.

· · · · ·

Almost immediately, the battle with Brelex and his army took a grim turn. The Grey Knight's seasoned forces cooly cut their way through the young solders led by Halmar and Dainwirth Lir. Though game, the inexperienced warriors were no match for Brelex's battle-tested and avaricious troops. Chrysalis' solders slowly lost ground.

It was not long before Brelex, the Grey Knight, stood face-to-face with Halmar, one of the Red Knight's most loyal and most-accomplished knights. Their eyes met in an icy stare. Wordlessly, they rushed at each other, their swords clanging together. As powerful as Halmar was, Brelex at least matched and likely exceeded the veteran knight's strength. The Grey Knight's thrust forced Halmar to lose his balance, and he was thrown from his horse.

Brelex turned and grinned menacingly. He charged at Halmar again, driving his horse toward the fallen knight in a vicious attempt to finish him. Halmar lunged away at the last moment, barely avoiding the blade. Brelex turned and rushed again, but Halmar deftly caught the Grey Knight's sword with his own, toppling Brelex from his own horse.

The Grey Knight leapt from the ground angrily and stalked Halmar. The knight faced Brelex squarely, both of their horses lost in the clouds of battle, only the skill of each warrior remaining between them. For the first time, Halmar noted the sheer size of the giant Brelex.

"You are an old man," Brelex spit at his adversary. "You have no place on a battlefield. Prepare to die."

"Prepare yourself," Halmar responded. "There's nothing worse than a knight whose mouth works faster than his sword."

Brelex growled and once more rushed Halmar. Their swords met in mid-air. Again and again, their blades pierced the air, each knight using all the force and skill they could muster. Brelex remained the aggressor, and Halmar was forced to parry his opponent's constant attack. Their weapons battered at each other's defenses, slicing at the light armor each wore for protection. At length, Halmar's strength waned under the furious assault of the Grey Knight. Halmar's skill was great, but paled when pitted against one of the strongest and most ferocious of all warriors in Ambrasian. Brelex slashed at Halmar quickly, catching his arm and cutting it deeply. Brelex swung again, planting his sword in Halmar's chest. The knight dropped to his knees.

"Slime," Halmar gasped. "You will not defeat us."

Brelex laughed cruelly.

"You certainly won't stop me," he scoffed, and drove his sword home one more time. Halmar collapsed, blood pouring from his lifeless body.

Brelex pulled his sword roughly from Halmar's corpse and went in search of his horse. But as he turned, a young scraggly soldier who seemed no older than a boy blocked his path.

"Out of my way," the Grey Knight demanded. "You are hardly worth my time."

The unlikely warrior stood his ground.

"You have killed my friend," Dainwirth Lir said shakily. "You will have to kill me to pass."

Brelex stopped and looked contemptuously at his scrawny opponent.

"So be it, fool," Brelex said, once again bringing his sword to an attacking position. "Another one with a death wish."

The Grey Knight advanced toward Lir.

•　　　•　　　•　　　•

Roanan left the battle briefly and rode alongside the Wizard Tabeus. The recent turn of events greatly dismayed the Red Knight.

"Halmar is dead," he said, fighting the sadness in his voice.

"That is unfortunately true," Tabeus said. "He and many others. Halmar fought bravely, but the Grey Knight was too powerful a foe."

The Red Knight remained silent, considering the grave circumstances.

"Brelex's army has ours in serious danger," the Wizard said. "Nor does the rest of our army fare any better against the vast number of Drens that oppose us."

Roanan nodded and peered back over the battlefield. Tabeus' assessment was inarguably correct. Drens were everywhere and their flow seemed unabated. The young warriors led by Halmar had become even more disorganized and disoriented after the knight's death. The surprising quickness of Maldur's forces had neutralized even the accuracy of the Elvii's arrows. Siora's forces were hard-pressed by a troop of the foul beings attacking in the Great Forest.

"It appears to be grim," Roanan said as he assessed the scene.

The Red Knight seemed to go deep within himself for a moment, then just as suddenly appeared to become infused with new vigor.

"We shall just have to fight harder," he concluded.

The Red Knight waved toward Toranis who rode nearby. The young knight quickly joined him.

"This way," Roanan cried, pointing Infernus toward the battle.

"Right behind you," Toranis agreed.

Together, the two rode into the thick of the conflict, and with sudden fury, charged an oncoming group of Drens. Tabeus watch as their swords hewed this way and that, Roanan's Infernus and Toranis' own noble blade cleaving a divide through the dusty terrain. In a few minutes, the two knights emerged unscathed. Roanan had killed twenty-two Drens, Toranis another ten.

"That may hold the flood temporarily," Tabeus said. "But it is the proverbial finger in the dike. Even you cannot defeat an entire army."

The Red Knight was about to respond when he suddenly turned and avoided the edge of a Drens' sword. In one motion, Roanan raised Infernus and swung powerfully, slitting his enemy diagonally from his shoulder to his waist.

Roanan turned toward Tabeus with conviction.

"We shall not surrender," Roanan said. "We cannot. For the sake of Ambrasian as we know it, we must emerge victorious, somehow, some way."

Without awaiting a response, the Red Knight urged Alajar forward, and with Toranis by his side, he thundered back into battle.

Tabeus looked quietly at Raven gently perched on his should and noticed the faraway look in the bird's eye.

"What do you see?" the Wizard asked.

"Hope," Raven answered. "And hope again."

On the edges of the Great Forest, Roanan's forces were just as challenged as elsewhere.

"Stay focused!" Siora shouted to his Elvii comrades. "Help will arrive! Until then, aim true and fight bravely."

The Elvii were under attack and the Drens had proven quicker than Siora had imagined. He fervently wished that help was in fact on the way, as quickly as possible. But as he spoke the words, the Elvii knew it could well be an empty promise. The rest of Roanan's forces were as hard-pressed as the Elvii and a sense of hopelessness had pervaded the troops.

A group of Elvii marksmen shot simultaneously, killing a dozen Drens. But the enemy continued to advance and their numbers were overwhelming. Elvii continued to drop in their enemy's relentless path, and Siora grieved the sudden mortality of an otherwise long-lived race. Many of the Elvii were forced into hand-to-hand combat, and the sheer strength, viciousness, and number of Drens challenged even their speed and skill. For every Dren the Elvii killed, it seemed that three took their place.

"Filthy beasts, they are," Siora muttered. He loaded his bow and fired quickly, killing an onrushing Dren. "Even Maldur is tolerable compared to these abominations."

Siora shook his head in an odd mixture of disgust and sadness. His comrades through generations were dropping one-by-one around him. The Drens continued to pour in, forcing the Elvii deeper into the forest. Soon, the undergrowth would become too thick for even the Elvii to travel swiftly, and as a mass they would be forced to turn and battle the Dren herd solely in hand-to-hand combat.

And now, Siora saw something that made him even more angry and desperate. The Dren lieutenant, Izuburu-Gy, was leading a troop of Drens to the edge of the forest. The lieutenant and each of his companions carried a flaming torch.

"Set fire at will," the Dren leader proclaimed. "Burn the entire forest to the ground if you must!"

Quickly and without remorse, each Dren brought their fiery weapons to the trees before them. Setting fire to the ancient and beautiful Great Forest, these vile creatures–hell bent on destruction–would not only annihilate the Elvii, but many other inhabitants of the primordial woods. As the flames crackled and enveloped the edge of the forest, Siora bellowed a great cry of woe and thrust himself once more into battle.

•   •   •   •   •

"The Oracle has given my strength I never thought possible," Maldur beamed as he peered with satisfaction at the surrounding fighting. "I can feel it coursing through my veins. The battle is going better than even I could have hoped."

The Black Knight sat haughtily in the middle of the battlefield, proudly surveying the carnage and urging the Drens onward. Presently, he spotted Celidia from the corner of his eye.

"Fight, you moron," she shouted using her powers to project her voice over the sounds of battle and across the plain. "Do you think you are out here for decoration?"

Maldur scowled and turned towards three of Roanan's oncoming warriors. With short, swift and powerful blows, he disposed of them easily.

"Satisfied?" he asked turning back toward Celidia.

"Behind you," the Sorceress shouted.

Maldur turned and saw another soldier rushing toward him. Moving quickly, the Black Knight faced his opponent squarely. After a furious but short battle, the soldier dropped. Maldur again looked smugly toward Celidia.

"At least he can fight," she muttered, then moved her attention elsewhere.

Shortly thereafter, the Sorceress retreated from the battlefield and moved back into the outer chambers of the Watchtower, Celidia went alone into the room holding the Oracle. Eyeing the great prize, she knelt before it. Though Maldur spouted loudly of the Oracle's affect, the Sorceress knew she had not yet fully harnessed its power.

The Oracle was radiant and pulsating, spewing its power to those that possessed it. Or was it the Oracle that held them in its possession? At this moment, Celidia did not even consider the thought.

"Give me strength," the Sorceress intoned, "and my strength will become one with yours. Our power will flow into the limbs of my warriors and make them invincible in battle."

As Celidia muttered her evil chant, her will became more enmeshed with the power of the Oracle. She was mastering its secrets more and more. And as those powers increased, the Drens suddenly burst forward with new-found fury, battling even more fiercely. Stunned by the rage of their enemy, Roanan's forces fell back even further as Chrysalian blood drenched the bleak landscape.

• • • • •

Dainwirth Lir had proven to be a more difficult foe than Brelex had expected. The lank, ill-coordinated young soldier had stood his ground, matching blows with the older, stronger and more experienced Grey Knight. Even Lir could not explain what maintained him in this hopeless quest. Perhaps his earlier embarrassment against Maldur had lifted him to feats that even he was unaware that he was capable. Or possibly his desire to avenge Halmar's death spurred him onward. For Lir, however, there was little time to consider his performance. He was literally in the fight for his life against one of the most feared warriors in Ambrasian.

Brelex pushed himself away from Lir.

"You have been lucky so far, you sorry excuse for a warrior," the Grey Knight mocked. "I shall finish you surely now."

"I would think a knight of such acclaim would fight with his sword instead of his mouth," Lir responded more bravely than he felt.

Brelex spit out his mocking words.

"Your friend said the same thing," he said. "You see his fate. Maybe I can put both of your heads on a spike you can share."

"I will not let you dishonor a knight as fine as Halmar," Lir responded.

But the young soldier's words were tinged with trepidation and he stood near exhaustion. The task before him seemed insurmountable. Thus far, he had somehow held his own against Brelex, one of the most feared warriors in all of Ambrasian. But how long could he last before the Grey Knight added to his body count?

Brelex again advanced angrily toward Dainwirth Lir. The Grey Knight raised his sword high in the air and it came crashing down. Lir blocked it at the last moment. Once more, Brelex swung and again Lir met his blow, staggering momentarily.

The Grey Knight continued his offensive and his blows became more telling. Lir began to weaken, and the tip of Brelex's sword drew blood more than once. Lir offered less and less defense and now appeared an easy target. But as is sometimes the case when victory is so near, the Grey Knight grew overconfident and careless. As Brelex raised his sword higher than necessary to finish Lir, he left an opening in his armor that the young warrior saw only for an instant. Summoning what little strength remained, Lir drove his sword toward Brelex in one short motion. He caught the Grey Knight in his side, and Brelex howled in pain and disbelief. With eyes agape, the Grey Knight watched in horror as Lir pulled back his blood-stained sword and swung again, cutting sharply through the now gaping hole in Brelex's armor and opening his belly. Against all odds, Brelex dropped his sword as he fell dying to the ground.

Stunned, Dainwirth Lir stood over his fallen foe blindly and unmoving. Slowly, he pulled himself from his stupor and shook his head in awe and shock. He, an ill-trained, ill-made solder, had somehow defeated the mighty Brelex . . .

As Lir stood oblivious to the action around him, one of Brelex's soldiers drew his sword. Moving quickly behind Lir, the warrior poised himself to avenge his leader's death. Seeing this turn of events from a distance, Mendelheimer realized there was no time to warn the young soldier–he wouldn't hear him anyway in the din of the battle surrounding him. The minstrel drew his own sword, leapt off Preston–who refused to budge–and ran as hard as he could down the hill. Brelex's soldier raised his sword and prepared to bring it down upon Dainwirth Lir. He began his motion, and the sword flashed down toward the unsuspecting Lir. But the attack fell astray. The sword fell harmlessly as the warrior collapsed to the ground, gasping in shock. Lir turned, and slowly collecting his wits, realized what had happened.

"Mendelheimer," the young soldier said. "You saved my life."

The minstrel bowed.

"It is my pleasure," he said. "I felt that I had to make a contribution, and I did not think this was the appropriate time for a song."

•   •   •   •   •

"Brelex is dead! The Grey Knight has been slain!"

The cry shot over the battlefield. It was truly the first good news is a day riddled with gloom for Roanan and his army. For a short time, buoyed by this heartening news, the soldiers fought with renewed strength, driving back the Drens and the now leaderless army of Brelex. But it was not to last: led by Celidia's channeled power of the Oracle and the barked orders of the Black Knight, the dark armies reorganized and again turned the tide of battle in their favor. With Roanan's army still hopelessly outnumbered, the sheer mass of Maldur's forces took its toll once more.

As the battle again turned against the Red Knight's army, Tabeus watched the scene grimly, losing more hope each instant. But at the same time that his eyes told him the story of a lost battle and a lost world, those senses that only a Wizard can tap told him a story of deception and greed of a decaying heart of evil. Slowly, Tabeus came to realize that the magic of the Oracle permeated the battlefield, and that Roanan's forces fought not only the warriors before them, but the perverted power of the Oracle itself.

"That explains it," the Wizard said knowingly. "I knew something was awry. This is why the Drens rise even after they are struck down and are seemingly tireless in a never-ending day."

Tabeus shook his head sorrowfully.

"Oh, Celidia, a powerful sorceress you may in fact be to tap the power of the Oracle, but you are not a wise one," the Wizard said. "Do you know the perils of using magic to determine the battles among the races of Ambrasian–or do you not care? Your victory will be an illusion. Wizards and magicians, enchantresses and sorcerers all will pass through this world and never return. But the peoples of Ambrasian will remain. This is their world to form, and theirs to rule. How long do you think your magic will hold against the endless fury of time?"

Tabeus looked across the battlefield toward the dark forces.

"You may pervert history today," the Wizard warned, "and your perversion may last for a short ripple in that span. But at what price? Power gained by magic is no power at all. Retaining that power will take all of your will: it will eat at you and rot you, consume your being, and become more of a burden than a pleasure. But you will not be able to give it up. That power will eventually destroy you, and nothing will remain. No one will remember, no one will regret."

The Wizard leaned hard on his staff.

"Until that time, however, the wicked Queen Celidia would reign with terror, with a greed, and with a cruelty unknown before her. And as she herself is being destroyed, she would destroy Ambrasian along with her. Perhaps you deserve that fate, Celidia. But the rest of Ambrasian does not."

Tabeus paused, raising himself majestically to his full height.

"My magic cannot be directed against those warriors in the midst of this battle," the Wizard said. "But magic can counter magic used for evil. I must break Celidia's will from the power of the Oracle."

The Wizard outstretched his arms and fervently chanted an ancient spell. Immediately, he was flung back against the stone that lay behind him. Rising in shock, the Wizard trembled in surprise.

"She is stronger than I suspected," Tabeus said. "The old magic retains great power."

"Doubtless it does," said a voice from behind him. "You cannot break that bond alone. Nor could I. But if we join our powers, together we may have a chance. We must work together."

Tabeus turned, and a look of joy, vexation, and amusement quickly crossed his face.

"Karmin!" he exclaimed. "Why you . . .I thought that was you following us. You haven't been as clever as all that."

"Nor did I try to be," Karmin answered, her long robe providing an ironic beauty to the dust-filled battlefield. "If I did not want you to see me, you surely would not have detected my presence. I thought the knowledge of my proximity would provide you with some sense of comfort. But perhaps I overestimated you."

Tabeus began to snarly a reply, but Karmin cut him short.

"Enough of all that," she said. "It is time to put away any petty differences we may have. Celidia controls the Oracle, and as long as she does, there can be no victory. We must break her will from the power of the Oracle. Only our powers – together – can accomplish that. Separately, we will surely fail. Will you join me now?"

Tabeus paused for only a moment.

"Just my luck to be stuck with a meddling old crone as a partner," he chuckled.

"Meddling?" Karmin laughed. "Old crone? Wizard, need I remind you you are more ancient than the mountains of Isalis. If we should succeed today, we shall see who better fits the description of an old crone."

Tabeus smiled for a moment, then turned grave once again. He gazed onto the grim sight of the battlefield where Maldur's forces were cutting a trail of destruction through Roanan's over-matched army.

"Success," he said grimly, "seems distant and unattainable. Yet we must do what we can to give Roanan a chance. Let us join our powers now."

●   ●   ●   ●   ●

In the midst of the battle, there was no more optimism. Siora's Elvii had been forced back into the forest as far as they could easily retreat, and before them the woods lay in flames. The forest had become too dense to move quickly, and hampered by the undergrowth, the Elvii were no match for the ferocious Drens. That which had provided the Elvii with natural protection for centuries had now become their foe. The Elvii now faced the choice of meeting their charging enemy head on or suffer death in the flames that engulfed more and more of the land.

The rest of the army fared no better. Roanan's forces fought bravely, but they were badly outnumbered and tiring. The Drens, on the other hand, still seemed powerful and fresh, gaining strength even as the battle dragged. With agonizing slowness, Roanan's army gave ground. Some outlying troops appeared on the verge of fleeing, and likely would have done so if there was an easy path to escape. Roanan himself emerged from the clouds of dust dirtied and bloodied, but unscathed. The Red Knight had fought valiantly, and Infernus had left its mark. But one man—even one as powerful as the Red Knight—could not defeat an entire army, and the army of his enemy was vast by any measure.

Roanan searched out Tabeus, and when he finally found him, gazed at the Wizard with a hint of desperation.

"My friend," the Red Knight said hoarsely, "hope fades."

The Wizard suppressed a tear.

"Fades, perhaps," Tabeus said, "but never disappears."

"That is true, Red Knight," a voice interrupted as a figure emerged from behind Tabeus. "While the sun still shines in the sky, hope remains."

"Karmin," Roanan said in surprise as he spotted the robed figure approaching him.

"Yes," Karmin answered. "The Wizard and I are only now beginning to battle the power of Celidia. But even so, the battle of swords must also be won. One victory cannot occur without the other."

Roanan and Tabeus looked out onto the battlefield together. A tremendous surge by the Drens had sent Roanan's army reeling backwards. Fresh blood stained the ravaged earth. The Wizard and the Red Knight viewed the scene with despair. Defeat seemed inevitable.

And then, in little more than an instant, all changed.

Suddenly, a huge storm cloud appeared over the flames of the Great Forest. Heavy torrents of rain came crashing from the sky, quashing the fires below, its ferocity blinding both Elvii and Drens alike. The remainder of the battlefield was strangely clear, but one of the Drens' tools of destruction was extinguished. Roanan turned toward Tabeus once more.

"You see," the Wizard said. "Help arrives. The Weathermaster sends a storm to fight the blaze of the enemy."

Roanan smiled weakly.

"So he does," the Red Knight said. "However, I fear a rainstorm will help little in the final . . ."

Tabeus raised his hand.

"Look," the Wizard said. "Aid arrives in every direction."

Roanan turned. From the southwest, the sky darkened and a cold wind swirled through the battlefield. A thick black cloud layer moved over and across the Red Knight's army. As the rapidly moving mass reached the forces of Maldur, the clouds dissipated and vanished. In its place, the air was suddenly filled with arrows that sped downward, striking down suddenly confused Drens and Brelex's men by the score, giving Roanan's army new life.

"What the . . .?" Roanan wondered, and then a sense of realization crossed his face as he watched the strange scene. "The Reomites!"

"Yes," Tabeus said, "just as they promised, they have come at your most desperate hour."

In just a few more moments, there was another loud cry from the southern edge of the battlefield. The Red Knight turned once more, and squinting his eyes, tried to see what now caused this new confusion. In the distance, he saw a dark mass. For a moment, his heart sank.

Not more Drens, the Red Knight prayed.

But as the horde came closer, Roanan made out the colors that flew before the onrushing army.

Could it be? he thought. *It is!*

Unquestionably, the red and green flags of Chrysalis and Selin advanced proudly before the throng. Lasarion and the army he had somehow cobbled together on his journey had miraculously arrived in time and were now coming up behind the Maldur's fighters, forcing them to fight from both the front and behind. Lasarion and Alexandra led the charge, both cutting down their foes on the left and the right.

Roanan turned to Tabeus. Even the Wizard seemed somewhat surprised. But the Red Knight thought, for a brief second, he had detected a knowing smile on the face of Raven, perched delicately on the wizard's shoulder.

And now, in yet another part of the field, one more disturbance flared. Roanan quickly turned back and saw its cause: Icyx. The brownish-white beast was taking great strides as he moved directly toward the battle.

"Tabeus!" the Red Knight shouted in dismay.

"We have nothing to fear from the beast!" Karmin assured Roanan as she joined the group.

"What?" Roanan asked. "He nearly single-handedly destroyed Necinia."

Karmin raised her hand calmly in reassurance.

"Celidia may have released the monster to cause havoc," Karmin explained. "But then, when it was no longer useful, she forgot about the beast. Once Celidia had full control of the Oracle, she deemed that Icyx was not essential to her task."

Karmin paused, considering the circumstances around her.

"She badly miscalculated," Karmin said. "The magic of Celidia pales before the powers of good that permeate Ambrasian. The Sorceress shall be sorry she ever awoke Icyx from its long sleep and then ignored its fate."

Karmin pointed toward an area of the battlefield beyond Icyx.

"Look closer, Red Knight," she said. "Even more help arrives, from those whose existence you may not have even been aware."

In fact, following Icyx in the field marched five hundred Regalan warriors, both male and female, half brandishing long swords while the others cocking their bows ready to fire on the enemy before them.

"I have heard legends of a walled city far to the north," Roanan said in wonder. "Could it be?"

"You surmise correctly," Karmin affirmed. "Regala has been hidden in the mountains for many generations, but now they have emerged. Their regent, Vandelyise, has cleared the mind of Icyx and now she herself leads her forces into battle to aid us. The Drens have never seen warriors use a long sword to such lethal effect."

Roanan thrust Infernus high into the air in exultation.

"This day will still be ours," he cried, and then drove Alajar back into the thick of battle.

This swiftly the tide turned. It was as if all Ambrasian had at this moment awakened to the evil that was Maldur and Celidia. Buoyed by new hope and aid from every side, the Red Knight's forces fought brilliantly. Brelex's army, once on the verge of ripping decisively through Dainwirth Lir's troops, were now buffeted between his and Lasarion's oncoming army. The Reomites took the forms of swords, arrows and lances and struck down row after row of befuddled Drens. Icyx tore through Maldur's forces with an unstoppable, chaotic fury, impermeable to the battlefield's weaponry. Regalan swordsman speared Dren after Dren, and those that avoided the fate of the long sword found their archers just as deadly as that of the Elvii. With Roanan and his army fighting with new-found strength, the Drens were thrown into utter disarray. With enemies now in every direction, the Drens' attention was diverted from the Elvii and they became easy prey for Siora's marksmen. Arrow after arrow sizzled through the air with sparkling accuracy.

What was once bleak and hopeless had turned into Ambrasian's finest hour. The Red Knight led the charge, his sword moving with lightning speed as it carved deeply into Maldur's forces.

Celidia now looked upon the suddenly transformed battlefield with anger and dismay. Preparing to summon even more power from the depths of the Oracle, the Sorceress instead felt the first abrupt jolt of resistance. Tabeus and Karmin had begun to assail the evil magic of the black queen.

Celidia jumped back in shock then looked angrily across the battlefield.

"I am not defeated yet," she cursed.

•　　•　　•　　•　　•

Lasarion's arrival into the battle in the nick of time was truly a tribute to both his resourcefulness and dedication as well as his implicit trust in Alexandra. When he gazed at the underground river, the knight was undeniably full of wonder. But even more wondrous were the four tall ships docked on the river's bank, awesome in their splendor and pristine condition.

Lasarion looked quizzically at Alexandra.

"How?" he asked.

"I am not entirely sure myself," Alexandra explained. "The river has roots deep in the mountains, but it remains underground until it reaches the spot where the Lorimen River meets the great Sylil. There it emerges, but in a way that only a few have ever discovered, hidden by some ancient charm. From there, it is but a half-day's ride to the Watchtower."

"But the ships?" Lasarion interrupted. "From where did they come?"

"I was getting to that," Alexandra answered in an annoyingly leisurely pace. "Long before you arrived in Selin, the winds of war had reached even us. We knew Brelex was mustering a great force, and if Balinwald fell, Selin would be an easy target. Still, my father was difficult to stir, and the population followed in his blissful and ignorant lethargy. As I have mentioned to you before, but unbeknownst to my father, I sent several brave knights into Balinwald to discover what knowledge they could. On one excursion, Brelex's agents nearly discovered them. They fled into the mountains and by chance or some magical intervention, they discovered the river. They followed it to find where it would lead and then returned."

"The ships?" Lasarion asked once more, somewhat vexed.

"The ships," Alexandra said, "were here when my knights found the cave. They are apparently the remnants of a great kingdom of old. They are vessels built with the old magic that surrounded Ambrasian when it was young. Perhaps they are even Elvii ships, or those of a race lost when the old magic faded away. In any case, they are remarkably well-preserved, sleekly built, and designed for speed. So if you truly wish to reach your king in time, stop admiring them and order your men aboard."

Lasarion began to respond then thought better of it. After a moment, he did as Alexandra suggested and the army boarded the ships with all possible speed. With little time lost, the army and their mounts were speeding up the brisk river. The ships seemed nearly to navigate themselves, and by early the next morning before dawn had burst from the underground caverns and were blazing across the Karmana countryside.

Once the ships docked in early morning, Lasarion led his troops on a last frantic rush toward the battlefield still to the north. They arrived on the dead run. In normal circumstances, the soldiers and their steeds would already have been fatigued, but the sight of the woeful condition of Roanan's troops gave them new energy. They stampeded into battle with Lasarion and Alexandra at the forefront, catching much of the opposing army unawares and pinning them between themselves and Roanan's warriors.

"You made it," Alexandra gasped just before Lasarion's army was ready to join the battle.

"With your help," Lasarion said, gave her an affectionate glance, and stormed into the fury.

Buoyed by the turn of events and reinforcements from every side, the Red Knight's army methodically carved through Maldur's forces. But some pockets continued to retaliate with ruthlessness. Dren lieutenant Izuburu-Gy and his small band of fighters fought furiously, inflicting grievous injury to all that came near them.

Finally, they came face-to-face with a group of soldiers led by Toranis. The knight had dismounted his horse some time ago when the fighting became too closely cropped but had battled his way across the plain. The young knight, infuriated by the wanton violence of Izuburu-Gy's troops, stampeded toward the Dren horde.

"Your reign of terror is over," Toranis cried.

Izuburu-Gy laughed mockingly.

"We shall see, Cadaren scum," he spit at his foe. "You look like dinner to me."

The two groups clashed, Chrysalian warriors taking their Dren opponents to task as the rest of Maldur's army began to collapse around them. Toranis and Izuburu-Gy now faced each other, their swords clanging together time after time.

Toranis' swordsmanship had improved greatly since his encounter with the Drens near the Hall of Karmana, but Izuburu-Gy was a skilled and vicious fighter on his own. The Dren lieutenant was larger and stronger than most of his race and an experienced fighter. He slashed his weapon quickly and accurately and used his unnatural quickness to evade Toranis' blows.

As the larger battle continued around them, the fight between Toranis and Izuburu-Gy took on its own drama. Back and forth they attacked and parried with powerful blows. The Dren attacked with a sudden combination. Toranis blocked the first swing, but Izuburu-Gy slashed again quickly, a blow that Toranis could only partially deflect. The blade caught the knight on the shoulder leaving a thin line of fresh blood. Toranis grimaced in pain.

Izuburu-Gy laughed wickedly and launched an even more aggressive attack, sensing victory. But the knight blocked the Dren's sword, called on some inner strength heretofore unknown, and became the aggressor. Izuburu-Gy blocked Toranis' blows once, twice, and even the third time, but on the fourth strike, the knight cut deeply through the Dren's chest. Izuburu-Gy dropped his sword as he grasped the wound and looked up at Toranis. The last thing Izuburu-Gy saw was the knight's blade just before it cut the head from the Dren's body.

•   •   •   •   •

Celidia now watched the battle from near the Watchtower with dismay and growing terror. The Drens and Brelex's troops were in complete chaos. The Weathermaster's rains had doused the fire in the Great Forest and her army was systematically being cut down from both front and behind. The Sorceress herself felt the power of Tabeus and Karmin growing stronger each moment. She knew command of the Oracle was slowly slipping from her control and she had to find a way to re-assert the mastery of her prize.

"No!" she screamed, knowing she had only one chance. "They will not succeed."

The Sorceress moved quickly, leaving the Watchtower and finding the Black Knight as fast as she could.

"Maldur," Celidia said desperately, "you are our last hope. You must find Roanan and destroy him. The Red Knight's forces cannot win if they lose their King. The day can yet be ours. Slay him."

The Black Knight nodded from atop his horse.

"Roanan is mine," he spit. "I will cut him to pieces."

Maldur drew his sword and turned his head.

Celidia threw her hands up in disgust.

"That way," she said, pointing in the opposite direction. "Must you always be such a moron?"

Maldur turned again and spotted Roanan almost immediately. In an instant, with some sixth sense, the Red Knight returned the stare. Hatred burned from the eyes of Maldur; a mixture of mission and destiny from those of Roanan. Slowly, the two knights battled their way across the field. What warriors foolish enough to challenge them fell quickly. As though some stronger force controlled the ebb and flow of battle, both Drens and soldiers gave way for the inevitable confrontation. Soon, a wide clearing appeared between Roanan and Maldur. For many moments, the Red Knight and the Black Knight remained on their horses, motionless, as the fight raged all around them. Tabeus stood across the battlefield, watching intently but helplessly, already fully engaged with Karmin in the battle with Celidia of control of the Oracle. Mendelheimer crossed his fingers and whistled out of tune.

The many heroic feats and tragic losses of life this day were now merely a footnote to this confrontation. Here was where the battle was to be ultimately won or lost: the Red Knight against the Black Knight, Roanan against Maldur, the two most powerful knights in Ambrasian, Maldur made stronger by the corrupted power of the Oracle. It was a battle made for legends, the stuff of myths if there were a more competent chronicler than Mendelheimer on the field to record it.

Finally, after a few interminable moments, Roanan and Maldur began their approach as if in slow motion. Though the battle raged all around them, a cone of ominous silence seemed the envelop the space between them. Their movements were calculated and cautious. But as their speed increased, the two knights took on an awful beauty, ferociously graceful and elegantly powerful.

Perfect mechanisms of death.

The Red Knight and the Black Knight met each other in the middle of the field. The swords slashed through the air, meeting each other in a tremendous crash. The horses veered. Roanan and Maldur turned and met again, the force of their blows knocking each off of their mounts. Both were up quickly, their eyes burning as they stalked each other mercilessly. Each measured his foe as they paced in a circular path. The Black Knight struck first, moving in one quick motion toward Roanan and thrusting his sword at the Red Knight's mid-section. It struck harmlessly off Roanan's shield. Roanan swung Infernus toward the Black Knight from the right, but his blow was also blocked.

"Your courage betrays you," Maldur bellowed mockingly. "You have come all this way only to meet your death, Red Knight. Your reign will be short, King Roanan."

The Red Knight shook his head.

"You are arrogant until the end," Roanan said. "Surrender, Maldur. Look around you. Your quest is lost. Your army is scattered and defeated. Stop this senseless bloodshed and spare yourself."

The Black Knight spit on the blood-stained ground.

"Noble words to disguise a weak sword," Maldur hissed. "Surrender? I am the strongest knight in the land. You are nothing, soon to be less than nothing. All you have is because you were lucky enough to be born into nobility."

Roanan allowed Maldur's words to pass through him without reaction.

"We will battle as you wish," Roanan answered. "Though I ask you to reconsider."

"Fight," Maldur screamed. "I am not here to argue."

To accentuate his point, the Black Knight delivered a powerful blow that Roanan was barely able to block.

Celidia watched from a distance.

"Amen to that," she said when she heard Maldur's words.

The fight continued in earnest, rising and falling in intensity like some ferocious concerto. Roanan and Maldur struck blow after blow that would have finished a lesser knight. Still, the combatants seemed not to tire. In reality, the battle grew in greater ferocity and the blows more deadly. Time and again, over and over, the Red Knight's sword met the Black Knight's. The thunder of death filled the air as the battle became increasingly more vicious. The lightning strokes were rapid, unerring, and filled with raw power. One slip by either knight meant certain death.

The blows ripped back and forth, with both Roanan and Maldur calling upon all of their skills to remain alive. The seemingly endless skirmish was a furious dance in the blood-riddled dust of the battlefield, its action so fast and ever-changing that those who observed it could hardly follow the flow of the battle. There were no words spoken; Roanan had offered a peace and Maldur had rejected it. Now the fight raged, with no rest nor lull, no chance to yield. It would cease only when one fell.

At a time when their bodies should have been on the verge of collapse, Roanan and Maldur both found some inner force within them kept them fighting. For the Red Knight, it was a fight for survival, for himself and the world he knew. For Maldur, hatred and greed propelled him forward.

As the battle progressed, Maldur's sword tore down toward Roanan. The Red Knight blocked it with his own but lost his footing in the process. He regained it before he fell, but Maldur quickly seized on his opportunity. The Black Knight swung mightily. Roanan somehow blocked the blow, the blade stopping inches from his neck. Maldur swung again with all his anger and strength. The Red Knight ducked under the fierce but uncontrolled attack, avoiding the Black Knight's sword and thrusting his own upwards. Suddenly, Infernus glowed with power. The blade caught the careless Maldur undefended, tearing through his chest and piercing his heart. Blood gushed from the Black Knight as Infernus penetrated even more deeply. Maldur's scream was cut off abruptly as he dropped to the ground, a dark puddle forming around him.

"I don't want to die," the Black Knight whispered, fear now in his voice.

Roanan rose and yanked Infernus from the crumpled body below him.

"You should have thought of that sooner," he said flatly, and watched the life leave Maldur's eyes as they stared into the sky.

The Red Knight stood over the Black Knight's body, the corpse of the power-hungry knight who had shamed his title and brought so much pain into the world. Now, Maldur lay defeated and harmless. After a few seconds, he walked away and did not look back.

Celidia watched the final moments of the battle in alarm. Yet her terror increased even more when, moments later, a tremendous jolt yanked control of the Oracle from the Sorceress. Tabeus and Karmin had joined together to sunder the magical bond the Sorceress had forged. Horrified, Celidia wasted no time in plotting her escape. She quickly wrapped the Oracle within the folds of her gown, moved hurriedly throughout the hidden pathways of the Watchtower, and disappeared from the battlefield.

They will not regain my prize, Celidia thought. *They may win the battlefield, but they will not win the day.*

After the death of Maldur and the loss of the Oracle's power, the forces of the East ran about in utter terror and confusion. They were quickly dispatched. What remained of Brelex's army surrendered after being surrounded by the forces led by Lasarion and Dainwirth Lir. The Drens–thoroughly thrashed by the combination of Roanan's army, the Elvii, the Reomites and Icyx–tried an ill-advised, hasty retreat back to Damora. Their attempt was haphazard and disorganized and most were slain trying to flee. Only a few of the vile beasts escaped. As Roanan's army learned this day, Drens were never taken captive.

Two hours after the Black Knight's death, his great force had been divided, scattered and totally routed. Their threat, so real and on the brink of victory only a short time before, now seemed a distant nightmare. Roanan found Lasarion in the waning moments of the battle. Wordlessly, the two Chrysalian knights who had led the armies through different paths to this day of victory, came to each other weary but triumphant and embraced.

At the edge of the battlefield, Tabeus moved along quickly, his staff at his side, Raven chattering on the Wizard's shoulder. He knew the task was not yet completed. Tabeus still had an appointment with Celidia, though it would be an unwanted rendezvous by the Sorceress.

CHAPTER 27
THE FINAL BATTLE

There was a joyful yet bittersweet reunion at the center of the battlefield. Toranis, Dainwirth Lir, Mendelheimer, and Siora soon surrounded Roanan and Lasarion. Toranis' wound to his shoulder had been dressed and heavily wrapped. The rest had somehow escaped the battle mostly unbloodied and uninjured.

But the triumph of the day had come at a great cost. Roanan moved to the spot where Halmar had fallen and knelt over the lifeless body of the great knight, gazing down quietly.

"My friend," he finally whispered, "the time we promised each other will have to wait."

After a few more moments, Roanan walked away, slowly moving from body to body. The Red Knight understood more fully the great cost of this victory.

On another part of the battlefield just to the south, Karmin and Vandelyise found each other.

"This is a reunion long in the making," Karmin said. "It has been what—fourteen hundred years?"

The Regalan smiled.

"Give or take a hundred years," Vandelyise smiled. "But who is counting? Fortunately, it was not a moment too late."

Karmin nodded in agreement and turned more serious.

"Thank you for your aid," she said to the Regent. "You are truly a remarkable leader."

Vandelyise acknowledged her distant cousin, and together they both turned and looked toward the distance.

"Unfortunately, I must cut this reunion short," Karmin finally said. "There is one more task that needs to be completed before we can claim victory."

Vandelyise nodded in understanding.

"Go," she said. "The Wizard is already on the trail."

•　　　•　　　•　　　•　　　•

Many were killed, and more were wounded. The battlefield was strewn with bodies of the dead and dying, the injured and the mutilated. The Red Knight ordered proper care for all in need. In time, the dead would be assembled on pyres by both soldiers and nearby residents. The thousands of bodies would be put to the fire. The army would remain until the tasks were complete. In time, those who had assembled here for such an epic battle would disperse. The events of the day would be remembered for many generations. The scars that the battle inflicted on the land would eventually heal, though it would take years and perhaps decades and even centuries. Who could tell if those that fell would linger and, as many battlefields, would prove haunted by the spirits of the combatants.

As Roanan walked solemnly through the victims strewn across the battlefield, a glint of recognition crossed his face as he spotted one of the soldiers who had given his life in this fight. He knelt down and examined the body before him more closely. A tear coursed the Red Knight's face for the first time. The soldier was none other than Thelin, the poor farmer he and Lasarion had saved from bandits many months before. Thelin had answered the call to arms and joined the army sent out to save his land. He had paid the ultimate price.

"I am told he fought valiantly," a voice said behind the Red Knight. "Though he needed to be equipped with a sword once he reached the Hall of Chrysalis, he wielded it well and took down many enemies before he himself died at the hands of a Dren battalion."

Roanan turned and looked up to Lasarion, who remembered the encounter just as plainly as the Red Knight.

"His family is left behind," Lasarion said.

"We will make sure we care for them," Roanan said. "They should not be additional victims of this battle."

Lasarion nodded in agreement and together, the two continued to pay their respects to the fallen soldiers as they walked across the plain. While doing so, Roanan and Lasarion exchanged their respective tales of how they arrived at the day's battle. The Red Knight listened in amazement as his faithful knight described the battle with Ravager and the ensuing journey across southern Ambrasian. And then, the warrior came to Alexandra. After Roanan heard that tale, he looked about the field.

"I must meet this individual who has so flustered my courageous knight and cousin," Roanan said with a smile.

In short order, he had spotted Alexandra, armored and covered with the blood of her opponents, but unharmed. The Red Knight looked at her in wonder.

"If all I hear is true," the Red Knight said, "you are a truly remarkable Cadaren."

Alexandra strode confidently to Roanan, eying him carefully.

"I am," Alexandra agreed. "And you better be a most remarkable King for all we went through to get here."

Lasarion's mouth gaped open. He tried to stammer out some words but was speechless. Alexandra winked. Roanan laughed heartily and patted his most trustworthy and noble knight on the back.

"She's yours if she'll have you," Roanan told Lasarion. "Good luck! You'll need it."

The conversation soon turned more serious, and the Red Knight was deeply distressed that Athena had not been saved. Remembering his promise, Roanan felt personally responsible that the princess was still captive. Much as he hated to acknowledge the fact, Roanan knew his battle was not yet complete.

This was made doubly clear when the Red Knight scanned the battlefield and found no sign of the Wizard Tabeus.

"Where is . . ." Roanan began, then answered his own question.

"The Oracle."

. . . . .

Celidia had slipped quietly from the battlefield and focused entirely on maintaining her now tenuous hold on the Oracle, fled quickly toward Damora. Her plan was to hide in the depths there until she could reestablish control of the Oracle and reemerge in fully glory. But Tabeus and Karmin had guessed her flight and as they regained more and more control of the Oracle, were led to it by its power. They wasted no time in pursuing the Sorceress.

Into the marshes Celidia plunged, choosing her path carefully, leaving no trail to follow. The Sorceress' simple tricks and spells, however, did not fool the Wizard nor Karmin, and together they prepared to unsheathe their full glory and power.

For a short time, hearing no one in pursuit, Celidia thought she had escaped and already began to plot her revenge. But her hopes were dashed when she heard Tabeus' voice in the distance echoing all about her.

"Celidia," he commanded, "flee no more. You cannot escape."

The Sorceress considered her options. Finally, she turned and saw the Wizard through the mists of the Damoran marshes. Tabeus stood powerfully and majestically, his staff glimmering, Raven's wings were outstretched.

Celidia raised her arm and pointed her finger at the figure of the Wizard.

"You cannot stop me alone," the Sorceress said. "And your precious Karmin is nowhere to be seen. Now, Wizard, feel the power of the Oracle."

From the gem-encrusted ring on Celidia's finger, a powerful burst of energy exploded toward Tabeus. But the vision of the Wizard vanished and the Sorceress' blast did no more harm than splitting a tree. In an instant, Tabeus reappeared to the left of the Sorceress.

"Your power fades," Tabeus mocked, "while mine grows stronger. Until now, I have harnessed my magic. But your use of the Oracle for evil has freed my own for good. And as time passes, my strength continues to blossom while you become a shell of your former self."

Celidia scowled, anger coursing through her body.

"Do you take me for a fool?" Celidia asked. "You cannot scare me with your childish tales of bravura."

"Tales?" Tabeus chuckled. "Do you mistake me for Maldur?"

"No one is that stupid," Celidia acknowledged. "But you are old and boastful. Do not be overconfident. Your power is as brittle as your ancient bones."

The Sorceress fired an even more powerful blast of energy at the Wizard. But Tabeus casually vanished once again, this time reappearing to Celidia's right. Again, the Sorceress did no more harm than setting a nearby bush ablaze, which Tabeus extinguished with a flick of his hand.

"What trickery is this?" Celidia hissed. "Are you done with your carnival games, old man?"

"Frustrated?" Tabeus mocked. "Are you beginning to doubt your powers?"

The Sorceress spit, her saliva bubbling in the marshes around her.

"Illusions you have aplenty, but no substance," she said. "You cannot harm me. Your magic is ancient and shriveled."

Tabeus chuckled and stared intently at the Sorceress.

"No?" the Wizard questioned. "Perhaps you are right, perhaps not. Why do you hesitate?"

Celidia's face flushed with new-found anger. She sent another burst toward the Wizard. This time, Tabeus did not vanish. Instead, he raised his staff, met the burst with his staff, and re-directed it to a nearby tree. The tree exploded in a blaze of flames and then disintegrated.

"My, my, my," the Wizard whistled. "Getting perturbed, are we?"

Celidia smirked coldly.

"You cannot stop me, you moldy bag of bones," she said, and lifting the Oracle, turned away.

"Stop!" Tabeus pronounced. "Your journey is over, whether or not you realize it."

The Wizard raised his arms upright and an explosion of thunder and lightning filled the air. A strong, cold wind threw Celidia backwards, and she plummeted to her knees.

"I cannot be your judge," Tabeus boomed, "but I can gladly be your captor. You have abused your power and have been overcome with greed. You set yourself up as a queen–but your rule promised to be as bleak as your soul. But now, Celidia, your menace is over."

The Sorceress now looked at the Wizard with desperation.

"Fool," the Sorceress hissed desperately. "What will you do with the Oracle? Return it to Karmin, that airheaded buffoon?"

Celidia thought she caught a quick glimpse of hesitation cross the Wizard's face. It lasted only a moment, but the Sorceress believed she had struck a vital chord.

"You too can have the power of the Oracle," she continued, changing to a conspiratorial tone. "I will share the power with you. We can rule Ambrasian together."

But Celidia, in her greed and short-sightedness, had overplayed her hand and forgotten that Tabeus had no desire for power. The Wizard's feint had caught her, and she had fallen into his trap. In that moment, Celidia had shown herself to be the vain, power-hungry despot all suspected. And Tabeus, who had never thought otherwise, smiled inwardly at the Sorceress' feeble attempt at persuasion.

"You are finished, Celidia," he said with determination. "You have no power to share–only hatred."

"I'll kill you!" she screamed and unsheathed a dagger hidden in the folds of her gown. Quickly, she lunged at the Wizard, the blade glimmering of its own accord. But Tabeus, with agility that defied his aged appearance, easily skirted the blow. Tabeus waved his hand, and Celidia's knife was turned into a writhing snake. The Sorceress shrieked and threw it away.

"Don't enjoy being toyed with?" Tabeus taunted. "Certainly, it's something you've mastered."

Celidia snarled. The Sorceress turned and moved away from the Wizard, clutching the Oracle. Tabeus' face grew grave and the playfulness in his eyes burned away. He raised his staff and spoke ancient words of the old magic. Suddenly, out of the shadows, Karmin emerged and joined the Wizard in the chant, raising her arms and causing the very elements about her to realize the Sorceress' evil.

The Oracle suddenly glowed brightly. A swirling wind encircled the Sorceress, growing more ferocious with each passing moment. Then, two powerful bursts of power emanated from Tabeus' staff and Karmin's very being, flinging Celidia to the ground, separating her from the Oracle of Karmana. The Sorceress dived to regain her lost prize. But Tabeus flung her aside again. With another wave of his hand, the Wizard raised the roots of a nearby tree from the ground and wrapped them around the struggling Celidia.

"You are finished," the Wizard said calmly and turned away.

Celidia began to say something, but Karmin waved her arm and one of the tree's limbs clamped itself around the Sorceress' mouth.

"You have nothing more to say that we have an interest to hear," Karmin said and joined the Wizard.

At that moment, Roanan came into sight riding hard atop Alajar.

"Now you show up," Tabeus said, but his grave expression faded and he broke into a wide smile as the Red Knight approached. "You missed most of the pyrotechnics."

Roanan surveyed the scene in front of him.

"It appears that you and Karmin have things well in hand," the Red Knight said.

Roanan leapt from Alajar and embraced the Wizard.

"It is good to see you, my friend," the Red Knight said. "Against all odds, we were victorious after all."

After a moment, Raven swooped down from a nearby tree and perched on his familiar place on Tabeus' shoulder.

"Good work, boss," he whispered.

Tabeus smiled. Roanan looked quickly at the bird and shook his head.

"Did he . . .?" the Red Knight began.

"Did he what?" the Wizard asked.

Roanan considered the question again.

"No, never mind," the Red Knight said. "I don't want to know."

Roanan and Tabeus finally separated, and the Wizard turned and faced Karmin.

"I believe you will find the Oracle of Karmana over there," he said, pointing toward Celidia. "I suggest you return it to your rightful place as quickly as possible."

Karmin nodded in agreement and looked at both Tabeus and Roanan.

"We owe both of you a great debt," Karmin said solemnly.

"All of us had much at stake," Roanan said. "We achieved victory by relying on the talents of each other. Let us hope this serves as the beginning of an even more glorious future among the free peoples of Ambrasian."

Tabeus cleared his throat, looking mischievously at Karmin.

"I, for one, will never let you forget that you are in my debt," the Wizard said to Karmin with a broad smile. "I intend to remind you of that at every opportunity I receive."

Karmin smirked.

"I am sure that is true," she said. "And despite that, you are always welcome in Karmana."

Roanan now turned his attention to Celidia and walked to the spot where the Sorceress was now held captive. He studied her carefully.

"So the feared Sorceress Celidia has been reduced to this?" Roanan mused. 'I am sorely disappointed."

Celidia hissed, but the tree's limb prevented her from responding. Roanan smiled and turned away from the captive and toward the Oracle. Instantly, the Red Knight was awestruck.

"It's beautiful," he said.

Tabeus and Karmin came up next to Roanan.

"Yes it is," Karmin agreed. "Yet its power is far greater than its beauty. The Oracle has been recovered and we can dream of a future of peace."

Karmin turned her attention toward Celidia.

"You are a disgrace to your sisters," she said and looked away.

Roanan admired the Oracle for a moment longer. However, he knew his victory was net yet completed. The Red Knight looked at his friend Tabeus.

"There is still one more task I must accomplish," he said.

"I know," Tabeus said. "You must leave now."

As Roanan mounted Alajar and moved as quickly away as he was able, Tabeus looked at Karmin more closely. After a few moments, she noticed his unusual attention and looked at the Wizard questioningly.

"Is there something that draws your eye?" Karmin finally asked.

"A streak of grey has developed in your hair," the Wizard said. "See for yourself."

Tabeus opened his palm and created a reflecting mirror in the air. Karmin looked and saw the streak for herself. She held back a gasp, then willed herself to regain her composure. It took a moment to resolve herself to a hint of age after an eternal youth.

"No doubt there is," Karmin acknowledged. "I believe I will keep it as it is. It will serve as an apt reminder of the events of these days and the importance of keeping vigilant."

Tabeus chuckled softly.

"With age comes wisdom," the Wizard said.

Karmin looked at her companion.

"You would know," was her retort.

•　　•　　•

With Celidia defeated by the powers of Tabeus and Karmin, Roanan now turned toward the last piece of unfinished business. The Red Knight joined Lasarion once again, and with an air of resolve hiding their exhaustion, announced their next step: to return to Balinwald and try to rescue the kidnapped princess, Athena.

Quickly, those closest to the Red Knight assembled near him. The force that was to accompany Roanan would be small, designed for speed rather than brute force. But even then, would it be fast enough? Athena had now been missing for days in the hands of renegade soldiers.

Brelex's compatriots who held the princess were surely waiting for their leader's return. But the Grey Knight now lay dead on the battlefield, and his defeat had dashed any hopes of victory by his allies. With the cause lost and the army defeated, how long would Athena remain safe? The odds were not in Roanan's favor.

Word would travel swiftly, and with the news, the princess's safety was even more imperiled. Surely some of Brelex's former army had escaped in the chaotic final moments of the battle. They were no doubt even now well on their way to Balinwald. The princess's head would plainly be viewed as apt revenge.

Roanan's flight would have to be a desperate one. To some, it would be seen as superfluous: the battle was over, the threat has passed. Maldur and Brelex were slain and Celidia captured. Roanan and his party would have to search throughout the countryside for however many days or weeks with no assuredness of success. While Athena would be yet another tragic loss, there was little hope of finding her alive. Meanwhile, Ambrasian was sorely in need of healing and leadership. A lone princess, some reasoned, was an acceptable price for victory.

But it was not an acceptable to Roanan. He had pledged that he would save the last heir to the throne of Balinwald and he intended to keep that vow. While that promise now seemed made so long ago, it was truly made just a short time in the past.

"We must go with all haste," Roanan said suddenly and decisively, "and hope for the best."

The Red Knight studied his company carefully.

"Lasarion, you have travelled far, but . . ."

"You could not keep me from accompanying you, my Lord," Lasarion said hastily.

Roanan smiled knowingly.

"Well, if he's going," Alexandra concluded, "then so am I."

The Red Knight chuckled.

"So be it," he said. "I can see arguing would be futile. Lir?"

Dainwirth Lir answered by mounting his horse instantly.

"Lead me to these scurrilous villains," he boomed.

Roanan raised his eyebrow.

"You have been hanging about Mendelheimer too long," he said.

The Red Knight also chose Dakar and Toranis to ride with him, once assured that the injury to Toranis' arm was not serious enough to cause additional harm. To the Elvii-king Siora, Roanan bid his farewell.

"Your Elvii lands are once again safe," the Red Knight said, "and your task here complete. I don't know how I can ever thank you and your people."

"Our appreciation for one another is mutual," Siora answered. "We Elvii played only a small part in today's victory. This is the Red Knight's triumph. Perhaps the Chrysalian King will honor us with a visit to Necinia."

Roanan smiled, a mix of joy and shock. The Red Knight and Siora had this conversation once before, but now it seemed a much more achievable sojourn.

"An Elvii inviting an outsider to the Elvii lands? This is one invitation I must take up one day," he said.

Siora bowed.

"And perhaps the Elvii will find an occasion to once again travel to Chrysalis," he said.

"That," Roanan answered, "would be a true honor. You are welcome at the Hall of Chrysalis any time."

The Red Knight clasped Siora's hand.

"Farewell, my friend," he said earnestly.

"Farewell," Siora said, held onto Roanan's hand for a moment longer, then bounded into the forest and disappeared.

Finally, Roanan turned to Tabeus, who had joined the quorum once custody of Celidia had been transferred to the guards.

"My dearest and most trusted companion," the Red Knight said, "you have travelled long and far. But this is not your battle. Perhaps you and Karmin could care for what needs to be done here and lead the army back to their homes."

The Wizard smiled in acceptance.

"I will stay and finish what we must do," the Wizard assured Roanan. "And I will bring your army home. It will be my personal pleasure to escort Celidia back to whatever punishment awaits her."

Tabeus allowed himself a chuckle, then turned serious again.

"But I think you would be wise to take Raven with you," he said.

"Raven?" Roanan asked, confused to the role a bird would play in this quest.

"Follow him," Tabeus said, "and he will lead you to where you need to go."

The Red Knight smiled knowingly.

"Have you also figured out how we can reach the princess in time as well?" Roanan asked.

Tabeus raised his finger crookedly.

"As a matter of fact," the Wizard started, "I have developed a plan."

On cue, a strong wind swirled through the battlefield and came together in a long funnel, rising about the scene like a runaway tornado. Then, a bright light flashed through the sky. When Roanan opened his eyes, a flock of the huge scavenger birds like the ones that had circled the battlefield now flew about him.

"We offer you our aid once more," the bird closest to him said to Roanan, and the Red Knight immediately recognized the voice.

"Phelin," Roanan shouted. "You are a Reomite of your word! It is now I that am in your debt–and still you offer even more aid?"

Phelin cawed, a noise Roanan recognized as a laugh.

"The freedom you have granted us," the Reomite answered, "is worth more than we could ever re-pay. And your warriors have no other chance to reach your princess in time. By horse, it will take two days to reach your destination. But in this form, we can bridge that same length in but a few hours. And we are undoubtedly large enough for your and your men to ride on your backs–though I fear your horses must stay behind. Shall we take one more adventure together, Red Knight of Chrysalis?"

Roanan laughed despite the circumstances.

"I accept your offer, Phelin," the Red Knight said. "Let us finish the final chapter in this battle. Your friendship is one that I will long cherish."

Phelin flapped his long wings.

"Let us both ensure that friendship grows and flourishes in the years to come," the Reomite said. "But now, let us depart. We Reomites have already stayed too long from our land of Arminan and must return shortly, for our lives are inextricably linked to our land. Let us waste no more precious time and be on your way to save this princess of yours."

Roanan glanced back at Tabeus.

"Care for Alajar," Roanan implored.

Tabeus nodded.

"Of course," the Wizard said, "as you must care for Raven."

As Roanan and his small band mounted the winged Reomites, a bedraggled form rushed toward them.

"Wait for me!" he cried. "I must be a member of the party."

"Mendelheimer!" the Red Knight cried. "What are you doing?"

The minstrel stumbled onto one of the Reomites, nearly collapsing and out of breath.

"Historian . . .," he huffed. "How can I document your great feats if I am left behind?"

Mendelheimer paused, puffing out his chest.

"Besides," he said, drawing his sword, "I am now a proven warrior."

He looked back to no one in particular.

"Watch Preston," he yelled as the Reomites took off, taking a sharp angle into the sky.

The Reomites punched through the clouds and hurtled toward their destination at incredible speed. In the lead was Raven, who moved with a pace unexpected for his small size. On and on the Reomites flew, the Ambrasian warriors on their backs: Roanan and Lasarion side by side, with Alexandra nearby; and Dainwirth Lir, Toranis, and Dakar only slightly behind. Somehow, Mendelheimer and the Reomite he rode had found their way to the back of the flock, and the minstrel struggled to keep up.

"Uncooperative bird," he muttered.

"Idiot minstrel," the bird responded.

The flock stormed through the skies, moving like a gale force over the skies of Ambrasian. With Raven untiringly leading the way, the Reomites and their riders bore slightly southwest of the Sylil River and made a great path flying over the center of Karmana.

The riders soon passed over a small band of warriors that rode an uneven line over the plains. They were the remnants of Brelex's army, returning to Balinwald in a disorganized retreat.

Dainwirth Lir and Toranis spotted the ragged band first and were ready to swoop down and attack.

"Let's finish them," Lir said.

Roanan, however, waved them off.

"Leave them be," the Red Knight said. "They pose no threat and we have a graver task."

Besides, Roanan thought, *they have nowhere to go and they will soon meet their own ends.*

In truth, the Red Knight was correct. News of Brelex's defeat reverberated through the countryside and the ragged band of survivors were already being peppered with surprise attacks by the farmers and townspeople along the way. The soldiers left behind by Lasarion reinforced by local residents who had volunteered to strengthen the garrison would greet those who finally reached the Hall of the Grey Knight. Those who didn't surrender would fall in their tracks.

Leaving the remnants of Brelex's army to their ultimate fate, the Reomites flew onward.

•   •   •   •   •

Still miles away, hidden deep in a valley of the southern kingdom, the bandit crew that held Athena now grew anxious and concerned. Each sound they heard raised both their suspicion and their trepidation. Though they had not come across the tattered remains of Brelex's forces, news travelled in many strange and mysterious ways in Ambrasian. Trees whispered tales in the wind, birds flew in every direction chattering endlessly, and streams sang merrily on their way to the distant seas. Many voices spread across the land, some of good and some of evil. Certainly, the tale of the battle at the Watchtower now echoed through those curious and uncharted paths.

How the hint that something was astray in Brelex's grand scheme came to his compatriots was impossible to determine. But their suspicions continued to increase until they were certain that their cause was crushed. Once the protectors of Brelex's war prize, they were now fugitives from Roanan's justice. Suddenly Athena, held for Brelex's triumphant return, now became excess baggage that threatened discovery of the fugitives. As it became more and more clear that the Grey Knight was lost, Athena's safety became tenuous.

The warriors talked among themselves.

"Let's kill her and escape while we can," one said. "If they have defeated Brelex, we must flee as quickly as possible and find some refuge."

Another scoffed at the notion.

"There is no hurry," he responded. "Who will look for us after such a battle? Thousands have died, kingdoms have been won and lost. More than likely, we will be forgotten never to be remembered. And even if we are, it will take days for anyone to reach Balinwald. After that, they must still find us in this hovel."

The speaker leered lecherously at the captive princess.

"In the meantime," he said, "our prize can amuse us. There is plenty of time for all of us."

Athena squirmed in a vain attempt to escape. She was bound securely. The ominous thought of Brelex's future return had been cast aside, but in its place now stood an even more gruesome immediate danger. Hope failed as the bandits leeringly approached the fair princess. One grabbed her and ripped at her gown.

Suddenly, there was a great stir outside and gusts of wind ripped through the cavern the bandits had chosen as their hideaway. Brelex's men turned toward the opening of the cave and saw Raven, hovering proudly and cawing a great clamor.

"Damned bird," cried the one closest to Raven and advanced on him, sword in hand. Raven led him from the cave as the bandits watched the scene with amusement. But their laughter quickly faded as they watched their partner step outside and be pulled upward from their view.

"What is this?" one cried. Simultaneously, all but one drew their swords and ran for the mouth of the cave. The last stayed to guard their prize.

When the remaining soldiers of Brelex's army reached their destination and looked up, they stepped back in shock. Nevertheless, the sight of Roanan, the rest of his knights, and the Reomites did not frighten them into surrendering. Realizing that their fears of Brelex's defeat were confirmed, the leader of the bandits thrust his sword upward and rushed forward. Whether it was to revenge the death of his leader or some unexpressed death wish, history would never know. His followers took up their swords and followed him into the poorly considered battle.

The fighting was swift and furious and ended nearly as quickly as it began. With the Reomites lending themselves to the battle and Roanan and his finest knights taking on the bandits as they came forward, Brelex's men were overwhelmed and fell quickly. Roanan's forces suffered no casualties.

In a short time, Raven led Roanan into the cave. The torches had gone out during the battle, but Roanan found his way through the darkness and re-lit the flames. As he reached the inner chamber, he found Athena at knifepoint, her last remaining guard standing behind her with the tip of his sword at her throat.

"Let me go or I will kill her," the soldier said, doing his best to keep his voice even.

"You cannot escape," Roanan said calmly, Infernus beginning to glow. The rest of his knights stood behind him. "You are cornered and outnumbered. Surrender and you will be unharmed."

The soldier became more agitated.

"I'll kill her, I swear," he shouted more desperate.

What the soldier did not see, however, was that when his comrades had accosted Athena just a few minutes earlier, they had unintentionally loosened the binding around her hands. With her final guard momentarily distracted by the fighting outside the cave, the Princess had slipped a nearby blade beneath the folds of her gown. Now, with her captor concentrating on the Red Knight, she quietly pulled out the blade once again, thrust backwards and stabbed Brelex's last soldier in the belly. He let his hold on Athena loosen, and in a flash, Roanan moved in and finished the guard before he could react.

The Red Knight turned to ensure the safety of Athena and found her in the warm yellow light of the cave.

It was the first time the Red Knight had laid eyes on the Princess Athena.

CHAPTER 28
A MEETING OF TWO WORLDS

Aboard the Explorer, the crew watching the conflict and its aftermath in near silence. Most of those aboard had never seen such wanton destruction and bloodshed. Their reactions ranged from shock to horror. Some became physically ill. Their reactions changed from revulsion to wonder as they watched Tabeus and Karmin subdue Celidia with an unexplainable series of actions–and magic, for lack of another description. Even Kevo had stopped trying to interpret the activities on the planet, choosing instead to focus on data collection of as much information as possible.

After the battle, emotions were mixed. Captain Evenru appeared relieved that Ambrasian had been "saved" from evil forces and seemed more secure in the ship's mission.

"Good appears to have won the day without our intervention," the Captain finally said.

"History will be so relieved," Kevo said flatly.

Can artificial intelligence be sarcastic? Evenru wondered as he stared over at the AI.

Officer Kalli studied his captain carefully.

"You know, some people believe the mere act of observation can alter the result," she finally said.

Evenru gave her a look of disdain.

"I'm not a philosopher," he responded.

"What if evil would have won?" Kalli persisted.

Evenru paused for a moment.

"Then we would have done the same thing we are going to be doing shortly," the Captain said. "Complete our mission and go on to our next assignment. No matter the outcome of today's events, no one can predict what will become of this planet and its residents."

The Command Center door whistled open and Officer Penra disrupted the conversation between Evenru and Kalli with an immediate concern that required direct action.

"Captain," Penra reported, "during the battle, one of the Reomites collided with Drone A6174 and disabled the device. It subsequently crashed in a remote area. We have located the drone just east of the battlefield, at coordinates 4369 by 2197."

The Captain sighed, wondering what else could go wrong.

One more complication I don't need, he thought.

"Can we order the device to self-destruct?" Evenru asked.

Penra worked the controls growing more frustrated as he did so. His efforts were fruitless.

"The communications protocols on the drone have been compromised," Penra reported. "It is not responding to any of our commands. And . . ."

The officer paused.

"And what?" the Captain demanded.

"The cloaking mechanism on the drone appears to have been damaged as well," Penra reported. "It is no longer functional. The device is visible from the ground."

Evenru looked at his young officer in disbelief. He shook his head in disgust.

"In other words, our technology is lying for anyone to find in the middle of a field?" he finally asked.

The officer cringed.

"Not exactly in a field," Penra said, his anxiety increasing as the Captain's facial expressions belied his anger. "But admittedly easy enough to locate."

Evenru sat back in his chair. The lights on Kevo's console blinked rapidly.

"Captain," the ship's AI chirped, "need I remind you of the Galactic Command Order 7A, which explicitly prohibits allowing a planet's development from being altered by our advanced technology. Specifically, the Order states . . ."

"I know what the order says," Evenru said, cutting off Kevo's dissertation. The captain looked at Penra.

"Well," he said. "It's your drone. You're going to have to go down and get it."

"But Captain . . ." Penra objected.

"No buts," Evenru said. "The new terrestrial landers are equipped with cloaking mechanisms. Get down there, retrieve our drone, and get back here."

"Yes, Captain," Penra responded and left the Command Center. "Kevo, please prepare Lander One for takeoff."

·   ·   ·   ·   ·

Standing in front of the Watchtower, Tabeus surveyed the wanton destruction before him. Victory had been achieved and the future of Ambrasian secured. But at what price? The battlefield had turned a dark crimson with the blood of the combatants. Thousands of dead from both sides lay before him. Many thousands of others lay injured or maimed. Arms and legs—and worse—lay detached from their owners. There would be no glory for many. Families had been torn asunder, entire bloodlines eliminated.

"A terrible price," the Wizard muttered as he turned and walked away from the carnage.

A short while later, Tabeus sat in contemplation, some distance away from the activity of the battlefield.

Could this have been avoided, he wondered. *Could victory have been attained in some other way?*

After some time, he looked up into the sky. A moment later, his attention focused, he arose and peered intently, looking beyond the capabilities of his normal vision.

Aboard the Explorer, Officer Kalli watched Tabeus with growing alarm as she ascertained the direction of the Wizard's gaze. Finally, the Lux officer showed signs of panic.

"Captain," Kalli said. "He sees the drone."

The Captain looked at his officer incredulously.

"Impossible," Evenru said. "The drone is cloaked. It's completely invisible to everyone on the planet."

The officer looked at the screen again and grimaced.

"Well, captain," Kalli said. "If I were you, I'd look for myself."

The Captain walked up and looked more closely at the screen.

"What the hell is he doing?" he asked.

Tabeus stared straight at the invisible drone, fury growing in his eyes. He raised his staff and shouted angrily.

"I hope we have sufficiently entertained you," the Wizard admonished, raising his voice. "Have you watched enough slaughter for one day? Have we satiated your macabre curiosity?"

The Captain shot a shocked stare at Kalli.

"Is he talking to us?" he demanded.

The officer shrugged.

"It appears so," she confirmed. "Either that, or he's gone mad."

"How does he know we're here?" Evenru asked, mostly to himself. "And even more so, how does he know who we are?"

The Captain continued to watch Tabeus as he stared at the unseen drone in growing agitation.

"Do you think I'm a fool?" the Wizard screeched. "Your technological machinations are not so impressive as you may think. I've seen much better."

"Are you kidding me?" Evenru pondered, transfixed by the scene unfolding on the screen.

"I'm collecting as much data on the being as I can," Officer Kalli said, madly moving through prompts on the control panel.

"Kevo, is that cloak working?" the Captain demanded.

"Affirmative, Captain," the AI responded. "The cloak is fully functional."

"Functional," Evenru said, "but not terribly effective."

Tabeus laughed grimly, anger flashing across his aged features.

"And what do you think you will find?" the Wizard taunted as if he knew he was being recorded. "Fools and cowards all of you. You are nothing but voyeurs. None of this bloodshed had to happen. You could have prevented it. What kept you from doing so? Some noble proclamation to not interfere with native cultures? Do you think the families of the thousands who died here today believe you acted with nobility? I would venture to say not. They would think you are complete cowards. But you followed the orders of some faceless command a thousand light years away."

Captain Evenru and Officer Kalli looked at each other.

"He's lecturing us, Captain," Kalli said, with some consternation.

"I can see that he is," Evenru said. "And quite knowledgeably. In fact, far too knowledgeably for someone living on a planet with this level of development."

Tabeus caught their attention once again.

"Your presence is no longer welcome," the Wizard proclaimed, "Your secret surveillance will no longer be tolerated. And whatever invitation was accorded to you is now rescinded."

The Wizard suddenly thrust his staff powerfully into the air with such ferocity that Evenru and Kalli jumped backwards. Instantaneously, the cloaked drone exploded in mid-air. The destruction complete, Tabeus turned back toward the battlefield.

"We are done being someone else's amusement," the Wizard said sternly. "Now, it is time to get these soldiers home to their families."

Aboard the Explorer, there was momentary chaos.

"He destroyed our drone," Kalli exclaimed in shock.

"With what?" Evenru asked sneeringly. "His magic wand? Run the diagnostics again. There must be some other explanation. Perhaps some malfunction."

Lights flickered crazily across the ship's console.

"Captain," Kevo reported after some time, "for whatever reason, we have lost contact with the drone, which appears to have been destroyed through an unidentified catastrophic event."

Evenru stared blankly at the console.

"That's all you got?" he finally asked.

"What more do you require?" Kevo asked flatly.

"Nothing, obviously," the Captain concluded.

Evenru returned to his command chair and dropped into it.

"When Penra returns, let's complete our mission and get the hell out of here," Evenru said. "I have had enough of wizards, dragons, and other fantastical beings."

The Captain turned toward the AI.

"Kevo, plot our course to the asteroid and run simulations to execute our plan."

•   •   •   •   •

Penra navigated the lander toward the surface of the planet. Even though the ship was cloaked, the officer took extra care to identify a discreet location to land, shielded by trees and several hills. Enough had already gone wrong on this mission and he didn't want to add any more "anomalies" to his report. Although atmospheric readings from the Explorer confirmed that Ambrasian was within the tolerable zone for habitability, the careful officer still double-checked before opening the hatch and stepping outside.

No data analysis, however, could prepare Penra for the stark difference between Ambrasian and his home planet of Lux. The color of the sun was redder than Lux's home sun, casting everything around him in an odd glow that disoriented the alien. The temperature was cooler and the humidity lower than which he was accustomed. The plant life around him looked unnatural and even the geography appeared as if it was designed by some abstract painter. So even though the Kevo had determined the planet was "habitable" for those from Lux, it was far from comfortable or inviting.

"Let's get this over with as quickly as possible," the young officer said to himself. "Retrieve the drone and get back to the ship."

Unfortunately, the drone had stopped transmitting shortly after it crashed. Penra had a general idea of its location and a terrestrial scanner to pinpoint its exact landing spot. The drone was constructed of composite material not known in nature, so the officer set the scanner accordingly. He received readings immediately.

"The drone should be about three-hundred meters to the east," Penra said, again to himself. Talking to himself seemed to quell some of the unease he felt on this strange planet. The officer walked in that direction, concentrating on his scanner. A few steps later, he felt his boot sink deeply and heard a loud squish. Penra looked down and saw that he had stepped into a wet and muddy marsh. He tried to pull out his foot, but the thick sludge resisted. After several more tries, he finally freed himself.

"I need to better watch where I'm going," he said to himself, smelling the stench of rotting vegetation.

That will have to be disinfected when I get back to the ship, he thought.

* * *

As Tabeus and Karmin took on the task of restoring order among the troops and organizing the journey home, they left their captive with a cadre of guards. Celidia was shackled and appeared to diminish as the Oracle was taken from her and its power yanked from her control. The guards began to lead her back to the scene of the battle, where she could be properly secured and escorted to a prison, impenetrable and so remotely located that she could no longer wreak havoc.

Celidia, however, was not so powerless as she appeared. The Sorceress emerged from her supposed helpless state and using some remnant of magic, unloosened her chains and freed herself. Holding the guards' attention in her gaze, she snatched a sword and cut down each of her captors in turn.

She dropped the sword in the dirt among the corpses and turned back toward the East.

'Damnable Roanan, that wretched Wizard, and the haughty Karmin ruining my plans," she cursed. "I must disappear and regroup to return more powerful and most unexpected. I am not finished yet, despite their victory celebration."

Celidia slithered away, quickly and quietly, unseen and unheard in the nearby din. She had travelled some time when she came across a metallic device of a design she had never before seen. She stopped and slowly moved closer to the apparatus, examining it closely.

The mechanism was made of a material unfamiliar to Celidia. Cylindrical with four appendages, the object measured more than a meter across. It was matte black, with various controls throughout, but appeared to have been severely damaged when it hit the ground.

"Whatever this is requires further study," Celidia said. "It may come in useful in my plans."

The Sorceress smirked, knowing intuitively she had found something more valuable that even she could understand at the moment. She picked up the device and stepped away when she heard a rustle. Seconds later, a strange looking being oddly colored and in a uniform she did not recognize appeared in her path.

"That does not belong to you," Officer Penra said.

Penra assuredly knew Celidia from the Explorer's observation and instinctively drew his weapon.

"And who–or what–are you?" Celidia challenged. "I have never seen your kind anywhere in Ambrasian and I have travelled to every corner of this land."

The Lux did not have an easy answer to that, nor did he wish to reveal his true origins.

"My name is Penra," the officer finally said. "That is my property, and I have come to retrieve it."

The Sorceress looked at the Lux with a mix of wonder and scorn.

"Have you now?" Celidia asked mockingly. "Then it must have some value and seeing that it is currently in my possession, I believe it obviously belongs to me."

Celidia studied the strange being in front of her more closely, then came to some inner conclusion.

"You must be one of those who have been spying on us," she said, then looked at the damaged drone. "And this must be one of your spying machines. Interesting. Very interesting."

Celidia's assertion shook Penra for a moment, then he regained his composure and raised his voice.

"That is not yours to use," the Lux officer said, "and I demand that you return it immediately."

The Sorceress chuckled, her face breaking into a wide grin.

"Demand, do you?" she said, sarcasm dripping from her voice.

She now looked at Penra with disdain.

"I have lost patience with you," she said with sudden contempt, "and I have tired of this debate."

Celidia raised her arm, a sphere of energy forming in her fist. Still disoriented from the unusual temperature of the light, the alien landscape, and the unbelievable threat before him, Penra raised his blaster toward the Sorceress.

"Stop immediately, I order you!" he said firmly.

A sinister glare came across Celidia's face as she prepared to dispatch her foe. She brought her arm back in a throwing motion and slung it forward. Penra saw the attack coming and fired his weapon directly into Celidia's chest.

In his desperate state, the Lux officer had not checked the setting on his blaster. It was programmed at a lethal power range.

Celidia's eyes went wide in shock as the plasma beam blew a gaping hole in her body. With some struggle, she desperately reached into the folds of her gown, throwing a tied scroll in the Lux officer's direction.

"What better than a quick and sudden death," she whispered.

Her gaze held for only a moment longer, then her body exploded. The Sorceress, her magic, and her evil intent succumbed to advanced science.

"Dammit," Penra said. His body was frozen for a few seconds. Then, the officer shook himself out of his paralysis, retrieved the scroll and the drone that the explosion had thrown near his feet, and ran back toward the lander.

The Captain will be really pissed, Penra thought to himself. *And I can kiss that promotion goodbye.*

•　　•　　•　　•　　•

Evenru stared at the screens and holograms before him in shock.

"You are freaking kidding me," Evenru cursed. "How could this mission go any more wrong? Get him back here and let's get the hell out of orbit as quickly as we can."

Kevo analyzed the location of Penra's ship.

"The lander should dock with the Explorer in nine minutes," the AI reported.

"Good," the Captain said. "As soon as we're secure, let's calculate our approach and finally deal with this asteroid. Then, we can head to our next mission–which hopefully, will not be as eventful."

Evenru continued to watch the various visuals as the lander approached the Explorer and settled into the ship's dock. As soon as the lander was secure and Penra was safely on board, Kevo navigated the Explorer away from the planet's surface toward the deadly projectile aimed at Ambrasian.

A few minutes later, Penra walked gingerly into the Command Center. Evenru stared sternly.

"What the . . ." the Captain began and Penra braced for a lecture of epic proportions. He was saved however–at least temporarily–when Officer Kalli burst into the room.

"Captain," Kalli said, "you have to see this."

Evenru looked at his junior officer in agitation.

"Kalli," he said, "you did see I was addressing Officer Penra."

Kalli nodded her head.

"Yes Captain, my apologies," she said. "But this is extremely important."

Evenru sighed and turned his full attention to Kalli.

"What's so critical?" he finally said.

"Kevo and I have been doing a detailed analysis of the various species found on the planet," she began. "At first, we were intrigued with the number of discrete intelligent species found in such a concentrated area. We began with the wizard who demonstrated such unexpected abilities."

"He among others," Evenru added. "What did you discover?"

The officer hesitated for a moment, seeming to check her results one last time before handing them over.

"Here, see for yourself," Kalli said, activating the electronic report. "Whatever species Tabeus represents is not native to this planet."

Evenru stared at the report as it identified the variances in DNA that could not occur naturally on Ambrasian. He then looked back at Kalli.

"You mean the wizard is an alien?" the Captain asked. "We have an alien among aliens?"

"That appears to be the case," Kalli affirmed. "And there's more."

"More?" Evenru asked, raising an eyebrow.

Kalli nodded her head.

"Once we realized the nature of the wizard, Kevo and I began a detailed analysis of all the species on the planet," she explained, then looked toward the command console.

"Kevo, do you want to complete the report?" she asked.

"My pleasure," the ship's AI said. "Based on the results of the wizard, we cross-referenced our analysis to other species. We have concluded that the Elvii, the females of Karmana, and even the Race of Cadaren all had their roots in other parts of the galaxy. In fact, in some cases, we have already identified the likely planetary origins of several species. Interestingly, not all alien species came from the same planet. Our conclusion is several intergalactic ships of various origins visited Ambrasian at some point in the past."

Evenru looked at the report in wonder. For a moment, he was speechless. Finally, he began to digest the information he had just received.

"Are there any native intelligent species on this planet?" he finally asked.

"One," Kevo reported. "The Drens. We believe that part of the reason they appear to be so uncivilized is that they are in an earlier stage of development than those who migrated to this planet.

"In fact," the AI continued, "there is some evidence that the Drens have been genetically altered by an outside force over time to increase their aggressiveness and decrease their cognitive development."

The crew pondered the results of the analysis for quite some time.

"So in essence," the Captain finally said, "more advanced species populated this planet and claimed it as their own, driving the native species back to the most undesirable parcels of land and hunting them down to defend their claim."

Kalli paused and considered the Captain's premise.

"That is one way to look at it," Kalli acknowledged.

"And to add insult to injury," Evenru added, "the native's natural development has been impeded to help maintain the superiority of the alien races."

Evenru shook his head, a hint of sadness in his eyes.

"That is a story not unique to this planet," Evenru concluded.

"That is true," Kalli agreed, then looked at the captain again. "We found one more thing."

"More?" Evenru asked incredulously. "How could there possibly be more?"

"It concerns Celidia," Kalli answered. "If you recall, she pulled a scroll from her robes just before she perished from her wounds. Penra received it and immediately transmitted its image to the ship. We have been analyzing it ever since . . ."

"And?" Evenru asked with some urgency.

"It appears that the revolt she started in Karmana began when she discovered the secret to allowing the males of her species to enjoy the same eternal life as the females," Kalli said. "The concept was seen as a threat to the society that the females of Karmana had fashioned. They had no appetite to have the males as equals. Celidia was exiled because her discovery would have totally overturned the Karmana society."

Evenru chuckled.

"They weren't ready for equal rights among the sexes," he said.

"Apparently not," Kalli agreed.

"It would seem that the peoples of Ambrasian suffer much the same shortsightedness as many others across the universe," Evenru concluded, "wherever they may have come from."

Evenru and his crew studied the various data and video they had collected from the previous days. Penra finally broke the silence.

"Captain," he asked, "did good actually win this battle?"

Evenru pondered the question.

"I presume," he concluded, "that only history will answer that. And history, as you know, is written by the victors."

Chapter 29
A View from Across the Solar System, Galactic Time Irrelevant

The monitoring station lie unseen in a barren section of Isalis unexplored by any race in Ambrasian. Even if some creature intelligent or otherwise would stumble across the location, the advanced cloaking system made the station undetectable to all—including the Lux.

Inside the station, two energy signatures reviewed the recent events.

"The primitive drones of the Lux nearly caused additional contamination," signature 113796241802 communicated, its thoughts empathically received by the second being.

"Agreed," signature 47536920196 transmitted. "This planet continues to attract multiple alien life forms as it has done throughout its existence. We will have to conduct further study to see why certain worlds such as this one serve as a vortex that draws explorers to it."

The second signature quickly recounted the arrival of the various species that now inhabited the planet, as well as others who studied Ambrasian without actually establishing a presence.

"When we first became aware of this world, do you remember the chaos we discovered?" signature 113796241802 communicated, adding an emotive that might be translated as a chuckle by other species.

47536920196 transmitted the equivalent of a groan.

"Species arriving with all levels of technology and understanding of the universe," it continued. "Those irresponsible races that concluded this planet would be an appropriate penal colony without consideration of the impact on the native race was nearly ruinous. The planet had already experienced so much contamination that it was impossible to revert to a natural state. Our efforts to provide some normalcy were unusual, to say the least."

113796241802 emoted agreement.

"If only the wizard knew from where the power of his staff was drawn," the signature thought. "Converting technology to magic in various forms was quite an inspired feat. With enough science, all magic is possible. Turning a Terantinian Rex into a dragon was quite remarkable."

47536920196 concurred.

"The Terantinian Rex was needed to exterminate the Aldian Harkan invasion," the energy transfer recounted. "That would have stripped all life from the planet. Dragons weren't a perfect solution—seeing they claimed their own victims—but were better than the alternative."

The energy transfer emoted the equivalent of a sigh.

"Many modifications needed to be accomplished," it continued. "It was not ideal, and it now may take thousands of generations for the Drens to reach their full potential. We will certainly need to continue to monitor this planet throughout its history."

The two energy signatures were silent for a moment as they considered a billion thoughts and observations.

"In the primitive mentality of this so-called Galactic Command, we have violated any number of their precepts," 47536920196 continued. "How little is their understanding of the universe. If only they knew how many of their lives would have been snuffed out by phenomenon natural or otherwise without our 'interference.'"

113796241802 transmitted thoughts of agreement.

"It is unfortunate their Galactic Command did not realize we would have never allowed the space object to destroy the planet," it communicated. "Much of what followed could have been avoided."

47536920196 concurred.

"It was important we understood how the object entered this system through the spatial rift," it continued. "This was a very unusual series of events. Now we will have to continue to deal with additional 'explorers.'"

Its companion communicated what sounded like a grunt.

"Now that Ambrasian been 'discovered' again by a new generation of space travelers, this planet will likely become an observational novelty once more," 113796241802 transmitted with some disgust.

47536920196 considered the information.

"That is true especially considering so much of what they observed is unexplainable based on their scientific and technological development," it added. "Other ships will arrive to try to provide rational explanations to irrational observations."

113796241802 processed the thought.

"In several hundred years," it said, "as Ambrasian follows normal planetary development, there will be those who make their own scientific discoveries. From there, a technological society will arise. Our own illusions and provisions will no longer be necessary and the world will no longer have use of 'magic.' Science will eliminate the need for magical solutions. Even the Oracle will become obsolete."

47536920196 paused in reflection.

"So many worlds," it pondered, "so much life. The universe teems with intelligent species at various levels of maturation. It stretches even our ability to monitor all that is happening."

113796241802 transmitted a tone of bemusement.

"It is fortunate that we do not have to construct such primitive forms of transportation to shuttle us about," it concluded. "Our ancestors long ago had to endure such means until we evolved."

The two energy signatures sensed a message from another part of the universe.

"Crisis in Galaxy J-134975," 113796241802 repeated. "C-Beams have been detected in the proximity. Immediate action necessary."

"Meet you there," 47536920196 responded.

In an instant, the two energy signatures had vanished. They would sense when they would again be needed in Ambrasian.

CHAPTER 30
THE AFTERMATH OF VICTORY

After being away from Arminan for so long, the Reomites now grew weak. Roanan wasted little time in freeing his allies to travel back to the Land of Mystery. Across the mountains and hills of Balinwald the flock flew, still carrying the Red Knight and his party, moving at the greatest possible speed. Though the Reomites never wavered, the Red Knight could sense that their suffering was greater than they let show.

Roanan could hear an audible sign of relief as the party crossed into Arminan at the border of Selin. The Reomites almost immediately grew visibly stronger, and by the time the flock had landed somewhere deep in the forest, the Reomites had once again achieved full vigor.

It was there, in the Land of Mystery–only a short time ago a land to be feared and avoided but now an oasis from the surrounding chaos — that Roanan first allowed himself a brief victory celebration. With Mendelheimer singing with gaiety and the Reomites providing ample food and drink, the Red Knight, his warriors, and Athena toasted their success into the night. Then, the excitement and adventure of the previous days finally caught up with them, and they felt the weariness of their bodies. In a short time, they fell asleep soundly, perhaps the first truly restful sleep they had allowed themselves in many a day. Alexandra fell asleep with her head resting on Lasarion's shoulder.

•   •   •   •   •

The next morning, the Red Knight awoke late and greeted his companions at a breakfast of fresh meats provided by the Reomites and prepared over an open flame. Then, they prepared to begin their journey back to Chrysalis. Roanan approached Phelin, who was now in the same shape as the bird that Roanan first saw when he met the Reomites some weeks ago and smiled broadly.

"Phelin, we have grown from adversaries to allies to friends," the Red Knight said. "I have much for which to give you thanks. Without the Reomites, Ambrasian may have easily fallen."

Roanan placed his hand on Infernus.

"My sword," he continued, "you have guarded through the ages. My wisdom, you have fostered. And in times most bleak, you have proven yourselves the truest of companions. May we never lose again what we have found."

Phelin flapped his wings softly. A tear escaped from the bird's eye.

"You are a most deserving King, Roanan the Red Knight," he said. "You are welcome to return to our land any time. We are forever in your debt, for you have freed us from our bond."

Phelin paused, seeming to wrestle with his thoughts.

"Perhaps the Reomites will visit Chrysalis one day, but when I cannot say," he mused, then broke into a hearty laugh. "But when we do, be assured you will not recognize us!"

Roanan smiled.

"I may not recognize your shape," the Red Knight admitted, "but I will always know the earnestness of your eyes."

It was in this mood of happiness and relief that the Reomites led the Red Knight and his companions out of the Land of Mystery and they began their journey home.

* * *

The winds of victory blew across Ambrasian and soon after emerging from Arminan, Roanan and his company were met by Chrysalian riders who brought extra horses. The party rode at a leisurely pace, Roanan greeting villagers and farm folk along the way who joined in the celebration. It was perhaps the most direct affirmation that the battle the Red Knight had waged was done so for good reason.

Even with the meandering pace of their return, the Red Knight easily reached the Hall of Chrysalis well before the rest of the victorious army. Roanan, Lasarion, Dainwirth Lir, Alexandra, Dakar, Toranis, Athena, and even Mendelheimer were greeted to a heroes' welcome. Throngs flocked outside the castle in celebration, forcing the Red Knight to post guards to ensure the victory party did not spread into the beautiful Chrysalian gardens.

Reports of the progress of the Chrysalian army continued to arrive. The force arrived at the Hall of Karmana, and from there, many of the knights and soldiers from Selin and Balinwald returned home before the march continued anew. Five days after Roanan's return, news of the sighting of the army reached the castle. And the celebration, which had begun to dwindle, renewed itself once again. The crowds swelled to near bursting, and the next day, the Red Knight rode out to greet the returning forces.

Tabeus had led the army home. To his right was Karmin, decked in splendor and brimming with happiness. To his left was Alajar, who perked up joyfully at the sight of his rider.

Roanan, Tabeus, and Karmin met in the middle of the wide field. They looked at each other solemnly for a moment.

"What does one say at such an occasion?" the Red Knight asked.

"Welcome home?" Tabeus asked, then smiled.

Roanan nodded.

"As good as anything, I suppose," he agreed. "Welcome home!"

The Red Knight glanced at Karmin, then back at the Wizard.

"I hope you two are getting along," Roanan added.

"We have found," Karmin started, then paused, "common ground."

Tabeus glanced over at the Regent and then back to Roanan.

"Just as she said," the Wizard said with a smile, then turned more serious. "We have developed a mutual appreciation for each other's talents and wisdom."

Roanan chuckled.

"I am glad to hear it," he said. "Now, we have a crowd to greet."

The Wizard nodded, and together, the three of them turned and began the short march to the Hall of Chrysalis.

• • • •

The celebratory scene at the Hall of Chrysalis was repeated throughout Ambrasian. A new energy and a new era of promised cooperation and partnership reverberated across the land. Kings and knights joined with commoners in festivities that cut across class and wealth.

Theopolis Fenton Ruck IV re-emerged, now selling various souvenirs and commemoratives of the great victory that ranged from flags and banners to carvings and illustrations of the key moments of the battle. Even Dainwirth Lir finally relented, purchasing a wooden carving depicting the moment when he had slain Brelex.

Nevertheless, a week after, many of the celebrations had ended and life in Ambrasian slowly returned to normal. To be sure, while much of the land celebrated the defeat of Maldur, Brelex, and Celidia, victory was not so sweet for many others. For those who lost husbands, brothers and sisters, it was a bitter denouement. Roanan provided compensation for those families that had been devastated, but even that provided little solace to those who had lost loved ones in their prime.

At a dinner in the Hall of Chrysalis, one of Roanan's guests asked of the progress of the annals of the War of the Oracle. In the battle's aftermath, the Red Knight had completely forgotten about Mendelheimer's promised tome.

"Why, I cannot say," the Red Knight answered. "The minstrel has been strangely quiet. Summon him."

It took some time to find the wayward minstrel, but he finally entered the Great Hall and faced the King, somewhat red-faced.

"Mendelheimer," Roanan said with a glint in his eye, "throughout our entire trip, I have suffered your readings of your work in progress of the history of the battle. Now the fight is over and I have heard nary a word. Haven't you completed your chronicle yet? The folk of Chrysalis grow restless."

Mendelheimer shuffled his feet and grinned sheepishly.

"Well, your highness," he said stuttering, "there has been a slight delay."

"A delay?" Roanan asked in mock concern. "I am shocked. However can that be?"

The minstrel looked about the room.

"Yes, well, while I was valiantly fighting in our rescue of Athena . . .," Mendelheimer began.

"Of course," Roanan laughed. 'I remember it well. Your contributions were invaluable. Go on."

"Preston was getting restless and even a little angry that I was gone," the minstrel continued. "So he, well, to put it bluntly, he . . ."

"Yes, what did he do?" the Red Knight pressed.

"He ate the draft of my history," Mendelheimer concluded.

Roanan paused.

"He what?" Roanan said holding back hysterical laughs.

"Well, sir," the minstrel said, "he opened up my storage bag, and I guess he got quite famished, and so, he ate it."

"He ate it?" Roanan repeated.

"Every last page," Mendelheimer said sadly.

Roanan dropped back in his chair and tried to remain serious for a moment. Then he laughed uproariously. Mendelheimer looked at him in shock, then dismay, then surrender. He, too, laughed, and soon, the whole hall was filled with uncontrollable laughter that did not cease for many minutes.

·   ·   ·   ·   ·

It was late that night when the village and farm folk of Chrysalis heard Mendelheimer's voice through the wind from the Hall of Chrysalis.

Once I saw a hero
And he rose up brave and tall
And in our most desperate hour
He never seemed to fall

And he brought us inspiration
When we seemed to need it most
But in his time of glory
He never seemed to boast

Yet he saved us all
He saved the world we know
And the beauty that it holds

When the war was finished
He turned and started down for home
For he had so much to do
And he had no time to roam

Well the legend of Roanan
Will live throughout the years
Of the strongest and the wisest knight
Who brought hope and vanquished fear

And the legend will continue
Of the Wizard and the rest
Who through their acts of courage
Saved Ambrasian from the test

And saved the world . . .

Chapter 31
Mission Complete,
Galactic Date 2142-08-17

The Explorer had broken orbit and now approached the planet-killing asteroid, X1-224. As the ship circled the interstellar object, Officers Penra and Kalli more carefully studied their target while Kevo collected as much data as the equipment on the ship would allow.

As they soon discovered, Asteroid X1-224 was no ordinary asteroid. The object measured nearly 50 miles in diameter and was travelling at 45,000 miles per hour. An impact on the surface of Ambrasian would have the explosive equivalent power of 5.13×10^{17} MegaTons of TNT. The impact would not only kill off all life on the planet, it would literally decimate Ambrasian. The impact would completely disrupt the planet and its debris would form a new asteroid belt orbiting in its place.

"This asteroid is much larger than originally anticipated," Penra said.

"It has an unusual shape," Kalli confirmed. "A significant portion of the object was not originally detected in our long-range scans. In addition, much of the composition of the asteroid is made of an unknown and virtually undetectable mineral, which was a major reason our scans underestimated the size of of this object."

Evenru studied the newest data with a level of concern.

"Kevo, have you calculated the force required to accomplish our mission?" the Captain asked.

"Affirmative, Captain," the ship's AI responded. "The asteroid is far too large to attempt to destroy it. In fact, it's remarkable an object of this size still survives in the time frame of this solar system's life span. Any effort to destroy the asteroid would likely result in the object breaking apart into several pieces with unpredictable results as it approaches the planet."

The Explorer matched the speed of the asteroid as it hurtled through space. The ship's crew spent their time documenting the various features of the large rock.

"Our best course of action," Kevo continued, "is to use the ship's weapons to divert the asteroid away from its current course. Ideally, we will alter the X1-224's trajectory so we can create an orbit that will eventually lead directly into the local sun, destroying the asteroid and eliminating any threat in the future."

The Captain considered Kevo's recommendation and agreed that would be the optimal solution.

"Can we achieve that?" Evenru inquired.

"I have calculated the required force," Kevo answered. "We will have to employ both our hypersonic missiles and combat laser pods in a coordinated sequence to accomplish sufficient power to alter the asteroid's course."

"Then let's get started," the Captain said. "We'll need to calibrate the weapons systems accordingly."

Kevo altered the course of the Explorer to reach the appropriate location in relation to the asteroid. The plan called for the hypersonic missiles to detonate sequentially in proximity to the asteroid without hitting it, using the concussive force of the blast to alter its course.

"Weapons in position," Kevo reported.

The Captain double-checked all the pre-sets to ensure accuracy. It was more habit than necessary. Kevo never erred in its control settings.

"Execute," the Captain said.

The missiles fired in order, followed by the laser pods. The first missile fired on cue, but the launch system on the second malfunctioned and sent the missile directly into the asteroid. The blast blew off shards of the object that went hurtling into space, while the main body continued its course toward the planet. The Explorer narrowly avoided one of the larger shards as it caromed near the port bow.

"Kevo, what the hell was that?" Evenru shouted.

"My apologies, Captain," Kevo said. "The hypersonic missile in bay 2 suffered a complete failure of its remote firing command. The asteroid shifted, but not enough to avoid the planet. We will need to repeat the process. I will personally confirm that the firing command system is operating properly on each missile before executing the sequence again."

The Captain sighed.

"Thank you, Kevo," the Captain said. "Please do so. And triple-check it to make sure it is working."

"Captain," Kevo objected, "there is no need for me to triple-check my actions."

"Do it anyway," Evenru said.

"Yes, captain," Kevo said, with a hint of confusion if that were possible.

It took several minutes to reset the missile sequence and confirm proper operations. Evenru had Penra and Kalli double, triple, and quadruple-check Kevo's work.

"I know the AI doesn't make mistakes," he said firmly. "But I still want to be sure."

Finally, Kevo announced that the sequence was again ready to execute. Penra and Kalli confirmed Kevo's conclusion.

"Let's get it right this time," Evenru said. "We haven't had anything go as planned on this mission yet."

Again, the missiles launched one after another, followed by the laser pods firing at twenty-four designated spots on the asteroid. The missiles exploded as planned, and the asteroid shifted, the laser pods enhancing the momentum of the shift. In two minutes and seventeen seconds, Asteroid X1-224 had assumed a new course well away from Ambrasian, one that would eventually lead it to a fiery meeting with the local sun.

The AI hummed for a few seconds as it analyzed the subsequent actions.

"Mission accomplished," Kevo reported. "The asteroid is on course to be captured by the local sun's gravitational pull and eventually destroyed."

The Captain sighed in relief.

"Very good," Evenru said. "Our work here is complete. We've been successful, though not without our share of hiccups."

Penra and Kalli stared at the Captain silently.

"Orders, Captain?" Penra finally said.

"Let's proceed to our next assignment," Evenru said.

Kevo calculated the course to the designated mission at Tannhauser Gate, and in a few minutes, the Explorer was traveling at maximum speed to the snakehole to depart this section of the galaxy.

• • • • •

On Ambrasian, the general population was blissfully unaware of the sequence of actions taking place in the skies above them. But as the allies of Chrysalis celebrated their recent victory, they were treated to a spectacular display of shooting stars flaming across the night sky.

"Look," Athena said to Roanan, showing her first signs of recovering from her ordeal. "Even the heavens celebrate your victory."

The Red Knight watched the fireworks above him and smiled.

"It is a good sign," Roanan agreed.

Elsewhere, Tabeus watched the display with bemusement.

"Now, the task is complete," the Wizard said to Raven, who nodded in agreement. "Ambrasian is safe."

CHAPTER 32
EPILOGUE

It was a time of peace and prosperity in Ambrasian. Karmana bloomed vibrantly once again, and in actuality, all the lands flourished as never before.

Dainwirth Lir took Halmar's place in Chrysalis' court, and together with Toranis and Dakar, formed the new backbone of Roanan's knights. And true to his word, the Red Knight gave Mendelheimer–and Preston– a home in the Hall of Chrysalis.

Tabeus and Karmin maintained their uneasy friendship, though the Wizard much preferred to journey to the Wizard's castle in the Northern Mountains, while the eternal maiden remained in the Hall of Karmana and in the gardens of her never-dying land. Vandelyise and the Regalans renewed more regular communication with their distant cousins, though still elected to stay in the quiet solitude of their hidden kingdom.

The western and southern kingdoms discovered a rebirth in both love and unity.

Lasarion eventually wed the Selinite princess Alexandra, and after the death of Sorick, pledged the loyalty of Selin to Chrysalis. Together, Lasarion and Alexandra oversaw a renewed prosperity and energy over the once isolated land.

Athena was the last heiress in the royal line of Balinwald, and she initially was much damaged by her ordeal. But the princess showed great strength and resilience and grew in both wisdom and strength. As queen of Balinwald, she championed the rights of females throughout Ambrasian. And in time, she and Roanan fell in love and united the houses of Chrysalis and Balinwald–and produced heirs to sustain the prosperity of Ambrasian going forward.

In this way, the lands of Selin and Balinwald, along with the Reomite lands of Arminan and the Elvii Necinia, all remained realms of their own, but were bound to the western kingdom by not only the pledge of allies but by the joining of families.

Some years after the events surrounding the Battle of the Oracle, Tabeus appeared unexpectedly at the Hall of Chrysalis. He moved through the chambers of the Hall quietly, looking even more gaunt than usual. He finally met Roanan in the King's private chambers.

"This is the last time you will see me," the Wizard said. "It is time for me to depart this world. I know it is in good hands."

"What are you saying?" Roanan asked with grave concern. "I don't understand."

"The time of magic is passing," Tabeus said. "An age of enlightenment will soon begin. I am no longer needed in the new world Ambrasian is about to enter. You and I have done our part to ensure the future. Now it is time for me to allow that future to come to pass."

Soon thereafter, the Wizard disappeared into the mountains of Isalis and was never seen in Ambrasian again.

The scattered remains of the Dren army disappeared back into Damora, and the race was little seen for many generations. Some in Ambrasian thought them extinct. But it was not so. Deep in the recesses of the dark eastern land, the natives of Ambrasian wondered if the future would provide an opportunity to reclaim their homeland.

•　　　•　　　•　　　•　　　•

The Explorer and other ships of its kind continued to explore the galaxy, discovering new wormholes - or snakeholes, depending on the home planet--and other wonders of space. Ambrasian became a notation in a catalog of inhabited planets, but a curious one that in fact drew the attention of those trying to make sense of its unique characteristics. The celestial body would be observed for a thousand years or so when its inhabitants would be ready to conquer the frontier of space - and themselves become explorers of new worlds.

Acknowledgements

From the time that my first book, *Pleasant Valley Lost*, was published in 2015, I have had an amazing partnership with Reagan Rothe and the rest of the team at Black Rose Writing. No publisher could be any more supportive of its authors.

When I first began writing fiction many years ago, most of my early works were in the fantasy and science fiction genres. This book, for all intents and purposes, goes back to my roots. I first learned the wonders of those genres in a Science Fiction and Fantasy class at Alvernia College (now University) taught by Sister Rosemary Stets and the late Beth Susmann. Later, those same two professors taught a Fiction Writing class where my first efforts–looking back, some good and some not so much– were committed to paper. This book would not have been possible without that early direction and encouragement decades ago.

Clearly, there are many previous authors who have influenced my writing and storytelling. A few who come immediately to mind are J. R. R. Tolkien, Thomas Malory, Isaac Asimov, Gene Roddenberry and the stable of *Star Trek* writers, the screenwriters of *Blade Runner* (obviously!), and George R. R. Martin, among many others.

Thanks to my family, especially my children who get drafted to read early drafts and who sometimes need to get my attention as I'm staring at my laptop screen. Special thanks to my daughter, Marissa, who helped me with the map illustration.

And to my readers who put up with my genre-shifting, my gratitude for your patience and ongoing support!

About the Author

Joseph J. Swope is an award-winning author, public relations professional, photographer, and university adjunct faculty member. He has lived and worked in Pennsylvania his entire career, which spans more than 35 years in both corporate and non-profit settings. *Where Magic and Science Collide* is his fourth book.

Note from the Author

Word-of-mouth is crucial for any author to succeed. If you enjoyed *Where Magic and Science Collide*, please leave a review online—anywhere you are able. Even if it's just a sentence or two. It would make all the difference and would be very much appreciated.

Thanks!

Joseph

Thank you so much for reading one of **Joseph J. Swope's** novels. If you enjoyed the experience, please check out our recommended title for your next great read!

Disturbed by Joseph J. Swope

Disturbed is set in the Coal Region of Northeast Pennsylvania, a grimly haunted region with a bloody history of conflict between oppressed miners and wealthy coal barons. Many believe that even today, the ghosts of the Molly Maguires — a secret Irish organization that waged war against oppressive labor practices in the 19th Century — still roam the landscape. Into this setting arrives Jonah Frost, a young man with a history of mental illness. Little does he know his new home is inhabited by its former resident, hell-bent on continuing her life's vendetta. Even as Jonah attempts to forge a new life and friendships, he must battle both his own demons and those from beyond the grave.

www.ingramcontent.com/pod-product-compliance
Lightning Source LLC
Chambersburg PA
CBHW011128100726
47898CB00009B/2898